Stoney Creek, Alabama

Jennifer Youngblood & Sandra Poole

Mapletree Publishing Company
Denver, Colorado

Printed in the United States of America
13 12 11 10 09 08   1 2 3 4 5 6 7

Cover design by Tamara Dever www.tlcgraphics.com

Bible verses quoted are from the King James Version.

**Library of Congress
Cataloging-in-Publication Data**

Youngblood, Jennifer Leigh, 1970-
 Stoney Creek, Alabama / by Jennifer Youngblood and
Sandra Poole.
    p. cm.
 ISBN 978-1-60065-103-8 (acid-free paper) 1. Fathers—
Death—Fiction. 2. Daughters—Fiction. 3. Alabama—
Fiction. 4. Psychological fiction. I. Poole, Sandra,
1948- II. Title.
PS3625.O974S76 2007
813'.6—dc22

                              2007015090
                              CIP.

Printed on acid-free paper

Mapletree Publishing Company
Denver, Colorado 80130
800-537-0414
www.mapletreepublishing.com

The Mapletree logo is a trademark of Mapletree Publishing Company

acknowledgments

It is with deep appreciation that we express our thanks to the following: Our husbands, Patrick and John, although there aren't enough words to convey our gratitude for their unfailing support in all of our endeavors. To see life through the color of their imagination is the greatest gift of all. Page Hopkins for being the best sister and daughter we could ever hope for. Jonathan and Robert for their support, laced with a sense of humor of course. Auston and Cameron, two future writers who have a world of possibilities in their grasp, for their enthusiasm and tremendous wealth of ideas. Shelby and Christy Edwards, Gail Overby, Dr. Larry Adams, and Dr. Priscilla Holland for reading the manuscript and offering great advice. Hanna Oliver for her creative ideas. Our editor, Janell Thompson, for helping us work out the kinks. Dave Hall and the staff at Mapletree Publishing for their continuing efforts in helping us take our writing to the next level. Jeff Youngblood for his input on law enforcement. Last but not least, all of our family and friends for their encouragement.

"To every thing there is a season, and a time to every purpose under the heaven."
—Ecclesiastes 3:1

chapter one

He was waiting for her to die. It was a simple fact that had been staring him in the face longer than he cared to admit. He sat rigid on the side of the hospital bed, his hand gripping the white sheets as he watched the only woman he'd ever loved slip beyond his reach. Her face was resting in the hollow of the pillow, barely resembling the beautiful, vibrant face he knew so well. Ever so softly, he touched her colorless cheek. It seemed such a short time ago that it had been rosy and so full of life. Now it was as stark and dry as parchment. Her eyes fluttered like the beating of a broken butterfly against the hard pavement, and he knew she was struggling to open them.

The hint of a smile stole across her cracked lips. "Avery," she whispered. He ignored everything else around him and concentrated on her emerald green eyes, which were still as clear as always. He winced at the pain he saw in them.

"I'm here," he said, unable to stop the thin line of tears coursing its way down his cheeks.

Her throat started working, and her chest expanded and contracted like a billow. Avery knew it was a struggle for her to speak. "We had some good times, didn't we?"

"We did," he said, barely aware that the words had left his mouth.

She raised her hand and touched his cheek, her frail fingers lingering there. "Remember our promise?"

I

He nodded.

She rehearsed the promise they'd gone over time and time again. "Only cry a day for me when I'm gone. That'll be enough."

Avery smiled. It was so like Susan to make him promise the impossible. She was dying as effortlessly as she'd lived. Neither life nor death had been that easy for him.

"Don't cry, honey. Death isn't all that bad—just another part of life. It's as much a part of life as the air we breathe." She gave him another weak smile. "It's not the end. It's really just the beginning."

His shoulders shook, and he tried to hold back the sob building in his chest. He longed to take her in his arms, but that was impossible. The doctors assured him that the medicine would help ease her pain, but Avery looked at the fluid flowing in the IV and could almost see what little life Susan had left draining out. He wanted her all to himself, away from the hospital, away from the smell of sickness and death.

She gripped his hand again, and he was startled by the strength of it. "Avery!"

"I'm here." He clenched her arms so hard that he left marks on them. "Look at me. Don't go." His voice broke. "Please, don't leave me alone."

For the first time in weeks, a peaceful expression came over her face. She smiled. "I'm going now. Take care of Cindy."

Her eyes closed for the last time.

*   *   *   *   *

The Lord is my shepherd; I shall not want.... Yea, though I walk through the valley of the shadow of death, I will fear no evil...

Avery stood dazed, listening to the bald preacher in his tight, black suit. The words swirled above him in a tumultuous jumble, and he tried—tried to reach through the haze and comprehend their meaning. He fixed his gaze on a nearby dogwood tree. Despite the fact that its dying branches had turned to claw-like fingers, a handful of leaves were clinging to the emaciated twigs. A gust of wind snatched the leaves off the tree. In a flurry of motion, the wind carried them high in the air, forcing them to dance madly to an unknown beat before dropping them still and lifeless on the ground.

Yea, though I walk through the valley of the shadow of death, I will fear no evil...

The circle of people around him, teary-eyed and stooped, were like vultures closing in. So much black. His eyes fell on the cold, marble casket, and he watched, mesmerized, as it was lowered inch by inch into the ground. This was real. This was now, and yet—how could it be?

Thou preparest a table before me in the presence of mine enemies...

An image of Susan, so full of life with her sparkling green eyes and blonde hair floated before him. They said it would be easier to let her go. They said he would finally have peace after the long, harrowing months he'd cared for her during the illness. But nothing could have prepared him for this.

Surely goodness and mercy shall follow me all the days of my life ...

A song he'd learned as a boy in church rippled through his mind. *I'll fly away oh glory, I'll fly away. When I die hallelujah by and by. I'll fly away.* Was that what Susan was doing? Flying away? Soaring high above him, weightless and free. Free as a bird. *No more sorrow. No more pain.*

Pain. So much pain. He wished it would cut him clean to the bone, open him wide and scoop out this terrible hurt.

His head swam and his lips quivered. Please. The silent plea lifted to heaven. Please, help me. How am I going to go on without her? Life was Susan. Without her—nothing.

*   *   *   *   *

"Avery." A distant voice swirled around him like an echo trying to penetrate, but he couldn't will himself to respond. He was as still as death, staring into the open grave. It was mesmerizing. A part of the earth, hollowed out and raked naked to swallow the memory of his love. Skin and bones, dust to dust. Where was the heart? Where was his Susan?

The voice came again, this time sharper. "Avery."

He felt a hand on his shoulder. "It's time to go."

Avery turned to face Judith. The raw hurt blurred his vision.

Judith cleared her throat. "Everyone has left. It's time for us to go too."

He glanced around the cemetery. "Oh. I'll be along directly."

He studied the flowers on the fresh grave. "It's a shame how many flowers are wasted at funerals."

Judith's jaw dropped. "What?"

"That's what Susan always said. She said that people ought to send flowers to the living, not wait 'til they're dead."

"Yep, that sounds just like something my sister would say."

Avery didn't reply. He was in another world. A world in which Susan still lived. How could they have possibly known that the seemingly innocuous lump in Susan's breast would turn out to be cancer? They certainly hadn't fathomed that three short years later she would be lying here. The flowers, so vivid and bright. How they mocked him, a smug reminder that not even Susan had the power to escape death. He groaned inwardly. *Oh Susan, look at all these flowers.* He looked up at the clear blue sky. It smiled when it should have cried. A leaden sky would have been more appropriate, or a gut-wrenching storm with enough thunder and lightening to shake down the mountains. His eyes lifted

4

to the nearby mountain. "Susan loved the mountains."

Judith's face tightened. "You need to ride in the car with Cindy over to the house. People are waiting for—"

"Let them wait!" A muffled sound rose in his throat, and he gulped it back down. All he wanted to do was run … run until he stopped hurting … run to Susan.

Judith's gasp brought Avery back to reality. He was seeing it all in slow motion, like a man awakening from a deep sleep. He looked past Judith and realized for the first time that his daughter was standing there. The fire flaming in Judith's eyes let him know that she would have given Avery a good tongue-lashing if Cindy hadn't been present. "You go on to the car. I'll be there in a few minutes," Judith told Cindy.

Cindy's eyes darted back and forth between Avery and Judith. "We just buried my mother. Can't you two just get along today?" A sob escaped and she turned and ran to the car.

Judith turned on Avery. "Look at your daughter. Do you think you're the only one who's hurting?"

He shook his head and ran a hand through his hair. "I didn't mean—"

"You've got to pull yourself together."

Before he could reply, she turned on her heel and walked across the cemetery. As usual, her posture was perfectly straight and her chin was in the air. Judith's back was so stiff that Avery used to joke to Susan that he was tempted to pull up Judith's shirt just to see if she had a board attached.

There had been a strong resemblance between Susan and her sister Judith. Judith was older than Susan and half a head taller. They both had the same blonde hair and green eyes, but Judith's features were more striking than her younger sister's. At first, Judith had caught Avery's eye, but it was Susan who had stolen his heart. There was something hard and impenetrable about Judith. Susan had compassion—something that Judith would never have.

Avery looked at his wife's grave. Enough flowers

had been sent from family and friends to fill a funeral parlor. The bouquets were now sitting beside the fresh dirt. If he stood there long enough maybe he could somehow use sheer will to bring Susan back to life. He knew it was useless—ridiculous, but he didn't know what else to do.

The image of Cindy that flashed through Avery's mind was the only thing that gave him enough willpower to tear himself away from the grave of his beloved. He turned and headed for the car.

* * * * *

Even though Avery assured Judith that he and Cindy would be perfectly fine, she insisted on staying an additional two weeks after Susan's funeral. He watched her place the last few items in a suitcase. She fastened it shut with a sharp click. Three nights ago, the tension between them had reached a boiling point. After a heated argument, Judith became sullen and withdrawn, speaking to him only when necessary.

"You sure you don't want me to drive you to the airport?"

"No, I can manage."

Judith picked up her suitcase, and Avery grabbed it from her. "Let me help."

She shrugged. "Suit yourself."

He knew that Judith could leave without resolving their argument, but he couldn't. He put her suitcase down. "Look Judith, it's not that I don't appreciate what you're trying to do. I just want you to understand where I'm coming from, that's all."

"I understand perfectly well."

His eyes narrowed. "What's that supposed to mean? Cindy's my daughter. Can't you understand that I want her here with me? She's all I've got left."

"Must we go into this again?"

"I hate for you to leave like this. For Susan's sake, please try to understand."

Judith gritted her teeth. "I am thinking about

Susan…and Cindy. Look at you. You can barely take care of yourself, much less a sixteen-year-old. I can give her the finest education money can buy and opportunities she'll never have in this place."

"What about love? Can you give her that?"

"You know how I feel about Cindy."

The nerve. Why should she remain untouched when he hurt so much? "The high and mighty Ms. Lassiter. Always the smug ice queen. Well, I'm not gonna let you prance away this time without knocking a few chunks out of your castle."

Her face paled.

"You know what I think? You're just itching to get hold of something you don't understand. You've always been jealous of me and Susan."

"What?"

"Our relationship. You don't even know what it's like to really love someone. I won't let you take away the only thing I have left."

"How dare you! I loved my sister too, and I'm truly sorry for your loss." She looked him straight in the eye, her voice quivering. "You don't know me at all."

"That's just it. I know you too well." He smirked. "You're so caught up in yourself that you wouldn't know what to do with Cindy if you had her."

Judith's hands went to her hips. "Why you sorry—"

Cindy ran into the room. "Stop it! Stop it right now! You're supposed to be adults, and look at you." Her voice crunched against itself like coarse gravel.

Avery cradled his forehead with his hand. When he spoke his voice was strained, the calm in the midst of the storm. "Cindy, Judith and I are having a private conversation right now."

Judith touched Cindy on the arm. "How long have you been standing outside the door?"

Cindy jerked away. "Long enough! She glared back and forth between the two of them. "You act like I don't exist! Why don't you ask me what I want to do? I'm a part of this too. She was my mother!" She looked at Avery. "Why didn't you come and get me when she was dying?"

His eyes widened. "What?"

"In the hospital. I was asleep in the lobby. You could've gotten me." Her hand went to her mouth, and she choked down a sob. "I never even got to say goodbye."

He moved to hug her. "Oh honey, I didn't think. I'm so—"

She flung him away. "I hate you!" Her eyes darted to Judith. "And I hate you too!" Avery winced at the avalanche of sobs that tumbled from Cindy as she fled the room.

Judith shook her head. "Look at the two of you. You're falling apart."

His voice rose like thunder. "That's enough!"

"I pity you, Avery. You're a blind fool." She reached for her suitcase.

They were at an impasse. They had said too much—cut each other too deeply. Avery stepped back and let Judith pass. The clicking of her stiletto heels on the floor was the only sound he heard until she walked out the front door and slammed it behind her.

*   *   *   *   *

Cindy went to Susan's closet and pulled down one of her sweatshirts. She put it on, then went to her room and lay huddled on the floor beside her bed. She buried her nose in the sleeve and let her mother's familiar scent envelop her. She'd shed so many tears over the past few weeks that she was surprised she had any left, but they still kept coming and coming until her eyes were big and sore. She let her mind drift into nothingness until she heard the knock at the door.

"Honey."

No answer.

"Cindy, we need to talk."

"Go away!"

"Open the door."

Why could he not see that she needed her privacy?

"Honey, I need to talk to you."

Why was it always about what he needed?

His knocking grew louder. "Cindy!"

She wiped her eyes with the back of her hand and jerked her hair out of her face. "Oh all right. I'm coming!" She opened the door then turned her back on him and sat on the bed. She could feel his eyes on her, but he didn't say anything. After a moment, he sat beside her.

She sniffed and looked down at her hands clasped in her lap. He touched her arm but she kept her eyes on her hands.

"Honey, I'm so sorry. That night your mother died, I was so upset—out of my mind. I didn't think."

A sob started building in Cindy's chest and she hiccupped it down. "I miss her." Her voice sounded small in her ears, too small to make any real difference.

He put his arm around her. "I miss her too."

Cindy shook her head. "She won't be here for my next birthday. Who'll bake my cake?"

Avery hugged her tight. "Oh sweetheart. We'll get through this. I promise you that we'll get through it together."

"So you're not going to make me live with Aunt Judith?"

"What? Of course not. We're going to stay here in this house." His voice broke. "And we're gonna keep your mother right here with us," he said, putting his balled fist over his chest. They let the silence settle between them before he spoke. "I reckon I'm gonna have to learn how to bake."

"The last time you baked Mom a cake it was only an inch tall."

"Yeah, I guess that baking powder I couldn't find in the cabinet was a little more important than I realized." He paused. "But your mother was a good sport about it. She ate as much of it as she could stomach."

"Yeah, beating her chest in between bites just to get it down her throat." Cindy laughed then realized what she had done. She shifted on the bed.

"It's okay to laugh. Your mother would want us to

be happy." Avery looked at her. "You know that, right?"
She shrugged. "I guess."
"We're gonna be all right."
She buried her head in the curve of his shoulder. "I hope so."

*   *   *   *   *

Avery got out of his truck and turned side to side, stretching his back. In his younger days, he never thought he would look forward to going to work on Monday, but the weekends loomed long and lonely since Susan passed. Lately, Cindy was spending more time with her friends, which was a good thing because it indicated that she was getting back to her normal self, but he missed their time together. He shook his head. The thoughts that rushed him were tangled ropes with no ends. Too much introspection could drive a man crazy. At least he could count on work to provide a much-needed distraction. He drank in a breath of musky air and exhaled slowly, letting the moisture linger on his tongue.

He turned and faced the mill. The sawmill resting in the shoulder of the mountain made a postcard picture. On the right he could see the log yard. Each stack of logs was marked with a different color, indicating when the logs had arrived at the mill. Over to the left were neat stacks of lumber waiting to be trucked to their final destinations. The mill itself was a two-story structure. The band saw and filing room were located on the top floor. The ground floor was a conglomeration of chains that moved the logs and lumber to the appropriate locations. Protruding from the left side of the building was a long chain where the finished lumber came out. It was known as the green chain because the lumber coming out was fresh and would need to be dried before it could be sold.

Even in its stillness the sawmill breathed of life. Its rawness was intoxicating. He didn't realize until

Susan's death how much he depended on the sheer routine of the mill to restore a measure of sanity to his life. He could go to work and get lost in the monotony of it all, much as he'd done for the bulk of his life. It was here that he could pretend Susan would still be waiting for him at the end of the day. It was here—where the forces of man and nature blended to transform ordinary logs into the building blocks of life—that the sawdust soaked into his bones as sure as life-sustaining marrow. Here, he might have a chance.

The spell was broken by wheels crunching gravel. Avery turned to see his secretary, Barb, drive into the parking lot. He watched her get out of her car. "You're here early."

"So are you." Barb smiled and mounted the stairs in front of him.

*　　*　　*　　*　　*

A couple of hours later, Barb came in holding the pink squares that had Avery's phone messages scribbled on them. He thumbed through the stack.

"Isn't it beautiful outside today?" Barb buzzed around the office, straightening the papers in his in-box and stacking files. Avery couldn't help but notice her snug jeans, tucked neatly in her high-top red leather boots. Finally, she sat in a chair across from his desk and ran her slender fingers through her thick sable hair. The faded jeans and denim shirt clung to her lean body in all the right places. She was a looker, and she knew it. The kind of woman who had trouble written all over her. Her hazel eyes sparkled with mischief. Only a blind man would fail to realize that she had her eye on him. He'd never taken her flirting seriously, but lately he was starting to feel like a coon on hunting day.

"How many trucks do we have coming in?" he asked.

"We have two scheduled for this morning and four this afternoon."

Avery leaned back in his chair. "Are the Whites on the list? They're supposed to bring in a load of cherry. We need to get it sawed and dried in time to ship to Thomasville. They're expecting their order in about eight weeks."

"I don't remember seeing them, but I'll check."

A couple of minutes later, Barb walked back into his office. "Sorry, they're not on the list."

Avery swore under his breath. "Would you please call them and tell them we need that load ASAP?"

She nodded.

"You're a gem."

She stopped midstream and turned to look at him. "Can I ask you something?"

"Sure."

"Do you have plans for this weekend?" Barb paused in the door and fidgeted with her long, perfectly manicured nails as she waited for him to answer.

Oops. He'd stepped right into that one. "Why do you ask?"

Her next words came out in a jumble. "Um, well, do you think there's—"

Sam Barnes, a shift supervisor, burst through the door, and Barb's words were lost in the commotion that followed. "Avery, there's been another accident! Buford's hurt—it's real bad!"

Before Sam could elaborate, Avery was out of his chair and halfway out the door. He turned to Barb. "Call an ambulance!"

"We've already done that," Sam said, running behind Avery.

Avery pushed his way through the crowd of workers and over to Buford. The paramedics were already there. "Get back," they shouted, then lifted Buford onto the stretcher and put him into the ambulance.

"Hang in there ol' timer," was all Avery had time to say before the doors closed.

*   *   *   *   *

Avery lightly trailed his finger across the gold letters that spelled *Walter Pike, General Manager, Sawmill Division.* He knocked once and then pushed open the door a hair and looked inside.

Walter was leaning back in his chair. One hand was holding the phone, the other was propped behind his neck. He motioned for Avery to enter. Avery pulled up a chair. He could tell from the forced sweetness in Walter's tone that he was talking to Maurene, his wife. "Honey, how could you let this happen? You were going to balance your checkbook every month. Remember?"

Walter groaned and Avery smiled inwardly. Everyone knew Maurene was a spend-a-holic.

"How much are all of the bank charges?" His voice crescendoed. "What? That's ridiculous!"

Walter glanced at Avery and then back at the wall. His face was beet-red. "I'll call Henry. See if he can erase those charges. That's highway robbery."

Avery knew that Walter was channeling his anger away from Maurene and straight to the bank. And if he knew Walter, Avery guessed that Henry Tate would most definitely forgive all of the charges.

Walter hung up the phone and shook his head. "I reckon Maurene thinks money grows on trees. That woman spends it faster than I can make it."

Avery remained silent. Even though Walter blustered and complained about Maurene, he would do whatever it took to keep her happy.

"Anyway, enough about that. What's on your mind?"

"I've been going over the report on Buford Phillips."

"And?"

"Something just doesn't fit."

Walter sat up in his chair. "Shoot."

Avery chose his words. "The report says that Phillips got too close to the band saw."

Walter nodded, a trace of impatience on his face.

"That's probably true, but why hasn't anything been said about the crack in the blade?"

Walter stroked his chin. "Did you talk to Buck? What about David and Ralph?"

"They all say ol' man Phillips was drunk. They said that if he hadn't been standing so close, the log wouldn't have hit him when it split off."

"I'm inclined to agree. It sounds like carelessness on Buford's part."

"Yeah, maybe...but if the blade hadn't been dull to begin with, the log wouldn't have split off. I checked that blade. There were cracks in it almost as wide as my hand." Avery shook his head. "Those guys know OSHA's requirements. I've cautioned them a hundred times. If this were the first time, it would be one thing. But, this was the third accident in a month. The first was the chipper incident, then the edger, and now the band saw. The only common denominator I can come up with is dull saw blades."

Walter walked around his desk and leaned against the edge. "There could have been a knot in that log." He folded his arms over his chest. "Look, I know how hard the last couple of months have been on you, losing Susan and all, then having to look after a teenager, but you've got to get a grip on yourself. I know the Bartons and so do you. They've always done a good job filing those saws. Let's not overreact."

Avery nodded. "Maybe you're right." He closed his eyes, and an image of Buford flashed before him. He saw again the shock and fear reflected in the man's eyes as the paramedics closed the ambulance doors. It was the last time Avery saw him alive.

"Look, if it makes you feel better, I'll talk to the Bartons myself. How about that?"

"I'd appreciate it."

Walter clapped his hands. "Good, then it's all settled. Unless I find out anything different from the Bartons, old man Phillips was drunk and got too close to the saw. That's our report."

"Yeah, at least for now anyway. I just hope OSHA will be satisfied with that."

In a couple of days, OSHA would be swarming like flies, checking everything from guards on the saws, voltage on the equipment, to making sure that "Joe Blow" was wearing a hard hat and steel-toed shoes.

Avery voiced their greatest fear. "If things are not just right, they'll close the mill." He shook his head. "Maybe I'm not cut out for this job."

He looked up and saw Walter studying him with concern. He had to fight the urge to run his fingers across the shadow stubble on his jaw. He knew he looked as tired and worn as he felt. He was giving everything he could to his work, trying to kill the pain, but nothing seemed to work. It was like the chipper was taking him out one piece at a time until he was as flimsy as a piece of balsa wood.

"Do you remember?" Walter motioned to the framed picture, displayed prominently behind his desk.

"How could I forget?" The print titled *The Goal Line Stand* depicted a legendary football play made by Alabama Crimson Tide. The print was by Daniel A. Moore, and it was the first of his many popular football paintings. Avery knew it was Walter's pride and joy.

Walter studied the picture, a tone of reverence in his voice. "Sugar Bowl, Superdome, New Orleans, 1978. National Championship riding on the line. Penn State was ranked number one. Lots of people didn't think Bama stood a chance. But there we were, fourth quarter, minutes to go...inside the Alabama one yard line, and it all came down to the goal line stand."

The painting captured the fierce battle taking place on the goal line. Alabama linebacker Barry Krauss held back Mike Guman, Penn State's tailback. Krauss' body stance was a combination of anger and determination. He was a rock, holding back the wave, pitting his strength against his opponent like it was the last battle on earth.

"Alabama was ahead, and Penn State got the ball

and was going for a touchdown. It was fourth down with seconds left in the game. Penn State made it to the goal line, but that's as far as they got. Alabama held them back to win the 1978 National Championship." Walter's voice grew more intense. "Two football teams and a stadium packed with over seventy thousand fans, and it all came down to a battle between two men. Do you think victory that day went to the strongest or the best? No!" He paused. "It went to the man who wanted it the most."

Walter turned to face Avery, his piercing blue eyes had the power to bore holes. "That's what we have to do. It's fourth down, seconds left. We've got to hold that line."

*   *   *   *   *

Avery's conversation with Walter did little to diminish his concerns. He had to get to the bottom of what really happened to Buford Phillips. He unfolded the directions Barb had given him.

Turn right when you get to the top of the mountain, go about three miles past the church, and the Phillips are in a white house off the road on the left.

Avery wasn't sure what he hoped to gain by visiting Buford Phillips' widow. No, that wasn't true. He knew what he was after—reassurance. Maybe this visit would give him the reassurance he needed to put those pleading eyes, Buford's eyes, out of his mind.

He rechecked the address when he saw the freshly painted white house with a swing on the front porch nestled at the foot of a hill. Huge shade trees surrounded the house. Over to the left fruit trees were planted in neat rows. Grape vines crawled up the fence, separating the house from the vineyard. Not your typical drunk's house.

A huge dog chained to a tree barked at him as he got out of the car. Was he at the wrong house? Avery cautiously knocked on the door.

"Can I help you?" An elderly woman stood at the

door. Her short, steel-colored hair stuck straight out like she'd stuck her finger in a light socket. Clear, mournful eyes stared back at Avery from her puffy face, and he realized with a jolt that she wasn't as old as he first thought, no more than ten years older than he.

"Ma'am, I'm Avery, the operations manager of the—"

"I know who you are. What do you want? My Buford's gone."

Avery cleared his throat and looked away from the woman's accusing eyes. She wasn't making this easy. "Um, I'm investigating his...death...accident, and I just wanna ask you a couple of questions."

Mrs. Phillips stepped back and let Avery through the door. "Let's go to the kitchen."

The cozy kitchen was neatly kept with a built-in stove on one side of the room and a refrigerator on the opposite wall. The door of the refrigerator was covered with tiny magnets holding up pictures of several children. A round table covered with a checked tablecloth was in the middle of the room with a bowl of plastic fruit in the center. Avery noticed a Reader's Digest, a cup of milk, and a plate heaped with chocolate chip cookies sitting on the table.

"I'm sorry, I didn't mean to catch you at a bad time."

Mrs. Phillips waved off the apology. "Have a seat. Buford talked about you sometimes. He told me about your wife. I'm sorry."

Avery nodded and swallowed hard. She of all people could relate to his loss. He'd come here to comfort her, not the other way around.

"Would you like some milk and cookies?"

"No, thank you. I would like to ask you a couple of questions about your husband if you don't mind." He cleared his throat. This wasn't going to be easy. "Mrs. Phillips, do you know if Buford was drinking the day of the accident?"

"Drinking! What are you talking about?" Patches the color of blood were making their way up Mrs. Phillips' neck.

"Look, I didn't mean to offend. I just have to know."

17

Now the patches were closing in like thunderclouds, making her neck a solid red. A tear formed in the corner of Mrs. Phillips' eye and dribbled down her round cheek. "Didn't you know Buford at all?" She dabbed at her eyes with her apron.

Avery shook his head. "What do you mean?"

"Buford ain't had a drop for over three years, not since he started going to church."

His eyes widened. "Are you sure?"

"I'm not sure of a lot of things, but I'm sure of that!" Mrs. Phillips closed her eyes as if she were in deep thought.

"Did he say very much about the sawmill and the people he worked with?"

"No, I just know that he thought a lot of some of the men there, and he worried about them. He said they were headed for trouble."

Avery jumped on her comment like a coon dog sniffing a scent. "What kind of trouble?"

The woman's thick lips clamped shut, causing her chin to wiggle. Avery was afraid he'd pushed her too hard. He sat back in his chair and tried to give her some space. Her jaw worked back and forth. A moment later she spoke. "He didn't say what kind of trouble. I reckon he just worried about them, that's all."

An alarm went off in the back of Avery's mind. She knew something. What was she not telling?

The silence stretched on until Avery spoke. "Thank you, Mrs. Phillips. You've been a big help. I'd better get going." He started down the steps.

"Avery?"

He turned.

"I don't know what happened that day at the mill, but I know it weren't my Buford's fault. He was a good man."

She closed the door, but not before he caught a glimpse of tears streaming down her face.

*   *   *   *   *

A nagging feeling gnawed at the pit of Avery's stomach. It was the same feeling he'd had just before Susan's death: the feeling of impending doom. He thought about his visit with Buford Phillips' widow. What was bothering him about that? Her denial that Buford had been drinking? No, that wasn't it. Of course she would deny that Buford had been drinking. Who wouldn't want to keep the memories of a departed loved one untainted? He didn't blame the poor woman for that.

Still, he admitted, Buford's drinking was mighty convenient for the mill and a lot easier to explain than a dull, cracked blade. He kept going over his conversation with Mrs. Phillips, dissecting every portion of it. She'd mentioned some trouble at the mill. Yes, that's what had been bothering him. What kind of trouble was Buford mixed up in?

Even if Buford had been drinking and had gotten too close to the saw, that still didn't excuse the poorly maintained equipment. There was only one way to be certain that the third-shift filers were doing their job. He would go and see for himself.

*   *   *   *   *

He parked several blocks from the mill and walked in the cover of the trees as much as possible. He had his flashlight but kept it turned off. He didn't want to give any advanced warning that he was coming. A thick blanket of fast-moving clouds battled with the light of the moon. Shadows rose and became slithery living shapes when a shaft of pale moonlight broke through the clouds. It was an evil moon. That's how his grandmother would describe it. The old woman was superstitious. He brushed off the thought and reminded himself not to become prey to such rubbish. Nevertheless, he stole a glance over his shoulder. Maybe coming down here at 2:00 AM wasn't such a good idea after all.

Avery made his way up the creaking stairs. He swore when he discovered the filing room was empty. There were saws scattered over the floor, all untouched by the filers. Where were they? Avery had hoped that his worries would be wrong and he would find the filers sharpening the blades.

If his suspicions were correct, those guys were responsible for several accidents and a death. They'd better have a good explanation.

After leaving the filing room, he walked outside and back toward his truck. A flicker of light bouncing off a stack of wood caught his attention. It was coming from the wood yard. Another beam of light flashed and then disappeared. Why would anyone be in the wood yard this time of night?

He moved in the direction of the lights, hiding behind one stack of logs and then another, to get a closer look at what was happening. As he stealthily made his way, he could hear voices floating in the night air. He treaded as lightly as he could and then cursed as his foot snapped a stray limb that had fallen from the log trucks. He halted in his tracks. No one heard him. So far so good.

Fifty yards up ahead, he could see a hauling truck surrounded by three or four men. His pulse quickened. They were loading logs onto the truck. He ducked lower to the ground and made his way to the large stack of logs nearest to the group. If he got close enough, he just might be able to hear what they were saying. He inched to the side of the stack so he could get a good look at the men. His eyes strained through the darkness. He could make out the filers. His pulse raced when he recognized another face in the group: Lewis Jackson, the first shift foreman.

Something had to be done. Theft was one thing, but what about Buford Phillips? Had the filers' negligence caused his death?

"Sherman, hand me that binding so we can get this load bound and out of here," Lewis said.

There had been several complaints over the past

few months from the loggers about being short on their pay. Lewis had dismissed their complaints, saying they were just disgruntled, overworked old men. Now Avery understood why. They were stealing logs that hadn't been receipted or scaled.

One of the men shined his flashlight in Avery's direction. Avery jerked back behind the stack of logs, causing his foot to slip. He threw out his hand to catch himself before hitting the ground. Pain wrenched through his hand when he sliced it on a piece of metal that had been left lying on the ground. His low moan pierced the night air.

"Did you hear that? Listen!" Lewis left the group and started walking in Avery's direction.

Avery was afraid he would hear his heart hammering out of his chest. He held his breath and tried to flatten himself into the logs. Lewis was only a couple of feet away. Run! his mind screamed, but his body was paralyzed. All he could do was pray.

"Come on back, Lew. There ain't nobody out here this time o' the night. We gotta get this load out before somebody does come."

Avery didn't exhale until Lewis walked away. His hand was throbbing, and he could feel blood oozing out with every beat. The front of his shirt and pants were covered with the sticky liquid. He closed his eyes and tried to stop his head from swimming.

He sat behind the stack of oak for almost an hour until he heard the log truck pull away and was sure that everyone had left.

* * * * *

Judge Crawford leaned back in his chair and drank the last sip of his coffee. He winced when it slid like mud down his throat. Nothing worse than cold coffee. He pulled out his planner and skimmed down the page for his next day's appointments, not really seeing the words. He shut the planner. His mind wasn't on anything except the phone call he received a couple of hours ago. After all these years on the bench, the surprises that cropped up still had the power to knock him off his feet. He straightened the papers on his desk and stared at the phone, attempting to bolster his nerve to call Harriett.

His fingers knew the number better than his mind. He swallowed as he waited for his wife to answer. "Hon, I've gotten held up tonight and won't be able to make it in time for dinner."

The silence on the other end stretched on. "Harriett, I know I promised we would go out to dinner tonight, but I just received a call about an important matter, and I have to go meet someone."

This time Harriet responded with a long tirade of complaints followed by insults.

"I'm real sorry, but you know how it is around here. It comes with the territory," he said, trying to keep the irritation out of his voice. He let her go on a little longer and squeezed in a goodbye when she paused to catch a breath. He hung up the phone and looked at his watch.

He didn't blame Harriett for being angry. Their marriage had been rocky the past few years since their children had married and moved away. Harriett already hated his long hours, and then she found out about Kim. That little fling had only lasted a few weeks, but Harriett had never forgiven him. He'd broken enough promises to her to last a lifetime, and a lifetime was probably how long it would take to make it up to her.

He picked up the note from the call he'd received earlier in the afternoon and stuffed it in his brief case. Yes, this could be the break he'd been waiting for. Everyone else had left the office hours ago. It was past 7:00 PM. He would have to hurry to get to his destination in forty-five minutes.

He locked his door and ran down the stairs. The extra twenty-five pounds he was carrying left him out of breath. He cursed when he remembered he was parked in the parking deck a couple of blocks away. He usually parked in his designated spot in front of his office, but a van had been parked there. Someone had moved it before he could have it ticketed or towed away.

Judge Crawford entered the parking garage. Footsteps on pavement—voices bouncing off walls. Was that what he was hearing? He scanned the parking deck. It was empty. That's another thing his job had instilled in him, paranoia. He opened the door of his new Mustang convertible, fastened his seat belt, and started the engine. He frowned. It was acting funny. He'd have it checked tomorrow. He turned the key again. This time the car exploded, and the upper floor of the parking deck collapsed with a deafening crash.

* * * * *

Avery ran his hand down the side of the Suzie Q, caressing her graceful, ageless lines. Susan had loved this boat. He remembered the first time he'd gone to Maryland with Judith to meet her family. There he saw Susan for the first time. It wasn't long until it was apparent to everyone that he and Susan were meant to be together.

On the third day of the visit, Judith insisted that he and Susan go sailing. It was then that he discovered Susan's love for the Suzie Q. She was in her element as she told him what to do and explained the rules of safety. Then she named off every part of the boat from the bow to the tiller. Her love for sailing was contagious, and it wasn't long before he felt the same way. No one was surprised when Susan inherited the boat after her parents passed away. Avery closed his eyes. He could see Susan on the boat with him, her green eyes sparkling in that mischievous way he loved so much—her deep tanned face with her sun-streaked hair blowing in the wind.

"Dad, you ready?"

Avery looked up to see Cindy standing on the pier. He watched her balance precariously, one foot on the pier and the other on the boat, before nimbly jumping into the boat. "Untie the rope and give 'er a push."

She tossed her honey-colored hair and saluted him in the mock solemnity only a teenager can perfect. "Aye, aye, skipper.'"

"Okay, let's get this show on the road. But first, I need you to check the bilge."

"You got it." She climbed down in the cabin while Avery took care of lowering the centerboard and rigging the rudder and tiller. A few minutes later, Cindy reappeared. "Bilge is clear, skipper."

He expertly guided the boat into the open expanse of the river and turned toward the breeze that kissed his cheek. He breathed a sigh of appreciation at the shimmering reflection of the afternoon sun on the mirror of glass around him. Sailing on the Tennessee River was a far cry from the Chesapeake Bay, but he loved it. March was one of the rare months that he could sail away from the shore without using his motor.

"Hold on." He and the boat were one, skipping over the waves like they could almost fly.

Cindy braced herself against the steady onslaught of bumping waves, her lean face eager with anticipation. The tenderness that welled in Avery when he looked at her hit him so strong it almost hurt. Out here, the problems seemed to melt away. It was just him and Cindy. Nothing else mattered. Cindy's athletic frame was softening into womanhood, and Avery knew it was only a matter of time before she became the spitting image of Susan. Cindy's uncanny resemblance to her mother had tormented him in the bitter months after her death. Cindy had needed him then, but he'd been too engulfed in his cruel hurt to open himself up to her. They were like the same poles of two magnets, feeling the same pain, the same emptiness, yet repelling each other away. Gradually, as the healing balm of time eased his grief, he'd gone the opposite direction, feeling the need to cling to Cindy. She'd been wary of his sudden interest at first but seemed to be warming up to him. Still, their relationship was fragile, a tender seedling taking root in soil of doubt. It was going to take time for it to grow into the sturdy oak it once was. She was his reason for living, and he knew he would do everything in his power to keep her safe. He just hoped someday she would understand.

When they reached the middle of the river, Avery dropped the sails and heaved the heavy anchor over the side. Cindy noticed the grimace on his face and the way he was protecting his hand.

He reached for his rod and reel. "Let's try it here. We'll see how they're biting."

"How's your hand?"

He flexed and winced. "Still sore, but okay." Cindy had asked him about his injury, and all he said was that he cut it at the mill. She accepted his sketchy explanation without question. "Hand me some bait, honey." The scowl on Cindy's face broke his thoughts and made him chuckle as she reached in the cup and pulled out a slimy worm. This was Cindy's least favorite part of fishing, but she never complained. It took him a fraction longer than normal to thread the hook. "Do you wanna take this one?"

"No, I can do it."

He stifled a grin. "Okay."

She reached for another worm and shuttered as it slithered around her fingers when she tried to hook it. "Yuck!" She dropped the worm, handed the rod to Avery, and smiled sheepishly. "Thanks, Dad."

It was one of those rare moments when they could shut out the world and just be father and daughter. What he would give to make times like this last longer. But he knew it couldn't last. The problems at the sawmill were closing in. His stomach churned when he thought about his reason for bringing Cindy on the boat. It was time to do some serious talking. His grandmother always said if you looked deep enough into a pool of water, you'd find your future reflected. He looked over the edge of the boat and down into the water. There was no reflection, only muddy water staring back at him.

He cleared his throat. "Cindy, there's something I

wanna talk to you about."

She eyed him suspiciously. "What is it?"

"I've been thinking about what your aunt Judith said before she left. I think it might be a good idea for you to go and live with her for a while."

Cindy's face crumbled like a piece of wadded up paper. "What? Why?"

Oh, how he wanted to take her in his arms and hug her until that wounded look in her eyes disappeared. She'd been through so much. It seemed unfair that he had to hurt her more. If only he could unload his fears, make his daughter understand. He wanted to tell her that nothing short of fear for her life or his could ever separate them. But, he couldn't. Worry over him was the last thing Cindy needed. "Judith can give you so many more opportunities than I can," he finally said.

"This is my home. What about my friends? I want to stay here with you." Her chin quivered. "You promised. Don't you want me anymore?"

Avery clenched his fist. Everything he loved was being pried away from him, and he was powerless to stop it. He moved closer to Cindy. "I love you, honey. You know that. We'll be back together again before you know it."

"No, I don't know that you love me. I don't know anything anymore. I won't go. I won't go live with that stuffy old battleaxe. I hate her!"

"Cindy, be reasonable."

"You can't make me! I hate you!" She took her rod and reel and tossed it as far as she could and then watched in dismay as it sank to the bottom of the river.

Avery moved to the stern of the boat. He shook his head. "We'll discuss this later."

Cindy crossed her arms and moved to the bow, as far away from him as she could get. She turned her back on him, and for an instant, he wondered if she was going to dive off.

Dusk settled in, and the air became cooler as lights began popping out of neighboring piers and then stretching down into the water like long icicles.

Avery looked at his watch. Time to go. He didn't want to be late for his appointment. It was time to face the music. He pulled up the anchor.

The wind had died down, so he would have to use the motor. He turned on the switch and it stalled. He tried again several times to no avail. "Come on," he said, turning the switch with a vengeance. "We've gotta get home," and then, "there she goes," when the engine caught.

The people sitting on the pier were the first to hear the deafening blast invade the still evening. The boat changed to a ball of fire, sending splinters of debris shooting into the air like fireworks.

Then there was silence.

*   *   *   *   *

Cindy's head was whirling. Treading her legs through the water was like pulling a lead ball with a chain. She was cold, and everything was moving in slow motion. If she could just make it to her dad. Was that him holding out his hands calling her name? Or was it her mom? Just when she thought she'd reached the spot, there was no one there. Seconds...minutes went by—or were they years? Time ceased to exist. Her eyes closed against the hurling blackness.

*"If you believe in yourself and have dedication and pride—
and never quit, you'll be a winner. The price of victory is
high—but so are the rewards."*
—Paul "Bear" Bryant

chapter two

Ten Years Later

Ginger watched her best friend dip her hand in the chalk pack and look with eager anticipation at the massive wall in front of her. Sydney turned and caught Ginger's gaze. "Race you to the top?"

Ginger raised an eyebrow. Instead of replying, she shook her head and then waved her hand. "No thanks."

She watched Sydney maneuver up the wall like Spider Man, her blonde hair swinging. Admittedly, despite her best efforts, she was a tad envious of Sydney's lean, athletic frame. Ginger was always trying in vain to lose those last five pounds. "I can hear it now," she would often complain to Sydney, "here comes Barbie and her short, stubby sidekick."

The two girls met their freshman year at Texas Christian University when they were assigned as roommates. They were an unlikely pair, but they clicked. They had been inseparable until Ginger's marriage to Mark six months earlier.

Now Ginger and Sydney saw each other less but remained close. Today they were shopping for a dress for Sydney. Even though they both lived only five minutes from the mall in Ft. Worth, Sydney insisted on driving the extra twenty minutes to the Parks Mall in Arlington so she could go climbing on the wall at Galyan's Sports Center.

Ginger examined her nails. How many would she break this time? She thrust her hand in the chalk pack and then gave her harness a swift yank. She looked up at the gray knobs that looked like blobs of putty. It could be worse, she told herself. This could be a real mountain with no hand or footholds.

Ginger could feel every muscle strain in protest when she reached to grab the knob on her left. She held on for dear life and heaved her left leg up to a knob even with her chest. She tried to pull her body up and lost her grip. She fell about a foot before the harness caught her. She swung back and forth for a moment before looking up. "Hey Syd, let's grab some frozen yogurt at TCBY on our way home. I can just taste a white chocolate mousse waffle cone dripping with wet walnuts."

*   *   *   *   *

Ginger ate a spoonful of frozen yogurt and leaned back in her chair. "Now this is what I call recreation."

Sydney studied her friend and then shook her head. "What am I gonna do without you?"

Ginger's lively brown eyes grew filmy. "You don't have to go, you know."

The two sat quietly for a moment. There was so much between them. Sydney felt a lump rise in her throat, and she swallowed hard. "Yes, I do."

"How did Adam take the news?"

A brief smile flittered at the corners of Sydney's mouth. She shrugged. "About like I expected. The very notion of my leaving Ft. Worth to interview in some podunk town in Alabama that he's never even heard of is almost as unfathomable to him as my having the gall to leave him." Sydney frowned when she remembered the heated conversation she and Adam had the night before. She kept her voice light. "Aside from that...I think he's handling it okay." She forced a laugh. "You know me, Gin. I'll be all right. It's like you always say: I change boyfriends about as often as most women change hairstyles."

30

Ginger twirled a lock of glossy chestnut hair around her finger without responding.

"Hey, you could at least pretend to disagree with that last comment."

Ginger chuckled. "You're the one who said it." She shifted in her seat and started chewing on her lip. "Are you sure about this?" She looked at Sydney. "Adam Sinclair is quite the catch. And he's crazy about you."

"And I guess my recent inheritance doesn't hurt me any in his eyes either, does it?"

Ginger's eyes grew wide. "Surely you don't believe that. His family is just as wealthy as your aunt was."

Not a tenth as wealthy, she could have said. She stirred her yogurt. "Oh, I know." The truth of the matter was she'd already thought about what she'd be losing by leaving. She and Adam had met a year ago at a charity function. Her aunt was on the board of directors for the Kimbell Art Museum and had insisted that Sydney accompany her. Just when she'd resigned herself to another boring evening at a social parade, Adam's eyes caught hers through the crowd. She'd been instantly drawn to Adam's wry sense of humor and quick smile. There was a boyish charm about the way he brushed back the hair that kept falling over his left eye. He was everything she'd always wanted and yet...

Ginger seemed to read her thoughts, something she did quite often. "Adam is a hunk. I would've gone after him myself if it weren't for Mark." Sydney's expression didn't change. She was used to Ginger's teasing. "When do you leave?" Ginger asked.

"I have to be there by next Tuesday."

"Mom's gonna want to have you over for one of her grand send-offs, complete with lasagna and her famous chocolate cake."

"I wouldn't miss it for the world."

Ginger's family had practically adopted Sydney. At first Sydney had felt out of place in the Parkins' boisterous home where Ginger was the middle child of seven. She made up excuses so she wouldn't have to accompany Ginger on her visits home, but Ginger refused to accept any of them. Finally, Sydney gave up. She went to the Parkins' home and grew to love them as much as they loved her.

The biggest change in Sydney's life came when Ginger invited her to attend her church. Religion had never played a major part in Sydney's life, so she was reluctant at first. Ginger pestered her until she finally gave in. The Church and the Parkins had helped fill a void in Sydney's life.

Ginger interrupted her thoughts. "Even if Adam is mad at you, he won't be able to stay that way after he sees you in that little black Armani dress you bought."

Sydney chuckled. "Let's hope not. The thing cost me a small fortune."

"You can afford it, and besides, you needed something to wear to the club. It's not every day a girl gets to have dinner at the Colonial Country Club with the prestigious Dr. and Mrs. Peter Sinclair."

Sydney wrinkled her nose. She didn't relish spending one of her last evenings with Adam in the company of his nice but stuffy parents. She would have rather had a quiet evening alone with him. She paused.

"Adam is something, isn't he?"

Ginger nodded.

"Do you think I'm crazy for even considering that job in Alabama?"

Ginger's mouth pulled down at the corners. "To tell you the truth, I'm not sure what to think."

An uncomfortable silence passed.

"What does your heart tell you?"

Sydney shook her head. "My heart? I stopped listening to it a long time ago."

* * * * *

All Sydney had to do was play it cool. She wouldn't give too much information, just enough to appease them. She reached in her handbag for her compact and gave herself a quick once-over, applying a fresh coat of lipstick and dab of powder. She hoped the concealer would hide the dark circles under her eyes. In the past twenty-four hours, she'd gotten less than six hours of sleep.

Ginger had taken her to the airport the day before. She'd flown from Dallas to Birmingham where she'd rented a car and driven the remaining three hours to Glendale, a mid-size town located twenty miles from Stoney Creek. She'd thought about trying to get a room at the motor lodge in Stoney Creek but decided there would be a better selection in Glendale. She had purposely arrived early in the evening so she could get plenty of rest, but her mind wouldn't cooperate. She tossed and turned most of the night and drifted off to an uneasy sleep at 2:00 AM. Her mind plagued her all night long. She was too keyed up about the interview and too upset over Adam.

The plan was for Adam, not Ginger, to drive her to the airport. But he backed out at the last minute. Supposedly, an emergency had come up at the law office, but Sydney knew that was his way of telling her it was over. His caustic attitude made her wonder if there had been anything between them to begin with. Maybe it was just one more chink in the long chain of illusions she called relationships.

She opened her car door and swung out her legs. It took some effort to pry her mind away from Adam Sinclair and concentrate on her interview that was being held at the Chamberland Paper Mill Division, but if she got the job, she would work at the hardwood sawmill across town.

The entrance to the building was covered in large, double glass doors that sparkled in the sun. Fresh paint and floor polish invaded her senses when she stepped inside and adjusted her suit. The waiting room was furnished with a few chairs and a coffee table. The room's only décor was a plastic, green fern and two prints, one on each wall. The main wall was bare except for a window with a glass panel. A middle-aged plump receptionist sat behind it. She peered over her glasses.

"May I help you?"

"I'm here to see the plant manager, Mr. Jake Roberts."

The lady looked Sydney over from head to toe and then frowned. She glanced at her appointment book. "No, I don't have you down. You'll have to call back and make an appointment."

The hair on the back of Sydney's neck bristled. "I beg your pardon, but I already have a ten o'clock appointment with Jake Roberts. I've flown all the way from Dallas to interview with him."

The woman huffed. "What did you say your name was?"

"Sydney Lassiter."

"Just a moment please." The woman stood and took a couple of steps before turning back toward Sydney who was still standing by the front window. "Oh, have a seat."

"Thank you," Sydney said, mostly to herself.

The woman returned a few minutes later. "Mr. Roberts will see you now." She ushered Sydney down a long hall to an open door at the far end.

"Mr. Roberts, meet Sydney Lassiter." The woman sniggered and looked at Sydney like she was last week's garbage.

Sydney did her best to keep her face neutral despite the fact that she was seething inside. The receptionist seemed to think her interview was a big joke.

Mr. Roberts came from behind the desk and shook Sydney's hand. "Have a seat young lady." The expression on his face was stern even though he was attempting to smile. He was dressed in a flannel, checked shirt and wore black jeans. His round belly protruded over the front of his pants, making it impossible to determine if he was wearing a belt. His sleeves were rolled up to the elbows of his hairy arms, like he was planning on breaking away from his desk any minute to do manual labor. Heavy brows overpowered his tiny gold glasses, and a short, thick beard covered his face and swallowed his neck.

Sydney felt overdressed in her four-hundred-dollar powder blue suit from Nordstrom. She crossed her legs and cringed inside when she saw Mr. Roberts glance at her expensive leather pumps.

"Ms. Lassiter, you'll have to forgive Evelyn and me. It never occurred to either of us that Sydney could be a woman's name. Your resume was sent to us through a recruiter, and arrangements for your interview were made through them."

Sydney's eyes met his in a cool challenge. "Is that a problem, Mr. Roberts? My credentials and experience are still the same."

The furrow between his brows deepened as his reply stumbled out of his mouth. "Oh, no. I mean, it was just a surprise."

He picked up her resume and skimmed it. "Tell me something about yourself, Ms. Lassiter. You're from the Dallas-Ft. Worth area?"

"Yes."

Mr. Roberts scratched his head. "Lassiter...I know a Charlie Lassiter. Do you have any relatives 'round these parts?"

"No." She cleared her throat. "Both of my parents are deceased."

There was an awkward pause until "I'm sorry" stumbled out of Mr. Robert's mouth.

"I lived with my aunt until she passed away a couple of years ago." She waited for him to interject something here. When he remained quiet, she continued. "I attended Texas Christian University and earned a bachelor of science in business administration and recently a master's in industrial hygiene. I wrote a thesis on OSHA regulations and sawmills. I've co-oped for several summers at paper mills in the South, and I've spent a lot of time at the sawmills I have listed on my resume. I worked with the personnel at the South Peak Sawmill and helped them resolve some of their safety issues."

Mr. Roberts leaned back in his chair and stroked his beard. "How familiar are you with our operations?"

"I know that both the paper mill and sawmill are owned by The Chamberland Corp., and the sawmill was privately owned until a few years ago. I'm also aware of the safety problems at the sawmill."

He nodded. "Impressive. Before we get into the safety issues, let me tell you a little history about the sawmill. Chamberland decided to purchase it because it was one of their major suppliers of hardwood chips." He crossed his legs and tugged at his belt. "Since that time, there have been a slew of accidents. Most of them were minor until an employee was killed on May 15th when he fell from the steel beams of a lumber sorter to the concrete floor below. This spurred an inspection from OSHA, during which several other serious violations were cited. It's my job to find a safety expert to ensure that we not only pass the next OSHA inspection, but that we prevent this from happening again."

Sydney nodded and mentally reviewed the information she'd learned about the sawmill. That particular accident prompted OSHA to levy a $147,000 fine.

"We're looking at signing a twelve-month contract with the safety consultant we hire. OSHA will make follow-up visits during that period of time, and we want to be prepared." Mr. Roberts looked down at his desk. "Your resume indicates you have a master's degree in industrial hygiene." He paused. "May I call you Sydney?"

"Sure."

"Sydney, your credentials are impeccable, and it's helpful that you've co-oped at several sawmills during the summers while you were attending college." He perched his glasses on his nose and looked over them, giving Sydney the impression that she was being reprimanded by a school principal instead of being interviewed for a job. "I'll be frank with you. This is a tough assignment. Working in a sawmill with a bunch of uneducated, backward, loggers could..." He shook his head. "Well, it could seem like one long root canal. I know I could get in trouble for talking openly to you, but the fact of the matter is that most men couldn't handle this job. It's rough at that sawmill, and you would be required to visit the outlying woodlands to investigate safety concerns of employees. It's worse out there because it's totally isolated."

Sydney could tell right away where this was going. She had to find a way to convince him that she was the right fit for the job. She scooted to the edge of her seat. "Mr. Roberts, I've always been interested in safety since I was a young girl. When the recruiter told me you were looking for a consultant who could come in and help get the safety issues resolved at the sawmill before your OSHA inspection, I jumped at the chance. I've done a great deal of research on your company and the safety problems at the hardwood sawmill here. I want to work somewhere where I can make a difference." She paused and looked him in the eye. "I know that I can make a difference here if given the chance. Most companies think you have to be a man to know about safety, and that's just not true." She leveled her stare at him until he began to squirm. She wasn't going to budge an inch.

Mr. Roberts broke his eyes away from hers.

"Does that mean you're not going to give me a chance?" Sydney asked, trying to control the emotion in her voice.

"No, I didn't say that young lady. All I'm saying is that I'll have to think about this."

"I know my business, Mr. Roberts. All I'm asking for is a chance."

He stood and shook hands with her. "I appreciate your coming in today. I'll think about it and let you know. There are other applicants that we'll be interviewing, but we'll stay in touch."

Sydney hardly noticed the interested looks that the men passing her in the hall cast in her direction as she left the office.

She knew Jake Roberts had no intention of hiring her. She also knew that he would indeed hire her. Her ace in the hole would guarantee it. She got to her car and reached for her cell phone.

One call to the right person would be enough to sway Jake Roberts in her direction.

"As a bird that wandereth from her nest, so is a man that
wandereth from his place."
—*Proverbs 27:8*

chapter three

After the long, dusty drive from Ft. Worth, Stoney Creek was an oasis in the desert. Sydney drank in the lush, rolling hills sparsely dotted with modest houses and wooden fences. The mountains were so close she could make out the outlines of the trees with their varying shades of greens that looked like variegated shag carpet.

The scenery had started changing in Mississippi, where a string of stalwart pines lined the interstate on each side, their branches lifting high to hold hands with each other in the sky. But it wasn't until she crossed the Tennessee state line that a tingle of excitement crept up her spine. A few more miles into Alabama and the sky was turning bluer by the minute. A mimosa tree caught her attention. It was covered from head to toe with pink, fuzzy tufts that from a distance looked more like a flamingo convention than a tree. She rolled down her window, expecting to get a whiff of fresh air. Instead, the sulfuric stench of the paper mill hit her full force. The smell was a powerful reminder of her reason for coming to Stoney Creek. A shadow of fear lurked underneath her thin layer of optimism. She started to roll up the window and use the air conditioner instead but thought better of it. She might as well get used to it. It was the smell of home. At least for a while anyway. She eased off the accelerator.

If the rest of the world were moving at a minute's pace, then Stoney Creek was parked way back on the hour hand and not in any hurry to catch up. The Piggly Wiggly was a stark contrast to the posh cobblestone grocery stores in Ft. Worth. It was the main attraction in a strip mall constructed of dull metal that had zero aesthetic appeal. The film of dust and grime covering the sign had settled so inconspicuously over the years that it was as integral a part of the building as the windows and doors. She looked the other direction to see Jack's, a fast food restaurant.

"What the heck!"

Sydney's knuckles went white, and she gripped the steering wheel to keep from being thrown into the dash. She hit her brakes and pulled the weaving jeep to a halt on the side of the road and got out to inspect the damage. Her left front tire was in shreds with chards of metal poking through. She had a spare on the back of the jeep but had no idea how to put it on. She pushed a strand of hair out of her face and leaned over the driver's seat so she could rummage through her purse for her cell phone. What were the chances of getting Triple A to come out here?

A low whistle caught her attention, and she turned to see a man walking up beside the jeep.

"Looks like you could use a hand."

Sydney pushed the "end" button on her cell phone and lowered her phone from her ear.

"Yeah, I was just driving when the tire blew. I'm not sure what caused it. I must've run over something."

The man bent down to study the tire, giving Sydney a chance to get a good look at him. Her pulse increased, and she steadied herself. He was a little older than she. His medium brown hair was crew cut, giving his head a squared effect. Hazel eyes specked with green flecks set a little too far apart in his face emphasized a slightly crooked nose that looked like it had been broken a couple of times. She liked his chin most of all. It was strong and sure, the perfect match for his easy smile. His jeans and T-shirt seemed to be an extension of his muscular body. At first she thought he was a half a head taller than her, but after getting a good look at him, she realized he was probably a mere three inches taller. The extra height came from his leather boots. He stood and dusted his jeans then went around the back to retrieve her spare.

He changed the ruined tire in five minutes flat. It was refreshing to see a man use his hands so adroitly. She reached for her wallet. "How much do I owe you?"

He chuckled and Sydney flushed. Was he laughing at her? "You're not from around here, are you?"

"No, not exactly."

"If your Texas plates hadn't given you away, your question would've."

Sydney shook her head. "I don't follow you."

"Around here, people stop and help each other 'cause it's the right thing to do."

"Oh, I see." She rewarded her rescuer with a brilliant smile. "Thank you." She extended her hand. "I'm Sydney Lassiter."

He gave her a firm handshake. "Kendall Fletcher." He studied her with open curiosity, characteristic of a Southerner. "Are you passing through?"

"I'm moving here, actually."

"Oh?"

"I am going to be working at the sawmill."

He raised an eyebrow. His look of surprise both annoyed and amused Sydney.

"I'm the new safety consultant."

His recovery was quick. "Well, let me be the first to welcome you to Stoney Creek. I work at the high school."

"Are you a teacher?"

"I coach football."

Syndey nodded. That explained the muscular physique.

An awkward silence passed. "Well, thank you again." Sydney got in her jeep.

"Anytime." He turned to go and then in what looked like an afterthought, turned to face her. "Would you like for me to…I mean, if you'd like for me to show you around sometime, I'd be happy to." He became interested in some spot on the ground as he shuffled his boot in the dirt.

It was an obvious attempt to ask her out, but he'd turned the words around to sound like he was doing her a favor. Her first impulse was to decline his offer, but seeing the discomfort on his face made her soften. There was something childlike and simple about him that was different from the polished, confident men she'd known in Ft. Worth. "I'd like that," she said.

His genuine smile sent a blanket of warmth over her.

Before driving off, she looked in her rearview mirror and watched him get into his truck. She couldn't wait to tell Ginger about the renegade cowboy who'd come out of nowhere to rescue her.

* * * * *

The shrill sound of the train whistle made Sydney question her decision to rent a house a mere two blocks from the railroad tracks. She had a hard enough time sleeping as it was. Adding a train to boot would make it impossible. She edged her Jeep Liberty up the steep, narrow road leading to the one-lane viaduct. Twenty feet below, the train was whizzing past. She waited for the car in the other direction to cross over. Now it was her turn. Was it her imagination, or did the rickety thing creak under the weight of her jeep?

Once on the other side, Sydney's fears eased at the sight that greeted her. The house she had rented was nestled on a cozy street in the historical section of town. The big stately trees lining the road reminded her of the TCU Colonial District where her aunt had lived. An overwhelming feeling of loneliness surged as she thought of her aunt, and she pushed it away.

Sydney's house was yellowish beige with dark green shutters and a matching painted door. From the first moment she'd seen it, she'd been impressed with its large windows and wide front porch. She walked up the cobblestone path leading to the door and up the steps. She lifted up a nearby planter that was empty and found the key that Tess Lambert, her Realtor, had promised to leave.

Tess had wanted to meet Sydney at the house when she first arrived, but Sydney declined her offer. Tess was fine with that but told Sydney that she would be by next week to check on her.

Sydney was glad Tess wasn't here. The Realtor was nice enough, but nosy. Sydney wanted to get to know her house alone, on her terms. She stepped into the front room. Her footsteps echoed on the hardwood floor as she walked around the empty room.

Tess had shown Sydney this house last because she'd been certain that Sydney would prefer one of the newer ones with central heat and air. Dust particles went flying when Sydney turned on the wall air conditioning unit, and she wondered if Tess had been right. She spent the next few minutes wandering through the downstairs part of the house as she inspected the kitchen, bathroom, and bedroom. Next she walked back into the living room and then up the steps where there were two more bedrooms and a bathroom.

The movers would arrive the next day with her things. Tonight, she would sleep in a sleeping bag in one of the bedrooms. A shrill ringing caused her to jump, and she ran downstairs to answer the phone. She'd forgotten that it had already been installed.

"Hello?"

Ginger's warm voice came over the line and without warning, Sydney's eyes blurred. She dabbled them with her sleeve.

"Yes, I made it...everything's fine. No, I haven't changed my mind about coming here."

A few minutes later she placed the phone on the receiver and ran her fingers through her long hair. She'd sold her aunt's house and given up her life in Ft. Worth, including Adam, to come here. Was she crazy? Only time would tell.

Sydney walked out to the jeep and stopped. What was that smell? It was the scent of flowers, but Sydney couldn't put her finger on which one. Then it hit her. Magnolias. Sydney retrieved her sleeping bag out of the back of her jeep. A soft southern drawl drifted from behind the bushes. "Come here kitty. Kitty, kitty, kitty. Oh! There you are."

Standing on her tiptoes, Sydney caught a glimpse of a woman in her mid-sixties entering the house next door. Was that the woman's perfume she smelled? If so, she must've slathered on a whole bottle. The woman was wearing a white Hawaiian muu muu with a huge orange floral design. Not your typical southern attire, that's for sure. Sydney shook her head and made a mental note to ask Tess about her neighbor.

"And if a stranger sojourn with thee in your land,
ye shall not vex him."
—*Leviticus 19:33*

chapter four

Sean looked at the resume lying on his desk and then pushed his secretary's call button. "Barb, get me Jake Roberts on the phone. Now!"

Jake's voice came over the line. "Hey buddy, what can I do for ya?"

"For starters, you can tell me why in the devil you went behind my back and hired a female safety consultant."

There was a pause before Jake cleared his throat. "Now take it easy, Sean. Miss Lassiter came highly recommended, and her educational background and experience are perfect. She has a bachelor of science in business administration and a master's in industrial safety and hygiene."

"Yeah, I can see that. I'm looking at her resume right now. You know as well as I do that the words on this piece of paper don't amount to a hill of beans. What were you thinking?"

"But she has experience. She's even co-oped in a hardwood sawmill that's very similar to ours."

Sean blew out a breath. "Don't I have enough to worry about with this OSHA inspection coming up? Now you're giving me a woman to baby-sit?"

"Look man, I know you're upset and I don't blame you, but the bottom line is that she came highly recommended."

"Oh yeah? By who?"

Silence filled the phone, and Sean heard Jake sigh. "You know I'm not at liberty to tell you everything."

"Oh, I see. You'll hang me out to dry, but you won't tell me why."

"All I can say is that the decision came through ownership."

He paused. "Sounds like Miss Lassiter must have some friends in high places."

"Yeah, looks that way."

Sean grunted. "Well, that's just great!"

"Look, this is beyond my control...and yours. I suggest you get used to the idea because the decision is final. And by the way, she's reporting to work today."

"Fine!" Sean slammed down the phone.

Barb stuck her head in the door. "Everything all right?"

"Oh, it's par for the course."

"You wanna talk about it?"

He clamped his lips shut. "No."

His secretary stood tongue-tied for a moment. "Suit yourself," she said.

He didn't notice she'd left the room.

*   *   *   *   *

Barb took the gold compact out of her purse and powered her nose before expertly applying her burgundy wine lipstick. The lines around her eyes and lips were getting deeper. A regimented exercise program kept her body looking like a twenty-year-old, but all the exercise in the world couldn't seem to restore the vitality she'd had in her younger years. She lifted her chin and patted the flesh under her neck, commanding it to firm up.

It seemed hard to believe she'd worked at this mill as long as she had. It was supposed to be a temporary job, a rung on her way to the top. Now, two divorces and twelve years later, here she sat.

"Excuse me. I'm here to see Sean O'Conner."

Barb looked up to see the epitome of youth standing in front of her. "Have a seat. I'll be with you in a minute."

Her eyes followed the blonde as she seated herself near the window and gracefully crossed her legs. Small pearls adorned her ears, and her hair was twisted in a bun held by a simple pearl comb. She wore a white, silk blouse and pleated navy pants. Barb sucked in her stomach. You had to be tall and lean to get away with looking that good in pleated pants.

Even though Barb didn't have much to keep her busy, she kept the woman waiting for a few minutes. She raised an eyebrow. "Do you have an appointment?"

"Yes, I do."

"I doubt that."

Barb saw the look of surprise that flickered over the young woman's face. She watched her lean forward in her seat.

"Excuse me?"

"I said, what is your name?"

"Sydney Lassiter."

"Humph," Barb said and looked down at her appointment schedule.

* * * * *

Sydney studied the petite brunette and guessed the woman to be in her early forties. Good grief. What was the deal? Why was the woman being so hostile? The sound of a vehicle door closing caught Sydney's attention, and she looked out the window. Two men were getting out of a pickup truck. One of them was ordinary looking, but the other man looked like he just stepped out of GQ Magazine. There weren't many men who could compare with Adam Sinclair as far as looks were concerned, but even Adam paled in comparison to this man. He was about six foot, four inches tall and had an athletic but slender build. His dark hair and olive skin shimmered in the morning sun, reminding her of a Greek statue she'd seen in Rome, Italy. But there was nothing statuesque about this man; every inch of him screamed alive. For an instant, Sydney forgot her appointment, and her heart skipped a beat. This guy was dangerous, the kind of man who could distract her from accomplishing her goal. If he worked in the mill, she would stay as far away from him as she could get.

She watched the man walk around the side of the building and out of sight.

The secretary cleared her throat, causing Sydney's face to warm. She realized the secretary had been watching her and hoped her face hadn't revealed her admiration. Sydney turned to face the woman.

"Mr. O'Conner is out of the office," the secretary said. "You'll have to wait."

"When do you expect him back?"

Barb's eyebrow arched. "When he comes through the door."

Sydney nodded and leaned back in her chair. She tried to ignore the flash of irritation that sparked.

Twenty minutes later, Sydney was still waiting. She approached the secretary's desk. "Is there any way you can call Mr. O'Conner and let him know that I'm here? He is expecting me."

Instead of answering, the secretary pushed a button on her phone. "Sean, Sydney Lassiter's here to see you."

A voice came through the speaker. "Yeah, she's late. Our appointment was at ten o'clock. Obviously, punctuality is not very high up on Ms. Lassiter's priority list." There was a slight pause. "Tell her to wait another five minutes, will you Barb?"

"Will do." The woman turned to Sydney and shot her a look of triumph. "It will be another few minutes."

"I heard." Sydney's blood began to boil. "You knew who I was all along, and you knew that Mr. O'Conner was expecting me."

A red light flashed on the secretary's phone. Barb and Sydney stared down at it. "Yes?"

"Tell Ms. Lassiter that I will see her now."

"Well that was a mighty quick five minutes. Don't you agree?" Sydney asked.

48

Barb stood, but before she could move, Sydney walked around her desk and opened the door to the inner offices. "Don't bother. I can find my own way."

It wasn't very hard to find Sean O'Conner's office. The house, turned office, was little bigger than a bathtub. Sydney walked through the room, crowded with a copy machine, fax machine, and a few desks, then back to the closed door that read *Sawmill Manager*. She knocked once and then opened the door.

There was Mr. GQ himself, sitting in his chair with one foot propped up on his desk. He seemed annoyed that he had to remove it and sit upright in his chair.

"Have a seat," he said, not bothering to stand. "Ms. Lassiter, I presume?"

The man had looked so appealing from a distance. Her first impression of him vanished in the wake of his sour attitude. "That's right. But you can call me Sydney."

He attempted a smile, but to her it looked more like a grimace. "Barb, would you please bring us some coffee?" Sydney turned to look behind her. She didn't realize that Sean's secretary had followed her to his office.

"No, none for me," Sydney said, holding up her hand. "I don't drink coffee."

Sean raised an eyebrow, as if he couldn't believe she had the audacity to refuse his hospitality. "Well, I'd like a cup."

Sydney reached for her briefcase. "Jake Roberts and I discussed the fatal accident that occurred on May 15th. He gave me a copy of all the citations against the sawmill, two of which are alleged willful citations. I've been going over these and I—"

"I believe I asked for a cup of coffee." For a brief second Sydney thought he was talking to her, and then she realized his secretary was still standing behind her.

He motioned at the woman. "In case you didn't realize, that's your cue."

Sydney was itching to turn around and look but

she didn't dare. The devil secretary, a.k.a. Barb, had pulled out her pitchfork, and it was pointed right at her.

"Why anything you say, your majesty. You are the boss. Although some days I'm not sure why."

Sydney could hear her harrumphing down the hall. Even the room breathed a little fresher with her gone. She looked at Sean to see his reaction but his face remained neutral. He seemed completely unaffected. What kind of man was she dealing with?

Then Sydney noticed that he was staring at her. "I don't mean to be rude, Ms. Lassiter..."

He didn't mean to be rude? What did he think he just was? Sydney's eyes met his in a challenge.

"I mean you just don't seem like the type to be roaming the woodlands with all these back woods loggers."

"Exactly what type do I look like?" The words had come out before she could call them back. She shook her head and started over, trying this time to keep her temper in check. "I can understand why you feel the way you do, Mr. O'Conner, but I'm more qualified and competent to do this job than any man you'll ever find, and I guarantee you I won't let you down."

"Well, considering you were hired without my consent, I guess I don't have a choice, do I?"

She wanted to wither. It took her a second to find her voice. "No, you don't." She spoke her next words very deliberately. "I can do the job with or without your help. But it would be in both of our best interests if we work together."

He seemed to be weighing her words before he spoke. "Okay, what's your plan?"

His dark eyes were flashing like they held all the power in the world, and she wasn't sure if she'd gotten through to him or if he was just paying her lip service. "Like I said, Mr. O'Conner, Jake gave me a list of the OSHA citations. I'm also going to need some background information on the safety problems and the accidents that have occurred."

"First of all, call me Sean. I'm not your father."

Before Sydney could respond, Barb returned with the coffee. She gave Sydney a hateful look as she traipsed by. I know what's eating you, and Mr. GQ is all yours, Sydney wanted to yell.

"What're you doing?" Sean jumped up from his chair.

It took Sydney a second to realize what happened. Barb had spilt the entire cup of hot coffee into his lap. Well, spilt or dumped. It was hard to say which.

Without a word, Barb turned and fled.

Sean grabbed a box of tissues and began furiously wiping his pants. After he'd gone through the entire box, he grimaced at the dark stains that now had shreds of tissue mixed in. "Well, this is just great!" He looked at Sydney, who was trying her hardest not to smile.

"I apologize for Barb. I don't know what got into her. If you'll follow me, I'll introduce you to the rest of this crazy crew."

Sean led her down the hall where Sydney could hear laughter and a buzz of conversation coming from the far end. Before they went in, a deep voice boomed. "Stop accidents, my foot! I've seen this chick and believe me, when she walks through the mill and those guys down there get a look at her, she'll cause more accidents than an oil spill at the Talladega 500." The room exploded with laughter.

Sydney's face burned. Her eyes met Sean's. Neither of them spoke. Her first instinct was to run and catch the first flight back to Ft. Worth, but she wouldn't do that. There was too much at stake. Instead, she squared her shoulders and jutted out her chin. "I'm ready to go in now."

He held out his hand. "After you."

Sean scanned the room. "Guys, I'd like for you to meet Sydney Lassiter, our new safety consultant. Sydney, this is the gang."

Sydney smiled and waved. The men and woman sitting around the huge mahogany table stopped talking and looked at her. She wished she had a camera to take a picture of their facial expressions. They had to know that she'd heard the comment about her. After what seemed like an eternity, a tall, potbellied, burley man with a mustache and auburn hair stood. "I'm Joe Slaton, the manager for the outlying woodlands. Welcome aboard."

"Thank you," Sydney said.

Next, a short middle-aged man extended a limp hand to Sydney. "I'm Dean Moore the accountant for the sawmill."

An older lady stood and smiled at Sydney. "I'm Louellen Jackson, the mill's bookkeeper and payroll clerk."

"Hello Louellen, nice to meet you." There was a quiet dignity about the stately gray-haired woman that was a stark contrast to Barb's tartness. Her appearance was impeccable. It was obvious that Louellen had been a beauty in her day. Maybe this was someone she could be friends with.

"Louellen's been here longer than anyone," Sean said. "She's the historian around here."

Sydney made a mental note to remember that.

Sean introduced her to a couple of other men and then looked around. "Where's Buck? And Van Allen?"

"Van Allen's on vacation this week," Louellen said.

"And Buck?"

"Knowing him, he could be anywhere." Joe Slaton chuckled. Everyone except Sean laughed.

"I'll have to introduce you to them later. Van Allen is our lumber salesman, and Buck Gibson is our mill foreman."

Sydney had a thousand questions she would like to ask, including who made the wise crack about her, but decided that it was not the time or the place.

After everyone left, Sean turned to Sydney. "You've probably already noticed that we're short on office space." He pointed. "There's an empty desk over by the window in the conference room that you can use. I'll catch up with you later on this afternoon."

* * * * *

Calling Adam Sinclair was the last thing Sydney had planned to do. It was one of those things that just happened. Quite possibly it was the combination of her awful day at work and visit to the grocery store that culminated in her temporary lapse in good judgment. After her initial meeting with Sean O'Conner, she sat in the conference room, waiting for him to do as he'd promised and "catch up with her later on in the afternoon." When he never came, she went looking for him. He wasn't in his office or in the building. She could have asked his secretary where he'd gone but decided it would be best to avoid the demon woman at all costs. She asked Louellen and Dean. Neither of them knew the whereabouts of Sean or where the accident records were kept.

At five o'clock, Sydney called it a wash and left. She couldn't very well conduct an inspection of the sawmill in her silk shirt and open-toed sandals. Tomorrow she would come to work dressed appropriately so she could explore the sawmill on her own. Sean O'Conner might have pigeon-holed her today, but it wouldn't happen again.

She left work and went straight to the Piggly Wiggly to do some major grocery shopping. Things had been so hectic since her arrival in town that she'd bought only the bare necessities. Peanut butter and jelly was all she had to eat at her house, and the very thought of choking down one more sticky sandwich was enough to make her gag.

At the grocery store, when she walked down the aisles, every person in the store stopped what they were doing and stared at her. It was as if she were an alien from a foreign planet. She was: Ft. Worth. Everyone in the store seemed to know where they belonged. She watched the ladies talking amongst themselves in the aisles. They had so much to say to each other. She had nothing. Where did she belong?

Back home, Sydney opened her front door and went inside. She listened to the lonely whistle from the nearby train. That's when she decided to call Adam. She hadn't heard from him since she left Ft. Worth. Her fingers punched the buttons by instinct, and she waited for him to answer. After the fourth ring, she was about to hang up when his voice came over the line.

"Hello?"

"Hey, it's me."

When he paused, she knew that calling him was a terrible mistake. "How are you doing?"

"Fine."

She searched for something to say. "How's work?"

"Hectic, like always."

Silence.

"Look, I know things haven't been that great between us," she said, fumbling for words. "But I was just hoping that..." She stopped. Was that laughter she heard in the background? A girl's laughter? "Who's there with you?"

He snorted. "What is this? Twenty questions?"

"It was just a simple question."

Her hand gripped the phone. His silence told her all she needed to know.

Her voice broke. "Did I not mean anything to you?"

"You made your decision. It's too late to come crying back now. Grow up, Sydney," she heard him say. She hung up.

She stared at the phone. It took her a few seconds to realize it was ringing.

"Hello?"

"Hello? Is this Sydney Lassiter?"

"Yes, it is."

"This is Kendall Fletcher. Uh, we met a couple of days ago."

"I remember you." She knew the tone of her voice was coarse but didn't care. It felt good to vent her frustrations.

"I was wondering if you would like to have dinner with me this Friday."

"Let me check my calendar." She reached in the grocery sack and retrieved a box of Fruity Pebbles and glanced at the back. "No, Friday's not good for me."

He stuttered around a few seconds, long enough for her to fear that he wasn't going to ask her out for another day. "Saturday then?"

"Sounds good. What time?"

"Seven o'clock."

"Do you need directions to my house? Okay then, see you Saturday."

*   *   *   *   *

True to her word, Sydney's Realtor, Tess Lambert, showed up a week later to check on her. And as Murphy's Law would have it, her visit came fifteen minutes before Kendall Fletcher was to arrive for their date. When Sydney heard the doorbell, she felt a flash of irritation at him for arriving early. Well, he'd just have to wait.

In all honesty, she was more piqued with herself than Kendall. Around 5:30 she decided to go for a short jog, thinking she would have plenty of time to get ready. Unfortunately, time-management was one of her greatest weaknesses. She always tried to cram too many things into her schedule.

When she looked through the peep-hole and saw that it was Tess instead of Kendall, she frowned. Tess was donning green oven mitts clear up to her elbows, juggling two large casserole dishes.

"Tess, this is a surprise."

"Well, hidy Sydney. I hope this isn't a bad time."

"Well, actually...I was just—"

Tess breezed past her. "I'll just put these dishes in the kitchen."

"Those are for me?"

"I brought you a little taste of Stoney Creek hospitality masked in the form of squash casserole and blackberry cobbler. Or in the words of my mother, *comfort food.*"

"Thank you." Sydney tried to think. She hadn't had squash casserole in...she couldn't remember how long it had been.

Tess was like most Southerners. She'd driven Sydney around Stoney Creek, showing her property available for rent, and in the short span of an afternoon told Sydney her entire family history, going back a generation. Tess Lambert wasn't originally from Stoney Creek or *homegrown* as she called it.

"I'm a transplant to Stoney Creek," Tess said. "Although I try not to show it." She chuckled. "I love this little town, warts and all. Give it time, and I guarantee that you'll feel the same way."

Sydney bit her tongue and smiled.

Tess was examining the place. "Sure does look nice." She ran her finger over the dining room table. "Stickley?"

Sydney nodded.

Tess was from Charleston, South Carolina, and spoke in a drawling accent that sounded exaggerated, like she was playing Scarlett O'Hara on the stage. All she needed to complete the picture was a hooped skirt and parasol.

Sydney's polite façade was wearing as thin as a sheet of veneer. She looked at her watch. "It's so good of you to stop by, but I'm afraid I have an appointment."

"I didn't mean to keep you. It looks like you're getting along all right."

"Yes," Sydney lied, "it's starting to feel like home."

The two women walked back into the living room and past the front window where they saw Kendall pulling up. Tess gave Sydney an insinuating smile. "Oh, I see why you're in such a hurry to rush me out the door."

Sydney's face flushed. She could have strangled the woman.

"I wasn't aware that you knew our charming football coach."

"There are quite a few things that you don't know about me," Sydney said, giving the woman a withering look.

Tess laughed good-naturedly. "I look forward to getting to know all of those things. In Stoney Creek, everybody knows everything about everybody."

Now that was something Sydney could believe.

"Honey, I'm so glad that Kendall has you," Tess said, catching Sydney's arm. "He's had a rough time, losing his father and all."

Sydney stopped and turned to face the woman. "His father? Did he die?"

Tess leaned near Sydney and spoke in low tones. "Joe Fletcher shot himself. He told his wife not to bother him, that he would be out in the shed, cleaning his guns. Kendall was the one who found him."

Sydney's face drained of color.

"I just thought you ought to know."

The doorbell rang. Before Sydney could respond, Tess opened the door wide and took over the role as hostess. "Kendall Fletcher, you get yourself in here and give me a hug."

If Kendall was surprised to see Tess greeting him at the door, he didn't show it. He smiled and gave her a broad hug and a perfunctory kiss on the cheek. Sydney was still trying to digest the news that Kendall's father was dead. She looked at him, standing there on the porch and saw him not as he was but as the little boy he would have been. How could he stand it? Finding his father that way. She felt the sudden urge to throw her arms around him and tell him it would be okay.

"How's your mama doing?" Tess asked.

"She's feeling much better."

"I've been meaning to get over and see her. You tell her I said hello." Tess looked at Sydney and squeezed Kendall's arm. "This fella here is one of the finest you'll ever meet."

Sydney raised an eyebrow. "Is that so?"

"Sure is." She winked. "And a nice catch to boot."

Before Sydney could think up a reply, Tess started out the door. "Y'all have fun. I'll come back next week to collect my dishes."

She watched Tess glide to her car. She shouldn't have been surprised that Tess and Kendall were acquainted, but their familiarity awoke a yearning that confused her. All of the people in this town were so connected.

Kendall turned toward Sydney and looked at her. Time seemed to pause for one breathless second. He gave her a slow, shy smile that melted through to her toes. "Hey."

"Hi," she said softly. He was standing so close that she might've heard the beating of his heart or was it her own? She took a step back to recover herself.

He reached out to steady her while his hazel eyes flickered over her. "Why don't I have a seat while you finish getting ready?"

She looked down at her bare feet and then at his jeans, loafers, and white v-necked polo shirt. Color rose in her cheeks. She smiled. "Okay, I'll be out in a few minutes."

She headed to her bedroom. Her first impression of Kendall Fletcher had been wrong. She'd pegged him as insecure. He was the exact opposite. Beneath his shyness, there was a strong force. It was like he already knew.

She belonged to him.

"Even a fool, when he holdeth his peace, is counted wise..."
—Proverbs 17:28

chapter five

The warm morning air rushing in through the open windows felt good. Sydney drove to the sawmill, her hair whipping wildly. Her date with Kendall had been just the tonic she'd needed. It was the start of a brand new week, and this time she wasn't going to be intimidated by Sean or his devil secretary. She had just as much right to be there as they did.

"I have a job to do, and by golly I'm gonna do it," she said. A smile tugged at the corners of her mouth. Those were her father's words. She'd heard him use them many times.

She parked her jeep and got out, barely noticing the group of men standing nearby. She liked the sound her steel-toed shoes made when they crunched the gravel. She felt confident and knew it showed in her every step. This time she'd come dressed for business.

The wolf calls and leering remarks stopped her dead in her tracks. It was amazing how fast that one incident could strip away her courage, leaving her feeling like a helpless mouse being taunted by huge ugly cats. Her first impulse was to flip them off, but she refrained. She'd put aside such vulgar behavior long ago. Instead, she lifted her head and pretended they didn't exist.

She turned her head in the opposite direction when she passed Barb's desk.

"You might want to check your in-box."

Sydney stopped. "My in-box?"

"It's the last cubicle on the right."

Sydney studied Barb, who was looking very chipper in her tight pink blouse. Could it be that the woman had decided to be civil? "Thanks."

One look at the contents in the box doused any remaining spark of her good mood.

*　　*　　*　　*　　*

Sydney's voice trembled. "What is the meaning of this?" She shoved the papers in front of Sean's face.

"It's the minutes from the last safety meeting. I thought you needed to get a copy since you were not there."

She wanted to claw the smug expression off his handsome face. "Need to get a copy! This meeting took place last Friday after I left the mill. I just got the announcement for the meeting this morning in my in-box! I was here all last week. Why wasn't I informed?"

"You were."

"What?"

Sean spoke deliberately. "I told Barb to be sure you knew about the meeting. I'm sure all of this is just a misunderstanding." He picked up a paper from his desk and studied it as if Sydney wasn't there.

Refusing to be dismissed, Sydney stood her ground. "How can I ever gain these men's respect if they think I'm not interested enough in them to come to their safety meetings?"

"Look, I said I'm sorry. I'll talk to Barb and find out what happened." His dark eyes glittered in an open challenge, daring her to argue.

Rage boiled up in Sydney's throat. "Don't count on Barb to tell me anything. She just now told me that I have an in-box. *You'd* better let me know from now on, Sean O'Conner." Sydney slammed the minutes on his desk and stormed out of his office.

Sydney looked at her watch. After the blow-up with Sean, she'd decided to by-pass him by calling and scheduling an appointment with the sawmill foreman. She would take each key player and get to know them on a personal basis. Mr. Gibson was ten minutes late for their appointment, but that didn't surprise her. It seemed to be the norm in this place.

The foreman knocked once and then entered her office. Could it be? Yes, this was one of the men that had made wolf calls at her.

"How do you do, ma'am?"

"I'm fine." Sydney's lips formed a tight line. She stood and shook his hand. "Thanks for coming in. Have a seat, Mr. Gibson."

Buck Gibson was a small-boned man who carried himself rather confidently for a man who stood a mere half a head taller than she. A short, stubbly mustache covered his upper lip, and his dark hair was sprinkled with salt. His forehead was a shade lighter than the rest of his face, probably due to wearing a cap all of the time. He was trim except for a small, tight belly that barely extended over his belt-line.

His smile was cold, never reaching those dark fathomless eyes. She'd heard that Mr. Gibson had quite a reputation with the women. Sydney found that hard to believe. He might've been an athlete in his younger years, she conceded. Perhaps then he'd been passably attractive. Stoney Creek, it seemed, was a very small pond with lots of big fish.

He seemed to be sizing her up. "So you think you can stop these here accidents we've been having?"

"No, Mr. Gibson. I can't do it alone, but I think that together we can. But first we have to do an analysis to determine any possible hazards. We need to go over every nook and cranny of the mill. We want to catch the problems before they turn into accidents. Then we'll set up safety procedures and implement them." She thumbed through her file. "I've been going through the reports. In addition to the accident on May 15th, resulting in Timothy MacGregor's death, there have been several other accidents. Do you have any idea what's going on or what may have changed over the last few months?"

"Ma'am, if I knew what was hap'nin, I would've stopped it a long time ago." He looked her in the eye. "I do have a question, though."

"What's that?"

"How did a pretty young thang like you git a job like this?"

"Mr. Gibson!" Sydney could have screamed. "Have you not heard a word I've said?"

"Jest call me Buck, ma'am."

"Buck, this is very serious business. We have to work together to find out what's going on here. Are you with me on this?"

"Yes ma'am, I'm with ye. I'll do whatever you want me to. I'll even shave the beard off Lincoln if you want me to. You jest tell me, and I'll do it."

"Good," Sydney said, trying to ignore the man's uncomfortable stare. "The first thing we need to do is a thorough inspection of the mill." Sydney looked at her calendar. "Is tomorrow a good time for you?"

"You jest name the time and place, and I'll be there." He smiled again.

"I'll meet you here at 8:00 AM."

* * * * *

Sean looked toward the office and caught glimpse of Buck coming down the front steps. He waved then walked across the parking lot. "Buck!"

"Yeah boss. Whadda you need?" Buck tucked his flannel shirt deeper in his pants and sucked in his round gut.

"Where've you been? I've been looking for you. We have some business to take care of tonight, and we need to talk."

"I was settin' up a time to take an inspection with Miss Lassiter." He let out a low whistle. "She's a nice little piece of pie if you get my drift. She needs my help." He winked. "I'll help her and maybe she can help me."

Sean's face darkened. "She's off limits. Do you understand?"

"Now boss. Don't tell me you've already staked a claim on 'er."

"She's not your type Buck. Stay away from her or you're asking for trouble for all of us. The sooner she does her inspection or whatever it is she does, the sooner we can get her out of here. Do you understand?"

Buck spit on the ground. "Whatever you say, boss."

*   *   *   *   *

Sweat dripped down Sydney's forehead and pooled inside her safety goggles. Sawdust covered her clothes, and she could taste the grittiness. Buck kept their appointment and met her at 8:00 AM to do the sawmill inspection. He charged full speed through the sawmill, leaving her to follow behind, taking notes on her clipboard. They waded through the thick air, musty with cinnamon-smelling sawdust.

She stopped in her tracks and looked up. Buck didn't realize she wasn't behind him until he got to the exit door. He turned and came back and stood beside her.

"Why isn't that man wearing fall protection?"

He looked up. "Which man?"

Sydney pointed in the air. She couldn't believe her eyes. "That man on the lumber sorter. That's exactly how Timothy MacGregor was killed. And where are the guardrails?" She shook her head. "These are willful violations to the requirements of the Occupational Safety and Health Act and Regulations."

Buck looked at her like she was speaking a foreign language. She threw her hands up and headed to the exit door. "Didn't you guys learn anything from the last OSHA inspection?"

Buck followed her. "We'll fix all this, Miss Lassiter."

"You're darn right you will. I want to go to the wood yard now."

On the way, she noticed the hostile stares of the workers she passed and remembered Jake's prediction that these men wouldn't appreciate a woman telling them how to fix their problems.

Sydney was sweating buckets by the time they reached the wood yard. It would take her a while to get used to the sultry humid heat. She pushed a loose strand of hair under her hardhat, trying to ignore Buck's persistent ogling. She looked around at the huge stacks of lumber, some dried and some still green. After the logs were cut into lumber, they had to be dried. Some pieces could be dried in the sun but most were placed in a kiln where they were baked by electric heat.

The lumber was stacked on each side of the kiln, allowing for a narrow passageway down the middle. Buck stood with his arms folded above his belly and watched without speaking while she made several notations on her clipboard. "When was this built? The foundation isn't solid." She pointed. "See, the tracks are sagging."

"There ain't no telling," Buck said. "It was here when I got here."

She walked inside and inspected the inside walls of the kiln and then moved to the escape door in the back. The escape door was a necessary precaution in the kiln because once the main door was closed, it couldn't be opened from the inside. She tugged at the handle and tried to push open the door. It didn't budge. "What's wrong with this handle?"

Buck came up behind her, and she stepped out of the way to let him try. He grasped the handle and pushed against the door but to no avail.

"I reckon it's stuck, Miss Lassiter."

Sydney turned and walk out of the kiln. "I'm going around the back to see if anything is obstructing it from the outside." Buck followed close behind.

Once around the back, she could hardly believe her eyes. "Well, no wonder the door won't open. You have all this lumber stacked up behind it." She shook her head. "The handle's broken, and this lumber shouldn't be here."

Buck watched Sydney make another notation on her clipboard. His face darkened, and he cleared his throat. "Miss Lassiter, I know you mean well, taking all them notes and all, but Mr. O'Conner'll be fit to be tied when he sees 'em."

"It won't matter what Mr. O'Conner thinks if we don't pass that OSHA inspection. None of us will have a job."

"Yes ma'am, I see what you mean." Buck took off his hardhat and wiped his damp forehead. "I think there's another solution."

Sydney raised an eyebrow.

"Them guardrails, this escape door. I can git all this fixed, and you don't even have to write it down. That's all I'm sayin'."

Sydney's eyes widened. "Buck, Mr. O'Conner will have this report by Friday. I plan on talking to him about the guardrails and lack of fall protection today. That can't wait until Friday." She looked at his troubled expression. It wouldn't do to make an enemy out of him. She motioned to the kiln. "This can wait, however. If you get this fixed, it will not be in the report. Otherwise, I'll have to write it down. Fair enough?"

"Yes ma'am."

Every time the man spoke those words, they sounded patronizing.

"For every tree is known by his own fruit..."
—*Luke 6:44*

chapter six

Sydney paused a moment outside the door of Sean's office so she could observe him without being seen. He was studying his laptop screen, his face a mask of concentration. He kept his thick wavy hair too short. It was the kind of hair that was itching to be left unruly. His high cheekbones and strong chin were the perfect match for his wiry muscular body, and she wondered how many hours of exercise it had taken to chisel it to perfection. It was a shame for all those good looks to be wasted on such a jerk. He was perfect until he opened his mouth.

"Honey, are you gonna stand there all day gawking at him or are you gonna go talk to him?"

Thanks to Barb's constant barrage of insults, Sydney was becoming quicker on her feet. She leveled her gaze at the woman standing in front of her. "I haven't decided yet, not that it's any of your business."

"Humph!" she said and sauntered down the hall.

Sydney's face burned when she looked back at Sean and realized that he'd been watching the exchange with a trace of amusement in his eyes. He lifted an eyebrow.

"You wanna talk to me I presume?"

She tromped in and sat down in the chair in front of his desk. She wasn't going to mince any words. "I went on an inspection with Buck Gibson today. Do you want to tell me why those men working on the lumber sorter haven't been equipped with fall protection?" Before he could respond, she rushed on. "And why haven't guard-rails been installed?" She paused to get a breath. "Did you not read any of the citations that OSHA levied on the sawmill?"

"The fact that you did your little inspection today doesn't give you the right to come barging in here with that haughty attitude. In case you've forgotten, I am still the boss. You would do well to remember that."

His words took her aback, and she realized that it would take all the intestinal fortitude she could muster to go head-to-head with Sean O'Conner on a daily basis.

"Is that a threat?" She fought to get control of her emotions.

"I'm sorry. You're right about the fall protection...and the guardrails. It's really good that you're here. Our workers haven't been given the proper training on the use of fall arrest equipment. I've been so busy with all the other tasks, I'm afraid I haven't devoted enough time to safety."

"I would think that safety should always be a number one priority."

"You're right. Now that you've brought it to my attention, I'll see that those problems are corrected."

She watched him with an eerie fascination. What had brought about his sudden change in mood? His tone was conversational now, almost charming. He was playing her. That was the only explanation she could think of.

"Well, at least we're on the same page. That makes it easier to discuss my next topic."

"What's that?"

"I want to do some research."

"Research?"

"Yes, I want to study the accident reports for the past ten years."

"That's ridiculous. Why do you need to go back ten years? I don't understand how that could possibly help us now."

"Don't you see? I need to establish an accident trend so we can determine where our weaknesses are. There may be some clue. Someone may have found something out then that might help us now."

"Such as?"

She knew how lame her argument sounded, but she somehow had to convince him. "Take for instance the accidents that occurred over the past year. They're all so sporadic: one person fell and wasn't wearing the right equipment, another one got cut on an unguarded piece of equipment. The list goes on and on. I just don't see any consistency. The only thing they all have in common is human error—carelessness. I can't predict human error and therefore can't prevent it."

Sean leaned back in his chair and studied her. He threw up his hands. "Okay, go ahead if you think it will help. But Barb will pitch a holy fit when she finds out that she has to go back that many years and pull old folders. I promise you that."

"Well, it shouldn't be too hard of a task, considering that it is her job."

"...the eye is not satisfied with seeing..."
—Ecclesiastes 1:8

chapter seven

The eyes watched Sydney get into her jeep and head west in the opposite direction of town.

She pulled into the overgrown driveway of a moderate-sized older home. At first he thought she was lost and looking for a place to turn around. Then he realized she'd turned off the motor and parked. He pulled behind some bushes, took out his binoculars, and waited. He looked down at his watch. Five minutes passed, and she was still sitting in the jeep, staring at the house. He watched her get out and walk up the steps. She knocked on the door. No one answered. Why was she here?

Instead of going back to her vehicle, Sydney walked around on the porch. She stopped at an old rocking chair situated on the far end and paused long enough to caress the back with her hand. He watched through the binoculars as she walked down the steps and across the yard to a huge sycamore tree where a swing was hanging from one of the giant limbs. She took off her shoes and bag and laid them by the swing. A few moments later, her long, blonde hair blew through the wind while she swung higher and higher with her eyes closed and her head tilted back. Tears were streaming down her face, glistening in the afternoon sun.

"But the stranger that dwelleth with you shall
be unto you as one born among you."
—Leviticus 19:34

chapter eight

Had it sat in Texas, the moderate-sized stone house with its wide porch and sturdy square columns would have been worth a mint. The large picture windows on the front looked friendly, Sydney decided. She walked up the steps to where a large terracotta pot stuffed with red geraniums rested comfortably beside the front door. At the far end of the porch was a wooden swing held by chains that attached to the ceiling. Its bright, colorful cushion was inviting, like you could snuggle down in it and swing all your problems away. In another time Sydney might've done just that. Instead, she pulled her eyes away from the swing and faced the door. The butterflies in her stomach turned to swarming bees when she rang the doorbell. No one answered. She knocked lightly at first and then louder.

The door opened and she stood facing a mature woman whose height matched her own. The woman seemed just as startled to see Sydney.

"May I help you?" the woman asked.

"Mrs. McClain?"

"Yes." Sydney smiled thinly and repeated the words she'd rehearsed a thousand times. "Hi, my name is Sydney, and I'm the safety consultant for The Chamberland Sawmill. I apologize for barging in on you like this. I tried to find your phone number but couldn't."

The woman nodded. "It's unlisted."

"The reason for my visit today is that your son was a foreman at the sawmill. I'm doing a ten-year history to establish an accident trend. If we can learn from the past, maybe we can prevent the same accidents from reoccurring." Sydney's voice trailed off. She knew how lame her words sounded.

"Please, come in and have a seat," the woman said.

Sydney looked around at the living room. The wide plank wooden floors had been left natural except for a glossy finish coat. The walls were a shade of taupe and looked earthy against the khaki sofa and loveseat. A hemp rug the color of hay covered the span between the living room furniture, and a mahogany antique table rested in the center of it. The table was bare except for a glass vase of cut hydrangeas. White wooden blinds covered the windows, and a green fern rested on a plant stand. A large palm tree that reached the ceiling stood in one corner. The combination of the subtle colors and green plants had a soothing effect on Sydney's nerves.

She studied Mrs. McClain while trying to determine the best approach she should take. Mrs. McClain was approaching seventy. Her lined face was make-up free. Sydney hadn't noticed this at first glance. The woman's green eyes were so vivid that they didn't need any artificial enhancement. She wore her silver hair in a stylish blunt cut that rounded and bounced on her angular shoulders. Her pleated linen pants were rolled up at the ankles, accentuating white tennis shoes with no socks. Her pale blue T-shirt revealed tanned arms that were dotted with age spots. She was a little on the frail side but definitely didn't look her age. Her wide smile, revealing lots of teeth, was her best feature.

She was exactly as Sydney had imagined her.

Mrs. McClain cleared her throat, and the spell was broken. Sydney realized with a jolt that while she'd been studying Mrs. McClain, the woman was studying her. Her face warmed, and she reached up to smooth down her hair.

"I appreciate your letting me barge in on you like this," Sydney said. She waited for Mrs. McClain to respond. When she didn't, Sydney continued. "I understand that your son was the foreman at Chamberland Sawmill at one time."

Mrs. McClain's eyes looked through her. "Yes, a long time ago."

"Did he ever talk about his work?"

"No." Mrs. McClain looked directly at Sydney. "Those last few months before Avery's death were particularly difficult for him. His wife died with cancer, leaving him with a young daughter to take care of. Avery was distraught over his wife's death. I think he just went through the motion of living. A part of him died with Susan."

Sydney's hands began to shake, and she clenched her pants in an attempt to steady them. "How did your son die?"

"He was killed in a boating accident."

Sydney's skin felt hot but her insides were cold—cold and empty as death. She forced the next words out. "What happened to his daughter?"

Tears formed in the older woman's eyes. She shook her head slowly back and forth. "I was afraid that I'd never see her again."

Sydney fought back the burning in her own eyes. "Losing those you love is very painful."

The woman nodded.

"I lost my aunt a few months ago."

"I'm so sorry," came the soft reply.

All of the hurt and pain swelled inside of Sydney until the emotion was so great that she felt like her heart would burst. She attempted to speak, but her tongue lay like lead in her mouth.

The shrill ringing of the phone sliced through the tense silence. Mrs. McClain looked toward it, as if deciding whether or not to answer it. "I'll be right back," Sydney heard her say.

A tear escaped from the corner of Sydney's eye and she used her sleeve to wipe it away. What was she doing here? This was a mistake. She stood and clutched her purse under her arm. She stumbled to the door.

"Cindy!"

Sydney's hand dropped from the doorknob.

"Don't leave. I have something for you."

Tears were flowing freely down her cheeks when her grandmother returned, carrying a box. She handed it to Sydney.

"These things were your father's. He would want you to have them. I knew you would come back. Welcome home, Cindy."

*   *   *   *   *

Sydney paused and looked at the box before opening it. It was a tangible door to a past she'd never been able to close. How she'd longed to touch something familiar, something that had belonged to her dad. But now that it was in front of her, she was hesitant. It was like looking at Pandora's box. She took a deep breath and tore off the tape with trembling hands. She reached for the item on top, a picture of her and her parents on the beach, taken when they were on vacation in Florida. She rubbed her hand over her parents' faces. They looked so strong and full of life. She swallowed the sob building in her chest and placed the picture on the floor. The box contained a hodgepodge of items: bank statements, her dad's watch, family photos, all bringing back bittersweet memories. It was near the bottom of the box that she saw the worn leather book. She opened it. Could it be? Yes, it was her father's journal. She hadn't realized he'd kept one. She looked at the familiar handwriting and could no longer contain her emotions. She began to sob.

She let her emotions have full sway until there were no tears left. Her body felt heavy and cold. She reached for the chenille throw, dragging it across the foot of her bed and down to the floor where she was sitting. She pulled her knees into her chest and wrapped the blanket around her shoulders and hugged herself as tightly as she could. Her puffy eyes felt sore and big. She pushed back a strand of hair that had mixed with tears, getting matted to her face.

She replayed the conversation with Mrs. McClain over and over again in her mind. She tried to pinpoint the moment that her grandmother had recognized her. In her mind she saw again her grandmother's startled expression when she opened the door and guessed it had been then, at the very beginning. Sydney knew that she bore an uncanny resemblance to her aunt Judith. It had been ten years since the accident that had taken her father's life. She'd grown accustomed to her appearance. At first she could only see Judith when she looked in the mirror. But over time, she was starting to catch glimpses of herself now and then. Or maybe she just wanted to see Cindy so badly that she was only imagining it.

Aunt Judith never talked about Sydney's grandmother. Sydney had been brave enough to ask about her only once. Rather than answering, Judith shot one of her death glares that could stop an entire army in its path.

Sydney never asked again.

The dull pain in her left thigh was intensifying. She massaged her leg, even though she knew the pain was being generated by her mind. Doctor Anderson called it a *phantom pain*. "You had third-degree burns on your lower back and upper right arm," he told her. "We used your left thigh as a donor site for skin grafts. Your left thigh will be tender for a long time."

A dry chuckle escaped her throat. What would the good doctor think if he knew she was still feeling pain in her leg after all these years? She'd be a candidate for the funny farm for sure.

Her grandmother had known Judith. That was obvious. She'd taken one look at Sydney's face and recognized her, even after all these years.

She opened her father's journal. Her visit to the house where she'd grown up and then to her grandmother's brought everything full circle. Fresh tears welled when she saw again her father's bold, steady handwriting. She thumbed through the first few pages until a particular date caught her attention. Her eyes widened. The entry was recorded only a month before his death.

Went to Mother's today and sat out in the swing underneath the grape vines. I remember sitting there as a boy. There were so many dreams for the future. I feel so hollow inside. I'm trying to make sense of my life, and then I look at Cindy. She's withdrawing more and more into herself, and she's so pale. She's been cutting paper-dolls out of magazines again. Doc. Bradford says it's a form of coping that's normal for her age, but I'm not so sure. I need to spend more time with her. I love her so much. But there's this chasm between us. It keeps growing, and I don't know how to reach her. I'm not sure if I can. I just can't get rid of this fear that I'll end up losing Cindy too.

A tear fell on the page and mixed with the ink. Sydney blotted the page with the sleeve of her sweatshirt and tried to continue reading, but the words blurred. She'd forgotten all about the paper dolls. She used to search through magazines and cut out pictures of families. Pictures of a healthy mom and a happy smiling dad. How she'd wished that she could jump into one of those pictures and go to a place where everything was right again.

Seeing her grandmother had made her feel close to Avery. She'd hoped the visit would bring her comfort, but it had done just the opposite. All of the old hurt rushed back like a giant tidal wave, and she felt like the helpless sixteen-year-old of her youth. She closed her eyes, letting the tunnel of black thoughts suck her back until her memories took over. The last ten years peeled back like the tide recessing into the ocean, raking the shoreline bare. And in her mind, she was back...back to the accident that had stolen her father's life and left her scarred, back to when she was Cindy, back to where it all began.

* * * * *

Cindy would have given anything if she could have ripped the bandages off of her back and arms so she could scratch her tight, itchy flesh. It took every ounce of control she could muster to keep from screaming. The scrubs were the worst. She did scream during those, but the nurses seemed to understand. The doctor had explained that the scrubs, as painful as they were, were a necessary part of the healing process.

A plastic surgeon, the best in his field, had been called in to fix her face. She'd heard him telling her aunt Judith that most of the bones in her face had been shattered. She could have told him that. "It will require a full reconstruction," Cindy heard him say. She tried to convince herself that her physical pain was of little consequence. She was going to die anyway. She'd willed herself to die. What was the use of living? First her mother, and now her father.

"Cindy."

Cindy didn't turn her head toward the voice. She recognized it instantly. It was her aunt Judith. Judith visited her every afternoon. The bandages still covered her face but had been removed from her eyes. "It's a miracle," Dr. Anderson told Judith. "Her eyes are okay. They weren't damaged in the accident."

Some miracle, Sydney thought. Why couldn't her father have lived? Now that would've been a good miracle.

"Cindy," Judith said, her voice laced with frustration. "I'm not leaving, so you might as well turn around and look at me."

Cindy continued to stare out the window.

Judith cleared her throat. "I can't even begin to imagine how you must be feeling. As you know, your father and I didn't always see eye to eye. I know I'm not the easiest person in the world to get along with. I don't have Susan's gift for openly expressing my feelings. I'm only going to say this once. I will always be here for you. I wanted Avery to send you to me right after Susan died."

Judith paused, her voice heavy with regret. "The Lord has sent you to me. I don't care how much it takes. I'll spend every dime I have if I have to. I'll do whatever it takes to get you well." Her voice caught. "Just please don't shut me out."

The conviction of Judith's words penetrated Cindy's outer shell like a tiny ray of light and went straight to her heart. Tears trickled from under Cindy's bandages. Judith placed her hand on the bed beside Cindy's. Finally, Cindy moved her hand a fraction and clasped her aunt's hand. They sat there, holding each other. It was the only thing in the world that either of them had to hold onto.

* * * * *

Cindy gripped the sheets of her hospital bed while she listened to Dr. Anderson's instructions.

"As you know, Dr. Stanton did the reconstructive surgery on your face. He's here with me to check your progress."

Cindy nodded. Her face was completely covered in bandages. Today, the doctors were removing them. Her face felt like it was swollen to the size of a watermelon. She could only imagine how she must look. In a few more minutes, all the guessing would be over. She would know.

"Your surgery was successful," Dr. Stanton said. "Your face will remain swollen and tender for another week or so. That's normal. But today you will be able to get a general idea of how you now look."

"Are you ready?" Dr. Anderson asked.

Panic fluttered in Cindy's stomach, and she searched the eyes staring back at her from around the room until she found Judith's. She made eye contact with her aunt.

Judith's expression suggested that everything would be okay. It was the reassurance Cindy needed. "I'm ready."

One nurse handed Cindy a mirror while another started carefully removing her bandages.

"Now remember," Dr. Stanton warned, "your face is swollen and bruised. This will subside, and you will look normal."

The room became deathly silent when the last bandage was removed. Cindy raised the mirror, and one of the nurses gasped. Cindy's hand began to shake. She touched her cheek and the bridge of her nose.

Judith rushed to her side and clasped her other hand.

"What have they done to me?" Cindy whispered.

"The swelling will go away," Judith said.

"This is not me! I want my face! This is not my face!"

Judith touched Cindy's arm, but Cindy pushed it away. A muffled sob escaped her throat and then rage boiled up in her chest. She threw the mirror, sending it flying across the room where it shattered.

Cindy's reaction sent the nurses scurrying. One went to clean up the glass and the other to retrieve a sedative.

"Cindy, you're being irrational. You need to calm down," Judith said.

"The bones in your face were shattered," Dr. Anderson said. "Dr. Stanton had to reconstruct them."

"But I look like Judith! I used to look like my mother! I want my face back!"

Cindy started crying hysterically. The nurse returned with a needle. Cindy thrashed like a caged cougar.

*   *   *   *   *

The scene was too horrific for Judith to watch. She left the room.

She leaned against the wall outside Cindy's room for support. Judith couldn't get the image out of her mind. Her niece, so tiny and vulnerable, lying there with the bandages on her face and her blonde hair spreading like silk over the pillow. Then lashing out in pain and anger at her altered appearance.

Yes, she admitted to herself, she'd been jealous of the family that Susan had, the family that she could never have. But, she didn't want it like this. Not like this.

She thought back to the day when Avery had accused her of trying to steal Cindy away from him. He called her an ice queen. How she wished she could freeze her heart now and shield it from the pain she was feeling. Then she'd gotten Avery's letter. If only she'd gone that very day and gotten Cindy.

"The nurses gave Cindy a sedative."

Judith looked up at Dr. Anderson. He had followed her into the hallway.

He shook his head. "This is what I was afraid might happen. It was against my better judgment to make her look so much like you."

Judith's lip tightened. "She'll be all right."

He raised an eyebrow. "I'm not so sure."

Doubt crept up her spine. Maybe the doctor was right. She felt tired—tired and defeated. No, she wouldn't give in to such thoughts. She straightened her shoulders. Cindy would be okay. She was strong—strong and resilient like herself.

"I could've made Cindy look very similar to the way she did before. I still don't understand why you wouldn't agree to that. It makes no sense whatsoever."

"That's none of your concern, doctor."

Dr. Anderson closed Cindy's chart. "Ms. Lassiter, you've made this whole situation very difficult. I tried to hold a conference with you on several occasions, but you were unavailable, as you will recall."

Judith shifted her feet. The doctor was right. He'd tried to meet with her, but she'd always given some excuse as to why she couldn't be there. The truth was that she hadn't wanted to meet with him. That would have made everything seem too real. She hadn't been able to deal with the news he might tell her. And she didn't want to answer his intrusive questions as to why she wanted Cindy to resemble herself. She and Susan had looked so much alike that she assumed Cindy would be pleased. Maybe it had been a fairytale idea to think that she could make Cindy into something she could understand. That if they looked more alike then they would somehow be more alike. At any rate, she couldn't let them make her look like her old self. No matter what the doctor said. No, that wasn't an option. Too many risks. On the other hand, she should have thought it through. She should have realized—

"I take it you're available now?"

Judith nodded.

"Let's go down to my office, and I'll update you on Cindy's condition."

She followed Dr. Anderson to his office. "Cindy is a very lucky girl," he said. "Her lower back sustained the deepest burns. The skin in that area was irreparable."

Nausea swept over Judith. His words sounded so impersonal, like he was talking about a slab of meat, not her beloved niece.

"Are you okay?"

Judith raised her chin. "I'm fine. Please continue."

"We've been doing skin grafts on her back. We are taking healthy skin from her left thigh and grafting it on her back. Her right arm sustained a severe burn, but thankfully her scarring there is hypertrophic."

Judith raised an eyebrow. "In layman's terms, doctor?"

"Hypertrophic scars are thick, red, and raised. But they don't develop beyond the injury site. A surgical procedure called dermabrasion was done on her arm. Dermabrasion is used to smooth scar tissue by shaving or scraping off the top layers of the skin. It soothes the surface of the scar. Over time, repigmentation will return. Then the skin should closely match the surrounding skin.

"Cindy will need to wear a pressure garment on her arm for the next twelve to eighteen months. It will help minimize the hypertrophic scars that are already there and will help prevent others from forming."

The doctor studied Judith's face and then continued. "As I was saying, Cindy is very lucky. The burns on her arm don't extend to her elbow. From all outward appearances, she will look completely normal."

Judith sighed. "Good."

"I said she will look normal. I didn't say she would be normal. Cindy has been through a traumatic experience. She will need counseling. She manifests evidence of some psychological trauma."

Judith bristled. "My niece is strong; she'll get through this."

"I'm not so sure."

Judith's eyes met his. "It's not your concern. You did your part, doctor. I'll take care of the rest."

*　*　*　*　*

Sydney awoke the next morning to the incessant ringing of her alarm clock. She hit the snooze button and pulled her pillow over her face. All night long she'd dreamed of hospitals and Judith. She leaned over to her nightstand and clutched her father's journal, just to make sure it was real. She sat up in bed and held it to her chest.

Her alarm went off again. This time she had to get up. She threw off her covers and walked over to her jewelry box, where she retrieved a small key attached to a gold chain. Then she went into her living room and over to a secretary desk that sat in a far corner. She used the key to unlock the middle drawer and placed the journal in the far back section, beside the two newspaper articles.

She pulled out the articles and read them again. She must've gone over them a hundred times. One article told about the boat explosion that had injured her and taken her father's life. The other was about a Judge Crawford of Glendale.

The headline read, "Local judge killed in a car bomb." She skimmed the article until she got to the meat of it. "Judge Crawford was killed instantly when his car exploded. Investigators are still trying to determine the motive for the crime. Several suspects are being questioned. He is survived by his wife, Harriet, and their two children."

The judge was killed the same day as Avery. Judith had kept these articles together. Why? Did Avery and Judge Crawford know each other? Did the same person murder both of them? There were so many unanswered questions.

She would go over her father's journal with a fine tooth comb, looking for clues about his death. Sean O'Conner had unknowingly aided her quest by giving his permission to search through the old files.

She looked in the mirror that morning and saw not only Sydney Lassiter but Cindy McClain as well. She studied her reflection and vowed to the girl that she once was that she would use every resource at her disposal, including Judith's money if necessary, to find her father's killer and bring him to justice.

"Trust in the Lord with all thine heart;
And lean not unto thine own understanding."
—*Proverbs 3:5*

chapter nine

Sydney clutched her raincoat and looked out the
office window at the pouring rain. It had started
as a drizzling mist that turned into a downpour later in
the day. In Texas the storm would have blown in and
out in a matter of hours, but here the mountains
sometimes held the clouds for days.

The day had dragged by. Sydney did her best to
concentrate on her work, but her mind kept returning
to the journal locked in her secretary. She reached to
make sure the key was still attached to its chain. Tonight
would be a good night to go home and curl up with a hot
cup of chicken noodle soup, but she had another stop to
make first—her grandmother's house. After that she
would have the rest of the night to research the safety
files. That is, if she could ever get them from Barb. She'd
already asked Barb for them several times. Sydney
squared her shoulders. Time to bring this little charade
to a head. She had a job to do and was tired of tip-toeing
around Barb.

She walked up to the front and stood by Barb's desk.
"It doesn't look like this rain's going to let up. I think
I'll make a mad dash for the car. By the way, have you
had time to retrieve those files?"

Barb raised an eyebrow.

Sydney wished she could read Barb's thoughts. Then
again, maybe she didn't want to know. She was probably

hoping that Sydney would get so fed up of the headaches that she would leave the mill with her tail tucked between her legs. What was it going to take for Barb to take her seriously?

"I told you that I'll get to that when I can. Do you think that's all I have to do?"

Sydney looked Barb square in the eye. "Let's get one thing straight. I have a job to do, and I'm going to do it. You can either get on board with the rest of the team or you can get your purse and keep on walking, right out the door."

Barb just looked up at Sydney.

"I can promise you one thing. If you don't have those files on my desk by tomorrow morning, I'm writing a letter to Sean and sending a copy of it to Jake Roberts."

Sydney didn't wait for a response. She turned her back on Barb and headed out the door into the rain.

*   *   *   *   *

If Sydney ever wondered what type of reception she would get from her grandmother, she didn't have to wait long for an answer. She knocked once before the door opened, and she found herself being held in a tight embrace.

"I'm so glad you didn't wait long to come back. Come inside and take off that wet raincoat. You'll catch your death."

"Thank you," Sydney said, shaking off a shiver. Even though it was July, the rain brought a chill to the humid air.

"Come in the kitchen, and I'll make us a cup of herbal tea. Do you like herbal tea?"

A smile played around the corners of Sydney's lips. "It's my favorite."

Sydney watched her grandmother move skillfully around the cozy kitchen. Her sage-colored silk blouse and beige linen pants complemented the color of her kitchen. The walls were done in a soft butter hue that gave the hint of gold in certain light. It was the perfect backdrop for the bare maple cabinets. Subtle earth-tone tiles covered the floor and countertops. Glass canisters, filled with rice and assortments of beans, lined the counter top. It reminded Sydney of her dad's workshop. Sydney's mom was always kidding her dad about being organized like Stella.

Sydney walked over to the double French doors that led off the kitchen to a bricked patio. She noticed a jasmine vine twining plentifully up the wooden trellis. She watched water pour from the gutters, leaving puddles on the ground. Her gaze moved further. The two oaks were still there, their supple branches swaying back and forth, holding their own against the wind and rain. And then there was the persimmon tree, its branches more brittle and gnarly. Possibly the trees were bigger than she remembered, but she couldn't tell for sure. She'd played in that very grass. Those trees had been her trees, her domain to explore. It seemed weird to think that this garden had been here the whole time she'd been away. She'd been through so much and it looked untouched, almost as though she'd left it only yesterday.

She tried to picture Avery in the garden. He'd been here in this house. Maybe he'd stood in this very spot.

Stella gently touched her arm. "Here's your tea. Let's go to the living room. We have much to talk about."

Sydney sipped her tea. It was hard to know where to begin. She cleared her throat and looked at Stella's intelligent green eyes. "Could I ask you a question?"

Stella put her cup of herbal tea on the mahogany table. "Of course. I'll answer any questions you have, if I can."

Sydney swallowed hard. Only her shaky hands portrayed the tumultuous emotions that were churning inside. She wanted to scream at the top of her lungs, demanding to know why her grandmother hadn't contacted her during all of those years when it would have been so important. "Why didn't you write to me?"

Rather than answering, Stella rose from the sofa and walked out of the room. A moment later, she returned, carrying a stack of letters. She sat beside Sydney. "These are for you."

Sydney put down her cup and ran her hand over the stack of unopened letters in her lap, each of them stamped return to sender.

"But why?"

"Judith sent them back."

Sydney shook her head. "No, there must be some mistake. Why would she do such a thing? How could she?"

Stella sat quietly for a moment and then spoke. "Judith was a complicated woman. I don't fully understand her reasoning, but I believe she had your best interest at heart. Maybe she was trying to shut out a world of hurt. I think she felt that any communication with me would place you in danger. She was trying to protect you."

Sydney's eyes burned. "I know. After Judith died, her lawyer gave me a key to her safety deposit box. Inside I found a letter that Dad had written to her and two newspaper articles. Judith kept them all these years."

This caught Stella's attention. "Avery wrote Judith a letter? When?"

"About a month before he died."

"What did it say?"

Sydney took a deep breath. "He told Judith that he'd reconsidered her offer for me to come and live with her. He'd been trying to call her, but she'd taken a trip to Europe, so he wrote her instead. He told her that he would explain the details in person but the gist of it was that he felt I was in danger and would be safe with her."

"What kind of danger?"

Sydney shrugged. "The letter didn't specify. I think Dad deliberately kept it vague because he was waiting to explain it all to Judith in person. He never got the chance."

"You mentioned some newspaper articles. Were they about Avery's death?"

"One was about the boat accident that killed Dad and the other was about a Judge Crawford who was killed by a car bomb. Both incidents took place on the same day."

Stella's eyebrows knitted. Sydney could tell from the expression on her grandmother's face that she had her suspicions.

"Did Dad know Judge Crawford?"

Stella shook her head. "If he did, he never mentioned him to me. All Avery said was that he was concerned about some things."

"What things?"

"I don't know. He never told me."

"Did you read the journal?"

Stella's face was blank. "What journal?"

"It was in the box you gave me. I assumed that you knew about it."

"No. Shortly after Avery's death, I went to his house and boxed up those items. I wasn't even sure what to save. I've meant to look through them, but it was too painful."

Sydney nodded in understanding.

"Avery kept a journal?"

"He wrote in it right up until his death. I read some of it last night."

"Did you see anything that would help us know more about the cause of his death?"

"It was all so vague. Just bits and pieces." She massaged her throbbing temples. "Everything is just a big blur, and I don't know how to make sense of any of it."

"Why don't you start at the beginning? Tell me everything from the accident on."

Sydney closed her eyes. "I remember waking up in the hospital. I knew right away that something was wrong when I started asking about Dad. No one would tell me anything. Judith finally told me. The bones in my face were shattered, and I was severely burned. I went through surgery and then rehabilitation. The doctors pieced me back together."

Stella's face paled. "I knew you were injured, but I had no idea how bad off you were. You were taken to the hospital in Glendale where you remained unconscious. I stayed with you during the night and left the next day to go home and get cleaned up. When I came back that afternoon, you were gone. Judith had you transported to a hospital in Dallas."

"When did you lose contact with Judith?"

"I called her, and she told me that Avery had contacted her before his death, asking her to take care of you. She also let me know, in no uncertain terms, that you would remain with her. I received one other call from Judith about six months later, letting me know you were okay."

Stella's eyes seemed to plead for understanding. "You were better off with Judith. I knew that she would take care of you. But most of all, I knew you would be safe."

Sydney's head started to spin. She tried to make sense of it all.

"Don't judge Judith too harshly. She did what she thought was best for you. She loved you and was trying to protect you."

Sydney nodded. For all of Judith's faults, that was one thing she knew. "I always thought Dad's death was an accident. I never realized it wasn't until after Judith's death when I found Dad's note and the newspaper articles."

"We still don't know for sure whether or not Avery's death was an accident. We can't be too quick to rush to conclusions."

"Well, Judith obviously thought I was in danger." She threw her hands up in the air. "And the whole thing— Dad's letter, two explosions on the same day—it's all just a little too coincidental, don't you think?"

Stella looked Sydney in the eye. "Yes, you're right. Deep down, I've always questioned whether or not Avery's death was an accident. That's another reason I never fought Judith to get you back." She paused. "I guess I'm just afraid. You know what the good book says: 'It rains on the just and the unjust all the same.'" She looked up at the ceiling and then down at her hands. "I can't lose you again."

Sydney hugged her grandmother. Tears ran down both of their cheeks. Finally, Sydney pulled away and laughed humorlessly. "I always wondered why Judith made me change my name. She came in one day at the hospital and told me that it was time to start fresh. 'We're going to start our lives right now,' she told me. 'You need a new name.' She looked me up and down. 'What do you think about Sydney?' I liked the name but would've never told Judith otherwise."

Stella chuckled. "You were wise not to cross Judith." She reached for her cup. "How did she die?"

"Breast cancer, just like Mom. Judith didn't tell me at first. She suggested that I go to Europe for the summer. Now I realize that it was her way of getting me out of the way so she could go through treatments. When I came home and saw how skinny and frail she was, I knew something was wrong. She passed away a few months later."

Stella shook her head. "Judith was a piece of work. I remember the first time I saw her. Avery brought her by to introduce her. I took one look at her flaxen hair and stubborn chin and knew that Avery was flirting with trouble."

Sydney's eyes grew round. "What?"

"Didn't you know that Avery dated Judith first?"

Sydney shook her head.

"Avery was finishing up his last year at the University of Alabama when he met Judith at a fraternity party. He took one look at her and was smitten. I think he would've married her right on the spot if she would've agreed. But Judith wanted everything on her terms. It was all a game to her. She thought she had Avery wrapped around her little finger. What she didn't count on, however, was what happened when she took Avery home to meet her family. That's when he met your mother. Avery's infatuation with Judith paled like fool's gold beside the real thing.

"Susan was everything Judith wasn't. Her wholesome features had always taken backstage to

Judith's beauty, but Susan didn't mind. She was happy letting her older sister take center stage. Avery felt as though he'd discovered some rare flower that belonged only to him. He and Susan were inseparable from that moment on. I don't reckon Judith ever did get over Avery choosing Susan over her."

Sydney was speechless for a moment. She shook her head. "I had no idea. No one ever mentioned any of this to me." Sydney looked at Stella. "Before my surgery I used to look just like my mom."

"I remember."

A trace of bitterness returned when Sydney thought back to the day her new face was unveiled. "They made me look just like Judith. So much that even you recognized me after all these years."

Stella's laugh echoed through the room. "No, you're wrong. It wasn't Judith that I saw when I first opened that door." The conviction of Stella's words rang true. Her eyes met Sydney's. "I saw Avery when I opened that door. You may resemble Judith, but you're Avery through and through."

Sydney hugged herself. She stared into the distance, her blue eyes glazed. "Oh, how I wish that were true." She voiced the question she'd asked herself over and over. "Why do you think Judith made me look so much like her?"

"Did you ask her?"

"Right after the accident, I tried a couple of times, but she never would give me a straight answer. She told me that all of my bones were broken and that the doctors did the best they could."

"Hah!" Stella clamped her lips shut. "Sorry."

Sydney shook her head, barely acknowledging Stella's comment. "As time went on, it became harder to ask her about it. She didn't like talking about anything that was unpleasant."

Stella chuckled. "Sounds about right."

"But why? Why do you think she made me look like her?"

"Well, I think Judith in her own way was trying to protect you. Has anyone besides me recognized you?"

This caught Sydney off guard. "Well...no. But that still doesn't explain why she made me look like her. She could've had them alter my face without doing that."

"Who knows what Judith was thinking? Maybe she was trying to make you into the daughter she never had."

They sat in silence, each lost in thought.

Sydney spoke the next words softly, afraid of speaking them at all. "Dad and I had an argument that last day on the boat. He wanted me to go and live with Judith. He tried to talk to me, but I wouldn't listen." Her voice faltered. "I'd give anything to live that moment over again. If only I'd listened, given him a chance to explain." She shook her head.

"*If only* is a very dangerous phrase. It'll drive you crazy if you let it. Avery knew how much you loved him."

"Sometimes I just get so afraid."

She lapsed into silence. After a moment, Stella spoke. "Of what? Dying?"

Sydney mulled over the question. "No, I'm not afraid of death," she finally said. "It's not like I have a death-wish, if that's what you mean. It's just that there's no dishonor in death. Right after Dad was killed I wanted to die. I knew that every breath I took toward recovery led me further from him and Mom."

Stella cocked her head. "Do you mean to tell me that you don't fear death at all? I've lived all these years, and the thought of it still gives me the jitters."

"I guess I'm a little afraid of dying," Sydney admitted with a shrug.

Stella nodded. "It's always good to have a healthy respect for death." She studied Sydney. "There's no dishonor in living, either. Avery and Susan want you to be happy."

Sydney's hand flew up to brush aside the comment. "Oh, I know that. That's not what I'm trying to say." She tried to find a way to give voice to her fears. Some fears loomed so large that it was impossible to put them

into words. At times the guilt was almost unbearable.
Avery had asked her to check the bilge of the boat for
gasoline fumes. Was she not careful enough? Why didn't
she smell the fumes? If foul play wasn't involved, then
it could mean only one thing. The accident was her fault.
"Dad always said that the finest steel comes from the
hottest fire."

A smile curved Stella's mouth. "I remember."

Sydney looked at her grandmother and wondered if
she'd spoken too much. Stella's face was impossible to
read. The ticking of the clock on the wall grew louder.
The silence stretched like a rubber band between them.

Sydney swallowed in an attempt to moisten her dry
throat. "I'm just afraid I might not measure up. When
my time comes, and I'm put in the fire, I hope I can prove
myself and not crumble like rust under the pressure.
Or even worse, what if my time has already come and
gone? What if I've already failed and don't even have
sense enough to know it?"

Stella chuckled. "How like Avery you are—always
questioning everything. Let me ask you this. If you were
so afraid of facing the fire, why did you come back?"

"Maybe I shouldn't have. Believe me, I thought
about just turning my back and walking away. Judith
was very wealthy. She left everything to me. I never have
to want for anything again."

Stella smiled wisely. "No, you did the right thing.
You wouldn't have been able to escape the truth any
more than Judith could."

Sydney looked at Stella. "Oh? What truth was
that?"

"That the most important things in life can't be
bought with money."

Stella's comment cut right to the heart of the
matter, and Sydney laughed despite herself. "You sound
just like Dad."

"Sometimes you have to go back a few steps before
you can move forward."

The words sank into Sydney's mind; she filed them
away to ponder later.

Stella put her arm around Sydney. "You did the right thing by coming back. Just trust your heart and have a little faith. You'll see. That'll be enough."

*　　*　　*　　*　　*

Rain was pelting like bullets when Sydney left Stella's door and bolted to her jeep. Stella tried to convince her to spend the night, but she declined the offer. She'd only planned on spending an hour at Stella's house but had stayed three. Her intent was to avoid the very thing she was getting ready to do—drive down the dark mountain in the rain.

The curvy country roads leading from her grandmother's house to the main road were deserted, and she had the eerie impression of being the only person in the world. She inched her way to the main road.

She turned her windshield wipers up a notch and strained to see in the darkness. Her conversation with Stella was playing over and over in her mind, leaving her emotionally drained. It was when she turned on the main road that she noticed the headlights behind her. She remembered the game she played as a child when she rode in the backseat. She would look behind her and pretend the headlights were following. The warning Stella gave left her with the jitters. She repeated the same phrase she'd used earlier. "Sydney, please be careful. Just remember what the good book says, 'It rains on the just and the unjust.'"

*　　*　　*　　*　　*

Sydney's porch light radiated like a lighthouse. She grabbed her umbrella and ran to the door. She was just about to put the key in the lock when she stopped. Something wasn't right. Her heart lurched when she pushed on the door and it opened. Her panic returned with a vengeance. She glanced back at the deserted street and dark houses. She looked at the door, not sure what to do. Surely she'd not left it unlocked. Was she losing her mind?

She stepped over the threshold and looked inside. Everything appeared normal from what she could tell. She flipped on the lights in the living room and locked the front door. Then she closed all the blinds. Her first thought was for the journal. She went to the secretary and pulled on the drawer. It was still locked, just as she'd left it. Next, she went methodically through the house, flipping on lights. She paused at the bottom of the steps, looking up at the dark stairway. She'd have to check the bedrooms too. She could hear every creak up the stairs on her way up. She reached her hand in first and flipped on the light. Her pulse slowed down a notch when she saw the room was clear. She went next to the other bedroom and then backtracked, checking in the closets and even under her bed, just to be sure.

The train whistle sounded, making her flinch. She headed downstairs and caught a glimpse of herself in the hall mirror. She scowled at her pale reflection. If only Ginger could see her now. She was afraid of her own shadow.

A red light was blinking on her answering machine, and she walked over and pressed the button. Ginger's cheery voice came over the speaker, restoring a measure of reality.

Not waiting for Ginger's message to end, Sydney picked up the phone and dialed her number.

"Hello? Gin? It's me."

"Where've you been? I've been trying to reach you for hours."

The mere sound of Ginger's voice did more to comfort her than any spoken reassurance could. She flipped off her shoes and collapsed on the sofa. "I went to visit my grandmother."

Ginger was quiet for a moment. "Are you sure that was a good idea?"

Sydney sighed. "No, I'm not sure of anything anymore."

"Well, how did it go? Don't spare any details."

She smiled. She could just picture Ginger, wearing shorts and a T-shirt, lounging on her sofa. Ginger and Mark had recently moved to a trendy apartment in downtown Ft. Worth known as The Firestone. A major renovation project was under way in the downtown district of Ft. Worth. The intent was to revamp the area, making it a viable part of the city again. Old abandoned buildings were being turned into quaint shops, and classical apartment homes were cropping up.

Sydney started at the beginning and told Ginger about the visit to Stella's house, leaving out the unlocked front door.

"Wow," Ginger said. "You've had an eventful week." There was a pause. "Do you really think you could be in any sort of danger? No one except your grandmother knows who you are."

There was one other person who knew Sydney's true identity, but she didn't mention this to Ginger. She looked toward the door. "Don't worry. This place is just like Mayberry. I'm perfectly safe."

"Even so, you be careful." Then, characteristic of Ginger, she suddenly switched gears. "How was church Sunday?"

Sydney hesitated. "I haven't had a chance to go yet." Her voice trailed off as she braced herself for what was sure to come.

"Syd, you know how easy it is to get out of the habit of going. It's so important."

Sydney rolled her eyes. She knew that Ginger meant well, but going to church was at the bottom of her priority list at the moment. "I know I need to go. I plan to. I just haven't had time. Besides, I'm not even sure where the nearest chapel is."

"That's okay. I've already looked it up for you. Grab a pen and write down this address."

A dry chuckle escaped Sydney's lips. She reached for a scrap sheet of paper and a pen and took down the address.

"Promise me you'll go this week?"

Sydney was used to Ginger's bullying and wasn't going to be that easily swayed. "I'll think about it."

Ginger groaned. "You're impossible."

Sydney laughed. "I sure do wish you were here to keep me in line."

"Someone needs to."

"Well, Gin, it's getting late. I need to get some rest."

"Are you sure you're okay? You seem a little edgy."

Sydney forced a laugh. "No need to worry. I'm fine, really. Goodnight."

Even as she spoke the words, an uneasy feeling settled like concrete in the pit of her stomach. She looked toward the door. Had someone been in her house tonight? She brushed the thought aside and chastised herself for being so ridiculous. Still, she unclasped the chain from her neck and took the key and unlocked the drawer of her secretary. She felt a sense of relief when her fingers clutched the journal. She pulled it out and held it to her chest. Tonight she would sleep with it under her pillow. It was the conversation with Stella that had unsettled her. "Too many ghosts," she said aloud. What she needed was a good night's rest and some sunshine. She frowned. The rain had been relentless. She went to the window and looked through the blinds to see if the rain had stopped. No such luck. Had someone been in her house tonight? Was he out there, watching? The thought sent prickles over her. She looked at the empty street and then next door at her neighbor's open window. The lace curtain moved. Quickly, she closed the blinds and headed for the comfort of her bed.

"...joy cometh in the morning."
—Psalms 30:5

chapter ten

Sydney hadn't planned on dating Kendall. It just sort of happened. Kind of like the time she and Ginger went shopping. Ginger saw a brown sweater hanging on the rack.

"Try it on Syd."

Sydney wrinkled her nose. "That? You want me to try on that?" She walked away from the sweater to look at something else. "I don't think so."

Ginger wasn't going to give up so easily. "It's perfect for you."

"Brown's not one of my better colors."

Ginger groaned. "Just try it on."

"Okay!"

Sydney tried on the sweater. To her amazement and Ginger's delight, it looked great.

"It just goes to prove that you can't always tell how something's gonna look unless you try it on."

Trying it on. That's what Sydney was doing with Kendall. And so far, he seemed to fit.

She'd been surprised and a little disappointed that he hadn't called her after their first date. The weekend was approaching and no call from Kendall. She'd slept in on Saturday and was sitting at the kitchen table eating a bowl of fruity pebbles, still wearing the shorts and long T-shirt she'd slept in the night before, when she heard the roar of an engine outside.

If rednecks are going to race up and down the street, the least they could do is buy a muffler, she thought. She waited for the sound to pass, but it only got louder. Annoyed, she put her empty bowl in the sink and went into the living room to look out her front window. By the time she reached the window, the noise had stopped. She opened the blinds and frowned. Why was there a motorcycle in her driveway?

The knock at the door caused her to jump. She looked down at her clothes. She went to the door and looked out the peep hole, raking her fingers through her disheveled hair.

"Kendall, this is a surprise. I wasn't expecting...um...you." Her face warmed when she watched his gaze go from her face to her clothes.

He smiled boyishly. "I just thought you might wanna go for a ride."

Her eyes widened and she pointed to the bike. "On that?"

"Uh huh."

"But I'm not dressed."

He stepped inside the living room. "It's okay. We're in no hurry. I'll wait."

There were probably at least half a dozen reasons why she shouldn't go. She'd planned on spending her Saturday recouping and reading the journal. "Make yourself at home," she heard herself say. "I'll only be a minute."

"Make sure you wear jeans. I'd hate for those nice legs of yours to get scratched up on my bike."

She warmed at the compliment.

*　　*　　*　　*　　*

"How in the world did I let you talk me into this?" Sydney yelled, tightening her grip around Kendall's waist.

In response, Kendall's laughter floated through the air. She looked at the brilliant blue sky, feeling the wind whip through her hair. The sun had finally broken through the clouds, dispelling the rain. She could feel the warmth of Kendall's body against hers. They raced against the wind, down the secluded country road. Her heart was pounding in her ears. She felt more alive at that moment than she'd felt in a very long time.

The picturesque landscape, with the gentle sloping mountain covered with green trees, whizzed by them. She didn't know where Kendall was taking her and really didn't care. It was nice to let someone else be in control for a while.

Kendall slowed down the bike and maneuvered it to the side of the road where it came to a stop. Sydney loosened her grip on his waist.

"How ya doin'?"

"Great."

"I wanna show you something." He pointed to the mountain. "See that old steel cable?"

Sydney nodded. A rusty cable extended from the top of the mountain to the bottom and across the road to the other side. The thick foliage made it impossible to see where the cable ended. "Where does it go?"

"To an abandoned factory." He pointed. "The river is over there. The factory was directly on the river. Coal was mined on top of the mountain and then put in a cable box and taken to the river where it was loaded onto barges."

Sydney wasn't sure where this was going. "That's interesting."

"Just a little Stoney Creek trivia for ya." He smiled. "And a good excuse to get off of this bike and stretch my legs."

Sydney laughed. "Ah, now the truth comes out," she said, taking off her helmet and running her fingers through her hair. "Kendall, what is that over there in that field? It looks like hundreds of tiny a-frame tin huts."

Kendall gave her a quizzical look.

"Well?

"You're serious? You really don't know what those are?"

The condescension in Kendall's tone irked her. "If I knew I wouldn't have asked you."

"I'm sorry. I forgot that you're not a country girl. I guess they don't raise fighting roosters in Dallas-Ft. Worth, do they?" He laughed.

"They raise roosters to fight?"

"Sure, not only do they raise them to fight, they also raise them to sell. Each one of those birds could bring anywhere from $1,200 to $2,500."

Sydney wrinkled her nose. "Why would anyone do such a thing?"

"For money, of course. People bet on which one will kill the other first."

She cringed. "How barbaric."

Kendall eyed her with amusement. "Cock fighting has been around for thousands of years. Alexander the Great staged cock fights for his men the night before they went to battle."

"Why?"

"To pump up his troops. Make them more courageous."

She raised an eyebrow.

"It's true." He paused. "Do you eat chicken?"

She sensed a trap. "Well, yes. Of course."

"Do you think those chickens just lay down and die so you can have chicken McNuggets anytime you want to?"

"That's different."

He shook his head. "Some people think that game chickens have it much better than their counterparts."

She frowned. "How so?"

"Well, for one thing they're housed in separate pens. Chickens raised for human consumption live in cramped quarters and are debeaked and pumped full of growth hormones. Then comes the slaughter house."

She shuddered.

Kendall pointed to the huts. "These chickens each

have their own patch of grass and are usually very well taken care of because of their high value."

"Until they're killed."

His expression suggested that he would have liked to have said more but he didn't want their date to end in an argument. "Haven't you ever heard the guys at the sawmill talking about it? A lot of them go to cockfights."

The men at the sawmill never told her anything. As a matter of fact, most of them stayed as far away from her as they could get, but she'd never admit that to Kendall. "Maybe I should go check it out sometime."

"You've got to be kidding. You at a cockfight? I don't think so."

"Have you ever taken a girl with you?"

Kendall kicked at the dirt on the ground. "Yeah." He avoided her eyes. "But she didn't come from Dallas-Ft. Worth."

The remark stung, and she clamped her jaw shut.

He got back on his bike. "Let's ride some more." Maybe he was wondering where their conversation had taken a wrong turn.

Sydney sat down behind him and reached for her helmet. Kendall placed his hand over hers. "Not yet."

She looked questioningly at him for a split second before his lips met hers. His kiss was deliberately tender, and she felt her anger melt away. He pulled away and searched her expression for a reaction.

"I'd like to see you again."

She nodded.

"Tomorrow? Mama's makin' a big Sunday dinner. You'll get to meet her and Emma."

She would like to tell Kendall Fletcher that she and Emma had already met and had in fact been the best of friends. Furthermore, he would have been shocked to know how well acquainted she was with him. She thought back to her first official day in Stoney Creek when he'd replaced her flat tire. It was ironic that of all people, he'd been the one to stop. It was like fate was throwing them together. Even though she looked completely different, she'd halfway expected him to recognize her. It was a strange feeling to stand so close to someone she knew and have him think she was a complete stranger. Her face was this invisible cloak and no one could see the real her.

She shook her head and willed her mind to come back to the present. "I would love to, but I already have plans for tomorrow," Sydney said. She'd promised to have lunch with Stella.

He frowned. Kendall was obviously used to getting his way.

She arched her eyebrow.

"Come Monday then."

"Monday sounds good."

"Good, it's all settled." He studied her face. "Would you like to get a closer look at the old coal mine building?"

"Sure." She was having too much fun and didn't want the date to end anytime soon.

*   *   *   *   *

"Well, what do you think?"

The building, constructed of wood and cinderblock, was nothing special in and of itself. It was the way it sat directly on the sparkling river—the faded roof—the aged wood—everything combined to give it an element of mystery, like she was peeking into a patch of the past that the present forgot to sweep away. "It's hard to believe a place like this still exists."

"I used to play here." He pointed. "I'd climb on the roof and then dive into the river."

She frowned. "Isn't it too shallow?"

They were leaning against his bike, and he put his arm around her. "No, it's great. Hey, too bad we didn't bring our swimsuits. It's a perfect day to go for a swim."

A tight smile formed on her lips and she thought about her scar. She fought the urge to touch it. She'd lost count of the times she'd turned down invitations to swim parties. The vague explanations, last minute excuses. It all ran together. "Yeah, too bad."

He traced his finger along the curve of her chin before bringing his lips to hers. A moment later, he pulled away from her. "I sure am glad you decided to come to Stoney Creek."

She looked into his warm eyes. "Yeah, me too."

He smiled and moved to get back on his bike. "Now you'd better hold on tight 'cause I'm fixin' to take you on the ride of your life."

"The full soul loatheth an honeycomb; but to the
hungry soul every bitter thing is sweet."
—*Proverbs 27:7*

chapter eleven

S ydney maneuvered her jeep up the steep
mountain. Her stay in Stoney Creek was
definitely improving her driving skills. She was growing
more comfortable and even starting to enjoy the way
the jeep hugged the narrow windy roads. She glanced at
the clock on her dash, a quarter to six. Hopefully, she
would catch Walter at home. The motorcycle ride had
been relaxing. It was after three o'clock when she got
home. She'd then changed clothes and gone for a quick
run.

It's funny how far away Walter's place seemed when
she was a kid. Now she realized it was only a thirty-five
minute drive from town. She felt the familiar loneliness
sweep over her. She would always jump at the chance to
drive up to Walter's house with Avery.

She pulled into the circular drive and sat for a few
minutes, admiring the two-story gray house with its
large windows. Her eyes followed the sharp angles of
the steep pitched roof that afforded the house a sense of
grandeur. The exterior, a mixture of stone and wood, was
in keeping with the woodsy surroundings. The view was
the crowning pinnacle. It was just as magnificent as she
remembered. Walter's house was situated so close to the
edge of the bluff that it looked like it was digging its
heels into the solid rock to keep from being toppled over
the side by the sheer weight of itself. The back of the

house was made up almost entirely of glass, providing a panoramic view of the glittering lake below.

She got out of her jeep and followed the stepping stones leading to the front of the house. A white Cadillac caught her eye. Sydney smiled. She remembered Avery talking about how much Walter liked his toys. From the looks of things, not much had changed. In Judith's circle of friends, Sydney had seen her share of expensive homes, but she had to admit that Walter's set-up rivaled some of the best.

Walter had worked at the sawmill with Avery. She knew that Walter could have never afforded a place like this on a general manager's salary and wondered if he'd come into an inheritance. Or maybe he was a savvy investor.

The bittersweet memories that seeped into her blood were as tantalizing and unsatisfying as dry water. Memories of running wild and free without a care in the world. Memories of being swept up in the comfort of Avery's safe arms. It was all so close. So close she could almost close her eyes and touch him. The water, sparkling in the distance looked so wet and inviting, but she could never get to it. She was here where it was dry, thirsting for something that could never be quenched.

She willed her mind to be quiet, pushed once on the doorbell, and waited.

Maurene opened the door and looked Sydney up and down. Sydney could tell that there was no trace of recognition in her cool eyes. "May I help you?"

Sydney smiled politely and extended her hand. "Hi, I'm Sydney Lassiter, the new safety coordinator at the sawmill. I'm here to see Walter." Rather than shaking Sydney's hand, Maurene took a step back. Sydney's hand hung in mid-air for a second until she dropped it to her side.

"Come on in and have a seat. I'll get Walter."

Sydney nodded and stepped into the foyer. She tried to remember if Maurene had always been this unfriendly. Her hair was still bleached blonde, or rather white.

Maurene had always been fastidious about getting her hair set at the beauty shop every three days. She never washed and styled it herself. From the looks of her, Sydney figured that was still the case. She was an inch shorter than Sydney with a trim figure except for a slight round belly. She was wearing white pleated shorts and a sleeveless red button-up shirt with a collar. Even though Maurene was thin, she was out of shape. Her legs jiggled like jelly when she walked. Her white open-toed sandals revealed blood-red toenails that matched her fingernails. Maurene had aged tremendously. Her face was bloated, and the lines around her eyes and mouth were deep. Then again, it had been ten years since Sydney had seen her. She remembered Avery saying that Maurene was a lot shrewder than she acted. From the looks of things, she wasn't so sure.

The great room had natural heart pine floors that might have looked bare were it not for the plush colorful rugs scattered throughout the room. She walked over and sat down in an overstuffed brown leather chair that was situated near the stone fireplace. Her eyes went to the open ceiling and exposed rafters. One of the pictures hanging on the wall caught her attention. A Ben Hampton print titled *Rambling Rose*. It had been years since she'd seen one of those prints. This picture was one of two in a series. One print had pink roses and the other had blue.

Avery always said that Walter had two loves: football and hunting, in that order. She was reminded of the latter when she saw the mounted head of an eight-point buck on one of the walls. It was surrounded by prints of mallard ducks. A balcony wound around three sides of the room. The living room was a good size to begin with, but the open ceiling gave the illusion of never-ending space. The sitting area was arranged to face the glass wall so that the panoramic view of the lake took center stage.

Maurene entered the room and walked to the bar in the corner. "Walter'll be down in a jiffy."

"Thank you."

Maurene's hands shook when she poured herself a drink. She looked back at Sydney. "Can I get you something to drink?"

"No, thank you." There was something not quite right about Maurene.

Both Maurene and Sydney watched Walter descend the stairs.

He smiled affectionately and took both of Sydney's hands in his. "Hello, dear. You are a beautiful woman," he said, kissing her on the cheek.

"I hope I'm not interrupting anything. I probably should've called first."

Walter brushed aside her apology. "Nonsense. You're welcome here anytime. It's good to see you," he said in that low comforting voice that Sydney remembered.

She studied Walter, trying to reconcile this living flesh-and-blood person with the memory from her childhood. He'd been a distant figure then, a friend of her dad's. Nothing more. He was a little heavier than she remembered and walked with a slower gait. Gray sprinkled his once jet-black hair. And except for a slight receding line, it was still thick. She searched his brown eyes. What did she remember about them? They were kind. That was it. She was relieved to see they still held the same compassion.

"It's good to see you too," she said. Walter ushered her to the sofa and sat down beside her. All doubts about coming to see him fled.

Maurene walked to the sitting area and stood with one hand resting on the loveseat. Walter looked at Maurene, and Sydney thought she detected a look of disapproval on his face when his eyes got to the glass of whiskey. She wondered how such a distinguished man could have ended up with her.

"Maurene, this is Sydney Lassiter. She's the new safety coordinator down at the mill."

"So I've heard." Maurene took a big gulp from her glass.

Walter cleared his throat. "Dear, Miss Lassiter and I are going to be discussing the sawmill." He motioned to the empty loveseat. "You're welcome to join us."

"No, I have some other things to attend to. If you'll excuse me..." Maurene sauntered from the room.

Sydney couldn't help but smile inwardly. Walter didn't want Maurene to hear their conversation any more than she did. He knew just what to say to get rid of her.

Walter leaned back into the comfort of the plush sofa and crossed his legs. He reached in his shirt pocket and retrieved a cigar. "Now, shall I call you Cindy or Sydney?" He struck a match on his shoe and cupped it in his hands, lighting his cigar.

His candor caught her off-guard. "Um, Sydney's fine."

"How's your job?"

"It's working out just fine. I've got my work cut out for me. That's for sure, but I'm adjusting." She cleared her throat. She wanted to set things straight from the beginning. "Walter, I just want to thank you for putting in a good word for me. You're the reason I got the job."

Walter didn't make any pretense of denying what they both knew was the truth. "It was the least I could do." He looked away from her and out the window. "Avery was like a brother to me."

Sydney swallowed. "He felt the same way about you."

Walter nodded, and Sydney could tell from the faraway look in his eye that he was remembering. Finally he shook his head. "Look at you. The last time I saw you, you were a lanky teenager. Where in the world have you been all this time? I could've sworn you'd dropped off the face of the earth. The last I heard, you'd gone out of the country with your aunt."

Sydney nodded. Judith had taken her to Paris a month after she'd been released from the hospital. "It's to celebrate the beginning of our new life together,"

Judith said. Now Sydney wondered if the trip abroad had been Judith's way of protecting her. Sydney looked at Walter and realized that he was still speaking.

"I talked to your grandmother. She'd lost touch with you. We tried to find out how badly you were injured. And now after all these years, you can imagine how shocked I was when you called me about working at the mill."

"It's a long story. I'll tell you all about it some day." His silence let her know that he wasn't going to press her. She was grateful for that. "Does Maurene know about me?"

"No, I haven't told her. When you called, you mentioned that you were using another name. I assumed that you wished to preserve your anonymity." He looked her in the eye. "I suppose you have your reasons."

"Yes, thank you." She chose her next words with care. "I want to find out what really happened to my dad."

Walter frowned.

Sydney didn't wait for a reply. She wanted him to understand where she was coming from first. "That's why it was so important for me to come back here and work at the mill."

"Sydney, Avery's death was an accident."

"Was there an investigation?"

"Yes, there was. It was determined that the explosion was caused from gasoline in the bilge. You see, Avery went to the gasoline station and filled his tank. There was a leak. If it weren't for the fact that the fumes were so dense at the dock, the boat would've exploded right there at the fuel pump. When he got out in the water, he must've opened some windows. When he started the engine again, a spark caused the explosion."

Sydney's face was hot and she could not meet his eyes. "Accidents of a similar nature happen all the time," she heard him say.

There it was. That sick, gut-wrenching feeling she got whenever she thought about the bilge. "I don't know," she said. "I just think there has to be more to it than that. I can pay an investigator if I have to." The words came tumbling out and a lone tear trickled down her cheek.

Walter laid down his cigar and touched her shoulder. "It's okay honey." He paused. "You're so much like your father. That same wild imagination, always thinking there was something sinister behind everything."

"You really think his death was an accident?"

"Absolutely! Why would anyone want to kill him? Why would you think such a thing?" He looked into Sydney's eyes. "Did he ever tell you that he was in any kind of danger?"

"No, not really, but I remember he seemed really troubled about something the day of the accident. He said he had to get to an appointment."

"Sydney, that was ten years ago. A young girl's imagination can play a lot of tricks, especially if she's missing her father. " His explanation reminded her of a psychiatrist she'd seen in Dallas.

"But what about the—"

"Walter?"

Sydney and Walter looked up to see Maurene standing on the balcony. "Hank just called. He and Jo Ann are meeting us at the Riverton Catfish house in thirty minutes."

Walter forced a smile. "Okay. Thanks dear. We're almost done."

Sydney stood and smiled thinly. Before Maurene had interrupted them, she was going to tell Walter about the journal and Avery's letter to Judith. Walter would probably explain that away too. "I'm sorry. I've taken too much of your time as it is."

Walter reached for her arm. "I loved Avery. I can't even begin to imagine what you've gone through."

Sydney stared at the floor.

"But I do know one thing. Avery would want you to put all this behind you and live your life."

Sydney bit her lip to keep it from quivering. She nodded. "Thank you."

"Walter!" Maurene called from the balcony. "You know how Jo Ann fusses when we're late."

He rolled his eyes. "I said I'll be right up, dear." He walked Sydney to the door and gave her a hug. "Remember, you're family. If you need anything, all you have to do is ask. You're welcome here anytime."

"You were a good friend to Daddy."

"No," he corrected her, "Avery was a good friend to me. The best."

She smiled. "Thanks."

*   *   *   *   *

Walter watched Sydney leave. The layers of time pulled back, and the hurt was there again, festering like stagnant water. His conversation with Sydney had left him unsettled, giving him the uncanny impression that a trace of Avery's ghost still lingered in the air. Even though Sydney bore no resemblance to Avery, there was something about her—the stubborn set of her jaw—that was just like Avery. Time was irrelevant where death was concerned. Avery had taught him that. Even though Avery's death occurred ten years ago, it was always right there like bits of a kaleidoscope that shifted at random and displayed images across his mind. Usually he tried to crowd them out. This time he let them flow. He and Maurene coming back from eating dinner. Maurene fixing herself a drink. Maurene laughing, the high-pitched sound grating on his nerves. Looking out the window, the police car coming up the driveway. Maurene laughing, always drinking. Walter's clutch of anxiety at the grave expression on the sheriff's face. The sheriff speaking. "I'm afraid I have some bad news." Maurene crying, glass shattering, Walter collapsing...

He shook his head. What good could come from dredging up the dead? He'd loved Avery—more than anybody! But that was all in the past. Stirring up a hornet's nest wouldn't bring him back. He thought of Sydney, so young and vibrant. She had so much to live for. He'd spoken truthfully when he told her that Avery would want her get on with her life. That's exactly what Avery would want her to do. Somehow he'd just have to figure out a way to convince Sydney.

*   *   *   *   *

Getting ready for the OSHA inspection was slow going. Thanks to Sydney, safety regulations, which should have been established from the start, were now implemented. Now all she had to do was make sure the employees were following them, and that was no small feat. Last week she caught two workers not wearing their hard-hats and another without safety glasses. She sighed. Sometimes she felt like she was trying to accomplish the impossible.

At least she had the accident reports now. She looked down at the folders on her desk. Her conversation with Barb last week did little to speed the woman up. Maybe Barb had known that Sydney was bluffing when she threatened to write a letter to Sean and send a copy to Jake Roberts. Sean had been suspicious of her desire to dig back ten years to establish an accident trend, and she certainly didn't want to send any red flags to Jake. So she'd played Barb's little game. And now, a week later, she finally had the files. She could have jumped for joy when Barb barged into her office this morning and slammed the files on her desk.

There were twenty-six files in all. Each arranged in alphabetical order, according to the name of the person who'd been involved in the accident. Her plan was simple. She would search through the files and find the ones that took place six months before Avery's death. Then she would see if she could find some relationship between the accidents. With any luck, she might find some of the names in the journal. It was a long shot, but that's all she had to go on. Her intuition told her that Avery's death was connected with the mill. But how? Walter's words about Avery played over and over like a broken record. "That same wild imagination, always thinking there was something sinister behind everything." Was that what she was doing? Imagining things? Was it all just a wild goose chase? She shook her head at the thought of Stella. No, Stella suspected something too. Judith had also believed she was in danger. And Avery was solid as stone. If he believed he was in danger, then he had a valid reason. She looked at the stack of files. It would be like searching for a needle in a haystack.

"Well, hey there, Syd."

She instantly recognized the masculine voice and looked up. Sean O'Conner walked in her office and planted himself on the edge of her desk. Most people would sit in one of the chairs in front of her desk, but not Sean. He came waltzing in like he owned the place, as if his irresistible charm would cause her to melt. He even shortened her name, insinuating intimacy between them.

"What can I do for you?" she asked.

He flashed a brilliant smile. "How are things going? Are you getting us all straightened out?"

"Trying to."

"Are you settling into your new place? Making new friends?"

Her eyes narrowed. Where was he going with his little charade of friendliness? "I'm getting along just fine. Why?"

He shrugged and looked at her stack of files. "Just making sure Kendall's treating you okay."

Her eyes went wide. "How do you know about Kendall?"

"Word travels fast in Stoney Creek."

She nodded. "Obviously."

"So these are the famous accident reports that I've heard so much about from Barb."

"Yeah, after a week of stalling, she finally gave them to me today." She didn't bother hiding the frustration from her voice.

He opened one and began reading aloud. "Matthew Grider lost the tip of his index finger when he got too close to an edger. Ouch." He tossed it back on her desk and picked up another file and skimmed its contents. "This poor fella died."

She fought the urge to grab the file from his hands and instead picked up a pencil and began tapping it on her desk. Maybe Sean would take a hint and leave. No such luck.

"Buford Phillips was killed by a flying log that split off while going through the band saw." He pointed. "Look, it says he was drunk." He shook his head. "See, you're doing all this research, and you're only finding out what I could've told you from the beginning."

"Oh yeah, and what's that?" She reached and took the file from him.

"That these people had the same problem we do."

She raised an eyebrow. "And?"

"Stupidity."

She looked down at the file she was holding and tried to keep a poker face when she recognized Avery's handwriting. It was the same bold print that she'd seen in his journal. She couldn't have known it then, but Sean had unknowingly reached in the haystack and pulled out the needle for her. She read the description about how Buford was killed and then frowned. The writing in the next sentence had changed.

Buford Phillips was drunk at the time of the accident. That sentence was not written by Avery. She skimmed to the end of the report and noted that it was signed by Avery. She looked at the date—only a couple of months before Avery's death. Had the sentence been there all along? Or was it added after the fact?

"Hello?"

Color rose in Sydney's face. She looked up and realized that Sean was studying her.

"Earth to Sydney."

"Did you have something you want to talk to me about or did you just come in to shoot the bull? Because if you did, I have too much work to do to listen—"

His laugh cut her off. "It doesn't take much to ruffle your feathers."

She shook her head.

He picked up another file and started leafing through the pages. "Actually, I did come in here for a reason."

"Oh, yeah. What?" Her mind was still on the accident report.

"I've been doing some thinking." He paused just long enough to arouse her curiosity. "About you."

Her eyes shot upward and met his. He looked smug, satisfied. His tone remained conversational. "I ask myself: Why would a beautiful young socialite come to a town like Stoney Creek? Especially a lady so wealthy?"

His comment clutched her stomach like a vice. Blood rushed to Sydney's face, and her temples began to pound like the feathers of a caged bird. "What makes you think I'm wealthy? You don't know anything about me."

He shrugged. "You're right of course." His piercing eyes held hers. "How much do we really know about anybody? I just assumed." He raised an eyebrow. "Maybe you inherited your wealth?"

He knows, her mind screamed. Somehow he discovered who she really was.

"Why are you here, Syd? What are you looking for?" He motioned at the files. "Ten years worth of accident reports just to establish a safety trend? Come on. What kind of a fool do you take me for?"

Somehow she found the nerve to speak. "Get out of my office."

He stood. "Have it your way." He made it to the door and then turned back. "One more question."

She waited.

"Is the safety meeting still on for this afternoon?"

She fought the urge to laugh hysterically. "Why wouldn't it be? I sent the e-mail out last week."

He smiled. "Okay, see you there."

Her hands were shaking. She looked down at the files. Did Sean really know who she was? She shook her head. No, that was impossible. He was bluffing. She'd underestimated Sean O'Connor. She wouldn't make that same mistake twice.

"Be of good courage, and he shall strengthen you heart, all ye that hope in the Lord."
—Psalms 31:24

chapter twelve

K endall was no conversationalist, Sydney decided. The two rode in silence to his mother's house. She made a few surface remarks in the hopes of starting a conversation but had given up. She glanced at Kendall's profile. His jaw was relaxed and he maneuvered the steering wheel with one hand. He must have felt her stare because he smiled at her and took her hand. She smiled back and relaxed in her seat. Maybe silence wasn't so bad after all.

Sydney tried to remember how old she was when she first developed her crush on Kendall. There was a time when she'd lived for a kind word or smile from him. He was the star quarterback, and she was his younger sister's best friend. It was puppy love, adoration, and infatuation all rolled into one. Even so, that hadn't stopped her pulse from raising a notch when she realized it was Kendall who was helping her with her flat tire the day she moved to Stoney Creek.

They turned off the road and started up the long driveway. When the house came into view, Sydney felt like she was coming home. She was, in a sense. She'd spent countless weekends at the Fletcher's. Everyone always thought that Emma was rich because her house looked so impressive from the road. It was set high up on a hill with the winding driveway and pastures sprawled out below. Looking at it now, Sydney realized with a jolt that while the house was nice, it was not a mansion. It was, in fact, a modest brick home with a large sun-porch on the side. The home's only frills were the two thick round columns on the front. That's what made the house look so impressive from the street.

She waited for Kendall to open her door and was a little disappointed when she saw that he was almost to the house. She opened the truck door and hurried to catch up. One look at the anticipation on his face, and she forgot her irritation over his lack of courtesy. He was excited about her being there with him. That's all it was.

He opened the door to the porch. "Mmm. Something smells good." His voice floated through the sunroom. Sydney followed him into the living room. Emma was standing there, and she had to catch herself to keep from bounding into her arms.

"Hi there," Emma said, a broad smile on her face. She looked at Kendall with a hint of mischief in her eyes. "I've heard so much about you."

The color started in splotches on Kendall's neck and rose to his face. Sydney could tell that Emma was thoroughly enjoying her brother's discomfort. She smiled. "It's nice to meet you."

Emma was still as lanky as ever, which was surprising because Kendall was so muscular. Her brown hair was almost the identical shade of Kendall's, but it was curly where his was straight. She had it tied up with a red bandana.

"So tell me about the sawmill," Emma said. "It must be so exciting."

"Well, if you consider sweaty, old men exciting, then I suppose it is."

Emma laughed a loud, uninhibited laugh, and Sydney was delighted to realize that she still liked Emma. For some reason, it made her miss Ginger even more.

"What do you do for a living?"

"I'm a first-grade teacher."

"That's wonderful. It's a perfect job for you."

"Huh?"

Sydney's face grew warm. "I mean...um...what I meant is that it sounds like a perfect job."

Emma laughed. "It has its moments."

Kendall came up behind Sydney and put his hands on her shoulders. "Hey now, Sydney's my date. Don't monopolize her."

Emma winked at Sydney and stuck her tongue out at Kendall.

"Come on," Kendall said. "I want you to meet Mama."

They followed the appetizing aroma to the kitchen. Gail Fletcher's face broke into a smile when she saw them enter the room. She wiped her hands on her apron and pushed her glasses up farther on her nose.

"Hello, Sydney," Mrs. Fletcher said softly. "It's so nice to meet you."

Even as Sydney shook Mrs. Fletcher's hand, she noticed the cedar cabinets that reached the ceiling and a memory surfaced.

"Kendall tells me you're from Ft. Worth."

Sydney nodded. All the while her mind was going back to that night when she and Emma had decided to make a cake after everyone else went to bed. They could only find one cake pan, so they poured all the batter into it and then turned the oven up to 500 degrees so the cake would cook faster. When batter started pouring over the sides, the smoke from the oven set off the fire alarm. They took a cookie sheet and madly fanned the alarm, but the smoke was too thick. J. W. came running into the kitchen and gave them both a good scolding.

Sydney pushed away her memories and focused on what Mrs. Fletcher was saying. She was spacing out far too often. She had to remind herself that these memories were Cindy's, not Sydney's. It was all so confusing. Her identities were colliding, and she knew that she'd better get a hold of herself and keep them separate.

"Supper's almost done," Mrs. Fletcher said. "Kendall, you and Sydney go on back in the living room. I'll call you when it's ready."

Sydney walked over to the fireplace to get a better look at the pictures on the mantle. There was one of a teenage Kendall wearing his football uniform. She could tell from his disheveled hair and the grass stains smeared on his jersey that the picture had been taken right after a game. J. W.'s face was the epitome of a proud father as they smiled into the camera.

A pang of sadness wrenched Sydney's gut. It was hard to believe that J. W. had committed suicide. He was rambunctious and so full of life, more like Emma than Kendall. He and Avery had been good friends, and he even worked at the sawmill for a short time. What she remembered most about J. W. was that every year on the Fourth of July he was responsible for setting off the fireworks. People would come for miles around and gather on the lake to watch the spectacular show. One time she heard Avery tell Susan that J. W. was the driving force behind the fireworks. J. W. was the only one in Stoney Creek with enough knowledge of explosives to pull off such a feat, he said.

She reached for the picture. "Is this your father?"

"Yeah, that's my dad," Kendall said.

She waited for him to say more but the silence loomed.

"Our father died," Emma said.

Sydney studied her friend's face and waited for her to explain.

"I'm so sorry. How?" The question came out before Sydney could call it back.

Emma started to speak, then stopped when she saw the look of warning on Kendall's face.

"It's not important," Kendall said.

Sydney watched the exchange between the siblings. J. W.'s death was obviously not something Kendall wished to discuss. What had she seen in Kendall's eyes? Hurt? Anger?

If only he knew how much they had in common.

*   *   *   *   *

Sydney stepped onto her front porch and caught a whiff of magnolias floating in the air. She looked next door, and sure enough, there was her neighbor in her front yard, piddling around in her flower garden. She'd asked Tess about the woman. Surprisingly, Tess didn't know a whole lot, only the woman's name and that she was from Stoney Creek but had lived in Hawaii. According to Tess, Hazel had been back in Stoney Creek for about five years. "Except for a sister who visits occasionally, Hazel pretty much keeps to herself. It's probably just as well," Tess said in a whisper. "She's a strange duck."

This time, Sydney got a good look at Hazel Finch. Her figure was round, and she wore a loose floral muu muu, much like the one Sydney had seen her in that first day. This one was purple instead of orange. She wore a lei made of silk flowers around her neck. She peeped over her wire-rimmed glasses at Sydney, her tiny eyes sparkling with curiosity. Sydney chuckled. *She's as interested in me as I am in her.* Sydney couldn't decide who she reminded her of the most: Aunt Bea or Cinderella's fairy godmother. She looked at her watch and then at the sky. No time for introductions today. She'd have to hurry in order to get her run in before dark.

With every pound of the pavement, Sydney's tension eased a little more. Running was the best stress reliever in the world. She enjoyed the rhythm her breathing created as she became one with the pavement. She ran across the viaduct and then headed toward town, her mind alternating between Sean and Kendall. The two men were like dueling forces. Sean hadn't mentioned anything more about Sydney's background, and Sydney doubted he would. He was so pleasant at the safety meeting yesterday, almost as though the exchange between them hadn't taken place. Kendall was always polite on the surface, but Sydney sensed that some deep emotions were churning inside him. She wished he would open up and tell her what he was feeling. She laughed out loud at the irony of her thoughts. As much as she liked Kendall, she wouldn't dream of telling him who she really was.

She ran past a vacant dilapidated building. It still had the word *Grocery* printed across the front. Beside it was *Murdock's* dress shop. Her mother loved to shop at *Murdock's* and often took Cindy with her. Without fail, Cindy would end up playing in the front window with the mannequins while her mother shopped. She thought about the abandoned grocery store. Who built it? Why did it fail and *Murdock's* succeed? What were the owners thinking? Did their dreams collapse when they closed their store or did they just move on to another dream?

She'd been trying to get to the heart of Stoney Creek since she moved back here. She looked at all the venerable shops with their glass windows popping out like eyes, watching the town. They'd been here for years and would still be standing many years to come. Was that where the heart was? In the buildings? Maybe it was the collective will of the people. Were they really connected or just strangers living side by side in their separate houses?

She left the downtown area and ran toward the park, which was a gathering place for many of the locals. Not only did it have the expected playground, but a community swimming pool and tennis courts as well. The road around the park was half a mile. She would run around it twice and then head for home.

The blaring music caught her attention before she saw the truck. She veered off the road and slowed her pace on the grassy shoulder and waited for the truck to pass. The truck pulled beside her and kept the same pace. Its tires were so large they could have passed for tractor tires. The back end of the truck was jacked up, making the front look like it was perpetually going downhill. In a flash she took in the red dull paint covered with rust spots and the two men with their caps pulled over their eyes, their bushy hair sticking out the sides.

Well this was great. Just what she needed. A couple of rednecks gawking at her.

The passenger leaned out the window and gave a loud wolf call. She didn't even bother to look his direction but kept her eyes fixed straight ahead.

"Man o' man. Look at them legs!"

They made a few more comments, which she ignored.

"You think you're too good to speak?"

She just kept running while her heart beat wildly in her ears.

A car came up behind the truck, forcing them to go on. She blew out a breath. Thank goodness for the car. She was only halfway finished with her first lap around the park. She glanced at her watch and decided she wouldn't risk going around another time. It was getting late and the truck might come back. As it was, it would be dark by the time she made it back home.

A fragment of a documentary she'd seen on the discovery channel popped into her mind, causing her stomach to flip. She could almost hear the announcer's voice speaking. There must be a sixth sense that warns prey of impending danger. Does the lion's prey feel it seconds before an impending attack? Or does it rest in ignorant bliss until the instant of the kill?

For Sydney, it was the subtle changes that were the biggest clues. The feeling of being watched and then turning and seeing no one there; a prickling of the skin, causing the hair on her neck to stand; the rapid beating of her heart and sweaty palms for no apparent reason. Was paranoia getting the best of her? Was someone out there? Watching, waiting? It was the feeling she'd had the night she'd driven home from Stella's in the rain, when she came home to find her door partially open. It was the uneasiness in the pit of her stomach that she was feeling right now!

Sydney shook her head in an attempt to brush aside the oppressive thoughts. She was being ridiculous. Still, she couldn't help but note that the park was empty. She told herself that she would feel more at ease once she was out of the park and on the main road. She wanted to get out before the truck circled again. She rounded the last curve and started up the hill by the swimming pool. She hesitated when she saw the truck up ahead. It was sitting beside the entrance to the park. Her legs went weak. She would have to run by it to leave the park. There was no other way out. Darkness was descending rapidly, crickets screeched in the distance. Her eyes narrowed. Those rednecks were trying to corner her like a scared animal. She squared her jaw and increased her pace.

When she reached the truck, the man on the passenger side leaned so far out that he looked like he was going to topple out the window head first. "Hey, remember me?"

She lifted her chin and ran past him without speaking.

The driver started the truck and came up beside her. "What's your hurry, honey? You ain't too friendly, are ya?"

"It looks like you'd take a hint," she said with a confidence she didn't feel. "I'm not interested."

The man in the passenger side chuckled. "You hear that, Sammy? She ain't interested." This brought a loud chortle from the driver. "That's cause she don't know what she's missin'."

Sydney's heart felt like it would leap out of her chest as she increased her pace *again*. Another minute and she'd be sprinting.

The men found this amusing. "You cain't outrun a truck, darlin'."

"Is there a problem here?"

Sydney looked back in time to see Sean running up by her side. She was so relieved she could have kissed him.

"And just who do ya think you are?" The man on the passenger side scowled. They'd cornered their prey and weren't going to let her go that easily.

Sean stopped and Sydney followed suit. The truck stopped too. "Let me handle this," Sean said.

"I believe I heard the lady tell you she wasn't interested. You need to just keep on moving down the road." He eyed the men, daring them to defy him. "Do you have a problem with that?"

Sean's comment was the match that lit the stick of dynamite. The man in the passenger seat began swearing. "The only problem I have is with you!"

Sean pointed. "It's awfully easy to talk brave when you've got lug head over there to back you up."

Sydney looked back and forth between Sean and the men. The man on the passenger side was lanky, but the driver was big and burly. His arms looked bigger than Sean's legs. He must've weighed at least three hundred pounds. She was grateful for Sean's help but didn't want to see him get beaten to a pulp either. She tugged at his arm. "Let's just go."

"You're right," Sean said. "He's not worth it."

At this, the man in the passenger seat jumped out of the truck and lunged at Sean. Sydney stepped back. Sean sidestepped the man and then turned and punched him in the jaw, sending him sprawling headfirst across the pavement. This brought the big man out of the truck. "Look out," Sydney yelled but it was too late. He came up behind Sean and caught him in a choke-hold. The lanky man stumbled to his feet. He used the back of his hand to wipe the trickle of blood from his mouth. "I'll teach you a lesson, city boy." He moved to punch Sean in the stomach. In an instant Sean flipped the big man over his shoulder where he landed with a sickening *thud* on the pavement. There was surprise in the lanky man's eyes the split second before Sean punched him again in the face. The big man got up. Sean gave him two swift punches in the stomach, causing him to double over, gasping for air. The men backed away from Sean and stumbled to their truck. "Come on. Let's get out here. She ain't worth it, nohow!" one of them said. The engine came to life and they squealed off.

Sydney turned to Sean. He was shaking his right fist.

She reached for it. "Here, let me see." His knuckles were cherry red. She grimaced. "You'll have a big bruise."

He smiled humorlessly. "I guess you're worth it."

The joke went over Sydney's head. She was still reeling, but he didn't look nearly as affected by all this as she was. "How? Where—where did you come from? And where did you learn to fight like that?"

Rather than answering, he started jogging. "Come on. I left my car up at Brewster's."

"Brewster's?"

"Yeah, Brewster's Gym."

"Oh, I've seen that place."

She had to lengthen her stride to keep up with him. "You never answered my question," she said between breaths.

"We'll jog now and talk later. It's getting dark, and I don't want to be out here if those idiots decide to go and get their guns."

Her eyes widened. She looked sideways at him to see if he were serious. The smile on his face let her know he was teasing.

When they reached his car, he insisted on taking her home. She didn't argue. He opened the door for her.

"Ouch, that must've hurt?"

"What?"

He touched the scar on her right arm, and she realized that her sleeve had ridden up.

She tugged at her shirt. "I got burned when I was little. I pulled a pan of boiling water off the stove."

He shook his head. "You're lucky. It could've been much worse, I'm sure."

"Yeah, I'm really lucky," she said under her breath as he closed the door.

A moment later he started the engine.

"Okay, I want to know how you ended up at the park."

"I was getting a workout when I saw you jog by. You were keeping a pretty good pace, so I thought I'd see if I could catch up with my favorite co-worker."

"It sure took you long enough."

He laughed easily. "Oh, Syd, you're some piece of work."

She knew his remark was meant as a compliment, and it sent a warm glow rushing over her. She glanced at his handsome face and then looked away. First he was her accuser and now her rescuer. There were times when she hated him and then there were other times...No, she wouldn't let herself get caught up in the moment and make another dumb mistake. She'd learned that the hard way from Adam.

"Well, here we are," he said, pulling into her driveway. He lifted his sore hand off the steering wheel and clenched it. "I'm afraid you were right. I'm gonna have a nice little souvenir to show off tomorrow. It's already turning purple."

"I'm so sorry."

"Didn't your mama ever tell you not to go jogging alone?"

She laughed. "Is that an invitation?"

"Maybe."

He turned his face towards her. His nearness caused her pulse to jump.

Did he feel the same attraction she did every time they were in the same room? She willed herself to think of Kendall.

"Where did you learn to fight like that?"

He leaned back against his seat. "I grew up in a place called The Woodlands, just north of Houston."

She waited for him to elaborate. "And?"

"Have you ever been to Houston?"

"Once."

"Rough place."

She rolled her eyes. "Okay, anyway, I just want to thank you for what you did tonight. I would invite you in, but I have a few projects waiting for me inside..." Her voice trailed off and she thought about the files she'd left scattered across the kitchen table.

"It's all right. I would've turned you down. I need to get home."

This took the wind out of her sails.

"Goodnight, Syd."

That was her cue to get out of the car. She fumbled around for the handle. "Goodnight."

"The fool foldeth his hands together, and eateth his own flesh."
—Ecclesiastes 4:5

chapter thirteen

Sydney's nerves started jumping like the needle on a sewing machine when she rounded the last bend of Kendall's driveway. She didn't know what had possessed her to come here without calling first. Maybe it was the vulnerable expression Kendall had on his face when she asked him about his father. Maybe it was the warm welcome that Emma and Mrs. Fletcher had given her on Monday, or maybe it was to take her mind off Sean.

Well, it was too late to turn back now. She got out of the jeep. When Kendall took her home on Monday evening, he'd casually mentioned that he might call her for a date on Friday. She'd been expecting his call all week, but it never came. Something probably came up, she told herself. And then she told herself that she didn't care if he called or not. Now here she was on a Saturday afternoon, trying to track him down. Was she really that desperate? She looked up at the afternoon sun. It felt good on her face but did little to lighten her spirits.

She rang the doorbell and waited.

"Sydney, what a nice surprise. Come in." The genuine smile on Mrs. Fletcher's face made Sydney felt a little better.

They stood inside the porch while Mrs. Fletcher explained that Kendall was in the shower.

Heat rose in Sydney's face and her words stumbled

out. "I just thought I'd stop by and say hello. I didn't mean to bother him."

Mrs. Fletcher patted her on the arm. "Come on in the living room and have a seat. He'll be thrilled to see you."

Sydney wasn't so sure, but she followed Mrs. Fletcher in and sat down on the sofa. If Kendall was in the shower, then he obviously had plans—plans that didn't include her. "I really can't stay long."

"Oh, he won't be long. You just make yourself comfortable, and I'll let him know you're here."

She waited five minutes before Kendall came out, his hair still wet. He was wearing jeans, brown leather boots, and a red polo shirt. Rather than sitting beside her, he chose the love seat. He looked uncomfortable, like he might've been sitting on a pin cushion, and she wanted to crawl under the sofa. "I'm sorry to drop in on you," she began. "I just wanted to say hello." She knew her voice sounded too cheerful. "It looks like I've caught you on your way out the door." She forced a smile and stood.

Kendall followed suit.

Mrs. Fletcher came into the room. Her eyes flew to Sydney. "You're leaving so soon? You just got here."

"I can't stay."

Mrs. Fletcher spoke to Sydney but all the while her eyes were on Kendall. "I'm sure Kendall doesn't have any plans that don't include you, Sydney."

Kendall looked back and forth between Sydney and his mother. "No," he finally said. "I don't have any definite plans." Kendall's smile was so automatic that Sydney had the impression that someone was standing above him, pulling the strings on the corners of his mouth. "Would you like to go grab a bite to eat?"

Sydney felt like screaming. The humiliation made her nauseous. "Thanks, but I can't. Some other time, maybe. It was good to see you again, Mrs. Fletcher."

She turned to leave and Kendall scrambled to get the door. "I'll walk you out."

They walked to her jeep in silence. She went to open the door, but he stopped her.

"Um, I'm sorry I didn't get around to calling you this week." His voice trailed off, and he wouldn't look her in the eye.

Her face burned. He made it sound like she was some task that needed to be checked off his to-do list.

"It's no big deal. You don't owe me an apology." Her words came out clipped and cold. She shrugged. "See you around."

"I really would like to take you to get something to eat."

A harsh laugh escaped her throat. She tossed her long hair. "Yeah, I can tell. You made that really obvious a few minutes ago." She opened the door to her jeep.

"Wait. You just caught me off guard."

She turned to face him. "I just stopped by to say hello, and now I'm leaving." She glanced at his attire. "Besides, I don't want to keep your date waiting."

A slow smile stole across Kendall's lips. "You think I'm going out on a date?"

His words smothered her like a hot blanket and she tried to think of a reply.

"Why don't you come with me, and I'll show you where I'm going."

She looked at him.

"I would've invited you to begin with, but I wasn't sure how you would like this sort of thing."

She frowned. "Where are you going?"

"You'll just have to find out." He closed the door to her jeep. "It's too late to back out now." He put his arm around her shoulder and led her to his truck.

* * * * *

They drove past the Alabama state line and into Tennessee. Somewhere near Jasper, they detoured off the main road and headed into the sticks. Kendall seemed to know the back roads like the back of his hand, making turn after turn. Houses and barns were the only structures that dotted the sides of the road. Finally, Kendall slowed the truck and turned down a gravel road where tall pine trees grew in thick clusters.

"Where are we?"

Kendall smiled. "Just wait."

She only had to wait a couple more seconds before gawking in amazement at the grassy clearing up ahead. It was packed with compacts, luxury vehicles, SUVs, and pickup trucks. People were getting out of their vehicles and making their way to a large metal building. It was a city that had sprung up out of nowhere, right before her very eyes. "How did you find this place?"

"Only those who know where they're going find this place." He rolled down his window and reached in his back pocket for his wallet.

"That'll be ten dollars," said an old man who spoke with a slight lisp. He was missing his two front teeth.

Ten dollars seemed ridiculously high, considering that they were parking in a pasture. Sydney scanned the tags of the parked cars. Most were from Tennessee, but a fair number of them read Alabama. She was surprised to see a couple from Mississippi and one from Kentucky.

She glanced at her watch—six PM. "Are you going to tell me where we are or are you going to keep me guessing all night?"

He laughed. "You haven't figured it out yet?"

She gave him a blank look.

"We're at a cockfight."

Her eyes grew to saucers. "Really? Why is it out here in the middle of nowhere?"

"Cockfighting is illegal. Don't you know that?"

She stammered. "No, I didn't know. If it's illegal, why do they raise those roosters in their front yards where everyone can see them?"

"Because it's not illegal to raise them. It's just illegal to fight them." Kendall spoke in the tone he might've used to speak to a four-year-old who was slow to understand.

"Let's go," he said, getting out of his truck. This time she didn't wait for him to come around and open her door. She got out and quickened her pace to catch up with him. She was wearing shorts, and the tall grass beat her legs like a whip. Now she realized why Kendall had worn boots.

The door of the building was propped open with a rusty metal can that was wedged in the dirt. Kendall took her hand and led her inside. It took her eyes a minute to adjust to the dim lighting. When Kendall first told her about cockfighting, she pictured beer bellied rednecks huddled around a couple of roosters in an old barn. This place was the opposite end of the spectrum. Oh, there were a few rednecks, but there were businessmen too and a few women. There must've been around three hundred people present. The metal building didn't look all that large on the outside, but it was. In fact, it was a full-blown arena. The square pit, sitting a couple of feet off the floor, took center stage. Dirt covered the floor and each side was a good fifteen feet long, topped by a plexi-glass guard. Above that was netting. Aluminum bleachers like the ones at soccer matches were placed around the pit, allowing the spectacle to be viewed on all four sides. Caged roosters were housed against the walls behind the bleachers. They were crowing and pacing back and forth, anxious for their turn in the pit.

Kendall led her to the bleachers. Sydney looked to her side and saw two women sitting in a glass booth in one corner of the arena. One was holding a microphone to her lips. "Number 42 and number 36 to the scale." The other woman was writing the numbers and weight on a large chalkboard.

"What are they doing?" she asked Kendall.

"All of the roosters have to be weighed before the match."

"How do they know which ones to call?"

"They're matched up by a computer—I think—beforehand."

"High tech."

Kendall didn't seem to notice her sarcasm. He was too busy waiting for the next match to begin.

Sydney looked at the line of men waiting for their rooster's turn in the pit. They were holding them as carefully as a mother would cradle her newborn baby. One man with long, stringy hair and a thick mustache was even blowing gently on his rooster's face.

Kendall rubbed his hands together and leaned forward. "Here goes."

The referee was a stout man who was completely bald except for a ring of fuzz encircling his head. He motioned for the next participants to bring their roosters into the pit. He pulled out a cloth and wiped underneath the rooster's wings and head. Then he wiped its feet. After finishing with the first, he moved to the second.

Sydney pointed. "What's he doing?"

"He's wiping down the roosters."

"Why?"

"To discourage cheating."

Kendall didn't elaborate and Sydney could tell that he was tired of answering her questions. Still, she couldn't help herself.

"How does that discourage cheating?"

"Some people put strychnine or skunk scent on the blades."

"Oh." She frowned. "What's that on their feet?"

"Those are called gaffs. They're metal spikes attached to the rooster's legs."

Sydney's stomach dropped.

The referee signaled the handlers. Sydney thought they were going to let the roosters go at each other, but they kept holding them while thrusting them at each other in a mock attack. The roosters went wild, straining against their handlers to get at each other. This excited the crowd. An old man in a red and black plaid shirt stood. He waved a fistful of bills. "I'll lay 50 to 40," he yelled.

A man in a white dress shirt with the arms rolled up to his elbows jumped to his feet. "I'll take that bet."

A cloud of feathers rose in the air when the roosters were thrown together. The feathers fell like snow to the dirt, and the handlers reached to disengage their combatants. Blood poured down one rooster's leg and Sydney saw that the other rooster's gaff was embedded in his opponent's thigh. One of the handlers worked the gaff loose, and the roosters went at it again. This went on for a couple more rounds until the fight ended with one rooster lying in a heap, blood oozing from its mouth.

Sydney closed her eyes and tried to fight off the nausea. Kendall seemed oblivious to her trauma. "I'm gonna go place a bet. Do you want anything from the concession stand?"

She wasn't sure she'd heard him correctly. Surely he was kidding. How could she possibly want food after witnessing that slaughter?

He pointed toward the concession stand. "Hot dog, Coke?" Her head began throbbing. The crowd roared in eagerness at the impending next match. She shook her head. "No thanks. I'm not hungry."

Kendall was gone almost before she got the words out. She looked around at the other spectators. Heads were bobbing up and down like fans rooting for their favorite football team. There was a young boy sitting about four rows up from her. He was shoving the last of a hot dog in his mouth. Ketchup trickled from the corner of his mouth, and he used the back of his hand to wipe it away. The boy's father was sitting beside him. He put his arm around his son and pointed. Sydney looked at the object of their interest and saw the man with the stringy hair and thick mustache. He was the same man she'd seen earlier, blowing on his rooster's face. Now he was stroking its feathers. His pride and joy would be the next to fight after this match. The boy nodded and gave a thumbs up, and his dad headed down the bleachers to place a bet.

Sydney couldn't bear to watch. She averted her eyes, but not before she saw the feathers fly high above the pit. Was she the only one sickened by the blood bath?

She remembered the time she and Judith had flown to Hawaii. Sydney didn't realize it at the time, but she had an ear infection. When the plane lifted off, she felt like her head would explode. Everyone around her was perfectly fine. That's how she felt right now. She looked back at the boy. What kind of parent took a child to see this?

Kendall returned just in time to see the man with the mustache step into the pit. His rooster was magnificent. It had a mane of orange hackle feathers with arching black tail feathers. Its opponent was dirty white with matching tail feathers. Their beaks were almost touching when each man shoved his rooster back and forth, teasing the other. Excitement rippled through the crowd. A few of the spectators scrambled to place their bets. Others stood.

"This is a knife fight," Kendall said. This time he didn't wait for her to ask but went on with an explanation. "Each rooster wears a single wide blade. This is a quicker and deadlier fight. And the bets soar."

Sydney's heart sank. She was too sick to say anything.

"Pit," the referee yelled. She watched the roosters collide breast to breast in mid-air. It was beak grabbing beak, feet tangling in feathers and wings. Hackles rose like porcupine quills on both roosters. The white bird didn't waste any time. It attacked the orange bird with a vengeance, slashing it in the face. The crowd went wild, chanting and yelling, reminding Sydney of a scene in a voodoo horror movie. The orange bird went down limping, and the white bird attacked again. This time it put out the orange rooster's eye.

It was all over from there. They went another round before the white bird finished off his opponent. The magnificent orange bird fell to its side, coughing up blood. The man with the mustache looked at his fallen rooster in disdain before it was dragged away to make room for the next fight.

Sydney's head started to spin. She tugged on Kendall's shirt. "I think it's time to leave."

Kendall scowled. "Don't be ridiculous. We just got here."

"I'm sorry Kendall. I don't feel so—" *good* she was about to say but instead heaved. Vomit exploded all over Kendall.

He looked down at his clothes. "Yuck!"

The men sitting around them jumped back and cringed. Some of them muttered remarks Sydney wished she'd not heard. They could watch roosters massacre each other all day and not be affected, but for some reason, the site of a woman throwing up was too much for them.

She and Kendall made their way through the sea of people to the door. Sydney looked up and her throat caught. She thought she saw Sean sitting amongst the crowd. Their eyes met for an instant, and then he turned his face another direction. Was it him? She couldn't be sure. She strained to get a better look. Before she could, Kendall grabbed her hand and yanked her out the door.

"Let's go," Kendall said. "I should've known better than to bring you here."

"Just what does that mean?" she asked, gaining strength from her anger.

"I think you know."

They got in his truck, and he slammed the door.

"The wise man's eyes are in his head;
but the fool walketh in darkness."
—Ecclesiastes 2:14

chapter fourteen

Ginger's voice grew incredulous. "He took you to a cockfight?"

Sydney told Ginger how she'd dropped by Kendall's house and how Mrs. Fletcher had cornered him into taking her on a date.

"Evidently, Kendall had planned on going to the cockfight alone. He never would've taken me there on his own accord."

"Still," Ginger said in an exaggerated drawl.

"Oh, don't worry. I'm not in any hurry to forgive him." Not that he was asking for her forgiveness. They'd driven home from the cockfight in stony silence with the windows rolled down. Her clothes were crusty and her head pounding by the time they reached his house. Without a word, she got out of his truck. He might've been about to apologize, but the look on her face stopped him.

"Have you talked to him since?" Ginger asked.

"Not yet."

"Well if you ask me, I'd say you're better off without him."

Sydney smiled. That was always Ginger's response when another one of Sydney's relationships went south. "You're probably right."

They talked for a few more minutes with Ginger going on like a chatter-box. Her voice had an unnatural edge like it was about to lift off and take flight. She'd heard that tone before, whenever Ginger was holding something back. "What is it you're not telling me, Gin?" She gripped the phone and waited. She could just picture how Ginger's face must look right now. Ginger always had that same expression when she tried to figure out how to put something delicately. Her brow would be furrowed and her round eyes small.

"Just spit it out, Gin. I'm a big girl. Whatever it is, I can handle it."

"Adam's engaged."

"What?" Sydney's mouth went dry and she went to the sofa.

There was a long pause.

"Sydney, are you okay?"

Sydney ran her hand through her hair. "Yeah, I'm fine. It's just a shock, that's all. When did you find out?"

"I saw it in the *Star Telegram* this morning."

"Who's the lucky girl of the minute?"

"Alicia Thomas."

Sydney made a face. "Her?" A picture of Alicia, her big brown eyes and wispy auburn hair, came to mind. She was the perfect picture of a model with her pretzel thin figure and pouty lips. Sydney didn't know Alicia very well but had seen her often enough at the country club. She and Adam used to joke that she was one of those permanent fixtures in the elite social circle. Sydney had always thought she was a little too friendly with Adam. She'd mentioned it once, and he'd laughed it off saying that Alicia Thomas was too high maintenance for him.

Adam had hugged Sydney. "Besides," he said, nuzzling her ear with his lips, "I've got all I need right here."

He'd said it, and like a fool, she believed him.

"I'm sorry, Sydney," Ginger said. "I shouldn't have brought it up."

"No, I'm glad I know. For her sake, let's just hope that little miss Alicia can figure out how to hold onto him before some other bimbo comes along." She knew it was a cheap shot but couldn't help herself.

She and Ginger talked for a few more minutes, but Sydney's mind was far away. Ginger hung up only after repeated assurances from Sydney that she was fine.

Sydney stared unseeingly out her front window. Why was she so upset about Adam? He'd called it off weeks ago. After last night's fiasco with Kendall, maybe she should just give up on men altogether.

Deep down, she knew the real source of her anger. Adam was a shallow jerk, and she was better off without him. It really didn't have that much to do with him, only in a broad sense. The trouble was her. She'd never been able to hold onto a relationship for very long. Maybe they could see right through her beauty, straight to her inner self, broken and battered. Sometimes her longing for a family was so poignant that she feared it would overwhelm her.

She rose from the sofa to make her a cup of mandarin orange herbal tea. She would read more of Avery's journal. That would take her mind off Adam.

* * * * *

Sydney reverently took the diary from the desk and sat down by the window. When she discovered it in the box, she thought she would read the entire book in one sitting. That hadn't been the case. The memories it evoked were too painful. She could only handle small doses. She thumbed through the pages, her eyes skimming over the record of Avery's day-to-day activities, searching for the meaningful phrases. She caught one.

Tried to talk to Cindy today about Susan's death. It's impossible. Unfortunately, she's just like me. She keeps everything bottled up inside. Susan was the glue that held us together. It's all up to me now. I've never been much of a praying man, but I

*found myself on my knees last night, asking the
good Lord to make me equal to the task. Cindy's
counting on me. How can I help her when I can
barely even help myself?*

Moisture formed in Sydney's eyes. She stared out
the window. Avery's plea struck a chord somewhere deep
within the recess of her heart. She'd always thought her
dad was impenetrable granite. He seemed to take
everything in stride. She'd been angry at him for not
reaching out to her after her mom's death. Maybe they'd
both been trying to get through their loss the only way
they knew how. She was starting to see Avery in a new
light. He was strong, but also fragile and hurting. Her
life was a thousand pieces of shattered glass, and here
she was, sifting through the shards to find something
to hold onto. How much more could she pick up without
getting cut? She wiped away a tear and skipped to the
end of the journal.

March 3
*I think someone tried to kill me today when I
went to the log yard. Cecil Prichard was a
witness.*

The words leapt from the page and seared their way
into her mind. It was so typical of Avery to skip the
preliminaries and jump straight to the heart of the
matter. She could just picture the events he described.
The words came alive:

Avery's heart warmed when he spotted Cecil on the
far end of the yard, scaling logs. Cecil was one of those
timeless people who never seemed to age. He'd been
Avery's boss in the log yard the summer after Avery's
high school graduation.

"Hey, Cecil. How's it going?"

"Pretty good. We're getting further and further
behind though. I have a couple of stacks of logs that
ain't been scaled yet, and there are a couple of trucks

that ain't been unloaded."

Avery frowned. "Why hasn't Lewis gotten you some help?"

"I don't know. I mentioned it to him yesterday and he said he would."

"Don't worry, Cecil, I'll take care of it," Avery said, cursing Lewis' incompetence under his breath. He walked around the yard for a few minutes then over to one of the trucks that was piled high with logs.

"Look out!"

Avery turned in time to see the logs break free from their chain. The mountain came rolling toward him. His first instinct was to run and then he saw a bulldozer parked a few feet away. He jumped behind the safety of the huge metal cup just before the logs hit, nearly knocking over the dozer.

Avery came out from under the dozer, shaking. He dusted off his clothes and went to inspect the chain.

Cecil heard the commotion and came running. "Are you okay?"

"Yeah, but I need to have a look at that chain."

Cecil was quiet for a moment. He looked Avery square in the eye and lowered his voice to a whisper when he spoke. "Avery, I wanna give you some advice. You'd better watch your back."

"What're you saying?"

"Be careful."

With that, Cecil turned and walked away. Avery glanced around the yard. He hadn't seen anyone near the truck. Then again, he wasn't paying much attention. He looked down at the heavy chain and realized what Cecil had already figured out.

It had been cut.

That was the last entry. There was nothing else except a hastily scribbled note:

Appointment with Henry on March 25.

She stared at the page. It was the same date as the boat accident. That last day on the boat Avery had said that he needed to get to an appointment. Who was Henry? That name sounded so familiar. Where had she heard it? She reread the last entry. Was that when Avery had written his letter to Judith? She made a note of the two other names: Cecil Prichard and Lewis. She'd never heard either name mentioned before. She searched through the pages to see if Avery had written down Lewis's last name, but came up empty handed. She went to get her phone book and flipped through the pages to the p's. Par for the course—no Prichard. She put down the directory. She should have known it wouldn't be that easy.

She thought of another avenue. The personnel files. There would be an employment file on Prichard. Too bad she didn't have access to the personnel files. It would make matters so much easier. She knew better than to ask Barb for any more files. The last thing she wanted to do was arouse more suspicion. She thought of Walter. He would know. She frowned, remembering Walter's comment about Avery being paranoid. No, she wouldn't ask him yet. She'd gather more information first and then show it to Walter. He was a reasonable person. If she gathered enough evidence, she could persuade him to see it her way. She'd have to get the personnel files without Barb knowing. That was her only answer.

She placed the journal in the desk before heading into the bathroom. She sat down on the edge of the tub and turned on the water. When the tub was full, she slipped off her robe and got in. She closed her eyes and let the warm water and sudsy bubbles cover her body. Who did Avery have an appointment with? Henry who? What was his last name, and why did she feel like she should know? She leaned her head back against the cool tub and then sat right back up when the answer came like a bolt of lightning. She jumped out and threw on her robe. She went to the secretary and pulled open the drawer. She reached for the newspaper clippings and skimmed the one about the judge. Then she saw it. The judge's first name was Henry. Her heart began to pound. Avery had planned on meeting Judge Henry Crawford. What was the name of the judge's wife? She skimmed down the page. Harriet. His wife's name was Harriet Crawford. If she could get in touch with her then maybe, just maybe she could get some answers.

* * * * *

Sydney spent the next morning searching the Internet for Harriet Crawford. She began her search in Glendale. When she didn't find any listing there, she searched the state of Alabama. That proved fruitless as well. Finally, she searched the entire country and found only three listings. California, Michigan, and Georgia. She zeroed in on Georgia. The city was Alpharetta, near Atlanta. Her heart was in her throat when she dialed. A lady with a strong cultured voice answered on the third ring. When Sydney explained that she was looking for the late Judge Henry Crawford's wife, the voice grew suspicious, and she knew she'd struck gold. Sydney decided that honesty was the best policy. Even so, she hadn't intended to spell it out so bluntly. It just came out that way.

"My father was killed in a boat explosion." She enunciated the next words so the lady would get the full implication of their meaning. "The same day your husband was killed. I believe my father had an appointment with your husband on the day he was killed. I was wondering if you would mind if I paid you a visit?"

She was met with silence on the other end. "Who did you say you were?" the lady finally asked.

"My name is Syd—Cindy McClain."

There was another pause.

"I won't stay very long," Sydney added.

"You can come this Tuesday afternoon at 4." From the tone of the woman's voice, Sydney could tell it was Tuesday or never.

"That sounds great. Thank you, Mrs. Crawford."

The dial tone sounded in Sydney's ear.

*   *   *   *   *

It was a typical Monday. Sydney rubbed her tired eyes and stifled a yawn, trying to concentrate on the paperwork in front of her. She'd barely gotten any sleep the night before. Dreams of bloody roosters with wings flapping like propellers taunted her. One minute they were trying to peck her eyes out and the next they were piled in a smothering heap on top of her. Kendall stood in the distance, watching the scene with indifference.

"Rough weekend?"

"Something like that."

Sean was standing in the doorway. She studied his face and wondered again for the hundredth time if it was him she saw at the cockfight.

"Well, it's about to get worse."

She frowned. "What are you talking about?"

"Haven't you heard?"

Sydney remained silent.

"Crandall Martin, a second shift log handler, got trapped in the kiln Friday afternoon."

"Oh no," Sydney's hands flew to her mouth.

"By the time they got him out, he'd collapsed. He was rushed to Glendale Memorial and then released a few hours later."

"Why wasn't I contacted?"

"I was called."

"Well, why didn't you call me?"

He shrugged. "I figured what was done was done. There wouldn't have been anything you could've done about it over the weekend."

Sydney cocked her head. "Well, why didn't Crandall go out the escape door?"

Sean looked her squarely in the eyes. "The handle was broken, and if that's not bad enough, there was a mountain of lumber piled outside the door."

"What?"

"If the escape door had been working properly, he could've gotten out as soon as he got locked in."

She shook her head. "What are you saying? That this is my fault? I talked to Buck. I told him to make sure it was fixed. I—"

"Save it for the meeting."

"What meeting?"

"The meeting I called this morning to find out how a blatant accident could occur right under our noses." He looked at his watch. "It starts in fifteen minutes in my office."

"Why wasn't I informed?"

"Consider yourself informed." He turned on his heel and walked out the door.

"Bread of deceit is sweet to a man; but afterwards
his mouth shall be filled with gravel."
—Proverbs 20:17

chapter fifteen

The meeting began at 9:15 sharp. Sydney and
Buck Gibson sat in the vinyl guest chairs
opposite Sean's desk, and a folding chair was brought
in for Larry Welton, the shift supervisor. Sean was the
picture of a hard-nosed general manager with his stony
expression and hard jaw. He eyed his three subordinates.
"You wanna tell me how this happened?"

Sean fixed his eyes on Larry Welton, who scooted
forward in his seat. He was a frail man with red hair
and a long nose that was dotted with freckles. His thin
white shirt emphasized his sunken chest. "Well, um,
Crandall was stacking lumber in the kiln." His eyes
darted around the room then down at the floor before
continuing. "Um, we didn't realize Crandall was in there.
He was still in the back when we shut the door."

Sean shook his head and his mouth twisted like he'd
bitten into something rotten.

"He must've been in there for a while. One of the
men happened to walk by and heard 'im hollerin'. It was
terrible. Crandall in there hollerin' and beatin' and I'll
be doggone if the door didn't jam. We turned off the heat
switch and Mike Sutherland ran and grabbed a crowbar.
We wedged it underneath and started working it up. We
finally got the door open. It were a good thing too. If
Crandall'd been in there much longer, he might not've
made it." Larry seemed relieved that his narrative was

over with. He slid back in his chair and waited for Sean to speak.

"Why wasn't the escape door working?" Sean looked at Buck first and then his eyes settled on Sydney. "This is why we hired you—to prevent accidents like this."

She looked at Buck and waited for him to explain. She tried to make eye contact with him, but he wouldn't look at her. "On my first inspection with Buck, I noticed the broken handle and the lumber stacked behind the door. I mentioned these problems to Buck, and he assured me that he would take care of them."

Sean looked at Buck. "Is this true?"

Buck shifted in his seat, and his mustache twitched. "I don't remember discussin' no escape door with Miss Lassiter."

Sydney's eyes grew wide and she flinched like someone had doused her with a bucket of ice water. "What?"

Buck didn't look at her. Instead, he kept his eyes fixed on Sean.

Sydney continued speaking. "You and I discussed the escape door. You asked me not to write it up because of the flack you would get from Sean. I agreed to leave that out of the report as long as you took care of the problem."

Sean looked back and forth between Sydney and Buck. "So let me get this straight. You noticed that there were problems with the escape door, but you didn't put it in your report?"

Sydney's chest felt like lead. "I trusted Buck to take care of it. I assumed that he would." The words trailed off.

Sean leveled a stare at Buck. "Is this true?"

Buck's eyes shifted toward Sydney and then away. "No boss, it ain't true."

Sydney turned crimson.

"I remember that Miss Lassiter and I talked about the fall protection, but I don't remember talking about no escape door."

Sydney's eyes could have burnt right through the snake in the grass. Liar! she wanted to scream.

Sean looked at Sydney. "So it's his word against yours. Is that it?"

It was all she could do to keep from ripping Buck's head off. "It seems to be the case."

"I'm going to have to document this," Sean said. "Lucky for us Crandall wasn't seriously injured. If he'd been hurt badly—or worse, killed, OSHA would've shut us down."

"How nice of Crandall to be so accommodating," Sydney said.

Sean didn't flinch. "Larry, thanks for coming in. That's all."

Larry stood and scampered out the door.

Sean looked at Sydney. "When OSHA does a follow-up inspection, we've got to be ready."

She lifted her chin and her eyes met his. "Oh, we will be."

"I trust that from now on any safety violations that you find will be written in a report."

Sydney raised an eyebrow and looked at Buck. The coward. He still wouldn't look her in the eye. "You can count on it." She stood to leave.

A knock at the door caught their attention. Barb entered holding a large bouquet of red roses. She cleared her throat. "These are for Miss Lassiter."

All eyes went to Sydney. Her face burned. She glared at Barb. "You should've put them on my desk."

Sydney reached for the bouquet.

"Uh-uh, not so fast." Barb lifted the card and read it aloud. "'Please forgive me. Kendall.' How sweet."

Sydney snatched the flowers and card from Barb, who then turned and left. Sydney glowered around the room. Her gaze stopped at Sean. His eyes met hers and he motioned at the card she was holding.

"Lover boy has impeccable timing."

Sydney jutted out her chin. Her humiliation was complete, but she'd be darned if she let Sean O'Connor know it. "If you'll excuse me..."

Sean nodded.

*　*　*　*　*

Sean stood and closed the door.

He looked at Buck. "You wanna tell me what that was all about?"

Buck sat up taller in his seat and pulled his pants over his belly. "You ought to be thankin' me, boss." He stuck out his thumb and thrust it toward the door. "A couple more incidents like this and Miss Lassiter'll be out of here."

"Are you admitting that you sat here and told a bold-face lie?"

Buck shifted in his seat like a caged pigeon. "I'm not admittin' nothin'."

"I'm gonna ask you this straight out, and I want an honest answer. Did Syd—I mean—Miss Lassiter ask you to fix the escape door?"

"Syd, huh. I see how it is."

Sean's eyes narrowed. "What?"

Buck leaned forward. "You've got a thang fer her. Ain't no use denying it. I saw the look in your eyes when she got them flowers."

Sean almost came off his seat. He slammed his hand on his desk. "Don't you dare change the subject. A man was almost killed because you didn't do your job!"

"And just when did you start caring about people dying?"

Buck leaned back in his seat and retrieved a cigarette from his shirt pocket. It was common knowledge that Sean didn't allow smoking in his office.

Buck took a long draw on his cigarette and then exhaled. "Did I ever tell you that my ol' man used to raise hogs?" He didn't wait for Sean to answer. "One time he brought home two of the prettiest little pigs I ever saw. My brother, Vernell, got attached to 'im. Even named 'im. Not me. I just called 'im by what they was gonna end up *sausage* and *pork chops*." Buck laughed.

"It like to of kilt Vernell when my ol' man took his little pets to the slaughter house."

Buck took another puff.

"Miss Lassiter is a pretty little ol' thang. That's for sure." He looked at Sean. "And you're hanging onto her like a hair on a biscuit. But let's face it. When the chips all come tumbling down—and I expect they will—in the end, she's just a pork chop."

* * * * *

The afternoon dragged by. Sydney tried to bury herself in paperwork. She was still smarting from the morning's events. Part of the blame lay with her, she knew that. She should have never agreed to leave the escape door off her report. What was she thinking? And she should have followed up to make sure that Buck had kept his word. The truth of the matter was it had completely slipped her mind. If Crandall had died, it would have been on her head. She shuddered at the thought.

She looked at the roses. They were beautiful. She wouldn't let Barb's theatrics keep her from enjoying them. She rubbed her finger against one of the velvety petals. She inhaled deeply and let the sweet scent take over her senses. She frowned. Now she had to decide what to do about Kendall.

She turned her swiveled chair around and faced the window. She let herself get lost in the motion of the red birds fluttering in and out of the willow tree just outside her window. She watched a few more minutes before turning back to her desk.

"Time to face the music," she said, using her dad's words. She reached for her steel-toed boots that she kept stashed in the corner and then for her hard hat and clipboard. This time she was going to do an inspection on her own.

A cool breeze kissed her cheek after she finished her inspection, reminding her that fall was just around the corner. Fall was virtually nonexistent in Ft. Worth. She was looking forward to the changing leaves. She glanced up at the rolling mountain in the distance— Stella's mountain. She felt a pang of guilt for not visiting her more often. She made a promise to visit her this week.

Her thoughts returned to the inspection. She'd found a few minor safety violations. But on the whole, the sawmill appeared to be in good order. She walked around the huge stacks of lumber and stopped in front of a pile of cedar. She loved the cedar most of all. She took a deep breath and absorbed the clean, fresh scent. It was the smell of Home Depot, magnified a hundred times. She ran her hand over the rough wood, feeling the grittiness under her smooth fingers.

Avery flashed in her mind, and she could see him propped against one of the stacks of lumber, smiling like a king overlooking his kingdom. How he'd loved this place. Without warning, hot tears welled and voices from the past rang in her mind.

"Come on, Cindy. We have to go," Avery yelled. "Your mother will have dinner ready, and I told her we would only be gone an hour or so."

"*Please,* Dad, five more minutes," Cindy said for the umpteenth time and then dodged behind a stack of lumber.

"Sydney."

The voice jolted her to the present. She turned and stood face to face with Sean.

"What're you doing here?"

"I saw your jeep parked up front and came looking for you."

Sydney averted her face. Sean was the last person she wanted to see her in such an emotional state. He reached out and brushed a tear from her cheek. "Are you okay?"

His nearness was overpowering. Her heart beat bumped up a notch when she looked in his eyes. Was it genuine concern or pity she saw in them? "Yes, I'm fine."

She took a step back. "I was just doing a safety inspection."

"Look, about this morning—"

"You were right. I should've put the escape door in my report."

"You should've never trusted Buck."

She looked up at him. "You believed me?" It took a moment for the realization to sink in. "Why didn't you take up for me? You knew Buck was lying, and you let me take the blame. Why?"

He leaned against the stack of lumber and shoved his hands in his pockets. "Regardless of what Buck did or didn't do, you should've put the escape door in your report. End of story."

"I know."

"Look Syd, it's just real important that you know who your friends are and who your enemies are."

"Oh yeah, and which one are you?"

He looked intently at her.

"If you don't know the answer to that then I guess we're both in trouble," he said and walked away.

*"All the rivers run into the sea; yet the sea is not full;
unto the place from whence the rivers come, thither they
return again."*
—Ecclesiastes 1:7

chapter sixteen

It took Sydney a good four and a half hours to get from the sawmill to Mrs. Crawford's house. She'd left work at 10:30 to give herself plenty of time. Sean had stopped her on her way out the door and asked where she was going. She was still upset about the kiln ordeal and told him in no uncertain terms that it was none of his business.

"I don't work on an hourly basis. You and I both know I can come and go as I please."

"Take it easy, Syd. I was just wondering if you wanted to go jogging with me this afternoon."

How could he stand there and act like none of the events from the day before had taken place? "No thanks. I have an appointment."

*   *   *   *   *

Sydney reached for her directions as she turned into the driveway. She compared the number on the mailbox to the one on her paper: 315 Preston Way. She was at the right place. The directions she'd gotten on the Internet had led her straight here without any difficulty. Her eyes took in the stately Tudor home with its carpeted lawn and majestic oak trees. The front bushes, shaped in perfect squares, looked like they'd been given a severe haircut. She walked up the brick path leading to the door.

The sound of her high heels clicking on the bricks reminded her of Judith, and she wondered what her aunt would think about her decision to investigate Avery's death—not too highly of it, she would imagine.

She stopped and took a deep breath before straightening her tan skirt. She had chosen her attire, a skirt and matching soft beige blouse, in the hope that the tailored lines and subtle colors would give her an air of sophistication. Her hair was pinned up in a neat bun, making her look older than twenty-six. She summoned the courage to ring the doorbell and smoothed down her hair.

A woman opened the door.

"Mrs. Crawford?"

"No, I'm the housekeeper." She motioned. "Come this way."

When Sydney entered the foyer, her love for wood drew her attention to the detailed parquet floors. A portrait of a man dressed in a suit hung on one wall, and Sydney guessed it might be the face of a young Judge Crawford staring back at her. She followed the woman down a hall where tasteful rugs and antique furniture pieces were expertly positioned. The housekeeper stopped in front of a closed door and knocked. Sydney's knees went weak when she heard the commanding voice answer from within.

The first thing she saw was an older woman sitting in front of a large bay window. One afghan covered her knees and another wrapped around her shoulders. A book rested on her lap.

Mrs. Crawford was an imposing figure with her silver hair and black eyes. Even though she was sitting down, Sydney could tell that her height was an even match for her big-boned frame. She removed her reading glasses and put her book on a nearby table. As the two eyed each other, Sydney felt that the older woman was stripping her bare.

"Have a seat," Mrs. Crawford said. It was more of a command than a suggestion.

"I appreciate your seeing me. As I told you on the phone, I believe there's a connection between the death of your husband and my father."

"Go on."

Sydney pulled the newspaper articles from her bag and handed them to Mrs. Crawford. She reached for her glasses and began examining the articles.

"My father's name was Avery McClain. Does that name sound familiar to you?"

Mrs. Crawford looked thoughtful then shook her head. "No."

Sydney rushed on. "My father, Avery, kept a journal. He recorded that he had an appointment with Henry on March 25th."

Until now, Mrs. Crawford had been looking over the articles while Sydney was speaking. Those black eyes looked up, and Sydney detected a hint of frustration in them. "Was *Henry* the only name your father wrote? Wasn't there a last name?"

Sydney's face warmed. She'd anticipated this question. "I know this probably sounds strange to you, but I feel sure that it was your husband that my father had intended to meet. I just learned of my father's journal a short while ago. Otherwise I would've contacted you sooner."

Mrs. Crawford's face was unreadable. She seemed to be weighing Sydney's words. "What else makes you think there was a connection between Henry's death and your father?"

Sydney told her about the sawmill and how she thought Avery had stumbled upon some sort of illegal activity. The woman looked unconvinced. "Stoney Creek and Glendale are neighboring towns. Two men died in an explosion on the same day. And Avery had an appointment with—well, I believe with your husband on that same evening they both were killed. Don't you find any of this odd?"

Mrs. Crawford's eyes grew distant. "Henry and I had a rocky relationship. We were trying to patch things up." Her voice became husky. "He called me just before he left the office that evening to cancel our dinner reservation. I could tell he was anxious to get off the phone, and this made me angry. He said he had to get to an appointment."

Déjà vu hit Sydney. Avery said almost those exact words.

"Henry seemed almost feverish with excitement. He said he thought it might be the big break he'd been looking for."

"I don't understand. Your husband was a judge, not a detective."

"I didn't understand it myself. Henry was a maverick of a sort who thought it was his duty to expose corruption on any score. He was always delving into things—things that he had no business being in." She shook her head and looked directly at Sydney. "I've always thought that's what got him killed."

Sydney leaned forward in her chair. "Did he tell you who he was meeting?"

"No."

Sydney nodded. She felt like she'd been taken up on the highest point of a rollercoaster and then dropped. "Did they ever find out who killed Judge Crawford?"

"No, they never did." She shrugged. "Henry had many enemies." She turned and looked out the window. "I didn't believe Henry when he told me he had appointment." She bit her lip then her voice faltered. "I—I was afraid he was meeting another woman."

When she turned to face Sydney, her eyes were moist. "If what you say is true, then Henry was telling me the truth. All these years..." Her voice trailed off.

"Mrs. Crawford, are you all right?"

The woman didn't answer.

Sydney felt a touch her on her shoulder. She turned to see the housekeeper. "I think it's time for you to leave."

Sydney stood and sighed. She walked over and retrieved the articles from Mrs. Crawford's lap. "Yes, I believe you're right."

Conflicting emotions churned inside Sydney during her drive back to Stoney Creek. The unanswered questions were mounting. Her whole theory—her reason for moving to Stoney Creek—everything hinged on *if.* If Avery and Judge Crawford were planning on meeting, then Avery could have been the big break that Judge Crawford had mentioned to his wife. She had hoped that Mrs. Crawford would give her some concrete information that would help her link Avery and Judge Crawford's death. It was a pit of snarling questions that's bottom was growing more fathomless by the day. All she'd really gained from her visit was a splitting headache.

There was still Cecil Prichard. She'd have to find a way to get down to the basement to see his employment file. The basement door was always locked, but Sydney knew that Barb kept the keys in her desk. The ringing of her cell phone startled her. She reached to answer it and instantly recognized Kendall's hesitant voice.

"Sydney?"

"Yes."

"I've been tryin' to reach you. You haven't returned any of my calls."

Sydney kept her voice impersonal. "Yeah, it's been a crazy week."

"I need to talk to you. I'm comin' over."

"Kendall, it's not a good time. Besides, I'm not at home right now." There was a long pause. "I don't think this is a good idea. We're just too different."

"At least let me try to explain."

She winced. Was it hurt or desperation she detected in his tone? A part of her wanted to relent just to soothe him. He seemed to sense that she was wavering. "Five minutes of your time is all I ask."

"Okay. I'm headed that way. I'll meet you there in an hour."

* * * * *

Kendall was waiting when she pulled into her driveway. They walked up to her front door in awkward silence. She was too drained to make polite conversation. Kendall was the one who precipitated their meeting. It was his turn to make the first move.

"Have a seat." She walked past him to put down her purse.

Kendall sat on the sofa and began drumming his fingers on his thighs. She sat in the oversized chair across from him and waited for him to speak.

He cleared his throat. "Last weekend was a big mistake."

That was an understatement.

"I should've never taken you to a cockfight."

Never taken her? What about him? She couldn't understand why he would want to go to such a vile place. "I appreciate your coming here to apologize, Kendall. I really do. It's like I told you on the phone. The idea of you and me is great." She paused, searching for the right words to express her feelings. "But in reality—we're just too different."

"I didn't come here to apologize."

Her mouth dropped. "What?"

"I came to make you understand where I'm comin' from."

Her eyes narrowed. That's what this was about?

He looked her square in the face, his brown eyes pleading with hers. "I, um, I was ten years old the first time Daddy took me to a cockfight. I can imagine how it must've looked to someone who'd never seen anything like that before."

Sydney lowered her head and massaged her pounding temples. An image of the boy eating the hotdog flashed in her mind.

Kendall stood and came across the room and knelt beside her chair. He reached for her hand and looked right in her eyes. "I never meant to upset you."

A weak laugh escaped her throat. "Well, it wasn't like you intended for me to go. I kind of forced you into it."

He brushed a strand of hair from her face. His hand cupped the curve of her cheek and lingered there for a moment. She smiled. It had the magical effect of smoothing Kendall's features, melting the tension from his face.

"Just promise me that you'll never take me to that place again." She shuddered. "I've seen enough blood and guts to last a lifetime."

His hand left her face and went over his heart. "I promise." He smiled that slow smile that sent a spark of warmth over her. She thought—hoped that he would kiss her, but instead, he stood and rubbed his hands together. "All this talk about blood and guts is making me hungry. What do you say we go get a burger?"

She laughed. "Oh Kendall, you're a monster."

"...a poor man is better than a liar."
—Proverbs 19:22

chapter seventeen

Hey, Syd, aren't you going home tonight?" Sean stood in her office doorway. He looked as fresh as he did when Sydney saw him that morning. "Now that the OSHA inspection's done, I figured that you could rest easy for a while." He leaned against the door frame. "Congratulations on passing."

Her eyes met his. "Did you ever have any doubt?"

A smile tugged at the corners of his mouth. "Do I have to answer that?"

She shook her head. She'd had her doubts as well. All in all, the follow-up inspection had been anticlimactic. A frail man with hair black as shoe polish and suspicious eyes showed up and made notes of all the improvements. He passed them off and then let her know in no uncertain terms that he would be back periodically to check on the situation.

"Can I walk you out?" Sean asked.

"No thanks, I still have a few things to finish up."

"See you tomorrow."

Sydney was thankful that she could finally be alone to complete her mission. She had to find Cecil Prichard and talk to him. Even though the log accident occurred several years ago, it was doubtful that someone would forget an incident so serious.

It was time to go to plan "B." There had to be an employment file on Cecil Prichard, and this time she wasn't about to ask Barb for it. Sydney's palms grew sweaty. She stepped out of her office and tried to appear casual while checking to make sure everyone had left. When she'd finished her search, she headed for Barb's desk. It was common knowledge that Barb kept the basement key in her top right-hand drawer. She prayed that Barb's desk would be unlocked. It was. She clutched the key and made her way to the basement. She closed the door behind her and flipped on the light. The musty smell was suffocating. The place felt like a tomb. She pushed the thought away and willed herself to stay calm. Don't panic, she repeated over and over. Even though she tried to tread lightly, every step on the wooden stairs sounded like a jackhammer in her ears. It took her a minute to locate the filing cabinets. A dull light bulb, hanging by a cord, made her wish she'd brought a flashlight. She searched through the first two cabinets and came up empty-handed. On the third she saw the label marked "terminations." Surely Cecil Prichard hadn't been fired. She frowned. Avery described Cecil as conscientious. He'd been a devoted employee for many years. She shrugged. It was worth a look. She scanned down to the fourth drawer where the "P's" began. She pulled out the drawer and thumbed through the folders: Parker, Parkings, Perkins, and Persell. Then she saw it—a folder labeled Prichard. She reached for the file, intending to study it. First things first, she told herself, scribbling the address on her note pad. She was just about to search the files for Lewis when she heard the voice.

"Hey, is somebody down here?"

Sydney jumped and stuffed the folder back into the drawer and shut it.

"I said, is anyone there?"

It was Sean. He pounded down the stairs, and she was sure he would hear her heart running at full speed. She crouched in the corner beside a filing cabinet and tried not to make a sound. The footsteps were getting closer. Would he hear her breathing? Would he smell her perfume?

His cell phone rang. "Now?" He sighed. "Yeah, I'm on my way." He ran back up the steps and flipped off the light.

She waited a good five minutes after he left before she dared to move. It was pitch black, and she had to feel her way to the stairs. What would happen if Sean were waiting on the other side of the door? She opened it a fraction at first before getting the nerve to open it all the way and step through. She braced herself for the worst, but nothing happened. The office was empty. She was shaking all over like the mouse that managed to slip unnoticed under the sleeping cat's paw. She replaced Barb's keys, then darted out the door without looking back. She clenched her fist. She'd done it! She'd gotten the address!

If she'd stayed a few more minutes, she would have seen Sean step out of the office and lock the door behind him.

*   *   *   *   *

Sydney decided to go straight to Cecil Prichard's house. She stopped at a convenience store and asked for directions, and then headed down one of the many country roads that tangled like spaghetti noodles over the area. It wasn't until the sun started setting behind the clouds that she second-guessed her decision to drive out to a place she'd never been this late in the afternoon. She glanced at her directions and then at the gravel road. This was it.

Tall trees and thick hedges hovered over the narrow road, creating a gloomy tunnel. She had the eerie impression that she'd left the modern world. She reached over to make sure her doors were locked. The road seemed never ending. The farther she went, the more frantic the warning voice in her head grew. Just when she was about to turn around, she saw a small structure in the clearing up ahead. It looked like an abandoned one-room cabin, completely barren of paint. A couple of dead ferns in black pots hung from rusty clothes hangers that were bent around the beams of the porch. A rotten table with a broken leg leaned against one side of the house. At the far edge of the yard, Sydney could see the remains of an old ringer-type washing machine turned on its side in the tall grass. A few feet from the washer there was an old wrecked car filled with garbage.

She cracked her window.

"What do you want?"

The man's deep voice seemed to materialize out of thin air, causing Sydney's heart to jump in her throat. She looked toward the house for a face. Before she could answer, a pack of yelping dogs ran from behind the house. Thank goodness she was still safely locked in her jeep.

Sydney lowered the window a couple of inches. "Is this Cecil Prichard's place?"

"Yeah, but who wants to know?" The man appeared from behind the door. He looked to be approximately forty-five years old. His thinning hair was a dingy gray and stringy, like it had not been combed in months. The stained T-shirt revealed a frail, hairy chest. His bottom lip bulged with a dip of snuff or chewing tobacco. Dried stains outlined the corners of his mouth.

Sydney tried to slow her pulsating heartbeat. "My name is Sydney Lassiter. I work at the sawmill, and I just wanted to ask Mr. Prichard a couple of questions."

"Well, he ain't in no shape to be answering questions, but you might as well get out so long as you're here."

Sydney's first impulse was to step on the gas and get as far away as possible from this place, but she couldn't. She needed to talk to Cecil Prichard. He might be just the key to unlock the mystery of her father's death. She opened the door a fraction and the barking dogs jumped at her.

"Git out o' here." The man came down the steps and began kicking the dogs with his bare feet.

"Come on in here and meet the ol' man and my misses." He beckoned Sydney to follow him up the creaky steps. If Sydney thought the outside of the cabin had prepared her for what she would see inside, she was sadly mistaken. The scent of dogs and body odor hit her full force. Stacks of dirty dishes still caked with dried food littered the kitchen counter. Fruit flies were swarming around a heap of garbage in the corner. Empty beer cans were scattered around the room. A dirty throw rug covered in dog hair lay in the middle of the floor.

Sydney took a step backwards. "Where are your wife and father?"

"Well, to tell the truth, they don't live here no more. You just have a seat Miss...uh, what'd you say your name was?" The man motioned toward a ragged recliner that had a big grease spot at the top, no doubt caused by his hair.

Sydney's chest began to pound. Here she was in the middle of nowhere with this creep, and like an idiot, she'd followed him into his lair. What was she thinking? "No thank you. I came to talk to Cecil Prichard. Where is he?"

The man spit a stream of tobacco into a can close to where Sydney was standing. She looked down, expecting to see splatters of tobacco spit on her linen pants.

"Now don't you get sassy with me, Missy!" The man took a step closer to her, and she shrank back against the door. The mixture of body odor, tobacco, and beer were more than she could take. Panic convulsed through her.

"I've obviously come to the wrong place." She moved to open the door.

Before she could get it open, the man reached and closed it. "I'm Bernice Prichard. I'll talk to you. I expect you and me can find lots of interesting things to talk about." He laughed and leaned over Sydney with his hand against the door, blocking her way out.

"Get out of my way!"

"You shore are pretty when you're mad. It makes them big blue eyes shoot bullets."

She kicked the vile man between his legs as hard as she could. He cursed and doubled over in pain. She flung open the door and raced to her jeep, knowing that she only had a few precious seconds to get away. She barely noticed the barking dogs, chasing her to the jeep. She locked the door and started the engine. Through the rear-view mirror, she could see Bernice standing in the yard, shaking his fist as her tires sprayed gravel across the yard. She hadn't meant to kick him. Instinct had taken over. Maybe all of those self-defense classes Judith made her attend were worthwhile after all. What an utterly stupid thing to do. When would she learn to use good judgment? This was one incident that she would definitely keep to herself. She raced down the gravel road and offered up a silent prayer for her escape.

* * * * *

The incident with Bernice Prichard had shaken her up, but Sydney was determined to find Cecil. For several days her mind raced for a way to locate him. It finally came to her—the one person that would know: Barb.

She found Barb in the break room. "Can I talk to you for a minute?"

Barb placed her coffee cup by the pot and turned to Sydney. "I'm busy. Is it important?"

Sydney tried to keep her voice casual. She focused on the stack of papers in Barb's hand. "Do you remember a man named Cecil Prichard who worked at the mill several years ago?

Barb's face grew curious. "Yeah, I remember Cecil. Why?"

"I'd like to ask him about some of the accidents that were happening back then."

"You'd better let old dogs lie—if you know what I mean." Barb turned her back on Sydney and filled her cup with coffee.

"Barb, I need to know where he is."

"Is that right? Well, I guess you're just out of luck." Barb flashed a smile and walked away, sipping her coffee.

Louellen's cultured voice came from behind. "Cecil Prichard is in Shady Side Rest Home. It's located in Beline, about forty miles from here."

Sydney turned and faced her. "Thanks," she said with more gratitude in her voice than she wished to convey.

"You're welcome."

Sydney thought of something else. "Louellen? Have you ever heard of anyone named Lewis?"

Louellen's eyebrow raised. "Why?"

"I was going through some of the old files and came across the name several times."

Louellen studied Sydney and waited. Finally she spoke. "Yeah, I know who Lewis is."

"Well, do you know where he is or what happened to him?"

"Yes."

"Well?" she prompted. This was about as useless as trying to eat a bowl of cereal with a fork.

"He's dead." Louellen turned and regally walked away.

What was that about? Louellen had freely given the information about Cecil Pritchard, but when Sydney mentioned Lewis, Louellen clammed up.

*   *   *   *   *

The nursing home was a far cry from the Prichard's home place. Sydney couldn't help but compare the old shack and junky yard to the modern buildings with the meticulous landscaping. "Are you a relative of Mr. Prichard?" the girl behind the glass window asked.

"Yes, I'm his niece," Sydney said, hoping that Mr. Prichard had one.

After a few minutes of waiting in the lobby, a nurse appeared and escorted Sydney out of the administration building, across the lawn, and into the large room of another building where an elderly bald man sat in a wheelchair, looking out the window. He was neatly dressed and had a blanket spread over his legs. Although they were the same build, it was hard for Sydney to believe this was the father of the repulsive man she'd met a few days before.

"Cecil, I've brought someone to visit you." The nurse smiled and left Sydney with him.

"Cecil." Sydney held out her hand.

"Hello," he said, studying her face.

Sydney looked around to be sure the nurse had left before starting her conversation. "Mr. Prichard, you don't know me. My name is Sydney Lassiter, and I work for the sawmill where you used to work."

"Yeah." The man nodded.

He did remember! "Do you remember a man named Avery McClain?

"Yeah, I knew Avery." Mr. Prichard smiled and nodded again. "I thought a lot of Avery. He was a fine man."

"Mr. Prichard, do you remember the log accident in the wood yard where Avery was almost killed?"

"Yeah, I remember that. Like to have scared me and him both to death. That chain didn't just break, you know. It was cut."

"Can you tell me who would have wanted to do such a thing?"

Sydney held her breath and waited for an answer.

Then Cecil smiled like he recognized her for the first time. "Honey, I thought I were never gone see my little girl again. You do love your old daddy after all, don't you?" He held out his hands.

At another time and place, Sydney would have gladly offered her hands to someone like Cecil, but not today. "What? No, we were talking about Avery McClain and the log yard accident. Don't you remember? Just a second ago, you said you knew Avery. Listen to me!" She felt like shaking Cecil.

"Yeah." Cecil laughed. "You look just like your momma. Where is she?"

"Ma'am." The nurse patted Sydney's arm. "Don't let Mr. Prichard upset you. He don't mean to. He has Alzheimers."

Sydney nodded. She tried to sort through her mixed emotions. Yes, pity was the word she was looking for, but she wasn't sure who she was feeling sorry for—Cecil Prichard or herself.

"Even a fool, when he holdeth his peace, is counted wise."
—Proverbs 17:28

chapter eighteen

Fall came swiftly to Stoney Creek. Not that Sydney minded. She'd forgotten how beautiful the change of the season was in the Southeast. It was as if Mother Nature took pity on the suffocating, listless terrain and decided to brush a leaf here and there with a smidgen of scarlet or gold. Before long the mystical process caught like wildfire and the whole mountainside became ablaze with brilliant color. The air was so crisp that it gave wings to the soul. It was a day for healing. The kind of day that made you believe you could accomplish anything.

Sydney opened one of her bedroom windows. The wind felt good on her face. She turned her attention away from the window to the closet. Sydney's small closet was stuffed so full that she grabbed a handful of hanging clothes and put them on her bed, just so she could sift through what she had. She sighed. With all these clothes, it shouldn't be that hard to find one outfit. She tried on one thing and then another, tossing the rejects in a heap on her bed.

The plan was to meet Kendall at football practice and then they were going to dinner with a few of his friends. She knew that Emma would be there with her boyfriend, Chuck Lingerfelt. The only memory Sydney had of Chuck was that he was very quiet and had so many pimples that he'd been nicknamed "pizza face" by some of the meaner kids in school. Sydney wasn't sure who else would be there.

She pulled out a pair of linen pants and tried them on. Too dressy. She took them off and tossed them on the bed, reaching for a pair of jeans when her cordless phone rang. She searched frantically under the mountain of clothes to get to the sound. "Hello? Hi, Kendall...yes, I'm meeting you at practice. I promise I'll be on time."

She ended the call and then tried to squelch the irritation that surfaced. Why would Kendall assume she would be late? It was only practice. Why was it so important for her to be there for the whole thing? Kendall had been wound up tight as a toy soldier now that football season was getting ready to start. The pressure he was under must be incredible. She just needed to overlook his moodiness. Things would settle down once the season got under way.

*   *   *   *   *

The entire town of Stoney Creek, it seemed, had come out to see the first official practice of the season. Kendall had been holding practices for two weeks now, but this was the time when it became serious. Practice was held on a side field where the grass was splotchy and beaten down. The football stadium was reserved for game nights only. All summer long the grass on the main field had been nurtured and was now a thick carpet of green.

Sydney parked along the street because the parking lot adjacent to the field was full. She made her way up to the field and saw the spectators, mostly men, leaning against their cars and discussing the players. All of them, no doubt, had strong opinions about the plays Kendall was running and which players he should put in various positions. She scoped the crowd, thinking she might see Walter, but no such luck. She found a spot to stand and noticed an attractive black woman leaning against a green Mercury Sable. The woman gave Sydney a polite smile. Sydney returned the gesture and then turned her focus to the field.

She spotted Kendall right away. He was hard to miss and looked every bit the head coach in his tight gray pants and white shirt that clung to his muscular chest and arms. A burgundy cap was pulled down over his eyes, and a whistle was wedged in his mouth like an extra tooth. He was blowing it in rhythm. The players were lined up, performing drills. Sydney remembered seeing the players do this particular one when she was younger. They would run in place as fast as they could until Kendall blew the whistle, at which point they would hit the ground and then come back up to repeat the same process over and over.

Nostalgia swept over her as she caught a faint whiff of sulfur from the paper mill. Avery and Walter used to watch the practices just like the men who were here now. Sometimes Avery would take her with him, and if she behaved he would treat her to an ice cream at Randall's Diner afterwards.

"Who are you here to see?"

It took Sydney a moment to realize that someone had spoken to her. She looked at the woman she'd noticed earlier.

"Are you here to see one of the players?" The woman repeated.

"Not exactly."

The woman waited for Sydney to explain. Sydney stepped closer to the woman so she wouldn't have to yell. "Coach Fletcher's a friend of mine." Her face warmed and she braced herself for the woman to make some insinuating comment. Why did she feel like she was sixteen again?

"Oh." The woman pointed to the field. "Do you see that guy on the end of the first row?"

Sydney looked. "The tall one?"

The woman nodded and smiled proudly. "That's my son, Reginald."

Sydney wasn't sure how to answer. "He looks like a fine player."

"He's the quarterback." The woman extended her hand. "I'm Jarilyn Kelly."

"Sydney Lassiter."

Jarilyn flashed a brilliant smile. "You must be new to Stoney Creek."

"I moved here this summer from Ft. Worth. I'm the safety coordinator for the sawmill," Sydney said. She guessed Jarilyn to be in her late thirties. Her ebony hair was soft and rounded on her shoulders. Her large almond eyes were friendly. She was dressed in white slacks and a matching tailored jacket. A pale blue silk shirt underneath the jacket was the perfect complement for her chocolate honey skin.

"I work at First Federal Bank next to the Piggly Wiggly," Jarilyn said.

There was something warm and approachable about Jarilyn that put Sydney completely at ease. She learned that Reginald was Jarilyn's only son and the center of her life. Reginald's father had left the picture years ago, shortly after Jarilyn became pregnant. Jarilyn had moved from Birmingham to Stoney Creek because she knew it would be a good place to raise her son.

They made small talk until they heard Kendall blow the whistle long and hard, a signal for the players to huddle around him.

"It looks like practice is over," Jarilyn said.

"Yeah." Sydney wasn't sure where Kendall was going to meet her.

"I hope you'll come to practice again. It's nice to have someone to talk to."

More than you know, Sydney thought. Jarilyn couldn't possibly guess how much her friendliness meant. Sydney smiled and turned to leave. "It was nice meeting you."

"Wait—don't leave yet. I want you to meet Reginald."

The women watched Reginald approach them, carrying his helmet in one hand. His curly hair had soaked up his perspiration like a sponge and left drops glistening on the ends. A few drops broke loose and trickled down his face. There were deep smudges of dirt on his elbows and grass stains on his knees. When he got next to them, Sydney noticed how he towered over his petite mother. "Son, I want you to meet Sydney Lassiter. She's a friend of Coach Fletcher."

Sydney extended her hand. "Reginald, it's nice to meet you."

He smiled broadly, accentuating his clean even features. His handshake was firm and sure. "It's nice to meet you, Miss Lassiter. Any friend of coach's is a friend of mine."

"I hear you're quite the football player."

Reginald shifted uncomfortably under the praise, and that made Sydney like him even more. He looked at his mother. "I see Mama's been talkin' to you."

"I've just been tellin' the truth." Jarilyn pulled her jacket together and jutted out her chin.

"I'm gonna go to the field house and get my stuff, Mama."

"Hurry, Son. I'm sure you've got lots of homework."

He waved at Sydney before trotting off. "Nice meetin' you, Miss Lassiter."

Sydney looked at Jarilyn. "You have a fine son."

"Thank you. It's been hard raising Reginald without a father. Coach Fletcher's been a real blessing to him—a father figure for Reginald to look up to."

Sydney's heart glowed warm. Just when she thought she had Kendall figured out, there seemed to be another facet to his personality.

"I'm real glad Coach Fletcher has you. It's about time he started going with someone nice for a change."

The words broad-sided Sydney, leaving her speechless. She would replay them a hundred times in her mind and would berate herself for not asking Jarilyn to explain what she meant. But at that moment, no words came. She just stood there.

"Can I give you a ride to the field house?" Jarilyn asked. The practice field and field house were at opposite ends of the school. Even so, it was a short walk between the two because the players could take the path between the cafeteria and agricultural building, but cars had to drive all the way around.

"No, thank you. I'll just wait here for Kendall."

"You might as well get comfortable. It looks like he's gonna be a while."

Sydney looked at the field. Kendall was walking away from her to the field house. A tight cluster of men surrounded him.

"You sure you don't want a ride?"

Sydney shook her head. "I parked my jeep on the side of the road. I need to go get it, and then I'll just drive down to the field house." She forced a smile. "See you next time."

Sydney couldn't help but feel hurt. Kendall had asked her to come but hadn't bothered to see if she was waiting for him. Why would he go to the trouble of calling to make sure she was coming if he wasn't even going to notice?

*   *   *   *   *

It took Kendall a while to get rid of what he called the "Monday morning quarterbacks"—the well-meaning but intrusive townsfolk who thought they knew more about coaching than he did. In Stoney Creek, pacifying the town was such an integral part of coaching that it should have been included in his job description. He followed the last stragglers into the field house and scanned the room. "Josh, Dave, Sam, y'all come over here."

"What's up coach?" Josh wiped the sweat from his forehead with the back of his arm.

Kendall gave him a dark look. "You're going back to the field."

The player's eyes grew round and he pointed to himself. "Me?"

"Yeah, you and you and you," he said, motioning to

the other players who, by this time, were standing still like wide-eyed deer caught in headlights. "Let's go."

"What're we doing?" one of the players asked. They quickened their pace to catch up to Kendall. Rather than answering, he marched full speed to the practice field. The boys had no other choice but to follow.

Kendall halted when they reached their destination. "Take a good look. What do you see?" By this time, all of the spectators had left, leaving an empty field.

The boys' faces looked as blank as a sheet of new paper. "Huh?"

Kendall's eyes narrowed a fraction and he repeated the question. "What do you see?"

Dave kicked at the ground. "A field?"

Kendall's hand went to his hip and he glared at the boys. "What else?"

Josh looked down. "Grass?"

This brought a chuckle from his peers. "Dead grass," one of them added, and then they all snickered.

Kendall's face turned scarlet, and a marble appeared under his skin where his jaw came together. "This is hallowed ground—my world." He eyed his players, whose faces had turned the color of chalk. "Do you think this is some big joke?"

"Uh, no sir."

"What were y'all thinking? I'm trying to get this team in shape and y'all are out here goofing off. Do you think that's fair when everyone else is busting their butts?"

"But coach," Dave said, "I wasn't goofing off."

Kendall caught Dave by the shirt and pulled his face within an inch of his. "You're telling me you can't block any better than that? If that's what you're saying, then you'd better step down and let somebody else take your place because you ain't man enough to be on my team."

The boy's chin quivered. "I'm sorry, coach. I'll do better. I promise."

Kendall let him go with a push. He turned his attention from Dave to the other two. "What about y'all?

You were jumping off sides every play. You know that will cost us five yards every time we turn around. We can't afford that!"

They spoke in unison. "We'll do better, coach. We promise."

"Yeah, and you'll start right now. Give me twenty-five times up the bleachers. Now!"

*   *   *   *   *

Sydney pulled in front of the field house just in time to see a player exiting. She rolled down her window. "Excuse me, have you seen Coach Fletcher?"

"Yes ma'am, he went back to the practice field."

This was getting ridiculous. For a split second, she thought about leaving. Then again, it wasn't like she had any other plans. She was here and might as well go and find him.

She neared the field and heard a man yelling. It took her a minute to realize it was Kendall.

"Come on Josh, my mama can run faster than that. What're you gonna do when you get out in the world? Do you think people are going to care if you're tired? Now get back up there on those bleachers."

She watched one of the boys came off the bleachers. He doubled over and vomited on the grass. Kendall looked her direction, and their eyes met for a brief moment before she turned and began walking back to her jeep.

Kendall came running across the field after her. "Hey, where are you going?"

"I'm leaving." As if you care, she thought.

He caught up with her. "Why?"

"Because I'm tired of waiting!" She motioned to the field. "And look what you're doing to your players!" She ran a hand through her hair.

Kendall took hold of her arm. "Look, it's not as bad as it looked. You only saw the last part. Don't go anywhere. I promise I'll just be a few minutes. I've got to check on my boys at the field and then I'll go to the field house and get changed." He searched her face. "Wait for me?"

"Okay."

Kendall came out wearing jeans and a button-up shirt. She rolled down the window. A ghost of a smile touched his lips. "You're still here."

"Yeah, but don't think I didn't consider leaving."

This won her a full smile and he gave her a peck on the lips.

"Why were you making those players run bleachers after practicing in the heat? Don't you think that's a little extreme?"

"I had it under control."

Her eyebrow arched. "Are you sure about that? You pushed that one player to the breaking point. He was over there puking his guts up."

"Look, I know what I'm doing. Those boys are like my sons. They've got to learn to be tough. Do you think the other team is going to care if my guys are hot and tired?" He paused. "Besides, it wouldn't be fair to the rest of the team if I let them get away with goofing off."

She grinned. "Are you saying that I should mind my own business?"

"Oh I get lots of advice from people about how to run my team." He gave her an appraising look, taking in her jeans and simple v-necked red sweater. "But I have to say that none of them look as good as you."

Kendall wasn't one to throw around compliments. Her face warmed. "Thanks."

"Why don't we leave your jeep here and take my truck?"

*　　*　　*　　*　　*

"Which restaurant are we going to?" Sydney asked.

"We're not."

"What?"

Kendall smiled. "We're having dinner at someone's house."

"Oh? Whose?"

"An old friend of mine—Jessica Winters."

Sydney's eyes widened. She had to bite her lip to hold back the groan in her throat. Of all the people. She and Jessica had been friends, had hung out together at cheerleading practice, had even spent the night at each other's houses—until Sydney beat Jessica out of the head cheerleader spot. That's all it took for Jessica to turn against her and become her fiercest enemy.

"You'll like Jess. She's a lot of fun and an excellent cook."

A wrinkle formed between Sydney's eyes. So it was *Jess* instead of *Jessica*. Sydney's culinary skills were limited to chicken noodle soup and microwavable pot pies. Her thigh began to ache, and she rubbed it and grimaced. Was it her imagination or was it starting to hurt more often?

"Are you okay?"

Sydney plastered on a smile. "Of course."

"They left the driveway for us." Kendall drove in and turned off the engine. Even though it was dark, the headlights from the truck were bright enough for Sydney to detect that the brick house was new.

They got out and went to the door. Kendall knocked once and then opened it and motioned for her to follow. They walked through the living room, decorated in vivid reds and yellows, and into the kitchen. The dining room and kitchen were one large room separated by a bar. It was a cozy floor plan that leant itself well to entertaining.

Kendall put an arm around Sydney's shoulder. "Everyone, this is Sydney Lassiter."

From the grand way he announced her, Sydney half expected a drum roll to sound. Kendall's friends rushed to greet her.

Emma was the first person to her side. Sydney extended her hand, but Emma gave her a bear hug instead. "Hi, Sydney. It's good to see you again." The warmth in Emma's voice helped ease some of Sydney's tension. "This is Chuck Lingerfelt—the love of my life." Emma put her arm around his waist and gave him a tight squeeze.

Age had been good to Chuck. He'd filled out to match his height. His pimples were gone but had left pits in his cheeks. "It's nice to meet you," he said, giving her hand a swift yank, making Sydney think that Chuck's bashfulness had vanished with the years. His nose was too large for his face and jumped out at her. However, once she willed it to step back and get in line with his other features, there was something attractive about him. Sydney decided it was the sparkle in his eyes—or it could have been his full lips that looked like they could break into a grin at any given moment.

Sydney looked past Emma and Chuck into the kitchen where Jessica was standing. She was still as beautiful as Sydney remembered in a flashy sort of way. Her shoulder-length curly hair was almost black. She was as tall as Sydney but curvaceous where Sydney was athletic. Her brown eyes were like big balls of chocolate, and she had deep dimples in her cheeks. Jessica wiped her hands on a kitchen towel and then sauntered over to meet Sydney.

"Hello." Jessica extended her hand, her eyes raking over Sydney.

In the pause that followed, Sydney recognized instinctively where she would stand with Jessica. Jessica's dark, narrowed eyes were saying what her lips never would—that she was used to being the queen bee, unaccustomed to having any competition. Sydney met her eyes in a quiet challenge. Jessica smiled, but her eyes remained cold.

"Please," Jessica said in a stately manner. "Make yourself at home."

Chuck gave Kendall a shove. "It's nice to finally meet you, Sydney. You're all Kendall talks about lately, except football of course."

She looked at Kendall's face for validation, but it was a blank. What she did notice, however, was the scowl that crossed Jessica's features. It was quickly replaced with a wooden smile.

"Dinner's almost ready," Jessica said.

"Umm. Sure smells good," Kendall said. "What's on the menu?"

"Chicken parmesan, mandarin salad, and garlic bread."

Kendall smiled. "My favorite."

"I know," Jessica said.

Kendall's face turned cherry red. Sydney wondered if there had ever been anything between them.

Jessica called out to everyone, "Y'all go sit down, and I'll start putting the food on the table."

Sydney moved to join the group until Jessica stopped her. "Would you mind helping me in the kitchen?"

"Not at all." Sydney's mind went back to an incident that occurred when she and Jessica were in the fifth grade.

* * * * *

"Mom, I want that ribbon for my hair," Jessica said.

"Here, we'll cut it in half. Then you and Cindy will match." Mrs. Winters snipped the royal blue ribbon and handed a length to Cindy.

"Thank you, Mrs. Winters."

Mrs. Winters clucked her tongue. "Cindy, please call me Ruth. I'm much too young to be a *Mrs.*"

Jessica's eyes narrowed. "You cut mine crooked. I'm going to fix it." She grabbed the scissors and started snipping while Cindy tied her ribbon in a bow around her ponytail.

"Now mine's too short!" Jessica's lips formed a pout and her eyes went to Cindy's hair. "Hers looks good, and mine looks terrible!"

Before Cindy knew what was happening, Ruth reached out with the scissors and snipped the ends of her ribbon so it would look just like Jessica's.

"What would you like for me to do?" Sydney asked, trying to put the incident back in the past. That was a long time ago. It was possible that Jessica had changed over the years. She should at least give her the benefit of the doubt.

"Put the ice in the glasses, will you?"

Sydney nodded.

Jessica moved close to Sydney, and her voice lowered to a whisper. "I'm so glad you and Kendall are dating."

"Excuse me?"

Jessica charged on. "Kendall's been so down in the dumps these past few months. It's good to see him smiling again."

Sydney raised an eyebrow. "Why has Kendall been down?"

The corners of Jessica's full mouth turned down. "Didn't he tell you? I thought you knew."

"Knew what?"

At least Jessica had the decency to look embarrassed, whether or not that was truly the case. "Kendall and I were—um—we used to go together."

Sydney's mouth went dry.

"I broke Kendall's heart. I didn't know whether or not he'd ever get over it." She looked at Sydney. "I always knew he'd eventually settle...um, find someone else."

"Hey, what's takin' so long?" Chuck's yelled.

Sydney stepped away from Jessica and began chunking cubes of ice in the glasses.

"We're coming," Jessica called back at him. "Just be patient."

Jessica pulled out cans of Ginger Ale. "I'll pour, and you take them to the table." She smiled. "So glad we had our little chat."

Jessica filled the glasses so full that Sydney had to walk slowly to keep them from spilling on the floor. She finally got all the glasses to the table except for her own. She went back to retrieve it and noticed that there was only an inch of soda in her glass. She looked at Jessica who shrugged and said, "Sorry, that's all there was left."

* * * * *

Sydney took a bite of chicken parmesan. The fact that it was indeed very good made Jessica's earlier comments sting even more.

"Well, how do you like Stoney Creek?" Chuck drawled.

"I like it," Sydney heard herself say. How else was she supposed to answer that question?

Emma forked a chunk of chicken into her mouth. "That was a pat answer. Now tell us how you really feel."

Sydney's cheeks grew warm. "I do like it here. Really."

Kendall came to her rescue. "Now Sis, you leave Sydney alone. She's gettin' along just fine. I'm seeing to that."

"That's mighty kind of ya," Chuck said, and everyone laughed.

"You'll have to excuse my little sis," Kendall said to Sydney. "She never takes anything at face value—always has to get to the bottom of everything."

Emma frowned. "That's not true."

Kendall ignored her. "Only problem with that is that if you go sifting through a can of worms, all you find at the bottom is more worms."

This brought on an explosion of laughter from Chuck. Emma delivered a swift elbow jab to his ribs. She then looked across the table and stuck out her tongue at Kendall.

A moment of silence passed and everyone focused their attention on their plates. Jessica was the first to speak. "Sydney, Kendall said you work at the sawmill. Do you know Sean O'Conner?"

"Yes, Sean's office is next to mine." Sydney left it at that. She wasn't about to ask Jessica if she knew Sean, even though she did want to know. No, she didn't want to know, she told herself. Why did she care if Jessica knew Sean?

"Sean and I are dating," Jessica said.

"Oh really?" Sydney looked Jessica square in the eyes. "That's interesting. I don't think he's ever mentioned you."

Jessica's face grew red. But Sydney wasn't finished yet. "And since you mentioned being a heartbreaker, I figured it would be too hard to limit yourself to just one man."

Jessica gasped, and Kendall almost choked on his food. Oops. She'd done it again. When would she learn to keep that snake-fanged tongue of hers in its cage? In Judith's glitzy magazine cover world, cattiness was an accepted—even admired—trait. How she'd watched Judith and mimicked her. She'd reveled in the flash of approval she saw in Judith's eyes when she was brave enough to level her own witty remark. But once Sydney opened that part of herself, it became harder and harder to control it. It was a way to expel some of the poison that had seeped into her since the accident. Over the years her claws had grown a little too sharp, even for Judith.

The shocked faces, staring at her around the table, brought home the fact that she wasn't in Judith's world any longer but in a more polite society where she would do well to choose her words with care. She caught a glimpse of her parents mirrored in those faces. Would they be shocked to see how coarse she'd become?

She smiled through the chill and hoped her words would sound sincere. Maybe she could repair some of the damage. "Jessica, I would love to get this recipe. You really are a wonderful cook."

Jessica was too busy stewing from her earlier comment to answer, but at least Kendall seemed to relax.

"How's the team lookin'?" Chuck asked.

Thank goodness for trusty ol' Chuck. If Emma hadn't slung her arm around him to give him a big hug, Sydney would have.

Kendall helped himself to another piece of bread. "Pretty good so far. I've got ten returning seniors, including Reggie."

Sydney's ears perked up. "Reginald Kelly?"

Kendall cocked his head. "Yeah, he's our starting quarterback. Do you know him?"

"I met him and his mother at practice this afternoon."

Kendall and Chuck became immersed in football while Sydney made polite conversation with Emma. Sydney looked across the table with an arched brow and met Jessica's glare.

"You just remind me of somebody I used to know." Jessica tucked a wisp of curly hair behind her ear.

Sydney chuckled. "Yeah, I seem to have that face—you know, the one that everyone thinks looks like so and so." Before Jessica could respond, Sydney turned her attention to Kendall and Chuck.

Chuck rubbed his hands together and shook his head. "I can just taste that state championship."

Kendall leaned back in his chair and held up his hand. "Whoa now. Let's not get ahead of ourselves. We haven't even played our first game yet."

"You've got all the elements," Chuck said.

"What do you think about Kendall's team?" Emma asked.

"I think he's great." Sydney laughed and squeezed Kendall's arm. "Oh—I mean, I think it's great."

Everyone except Jessica laughed.

Chuck leaned forward. "Ken, do you remember that time we played Bessemer for the state championship?" A slow grin stole over Kendall's face. Chuck continued.

"The score was tied, fourteen to fourteen, and we were in double overtime. And there were only ten seconds left." Chuck let out a low whistle. "Right down to the wire, and then Willy kicked that beautiful field goal, smack down the middle. We beat 'em seventeen to fourteen. I'll never forget it."

"No, the score was sixteen to thirteen," Sydney blurted.

All eyes at the table whipped around to Sydney. Kendall spoke first. "She's right." He looked thoughtful. "How did you know that?"

It had just come out. Sydney wished she could crawl under the table. She knew her face was beaming like a neon light. "Do you think y'all are the only ones who talk about football? I hear the guys at the mill talking about it all the time." She knew her explanation sounded flimsy, but it was the best she could come up with at that moment.

"Well, what a coincidence," Jessica purred and rolled her eyes at the rest of the group. "Our little debutant is just full of surprises."

Sydney stared numbly at her plate.

"Wisdom excelleth folly, as far as light excelleth darkness."
—Ecclesiastes 2:13

chapter nineteen

A bittersweet feeling settled over Stella as she listened to her granddaughter talk. Sydney was so much like Avery. Having her here was like having a part of Avery back, but it also made her keenly aware of his absence. Stella sank deeper into the sofa and took a long sip of herbal tea. Sydney's visits had grown more frequent over the past few weeks, and Stella found herself looking forward to them.

She tried to put her finger on what was bothering her. A change had occurred in her granddaughter over the past few weeks, and Stella wasn't sure why. Sydney had learned from Judith how to appear as cool as a cucumber on the outside, but Stella knew that she had too much Avery in her to keep up that façade for long. Tension was boiling inside her like a pressure cooker. But then, Sydney had been like that since the first day she stepped back into Stella's life. Sydney's tension was mounting. That was the difference. Stella didn't know how much more Sydney could take before she exploded.

Sydney told Stella about her dead-end visit with Harriet Crawford and how frustrating it had been. She told her about the accident in the kiln and how Sean had let her take all the blame. Then she told her about visiting Cecil Prichard in the nursing home.

"Tell me more about Sean O'Conner," Stella said.

Sydney laughed humorlessly. "Oh, he's smart,

witty, handsome as sin, and mean as a pit bull. I think that about sums it up."

"It sounds like he keeps you on your toes."

"That's putting it mildly. I never know where I stand with Sean. One minute he's appearing out of thin air to rescue me, and the next he's hanging me out to dry."

Stella chuckled. "Sounds like a typical man."

"Things would be so much better if he would just stay out of my way."

Stella didn't miss much. She guessed that Sydney must have some feelings for Sean or she wouldn't have such a strong reaction to him. Countless times, she'd seen Avery react the very same way whenever he would have a disagreement with Susan. Stella steered Sydney in another direction. "Tell me more about that other young man—the one you're dating."

Sydney's countenance lightened. "Kendall?"

Stella nodded.

"He's everything Sean isn't—nice, cute, sweet."

Stella frowned. "Sounds like you're describing a pet. And you really like him?"

"We have fun together. And he's very—comfortable."

Stella set her cup on the coffee table. "Comfortable?"

"It just feels right when I'm with him. Having said that, there's another part of Kendall that I'm having a hard time figuring out. He doesn't express his feelings very well. I always wonder what he's thinking. He grew up in a completely different world than I did."

"A world that was stolen from you?" Stella watched Sydney's eyes widen.

"Well, yes. It's just that...in a lot of ways Kendall reminds me of—well—um." She stopped.

"Of who?"

Sydney shook her head. "Oh, never mind. I'm just rambling"

"Of Avery? Is that what you were going to say?"

Sydney's eyes met Stella's, and she nodded slowly. "Yes."

Stella moved over and sat next to Sydney. "I miss him too."

Sydney's eyes misted. "I just feel so helpless. I've tried so hard to find out what happened to Daddy, and here it is four months later, and I don't know any more now than I did when I first got here."

Stella took Sydney by the hand. "I've been giving this whole thing a lot of thought. Maybe it's time to let this go and get on with your life."

Sydney's eyes widened and she looked at Stella. "What are you saying? How can I possibly do that?"

"Hand me my Bible."

Sydney reached for it. She looked skeptical, like she knew where this was going.

It took Stella only a second to find her place. She began reading. "Ecclesiastes, Chapter 3. 'To every thing there is a season, and a time to every purpose under the heaven: A time to be born, and a time to die...a time to kill, and a time to heal; a time to weep, and a time to laugh; a time to mourn, and a time to dance.'"

Moisture formed in Stella's eyes. "And there's a time to move on. This whole thing—it's tearing you apart. I just can't bear to see that happen." She patted Sydney's hand and the two sat in silence.

Sydney withdrew her hand from Stella's grasp and shook her head. "I don't know if it's possible for me to go on. I'm so messed up on the inside. So many terrible things have happened. I just can't put it all out of my mind."

Stella understood, had even felt, some of those same feelings, but she knew how empty and useless hate was. It would destroy her granddaughter. She had to find a way to get through to her. "Do you remember when I told you that it rains on the just and the unjust?"

Instead of answering, Sydney stared in the distance.

Stella nudged her. "Sydney?"

"I remember."

"Do you know what I meant by that?"

Silence.

"If every person were immediately struck down the moment he did an evil deed, or if every person instantly rewarded for good deeds, there would be no freedom. God allows us to have a space in between so that we can choose how we'll act." Stella paused to see if she was getting through. Sydney's face was unreadable. Stella knew her next words would hurt, but they needed to be said. "Sometimes the Lord allows bad things to happen to good people."

Sydney's lower lip began to quiver. "Why would a loving God take away my parents?" she whispered. "He took away everything—my identity—even Judith."

"We don't always understand why, but if we continue to have faith, He'll help us through it," Stella finished gently.

"Those are just words. I don't feel God's love. I don't feel anything."

The bitterness in Sydney's voice took Stella aback, and she uttered a silent prayer so she would know how to respond. "You never met my mother—your great-grandmother Bessie. She died before you were born."

Sydney remained quiet.

"I grew up on a farm in a little bitty old shack of a house that got so cold in the wintertime that on sunny days, we'd go outside just to get warm." Stella chuckled. "Mama didn't own a car. She walked everywhere she went. She was always helping somebody. Whenever Mama went on one of her crusades I, of course, had to go with her. Sometimes we'd walk for miles down railroad tracks and old dusty roads. My feet would hurt and I'd start complaining. 'Come on, Stella,' she'd say, 'don't quit on me now. Them poor ol' folks ain't got nothing. They need our help.'" Stella laughed at the remembrance of it. "It never occurred to Mama that most people considered us poor." Stella paused. "Mama had a lot of heartache. My father died when I was two years old. She raised me and my two older brothers alone.

She had plenty of reasons to be bitter, but she stayed so busy raising us and helping the whole countryside that she hardly had time to think about it." Stella looked at Sydney. "And then there were the chickens we raised."

A smile crept over Sydney's face, and she shook her head. She loved hearing Stella's stories, even if they were a form of chastisement.

"We raised chickens so we could sell the eggs. One time we decided to keep a few eggs and let them hatch. Benny, my brother who was only three years older than me, and I watched those eggs for weeks. Finally, they started to get cracks in them, and we saw a little beak pecking its way out of one of the eggs. We got so excited that we started helping him. We pulled away a few pieces at a time—and just kept peeling until we'd exposed the entire chicken. We were devastated when our baby chick died a few hours later. I told Mama what happened, and her expression grew cross. I'll never forget what she told us. 'Ben, Stella, y'all done killed that chicken.'

"'We were just trying to help him,' we said.

"She gathered us close and explained that every baby chick had to fight his way out of his own egg. It was that fight that helped make him strong enough to survive."

Sydney felt her anger melt away. That story sounded familiar, and she thought she might have read it somewhere in a book. It was possible that the same experience had happened to Stella—but not probable. Still, Sydney appreciated what Stella was trying to do.

But Stella wasn't finished yet. "God doesn't give us hardships to tear us apart. He gives them to us to help make us stronger." Stella's next words were spoken with such strong conviction that they hit home, and Sydney felt a burning in her heart despite her best efforts to shut it out. "There's one thing I've learned. Whenever I've felt a great distance between me and the Lord, it's me who has turned away from Him."

*"Pleasant words are as an honeycomb,
sweet to the soul, and health to the bones."*
—Proverbs 16:24

chapter twenty

Cold, wet darkness closed in like a giant faceless mouth, devouring her. It was useless to fight. There was so much water, and she was so tired. But she must help him. She must get to the boat. She could feel the heat, the searing burning of her flesh, so powerful in its fury that even the blackest water couldn't shut it out. Her hand reached for something solid. Instinct told her that she must stay above the water. She must try and hold on. The hammering started in the distance. It was a steady rhythmic beat at first, and then it started racking her brain, crowding out everything else. Maybe she should sink into the darkness—anything to get away from the hammering.

Sydney jolted up in her bed. Her pulse was racing, and she was bathed in sticky sweat. She pushed her matted hair back from her forehead. The dreams had started in the hospital when she was recovering from the boat accident. Over the years they'd diminished to the point that she'd thought she was over them for good. Ever since her return to Stoney Creek, they'd come back. And they'd come with a vengeance. Last night's visit to Stella had prompted this dream. But wait. Where did the hammering come from? That was new.

It took her a moment to realize that the hammering in her dream was in reality a loud pounding on the door. She looked at her clock—8:30 on a Saturday morning.

She threw her off her covers and stumbled out of bed. She'd grown used to Kendall's unexpected visits, especially on Saturdays, but this was a little ridiculous. Kendall had held a late practice the night before to get ready for next week's game. What was he doing up so early?

There wasn't time for her to try and do anything with her hair. "I'm coming," she called. He must not have heard her because he kept pounding. "I said, I'm coming!"

She unlocked the door and removed the chain. "Come in," she said with a yawn.

"It's about time. I thought I was gonna have to call in the National Guard to get you out of bed."

All sleepiness fled when her mind registered that it was Sean, not Kendall, who had spoken. He barged past her, and she just stood there, staring at him with her hand on the open door. He plopped down on the sofa like he owned the place. "Good morning, Syd."

One hand went to smooth down her disheveled hair and the other tried to pull her T-shirt farther down over her shorts. His eyes flickered over her bedraggled appearance.

"I wasn't exactly expecting you."

His eyes danced. "You look fine. You ought to see me when I get up."

She gave him a courtesy smile and sat down in the oversized chair across from him. "To what do I owe this honor?" She looked at his sweatshirt, jeans, and hiking boots.

He spread his hands and flashed a disarming smile, probably hoping that it would melt her right into the floor. "What? I can't even stop by to see you?"

Her blue eyes met his with a trace of defiance. She wasn't in the mood for this. "At 8:30 on a Saturday morning?"

"I want you to spend the day with me."

"What?"

"Look Syd, things are always so tense between us at work. I thought it would do us both some good to spend some time together away from the mill."

Sydney shook her head. "I'm sorry, I have other plans today."

"With Kendall?" There was a challenge in his dark eyes that was scary and inviting at the same time. What was it about him that made her feel so alive? What was it that made her want to pit her will against his?

Her chin jutted out. "Maybe."

"I see how it is."

"Do you?"

Sean nodded and looked her straight in the eyes. "Loverboy's got you wrapped around his little finger."

Her eyes narrowed. "That's not how it is," she said, all the while remembering how she'd gone to Kendall's practices every day this week and sat there like a groupie.

Sean's voice became smooth. "Come on Syd, I don't wanna argue. It's a perfect day. Let's go have some fun. Do something spontaneous for once. You don't have to ask Kendall's permission. I'm going flying. Come with me."

She shouldn't have let Sean get away with that comment about getting Kendall's permission, but her mind was already jumping past that. "Flying? What're you talking about? Where?"

"The airport is in Rome, Georgia."

Sydney wrinkled her nose. "You fly planes?"

Sean nodded with a grin. "I have a pilot's license. It's awesome, Syd. You'll love it. Afterwards, I thought we could head down to Marietta and eat dinner."

She glanced at the door. What if Kendall really did show up here this morning? She didn't want to have to explain what Sean was doing at her house. She stood. "Make yourself at home. I'll go and get ready."

"Don't you want to eat breakfast first?"

"No, I'll grab something to take with me."

* * * * *

The drive to Rome was a feast for the eyes. They followed along the rolling hills that were splashed with the colors of fall. Sydney stole a sideways glance at Sean. He had one hand on the steering wheel while the other rested in his lap.

Sydney pointed. "Oh look, there's a *See Rock City* sign."

"Those signs are all over the Southeast."

I know that, Sydney was itching to say. I'm from here! She could have given Sean a little history lesson. For instance, how the signs used to be painted on the sides of barns.

While holding tight to the steering wheel with one hand, Sean reached behind her seat and retrieved a brown paper bag. He placed the bag in his lap and pulled out a moon pie. "Want one?"

"No thanks."

"These things are delicious. I discovered them when I moved to Stoney Creek."

Sydney remembered how Avery would bring home boxes of Moon Pies. They had a marshmallow center that was sandwiched between two graham crackers and coated with chocolate, vanilla, or banana flavoring. Susan used to tease Avery about bringing them home for everyone else because he was the only one who ever ate them. Sydney laughed. "Next you'll be offering me an RC cola."

"What's that?"

She shook her head. "Never mind." RC colas were a southern delicacy, ranking right up there with Wonder bread and potted meat.

Sydney leaned back in her seat. She knew she shouldn't compare Kendall to Sean, but the thought came barging through nevertheless. Sean was as relaxed as Kendall was uptight. He had a bold confidence that showed in his mannerisms, and he talked about everything. Sydney found herself laughing more than she'd laughed in weeks. Sean's wry sense of humor was a surprise that she hadn't anticipated, making her wonder what else she didn't know about him. She'd thought she had him figured out, but now she wasn't so sure. There were no uncomfortable stretches of silence with Sean like there were with Kendall, and Sean didn't stutter all over himself when he spoke. Sean O'Conner was a ladies' man in every sense of the word, and Sydney had to admit that she was no more immune to his wiles than any other woman. A picture of Jessica flashed through her mind, and she felt a stab of jealousy. She wondered what little Miss Heartbreaker would think if she knew her man was here with her. Sydney's blue eyes glittered in satisfaction at the thought.

"We're almost there," Sean said.

The time had flown by. It was an hour and a half drive to Rome, but it felt like they'd just left. "It's about time." A playful smile tugged at the corners of her mouth. She caught herself. What was she doing? Flirting with him? A warning went off in her head. *Don't be stupid. Keep your guard up.* She had enough trouble in her life without falling for the likes of Sean O'Conner.

When they pulled into the parking lot, Sydney reached for her door.

"Stop." Sean jumped out and ran around to open her door.

"Thank you." The warning was still going off, but she shut it out of her mind. The sun was shining, and the air felt good against her cheeks. She was going to stop analyzing everything and enjoy herself for once.

* * * * *

Sydney was amazed how easy it was to fly from a small airport versus a commercial one. There were no other passengers, no security checks, and no hassles. Sean stopped at the front desk and spoke to the attendant. He'd called ahead to reserve the plane, so everything was a cinch from there.

He walked outside with the attendant, giving her an opportunity to look around. The airport was tiny and looked deserted except for the one attendant. There were a few chairs in the main room and a handful of magazines on a square table.

A few minutes later, the attendant returned and told her that Sean was bringing the plane around. She walked through the double glass doors and waited. The plane was white with blue stripes. She felt her first shiver of apprehension when she realized how small it was.

Sean drove the plane around and turned off the engine. He got out and then helped her into the passenger seat.

"Watch your step." He put his arm around Sydney's shoulder and helped her to her seat.

He ran around and got in and handed her a set of earphones. "Put these on so that we can talk. Otherwise, the noise of the engine drowns everything out." He glanced at her. "Nervous?"

Her palms were sweaty. "Not in the least."

He started the plane and followed the instructions given by the attendant at the control tower, checking off each item as it was called out. The plane started moving slowly at first and then raced down the end of the runway. Sydney felt the adrenaline rush akin to riding a roller coaster when the plane lifted. She was struck by the lack of movement once they were in the air. She looked below them. The landscape got smaller and the trees changed to pencils with pom poms stuck on their ends.

She was amazed at how well Sean maneuvered the plane. "Look to your right," he said. She saw a cluster of buildings that encircled what looked like a castle. "That's Berry College."

"It's so beautiful up here."

"There's nothing else like it."

Sydney forced herself to pay attention while he pointed out various sites of interest. She tried not to think about the nearness of Sean or his strong, steady hands on the wheel.

The ride was over all too soon for Sydney. She loved being in the plane, soaring free like a bird.

When they got back to the car, Sean opened her door. A comfortable silence stretched between them. He started the engine and turned out of the parking lot. "Thanks for bringing me here. I had a really nice time."

Sean chuckled. "I'll bet you say that to all your dates."

Her face grew warm, and she changed the subject. "You're a good pilot." She studied his chiseled profile then cocked her head. "Where did you learn to fly like that? As a matter of fact, you're very cultured, considering you grew up on the streets of Houston."

"Woodland, north of Houston."

She smiled. "Close enough." She watched him squirm. Were her questions making him nervous? He was always drilling her. She was going to give him a taste of his own medicine for once. "Why did you come to Stoney Creek?" She motioned at the passing scenery. "I mean, I know this is a beautiful area, but I'm sure it took a lot more than that to attract the illustrious Sean O'Conner to backwoods Stoney Creek."

"Hey, I like Stoney Creek."

"So do I. Don't try to evade my question."

Sean looked in both directions when they came to the main highway. "I can't remember which way we turn."

"Turn left to go to Marietta."

"All right. Left it is." Sean looked at Sydney. "For an out of towner, you sure seem to know your way around."

Blood rushed to Sydney's face. "I never go anywhere without looking at a map first."

Sean raised an eyebrow. "I'm glad you had enough foresight to check your map before we rushed out of your house this morning."

There was nothing Sydney could say to get out of this one so she remained silent.

Sean broke the silence. "I don't know about you, but I'm getting hungry."

"Me too," Sydney said, glad he'd changed the subject. She relaxed in her seat, and then stiffened right back up at his next comment.

"So how are things going with Kendall?"

Discussing Kendall with Sean was the last thing she wanted to do. She already felt guilty for spending the day with Sean. "Things are fine."

"How well do you know Kendall Fletcher?"

Sydney frowned. "Well enough."

"Are you sure about that?"

"Just what are you trying to say?"

Sean shrugged indifferently, but Sydney noticed that grip on the steering wheel had tightened. "I just don't want to see you get hurt, that's all."

She couldn't believe what she was hearing. The next words shot out of her mouth. "Thanks for your concern, but I'm a big girl. I can take care of myself."

"Okay, whatever."

Sydney folded her arms tightly and turned away from him to look out the window.

*　　*　　*　　*　　*

It was dark by the time Sean pulled into Sydney's driveway. Things had loosened up between them at the restaurant, and Sydney found herself telling Sean about her life in Ft. Worth. She figured that was a safe subject and one that would help erase any doubts in Sean's mind concerning where she was from.

He turned off the engine and turned in his seat to face her. "Thanks for coming with me today."

"It was fun," she said mechanically, all the while waiting for him to spit out whatever it was he was trying to tell her.

"Look Syd, I know we don't always see eye to eye about the mill, and I know I'm not the easiest person to get along with."

Sydney rolled her eyes. "That's an understatement."

He tensed, and she instantly regretted her remark. "I'm sorry. Please go on."

"The safety procedures you've implemented have

really helped. I've seen a lot of improvement since you came."

She studied his dark eyes to see if the compliment was sincere. "Thank you."

He reached and touched a strand of her hair. His nearness was electrifying. When he drew closer, she realized he was going to kiss her. And she wanted him to. Why was she always attracted to the wrong type of guy? The warning bell was going off again in her head, and she made one last ditch effort to think of Kendall. But it was no good, she could see only Sean. She pushed the last fringes of doubt from her mind and closed her eyes and parted her lips. She waited. Nothing happened. When she opened her eyes, he was studying her. There was a trace of amusement glittering in his eyes. She backed away from him, heat burning through her veins. He got out to open her door, but she beat him to it.

It was an effort, but she managed to keep her voice light. "Well, it has been interesting. Goodnight." With that she turned and walked away before he could respond. She could feel his penetrating gaze eating into her back. She hurried up the sidewalk. He was still watching when she went into her house and locked the door.

* * * * *

"I can't believe you went out with that creep."

Sydney closed her eyes. She should have known better than to call Ginger. Ginger was used to hearing Sydney complain about Sean and had dubbed him *that creep*. "A temporary lapse in good judgment. I assure you."

"Does Kendall know?"

"No, of course not. But what if he did? It's not like I'm married to him or anything." Sydney tried to keep her voice indifferent, all the while wondering if Kendall had dropped by her house today.

"What were you thinking?"

The incredulous tone in Ginger's voice struck a nerve. Everything was so black and white with Ginger.

Ginger with her close family and perfect marriage. It was all too easy for her to sit back and cast judgment. "I guess I'm just not perfect like you," Sydney said. She regretted the words as soon as they left her mouth.

It took Ginger a moment to respond. "I'm not trying to judge you."

"It's been a rough day," Sydney said, trying to soften the blow.

Ginger slipped back into her guard dog mode. "He didn't try anything, did he?"

A dry laugh escaped Sydney's lips. "No, he was a perfect gentleman."

"Do you have a busy day planned for tomorrow?" Ginger asked. Her voice was innocent, but Sydney knew she was fishing. Ginger was dying to ask if she was going to church.

"No, I don't have much planned." She broke into a smile. "Except for going to church."

"Hallelujah!"

Sydney wasn't sure why she'd said that. She hadn't been planning on going. Maybe she'd told Ginger that because she felt guilty about snapping at her. Oh well. Whatever her reasoning, she'd committed to go, and now she had to follow through. She said goodnight to Ginger and hung up the phone.

She went to her front window and looked through the blinds, half expecting to see Sean still parked in her driveway. The driveway and street were both empty. She looked at Hazel Finch's house. The lace curtain moved, and Sydney imagined the old woman standing on the other side, her beady eyes watching through the window. Her face flushed. Hazel had probably been spying on her the entire time she sat in the car with Sean. There was no escaping the woman. It was like living in a fishbowl. Sydney snapped off her porch light and then flipped off the lamps in the living room. "Feast your eyes on that," she said and stalked to her bedroom.

*"And I give my heart to know wisdom, and to know madness
and folly."*
—Ecclesiastes 1:17

chapter twenty-one

It was a smaller building than the one in Ft.
Worth, about a quarter of the size. Still it loomed
larger than life. She sat in her jeep, trying to decide if
she was going to get out. Sydney had allowed an extra
fifteen minutes, but it hadn't been necessary. She found
her way here without a glitch. She'd promised Ginger
that she would go to church—and here she was, in the
parking lot. She smiled ruefully. If she turned around
now and left, Ginger would never know the difference.
Even as she contemplated it, she opened her door. People
were walking into the building. She gave her lipstick
one last check before grabbing her purse and heading
that direction.

"Hi, I'm Julie Parkinson. It's nice to meet you."

Sydney extended her hand to the petite brunette
who was so pregnant that she looked like she was going
to pop. Julie followed Sydney's gaze and rubbed her belly
in reply. "My doctor has promised that if I don't go into
labor by Tuesday, then he'll induce me."

"Mom, Derek won't give me back my car."

Julie looked apologetic and turned her attention to
the distraction. Sydney looked down at the little boy who
was furiously tugging at his mother's dress. He was the
mirror image of his mother with his brown eyes and dark
hair. Julie's face grew stern. "Kevin, what did I tell you
about bringing toys to church? You know the rules."

The little boy shrugged and she tousled his hair. "Now, you and Derek behave and listen to your teachers."

"Okay, Mom." He let go of her dress and ran down the hall.

Julie turned to Sydney.

"It looks like you've got your hands full," Sydney said.

Julie sighed. "I do." She pointed at her stomach. "This makes number four."

The woman couldn't be much older than her, and she couldn't imagine having one child, much less four.

Julie smiled brightly. "Are you visiting?"

"I live in Stoney Creek."

"That's great. Come on, and I'll take you to the women's class." Julie's friendly manner was infectious, and Sydney started to relax.

Sydney would rather have sat in the back, but Julie led her to the front row. There were about eight or nine other women in the room whose ages ranged anywhere between mid-twenties to seventies. A blonde with short wavy hair was conducting. She looked very stylish in her tailored navy suit. A song was sung and then a prayer was given, and then it was time for the blonde lady to speak again. She looked at Sydney and smiled.

"I want to welcome our visitor."

Before Sydney could introduce herself, Julie spoke up. "Sydney's not a visitor. She lives in Stoney Creek and will be attending church with us."

This brought a wide smile from the lady. "That's fantastic. We love having new members to join us. Would you please stand and tell us where you're from and a little about yourself?"

Sydney cleared her throat. "Um, my name is Sydney Lassiter. I'm from Ft. Worth, Texas. I live in Stoney Creek. I'm the safety coordinator at the sawmill."

"Welcome," the lady said. "We look forward to getting to know you."

Sydney sat down, and Julie leaned over and whispered. "You'll have to meet Tuesday Phillips. She's

216

the older lady in the back with the light blue blouse and white skirt." Sydney fought the urge to look. "Her husband used to work at the sawmill." Julie's whisper grew softer. "He was killed in an accident there."

Another lady stood and began teaching the lesson, but Sydney hardly noticed. Her throat had gone dry, and her mind was reeling with the possibility. Phillips! Avery mentioned Buford Phillips in his journal, and then there was the accident report. Someone else besides Avery had added that Buford Phillips had been drinking. Could it be the same person? Sydney's heart was pounding. She leaned over and whispered in Julie's ear. "What was his first name?"

Julie looked confused. "Who?"

"Mrs.—I mean—Sister Phillips' husband."

Julie paused. Finally she shook her head. "Sorry. It's on the tip of my tongue, but I can't remember."

It was all Sydney could do to hide her frustration. She looked up at the lady who was teaching the lesson and stared right through her, her mind a thousand miles away.

Fifteen minutes later, Julie nudged Sydney. "Buford," she whispered. "His name was Buford."

*　　*　　*　　*　　*

After the class was over, Sydney made her way to the back of the room where Mrs. Phillips was standing. She wasn't sure how to approach the woman and hoped the words would come.

Mrs. Phillips' warm smile was a good sign. She was at least a head shorter than Sydney, and her spiky gray hair shot out like a porcupine. She was as round as she was tall, reminding Sydney of a weeble wobble toy.

Sydney extended her hand. "It's very nice to meet you," she said and then plunged right in. "As I mentioned earlier, I'm the new safety coordinator at the mill. Sister Parkinson told me that your husband used to work at the sawmill."

The smile on Mrs. Phillips' face faltered, and her face grew clouded. She nodded.

"I was wondering if I could talk to you sometime about it."

Mrs. Phillips shook her head. "That was a long time ago. I'm trying to put all of that behind me. I'm sure you can understand." The woman turned to leave, but Sydney touched her on the arm.

"Please." Her voice came out hoarse. "I promise I won't take up much of your time."

Mrs. Phillips studied her. "Okay," the older woman finally said.

"Can I stop by and see you this afternoon?" Sydney was unable to hide the eagerness that crept into her voice.

"No, today's not a good time."

Sydney was crestfallen. "Tomorrow then?"

"That will be fine."

Sydney scrambled in her purse to find a pen and scrap of paper to write down the address.

* * * * *

It was nearing the end of church. Sydney let her gaze wander to the families who were sitting on the pews. The children were getting restless, and a few of the adults had dozed off. Julie Parkinson and her brood were sitting on the next-to-the-front row. Julie's husband had his arm draped around her, and she was leaning her head into the curve of his shoulder. Families. What must it be like to be a part of a real family? It had been so long for her that she barely remembered. These people—they all belonged. They had a place, people to love. Her stomach knotted. This was one of the reasons she avoided church. It was so hard to see this much love and know that she could never have it.

The notes to the closing song filled the room. She recognized it instantly, *God Be With You Till We Meet Again*. It was a song of parting and had a sense of finality.

Even though she'd joined the church after her parent's death, it was this song that reminded her most of them. The lyrics hit her full force. *God be with you till we meet again...when life's perils thick confound you...put his arms unfailing round you...*

Her mind stopped at that line. She ran it over and over again in her mind. Where was God when her parents died? Where was God when she was lying in the hospital? Where was He now? She tried to remember the advice that Stella had given her, but it was no use. *Put his arms unfailing round you.* She didn't feel God's arms around her. She didn't feel anything. She was utterly and completely alone, and no one, not even God, cared. Tears started gushing like a river down her face. When the closing prayer was over, she fled out of the room and to her jeep before anyone could see.

*   *   *   *   *

Sydney rounded the bend to Mrs. Phillips' house and had the impression that she'd left the twenty-first century and gone back in time about fifty years to the television show *The Walton's*. A picket fence across the front yard was the only thing missing to make the picture complete. She pulled into the driveway and heard the gravel crunch like crushed ice under her tires.

She knocked and then waited. A couple of seconds later Mrs. Phillips opened the door. Sydney pasted a polite smile on her face and hoped that Mrs. Phillips would remember her. Her fears vanished when she saw recognition in the elderly woman's features.

"Come in."

"Thank you." When Sydney stepped inside, a musty smell swept over her, and she had the feeling she'd opened an old trunk hidden away in an attic. It was as if the aged house had absorbed all of the woman's treasured memories in its gnarly walls.

"Please have a seat."

Sydney chose the plastic-covered couch. The material underneath was olive green with an intricate gold pattern swirled into it. She could feel it crinkle under her jeans as she sat down.

"Would you like a glass of lemonade?"

"No, thank you." How many people still offered lemonade to their guests?

"Water then?"

"Sure."

Mrs. Phillips returned with the water and a big platter of shortbread cookies. She handed Sydney her glass and then sat down in a recliner directly across from Sydney. She juggled her glass of lemonade in one hand and reached for a cookie with the other. "My doctor gets onto me all the time for eating too much sugar." She chuckled. "I told 'im that he done stopped doctoring and started meddling. It's patients like me that keeps him in bid'ness. Anyways, I reckon we all die of something sometime."

The hint of a smile crept across Sydney's face. She took a sip of her water and set it on the small round table next to the couch. A creamy lace coverlet caught her eye. She touched it. "This is beautiful. Did you make it?"

"Yes, it's called tatting."

"I know." Sydney rushed on. "My grandmother does it. She says it's a lost art."

"Do I know her?"

"Who?"

"Your grandmother."

Sydney's heart accelerated. She'd let her guard down. One slip of the tongue could ruin everything. "No, she lives in Texas."

"Oh, that's right. You're not from around here."

Sydney nodded. Mrs. Phillips' short hair wasn't silver like her grandmother's, it was slate gray. Mrs. Phillips caught her eyes and held them until Sydney broke away from the woman's probing gaze. There was a strength, no a light, in those weathered eyes that radiated like a beacon. Even the octagon-shaped glasses that Mrs. Phillips wore couldn't cover it up. It felt oddly

familiar. Where had she seen it before? Ginger! The
answer warmed into her consciousness like a ray of
sunshine on a cold day. She'd felt that same light in
Ginger. It was as if Ginger wore an invisible armor that
made her impervious to all the suffering that came from
living in this wretched world. Mrs. Phillips had it too.

"So your husband worked at the sawmill before he
died?"

"Yes, the sawmill. It always comes back to that."

The meaning in Mrs. Phillips' odd words eluded
Sydney.

"Buford worked as a log puller. They said he got
too close to the saw and a section of log hit him."

"Yes, I've read the report." Sydney said and then
wondered if she was giving away too much information.
Thankfully, Mrs. Phillips' expression didn't change.
Sydney struggled to keep her voice neutral. "The accident
report was filled out by Avery McClain. Did you know
him?"

"Mostly I knew of him. He did visit me once."

Sydney's throat went dry and she took a gulp of
water and swallowed hard. Don't probe too hard, she
told herself. If she appeared too anxious, Mrs. Phillips
might clam up.

"Mr. McClain seemed like a nice man. He visited
me right after Buford died. I don't think he believed what
I told him about Buford though."

"What was that?" The question came out in a half
croak.

"I told him the truth. He asked me if Buford had
been drinking, and I told him Buford quit drinking when
he started goin' to church."

"What else? Do you remember anything else?"

Mrs. Phillips munched on her cookie and took a
sip of lemonade. "Now, Sydney, tell me again. What
exactly do you do at the sawmill?"

Sydney could have screamed, but she kept her face
blank. "I'm the safety consultant. It's my job to
investigate accidents at the mill."

Mrs. Phillips nodded. "But this accident happened years ago. Why are you worrying 'bout it now?"

Sydney realized that Mrs. Phillips was a lot more perceptive than she looked. "I'm trying to establish an accident trend so we can prevent future accidents."

"I see." Mrs. Phillips placed her glass on the table. Sydney hoped that her explanation had sounded convincing.

"Whereabouts are you from in Texas?"

"Ft. Worth."

"I have a cousin that lives in Arlington. He and his family moved there 'bout five years ago. They say it's a dust bowl in the summertime."

Sydney scooted to the edge of the couch. She had to figure out a way to get the conversation back on track. Before she could think of anything to say, Mrs. Phillips asked her another question.

"How long did you say you've been a member of the church?"

"About a year."

"How long have you lived in Stoney Creek?"

"About four months."

"Well, yesterday was the first time I saw you at church."

Sydney's face warmed. "I've been really busy." She knew her response did little to placate the woman and feared that the next words out of Mrs. Phillips mouth would be a stern lecture on the importance of attending her church meetings. Her thoughts must've shown on her face because Mrs. Phillips chuckled.

Sydney glanced at her watch. "Mrs. Phillips, I have to get back to work. If you don't mind, I need to ask you a couple more questions."

The smile faded from Mrs. Phillips face.

"Are you telling me that Buford was a member of the church?"

Mrs. Phillips nodded.

Something wasn't adding up. "Members of our church don't drink."

Mrs. Phillips slapped her knee the way a teacher would when the student finally got the point. "Exactly!" "Did he tell you anything that was going on at the mill?"

Sydney could see the wariness in Mrs. Phillips' eyes before she finally spoke. "I asked him about it once or twiced, but Buford kept things inside. I always tried to give him his space. You know what I mean?"

Sydney nodded. The disappointment was so tangible she could taste it. The woman had to know something. But whatever it was, she wasn't telling—at least not today. Another question was forming in the back of Sydney's mind. It was about the light in Mrs. Phillips' eyes. She had to know the source of that light. Somehow the words forced their way to her lips. "How did you get through it? How did you pick up and go on after your husband's death?"

Silence settled between them and Mrs. Phillips pondered the question. "It wasn't easy. I guess I could come up with some pie crust answer. But the truth is that it's still hard sometimes, even after all this time." Moisture formed behind her glasses.

"I'm sorry. I shouldn't have asked such a personal question."

Mrs. Phillips brushed aside the apology and went on as if Sydney hadn't spoken. "I don't know how I made it through the first few weeks after he died. Everything was black. No matter how hard I tried, I couldn't break out of it. After about two months, things got real bad. I had so much anger boiled up inside that I felt like I was gonna fly off the handle. I knew I needed help. One Sunday I put on my best dress and hat and marched right down there to that church. You see, I weren't a member then. Buford had tried to talk to me about them things he learnt, but I wouldn't have no part of it."

Sydney nodded. "I can understand that."

"Anyways, I went down there and told them people that I wanted to know all the things they'd been teaching my Buford." She chuckled. "After they picked their jaws up off the floor, they started teaching me. Little by little, the darkness in me started to fade until one day I came home and opened my curtains and let in the light. I've been going toward it ever since." She looked at Sydney and saw that her eyes were as moist as her own.

"Thank you. That was a beautiful story." Sydney stood, and Mrs. Phillips picked up on her cue and stood as well.

"I have to get back to work." Sydney reached in her purse and retrieved a folded sheet of paper that contained her cell phone number. "If you think of anything, will you call me?"

Mrs. Phillips nodded.

Sydney took a step out the door before Mrs. Phillips stopped her. "There is something else."

Sydney turned.

"Buford tried to tell me something before he died." Mrs. Phillips shook her head. "I couldn't understand him." She leveled her eyes with Sydney's. "I do know Buford was worried about some of the men at the mill. I'm afraid he was involved in something."

"What?"

"I don't know. Buford was tryin' to straighten out his life. I think he tried to get out and was kilt because of it." The words came out in a hushed tone, as if Mrs. Phillips were speaking them for the very first time.

"Did he ever mention any names?"

Mrs. Phillips searched her memory. "The only thing he ever mentioned was that this one feller whistled the same tune all the time. It like to of drove Buford crazy."

"And you think this man was involved?"

Mrs. Phillips nodded. "I'm sure of it. Buford used to meet him at the sawmill late at night. Some nights I'd stay up till four in the morning walking the floors till he got home."

"And you don't know this man's name?"

"No, I don't think I ever knew—only that he whistled all the time."

Sydney clasped Mrs. Phillips's hand. "Thank you. If you remember anything else, please let me know."

*   *   *   *   *

Mrs. Phillips watched Sydney walk to her jeep. She wasn't sure what in the tarnation had possessed her to tell that young girl all them things. Things she'd never told another living soul.

She stood in this same door all those years ago and watched Buford leave, and somehow knew she would never see him again. Many considered her premonitions a gift, but to her it was a curse. Mrs. Phillips closed the door and tried to push away the nagging fear.

Sydney was in danger.

"Wrath is cruel, and anger is outrageous: but who is able to stand before envy?"
—Proverbs 27:4

chapter twenty-two

Sydney heard a single knock, then the door opened and Sean let himself in. He walked over and sat in his usual spot on the edge of her desk.

She turned in her chair. His nearness heightened her senses, like every inch of her body was standing at attention, but she didn't want to show it, especially not after he'd humiliated her the other night.

"It's Friday afternoon, Syd. Aren't you ready to get out of this place? I thought you'd be anxious to get home and get all dolled up for the game so you could cheer on the famous coach."

"What I do on my own time is my business."

His eyebrow arched. "It was just a simple observation, that's all."

She studied his face and then relaxed. Why was she always so sensitive where Sean O'Conner was concerned? He was probably just trying to make conversation.

"Well, if you must know, I'm getting your stuff ready for the safety training meeting on Monday."

Sean picked up a pencil from her desk and began fiddling with it. "I'm so glad you're keeping me on track," he said.

Sydney knew she'd touched a nerve and braced herself for the backlash. It never came though. In fact, it was fascinating to watch how quickly the irritation faded. His voice became conversational again.

"Hey, I just want to talk to you a minute about tomorrow."

"Tomorrow?"

"Yeah, Depot Days. I think you ought to be there."

Sydney planned to go to Depot Days. It was an annual celebration, centering around the old depot that dated back to the civil war. Her parents had always looked forward to the event. They would arrive early Saturday morning and then stay all day and go to the street dance that night. She could still picture them dancing close together. Figures in a music box, beating one heart, sharing one breath—locked so close together that the rest of the world faded away.

"Syd?"

Her face warmed and she looked up to see Sean studying her. She was glad he couldn't read her mind.

"Are you okay?"

"Yeah, just listening to you."

"I thought I'd lost you there for a minute."

"No, just waiting for you to continue."

"You've been saying you need to get to know the men down at the mill. I thought tomorrow would be a good opportunity. A lot of them will be there with their wives and kids. This is the biggest event in this town for the whole year. They're expecting hundreds of people."

"If hundreds of people are going to be there, I don't think they'll miss seeing me. What's the big deal about Depot Days anyway?"

It gave her a touch of satisfaction to see a cloud come over his handsome face.

"Depot Days ranks right up there with football and church in this town. You've been here long enough to know that." He paused. "Why do I even bother? Anyway, it was just a suggestion. Suit yourself." He shook his head and left her office.

Sean was right, of course. She needed to go to Depot Days, not only for her job, but for herself. She'd thought that Kendall would invite her to go with him, but he hadn't mentioned it. That was proving to be the story of her life. For a split second, she thought about calling Kendall and inviting him, but then thought better of it. She wasn't about to throw herself at him. She'd let him come to her.

*   *   *   *   *

The morning of Depot Days turned out uncharacteristically hot, letting the residents of Stoney Creek know that summer was still in control and not quite ready to relinquish her hold to fall. Sydney chose a pale blue cotton shirt and white cropped pants. Instead of applying makeup, she used a tinted moisturizer and brushed her lips with gloss. That was as good as it was going to get today. She grabbed her sunglasses and shoulder bag and went out the door.

When Sydney arrived downtown, the sidewalks were already filling with people who were waiting for the parade to begin. She decided to cross the street and go to the old train depot and watch the parade from there. She followed the brick walkway that led to a gazebo where lush ferns hung like feathery caps, providing some shelter from the sweltering sun. Not surprising, all the seating in and around the gazebo was taken. Her gaze wandered to the mounds of colorful petunias, marigolds, and daisies bordering the walkways. She loved the wise old two-story store fronts with their big glass windows and creaky wood floors. It was good to see Stoney Creek revitalizing the downtown district. The street lights from her childhood had been replaced with old fashioned lamp posts, and the white trim on the train depot looked like fresh milk glistening in the sun.

Sydney found a lamp post to lean against. It shouldn't be too long before the parade began. She watched the people buzz back and forth. A group of majorettes were setting up their snow cone booth, and a little boy was tugging at his mother's sleeve and pointing in the direction of a snack stand that was selling cotton candy, boiled peanuts, and popcorn. She closed her eyes and let the sound of the crowd take her to another time. Like an old movie reel playing the same scene round and round, she could see her parents laughing and dancing at the street dance—Avery's protective embrace, Susan's hair flying in the wind.

"Hey Sydney. Nice to see you again." Emma's voice broke into her thoughts. "Kendall's here. He's standing on the other side of the depot. I figured y'all would come together."

"No, I didn't tell him I was coming," Sydney said, looking at Kendall's younger sister.

Emma frowned and looked like she was going to question Sydney about her comment. Instead she said, "I love that blouse. Come on. I've got a blanket over here." Sydney didn't have a chance to respond before Emma caught her by the arm and maneuvered her through the crowd.

Sydney noticed several people gathered under the big oak tree next to the depot. From a distance, she could see two men engaged in what looked like serious conversation. When they got closer, she recognized first Sean, then Kendall. She frowned. "Why is Sean talking to Kendall? I was under the impression that they barely knew each other."

Emma cocked her head. "You know Sean?"

Sydney nodded.

"Oh yeah, that's right. He works at the sawmill with you. You were talking about him that night at Jessica's."

Sydney's face warmed, and she thought Emma might be attempting to bring up that disastrous moment when her tongue had gotten the best of her, but Emma's expression was without guile. Her curls bounced happily when she shook her head and chuckled. "Every woman in Stoney Creek under the age of sixty-five knows who Sean O'Conner is. He's gorgeous."

"You think so?" Sydney wrinkled her nose.

"Look at him and then tell me honestly. Is he not one of the hottest looking guys you've ever seen?"

Sydney glanced at Sean, not bothering to really look at him. She'd already committed him to memory anyway. "He's all right, I guess."

"You must really be nuts over my brother. That's all I've got to say." Emma grinned wickedly. "Chuck would just die if he heard me carrying on about Sean like this."

Sydney put her hand over her heart, feeling a little like she was in junior high again. "I'll never tell. It'll be our secret."

Emma stopped and stared at Sydney. "Talk about déjà vu. That was weird. You remind me of someone."

"Oh?" Sydney's heart began hammering in her chest.

Emma shook her head. "It's gone. Maybe it'll come to me later."

"Yeah, maybe."

Emma waved at Kendall to get his attention. "Look who I found standing all by herself."

So much for letting Kendall come to her. No matter what Sydney did, it always looked like she was throwing herself at Kendall's feet.

Sydney waved at Kendall but her eyes met Sean's. His expression was unreadable. She felt her face flush and wondered if Sean would tell Kendall that she'd been flying with him. Maybe he already had. Was that what they were discussing?

Emma plopped down on the blanket and motioned for Sydney to join her. "Here, you'll need this today." Emma reached into her bag and pulled out a bottle of insect repellent.

"Thanks," Sydney said, her mind still on Kendall and Sean. She looked around. "Speaking of Chuck, where is he?"

"He went down to Gulf Shores to visit his mother."

Sydney searched her memory. "Doesn't she live here?"

"After his father died, his mother bought a condo down there so she could be next to her sister." Sydney jumped when Emma slapped her ankle. "The mosquitoes are eatin' me alive." She doused herself with more repellent. "What happened to your arm?"

Sydney tugged at her sleeve. She knew she should have at least worn a quarter length sleeve. Now it was time to tell the age-old lie. "Oh, I got burned when I was little. My mom was making macaroni and cheese, and I pulled the pan of boiling water on top of me."

Emma grimaced. Both girls looked up as Kendall and Sean joined them.

"Well, well, look who decided to join us," Sean said to Sydney.

She didn't answer.

Kendall had that same awkward, constipated expression on his face like he wasn't sure how to approach Sydney. He sat down next to her and gave her a peck on the cheek, which she didn't acknowledge. What gave him the right to act possessive when he'd not even called to invite her to Depot Days? Kendall sensed her coolness and became fidgety. Color crept into his face. Sydney looked at Sean and felt her face flame when she saw his amused expression.

All of this was lost on Emma. She was too busy scanning the street to see when the parade would begin. She turned her attention to Sean. "Is Jessica coming?"

So it was true, Sydney thought. Sean and Jessica were an item.

Sean looked at his watch. "She should be here any minute now." He looked up and smiled. "Speak of the devil. Here she comes."

All eyes turned to Jessica. She made her grand appearance, looking terrific in her white pleated shorts and red shirt. Her sandals had just enough of a heel to emphasize her shapely calves, and her curly hair was expertly pulled up in a high pony tail. She removed her sunglass and put them on her head when she got close to the group. Sydney hated herself for it but couldn't stop the jealously that stabbed at her when Jessica sat down by Sean and gave him a quick kiss on the lips.

Jessica's makeup was perfect, making Sydney wish she'd done more to herself. Makeup wouldn't last long in this heat though. Before long Jessica would have mascara running down her face. Oh, one could only hope. Sydney shook her head. She was going to have to learn to temper these horrible thoughts.

"What have I missed?" Jessica asked.

"Nothing," Sean said. "The parade is just about to start."

After all was said and done, the parade really wasn't much to brag about. There were several civic groups with banners and the high school marching band. The cars came through last, as if signaling the grand finale. Girls wearing formal dresses were sitting on top of the cars waving and smiling while trying to keep perspiration from dripping in their eyes.

During the course of the parade, Jessica managed to position herself between Sean and Kendall. "Jess, I would've thought that you'd be up there too," Kendall said.

Jessica laughed and nudged Kendall with her elbow. "I'm afraid my time for that is past."

"Jessica was homecoming queen and county junior miss," Kendall said to Sydney.

"Oh," Sydney said, fighting the urge to roll her eyes.

"Our little Jess is a woman of many talents," Kendall added.

"Oh, Kendall, you're just biased," Jessica said, beaming.

Sydney couldn't handle any more. She looked at Jessica and smiled. "Then we didn't really need to come to watch the parade. We could've just sat and watched Jessica parade around."

Jessica's face went scarlet, and Kendall looked shocked. Sean was the only one who chuckled.

Sydney stood. "I'm going to get something to drink. Does anyone else want anything?"

"I'd like a Dr. Pepper," Sean said.

Sydney glared at him. Of course he wouldn't miss a chance to have her fetch something for him. "Anyone else?" Everyone else shook their heads. "Okay then."

So much for making a good impression. She should have kept her big mouth shut about Jessica. When would she ever learn?

She headed in the direction of the concession stand and then stopped in her tracks. Walter and Maurene were sitting in lounge chairs on the sidewalk.

"Well, hello," she said, a broad smile on her face. Walter looked up and then right past her like she was a stranger.

Her smile faltered, and she stumbled by them. She felt something touch her arm and looked up to see Sean standing beside her.

"Do you know them?"

"What?"

"That couple. It looked like you were trying to talk to them."

She shook her head, all the while trying to make sense of what had just happened. Why did Walter treat her like a stranger? Was he trying to protect her? Maybe he didn't want to arouse Maurene's suspicions. Yes, that was probably it. She had to agree that Walter used good judgment in pretending not to know her, but that didn't stop the hurt from washing over her like a tidal wave.

Sydney turned to Sean. "What are you doing here? I told you I'd get your Dr. Pepper."

"I decided to get some popcorn too."

"Oh? I'm surprised you could pry yourself away from Jessica for that long."

Sean laughed. "You're not jealous are you, Syd?"

"Of you? No, quite the opposite. I'd say the two of you are perfect for each other."

"Ouch! Somehow I don't think that was meant as a compliment." He paused. "I guess Jessica and I are about as well suited as you and Kendall."

She laughed. She hated to admit it, but Sean was right. She and Kendall were an odd match.

He linked his arm through hers and held her hand so she couldn't pull away. "Shall we?"

"Let's."

"Know ye not that they which run in a race run all, but one receiveth the prize? So run, that ye may obtain."
—*1 Corinthians 9:24*

chapter twenty-three

The phone call that Sydney received the next Monday morning was the very one she'd been hoping for, although it didn't quite turn out the way she expected it to.

"Sydney Lassiter?"

"Yes, this is she."

"This is Tuesday Phillips." There was a pause. "We talked the other day."

"Hello, Mrs. Phillips." Sydney's heart leapt. Maybe Mrs. Phillips had remembered something.

"I've been asked to help with an activity for the young chil'ren this Saturday at the church. I was wondering if you would mind coming along and helpin' too."

She'd given Mrs. Phillips her number in case the woman remembered anything about Buford's death. Now she was second-guessing that decision. The woman was as relentless as Ginger about church attendance. Sydney mentally reviewed her schedule for the week. There was Friday night's football game, but she didn't have any plans for Saturday.

"I really could use your help," Mrs. Phillips said. "And I know the chil'ren will love you."

"Okay," Sydney heard herself say. "I'll go."

"Good. It starts at 10:00 AM. I'll see you there."

* * * * *

Sydney pulled her windbreaker tighter around her. The October wind that whipped hair in her eyes was as crisp as a Granny Smith apple. There was a fresh rawness to the air that only an Alabama football Friday night could bring. It was as if the whole world had built up to that moment and could now begin anew. She'd attended some TCU football games in Texas, but all of them paled in comparison to this. A sea of fans swarmed the bleachers, hollering and hooting. The rest of the world may consider baseball the great American pastime, but here in Alabama, football was a religion.

The mouth-watering smell of hotdogs and popcorn floated from the concession stand, causing her stomach to rumble. She would have grabbed something before the game, but she and Kendall were planning on going out to eat afterwards. A flash of metal caught her attention, and she looked to see the band members, swinging their instruments to the rhythm of the tune they played. It looked like the JD section still sat beside the band. The *JD* stood for *Jack Daniels*, and members of this group brought plenty of it with them. Even if they weren't the rowdiest and most obnoxious fans in the stadium, the stench of booze drifting from their direction would have been enough to give them away.

More often than not, a brawl would break out in the JD section. A slow smile crept across Sydney's face. She remembered the time that two men got into a fist fight that ended when one man went sailing headfirst into the trumpet section. Band members, sheets of music, and instruments went flying. Sydney was standing on the field watching the scene unfold when the band director caught her eye. "Go get the police."

She had run to the concession stand and grabbed the first officer she saw. When she looked back, she saw that Avery had one of the men by the neck, holding him in the crook of his arm. He was carrying him down the bleachers so effortlessly that he might've been toting a sack of potatoes. Sydney's first thought was: *I've called the police on my own dad.* She soon learned that Avery wasn't involved in the fight but had, in fact, saved the day. The disoriented drunk kept falling over the instruments. Avery had retrieved him to prevent any further damage. So many memories.

Sydney paused to watch a cheerleader's blonde ponytail bob up and down with each jump. She then started up the bleachers, searching the faces in the crowd for Jarilyn. They saw each other the same instant, and Jarilyn half stood and waved to make sure Sydney could tell where she was sitting. It felt good to know that Jarilyn had been waiting for her, helping her to not feel so alone in this multitude of brimming people. The two women gave each other a warm hug and then settled in to watch the game.

"Wow, can you believe we're halfway through the season and haven't lost a game?" Jarilyn asked. "Coach Fletcher said there'll be some scouts coming out to look at Reggie in some of the later games." Her voice was a mixture of longing and motherly pride. The cold wind picked up and Jarilyn gathered her collar around her throat.

Sydney knew what a football scholarship would mean to Jarilyn and Reggie. She guessed it wasn't easy for Jarilyn to provide for the two of them on her bank teller income. Guilt rushed over her when she thought of all she had in comparison. "From what Kendall tells me, Reggie will have a long line of scouts wanting to come and watch him."

Jarilyn smiled appreciatively and then turned her attention to the field. She stood. "Oh, here they come."

Sydney watched the first player break through the story-high paper banner and then a long train of them followed. The band blared out the school's song, *Victory.* The cheerleaders followed the players, clapping and jumping. Kendall and his assistant coaches rounded out the back, walking with their chests thrust out like proud peacocks, their expressions stony and controlled. Sydney imagined that the coaches on the other side of the field were walking the same way. It was a spitting contest to see who was the meanest, who was the toughest. Kendall strutted back and forth in his jeans and tight-fitting polo, giving his players last minute instructions. Something about him reminded Sydney of the roosters just before the cockfight. No, not a rooster—he was a general in command on the brink of battle, lining up his troops to face the foe. There was a childish innocence about him that flowed clean and pure. An image of Avery flashed in her mind. She saw him standing straight and tall, ready to take on the world. Kendall looked back at the bleachers, and she wondered if he was looking for her. Jarilyn noticed it too.

"Looks like Coach Fletcher's checking to make sure you're here," Jarilyn said with a sly smile.

* * * * *

Sydney was here. That was good. Her cool manner toward him at Depot Days was perplexing. One minute she seemed fine and then the next, she was cool and distant. Then again, he never claimed to be an expert at figuring out the whims of the opposite sex. Sydney's moods were as changeable as the weather—typical of a woman. Things had been shaky between them lately, and Kendall hoped he could rectify the situation. He turned his back on the bleachers and erased all thoughts of Sydney. It was time to focus on the game. Now that was something Kendall knew.

Few people understood his passion for football. The notoriety he received was rewarding. He was a celebrity in Stoney Creek, but it was more than that. It was as much a part of him as breathing. Ever since he was a kid, he had either watched or played ball. He loved it all. The smell of freshly mowed grass on the field, the butterflies in his stomach just before the opening kick off, the sweat running down his face when he made a big hit. Nothing was as important as football. The ball was the beating, pulsing heart of the town and had come to symbolize everything that was good and right. He would do whatever was necessary to preserve it.

He spit in his hands and rubbed them together. This was his season. With Reggie and the other seniors, all the pistons were firing. He could feel the state championship in his grasp. The players lined up on the field. It was time to begin.

* * * * *

Midway through the third quarter, Sydney saw Sean running up the bleachers, his feet only touching every other step. Their eyes locked for a moment, and her heart skipped a beat. She scolded herself for not being able to control her emotions and wondered if she'd ever be able to make a commitment to one man. After all, she'd come to the game to watch Kendall. Her heart started racing full speed when she realized he was coming to sit with her.

She feigned indifference and pointed to the clock on the scoreboard, hoping that he'd get the hint that she couldn't care less where he'd been. "Running a little behind, aren't you? The game's almost over."

"I had to stay and take care of some problems at the mill."

"Is everything all right?" she asked, remembering the kiln door fiasco.

"Yeah, everything's okay. I just had to finish some paperwork. What's the score?"

"Zero to zero, and Glenwood has the ball." She turned. "Sean, this is Jarilyn Kelly. Her son, Reggie, is one of Kendall's players."

"Nice to meet you," Sean said.

Jarilyn nodded curtly to Sean and Sydney bit back a smile. Jarilyn was protecting Kendall's interest by showing her disapproval of Sean.

"Reggie's our quarterback," Sydney said.

"I know all about Reggie. He's a fine athlete."

"Thank you," Jarilyn said, turning toward Sean. "I'm very proud of him." She gave him a warm smile before turning her attention back to the game.

Sydney rolled her eyes. *Great.* It had taken all of two seconds for Sean O'Connor to win Jarilyn over. She couldn't help but compare Sean to Kendall. In some ways she understood him more than Kendall. After all, Sean was like her—handsome on the outside and flawed within. She studied Kendall's profile. Surely such an angelic face must be instilled with strong convictions and character. She made a promise to herself that she would forget all about this senseless attraction to Sean and transfer all her loyalty, her affection, to Kendall. Maybe he had enough goodness in him to save them both.

"How about getting something to eat with me after the game?"

It took a moment for her to answer, and Sean spoke for her. "Sorry, I forgot. I'm sure you already have plans with Kendall."

"What's wrong, Sean? Couldn't you get a date with Jessica tonight?"

"My, my. Aren't we touchy? Actually, Jessica's out of town."

Figures. Sydney's eyes narrowed. Sean was only sitting by her because Jessica wasn't available. Why was it that everywhere she turned, Jessica was right around the corner? There just didn't seem to be enough room for the both of them in Stoney Creek. They watched the game in silence from that point on.

Sydney focused her attention on Kendall, watching him interact with each player as they came off the field. She could see the tension in his neck and shoulders when Glenwood went for a field goal and made it. She closed her eyes and prayed that Kendall wouldn't look up in the stand and see Sean sitting beside her.

The band played *The Eye of the Tiger*, and Glenwood kicked off to Stoney Creek. Stoney Creek ran the ball back to Glenwood's thirty-five yard line. The crowd went wild and everyone jumped to their feet. Stoney Creek's players lined up for the next play in a shotgun formation. The ball was snapped. Reggie dropped back to find his receivers. The crowd continued to scream. Reggie drew back and threw to the wide receiver in the back of the end zone. The ball flew through the air, and both the wide receiver and cornerback leaped for it. The stunned crowd watched the ball slip through the cornerback's hands and into the waiting hands of the Stoney Creek wide receiver. He brought it in for a touchdown. The game was over. Another victory for Stoney Creek.

Sydney and Jarilyn were jumping up and down and hugging each other. "Let's go out on the field and congratulate them," Jarilyn said.

Sydney turned to leave and almost bumped into Sean. In all of the excitement, she'd forgotten that he was standing next to her.

He cleared his throat. "That offer still stands for a bite to eat."

She reddened. "No thanks. I need to go and talk to Kendall."

"Suit yourself," he said and walked away.

"For I was an hungered, and ye gave me meat; I was thirsty,
and ye gave me drink;
I was a stranger, and ye took me in:"
—Matthew 25:35

chapter twenty-four

Tuesday Phillips' broad smile was the first thing Sydney saw when she stepped in the room. "Sydney, I'm so glad you made it."

The activity had not yet started, and children were running wild in the building. Tuesday led her down the hall and into the kitchen. "The chil'ren are gonna be practicing for their program," she said. "Afterwards..." She motioned. "Honey, can you hand me that plate? Oh yes, like I was saying. We need to make some peanut butter and jelly sandwiches for'em. Hand me that knife in the drawer over yonder. Cut them into squares."

Sydney washed her hands and got down to business. All the while she tried to think of a way to broach the subject of Buford's death—a task that was proving to be impossible, considering that Tuesday was fluttering in and out of the room like a butterfly, not staying in one spot long enough for Sydney to ask her the simplest question, much less something more.

When the sandwiches were made, Tuesday ushered Sydney out of the kitchen, telling her that she would enjoy watching the children practice. The eager faces of the children were a stark contrast to the pinched expressions of the adult leaders who were trying their best to get the children to sit still and pay attention. A fair-haired boy sitting on the front row was having an especially difficult time. He was up more than he was down, much to the chagrin of his teacher.

Tuesday was quick to inform Sydney about each child. "See that there group on the back row?"

Sydney nodded.

Tuesday lowered her voice to a whisper. "They're all Nolans." She spoke the name with such significance that Sydney halfway wondered if Mrs. Phillips expected her to know something about them. "There are about five of 'em, I believe. Like stair-steps. Impossible to tell 'em apart." She shook her head. "Them chil'ren's father's a no-count drunk. Patsy, their poor mother, like to of worked herself to death, trying to keep 'em fed and a roof over their heads. I've been out to their trailer once or twice before. It ain't fit for pigs, much less all them chil'ren. Bless her heart, poor Patsy's in her late thirties but looks like she's in her fifties."

The oldest Nolan girl got up to say her part. Her voice was barely above a whisper, and she looked like the sheer act of public speaking put her on the verge of tears. Long black tresses framed her oval face, and her shirt was wrinkled and too big. Her hair would have been beautiful if it had been combed. The girl sat down and other children got up to say their parts, but Sydney didn't hear any of them. She kept hearing the little Nolan girl with her timid voice and shy eyes.

After practice was over, the children ran toward the kitchen like race horses that had been let out of the gate. The peanut butter and jelly sandwiches were a hit. Most of the children had already gone home when the oldest Nolan girl approached Sydney.

"Excuse me, ma'am."

Sydney smiled down at her. "Yes?"

The little girl shuffled her feet back and forth, and Sydney wanted to help her get the words out.

"Um, I was wondering if..." The girl looked at the floor.

Sydney bent down in an effort to hear her.

The words came out in a rush this time, almost as though the girl was trying to speak faster so she could bring herself to get it all out. "I was wondering if I can take them left-over sandwiches home."

Sydney paused. "I'm sure that'll be all right."

The girl's countenance brightened.

In an afterthought Sydney added, "You know you can eat as many sandwiches as you want while you're here, don't you?"

"I wanna take them home to my mama and brothers and sisters."

All of Sydney's personal worries vanished. She looked at the girl's thin frame and hollow eyes and wondered how often she went hungry. "Here, let me get you a bag. I'll wrap up these sandwiches, and you can also have the leftover jars of peanut butter and jelly." The bread was all gone, but Sydney gave her the rest of the potato chips.

When Sydney got ready to leave the church, Tuesday gave her a bear hug. "Thanks for comin' today."

An image of the Nolan girl flashed in her mind. "No, I'm the one who should be thanking you. I'm glad I was a part of this." It felt good to do something for someone else for a change. She reached in her purse for a pen and rummaged for a scrap piece of paper but came up empty-handed. She looked at Tuesday. "Do you have a piece of paper? I'd like for you to give me the address for the Nolans."

Tuesday's eyes widened.

"I'd like to do something to help them."

The older woman looked pleased. "Like I always said, the good Lord expects us to be his helping hands." She paused and her hawk-eyes studied Sydney. "Will you be at church tomorrow?"

Sydney met her gaze. "I can't make you any guarantees, but I promise I'll give it some thought."

* * * * *

A thousand scenarios ran through Sydney's mind, and a hard knot formed in the pit of her stomach. Perspiration broke out on her upper lip and nose, and she could feel her hands becoming wet and clammy as they drove up the mountain.

"Sydney, wait until you meet this ol' dude. He knows everything there is to know about football, or at least Alabama football." Kendall laughed.

His voice sounded like it was coming from far away. She looked out the window. Only a few more minutes before they arrived. Kendall recounted his and Walter's experiences and relationship. She didn't hear a word he said but managed to nod at the appropriate times. Her mind raced to think of ways to sidetrack him from going to Walter's house. Why hadn't she thought about a possible connection between Walter and Kendall? She could remember her dad telling her mom funny stories about Walter's obsession with football. It only made sense that he would know the head football coach for the local high school team.

Sydney finally managed to say, "Kendall, he sounds like a great guy, but I thought we were going to meet some of the other coaches and their wives for dinner."

"Honey, we are meeting them for dinner, but first I need Walter to look over some plays that I'm thinking about using in Friday night's game." Kendall reached and patted Sydney's knee. "You really don't mind, do you?" And then he gave her that boyish smile that she couldn't resist. She was also surprised that he'd called her *honey*.

"No, of course not," she said, praying all the while that Maurene would not give her secret away if she answered the door. She was also counting on Walter to remember her wish to remain anonymous. She valued her relationship with Kendall and eventually intended to tell him everything, but not now. He would never understand.

They approached Walter's drive and parked. Sydney noticed that the light in the foyer was the only one on. Please don't be home, she prayed.

Kendall smiled. "You're going to love Walter."

She got out of the car and smoothed the yellow cashmere sweater that had belonged to Judith. Somehow wearing Judith's clothes always bolstered her courage, allowing her to borrow a little of Judith's strength and determination. She needed all the courage she could muster tonight.

Kendall rang the doorbell and then turned and gave her an appraising look. "You look beautiful." Before Sydney could answer, he said, "Oh, I'll be right back." He turned and bounced down the steps. "I forgot my play folder."

Maurene opened the door. "Come on in." She swayed toward Sydney and gestured with one hand while holding up an empty martini glass with the other. Maurene blinked several times, trying to focus on Sydney's face. "Oh, you're that sawmill girl. Go on in. Walter's here..." She motioned. "Somewhere."

For the first time, and she hoped the only time in her life, Sydney was grateful to see someone drunk.

Walter entered the foyer. His eyes flickered over his wife and then settled on the martini glass. "Maurene, don't you think you've had enough?"

"Don't you try to tell me when I've had enough!" Maurene walked out of the foyer, almost tripping on her long silk robe.

"I'm sorry, dear. Maurene isn't feeling well tonight, but what a nice surprise to see you. What brings you to this neck of the woods?" Walter smiled and took hold of Sydney's hands.

"Walter," she said just as Kendall reappeared.

Kendall smiled. "Oh, I see you two have met. He turned to Walter. "Isn't she a beauty?"

"Yes, she is," Walter locked eyes with Sydney. "When Kendall told me he was dating a beautiful woman, I thought he was exaggerating."

Sydney's eyes pleaded with Walter's. *Please, please. Don't act like you know me.*

"What is your name?" Walter asked.

"Sydney Lassiter." She sighed and she and Kendall followed Walter into the den. The fire in the fireplace was the only light in the room. It was obvious that Walter had not been expecting company. He walked over and flipped on the light. An empty glass sat on the coffee table.

Walter picked up the glass and walked to the bar to pour another drink. "Can I get y'all something?"

"No thank you," Sydney and Kendall answered in unison.

"Well Sydney, tell me a little about yourself."

Kendall opened his notebook and spread several sheets on the coffee table. "We can't stay long, Walter. I just wanted to get your opinion on some plays for Friday night."

Sydney smiled. "Well, I'm from the Dallas-Ft. Worth area, and I'm here working for the sawmill on a safety consulting contract."

"That sounds like an interesting job for a young lady." Walter took a drink from his glass and then set it on the table.

Kendall shifted on the sofa. "Sydney, if you don't mind, we'll come back some other time so that you and Walter can get better acquainted. Right now, I need to talk to him about football."

"Sure." Sydney forced a smile. She was relieved that she didn't have to go through any more pretense with Walter, but a little annoyed with Kendall's attitude. "I noticed your library on the way in. If it's okay with you, Walter, I'll take a look around."

"You go right ahead," Walter said.

Memories rushed back when Sydney thought of the many times she'd been sent to the library to play while her dad and Walter talked about business. She'd forgotten how cold the room was. She rubbed her arms and looked around. Very little had changed. The world globe, the size of a beach ball, stood in a corner. Walter's football books lined the shelf nearest the window. The ornate Oriental rug where she'd played looked the same.

Sydney sat in an overstuffed leather chair and closed her eyes. She was grateful for Maurene's love of fine things as she covered herself with the plush throw that was draped over the arm of the chair.

She awoke to the smell of alcohol before she saw the face. It took a second for her mind to register that it was Maurene, not an apparition, that loomed over her. Maurene's bloodshot eyes were bulging and one side of her flimsy white nightgown had fallen down below her shoulder. Sydney tried to shrink back from the hideous expression that was only inches from her face. Maurene's breathing was heavy and raspy.

Before Sydney could say anything, Maurene was gone.

Sydney sat upright. Her body trembled. She tried to make sense of what had just happened. That's when she heard the loud voices.

Walter and Kendall looked up when Sydney entered into the room.

"What's going on? Is everything all right?"

"Everything is fine." Walter stood. His smile looked strained. "This young man of yours is a stubborn mule. He came all the way here to ask my opinion, and now he's arguing with me about football."

Kendall was glaring at Walter, and his face was red. She knew that people in Stoney Creek were serious about football, but this was ridiculous. "I'm sorry you feel that way, Walter," he said. He gathered his papers from the table. "It's just that I've worked so hard on this, and I thought you would agree with me, that's all."

Walter went over and put his hand on Kendall's shoulder. "Everything will go fine. I promise you that."

Sydney was amazed at the impact that Walter's small gesture had on Kendall. All the tension seemed to leave him instantaneously. Walter turned to Sydney. "Now, young lady, you have to get this rascal to bring you back when y'all can stay longer. We'll talk about something other than football."

"Thanks, I will," she said, looking at Kendall.

They made their way to the door. Sydney turned and saw Maurene standing on the stairs. Icy fingers pricked at her skin when Maurene's eyes met hers. Sydney locked the picture away to be replayed over and over a thousand times in her mind. Why did she look like the face of death?

"That which is crooked cannot be made straight."
—Ecclesiastes 1:15

chapter twenty-five

No matter how hard she tried, Sydney couldn't ever get any of the things she cooked to turn out right. She wedged her spatula under the bottom of a cookie. *Yuck* and then *ouch!* when she accidentally touched the hot metal cookie sheet. The cookies were charred on the bottom. Unsalvageable. What went wrong? She'd followed the directions on the back of the Nestle chocolate chip bag right down to the letter. She propped her hand on her hip and frowned. In two swift strides she walked to the garbage can and raked the cookies into it. So much for a home-baked treat. She'd have to go to the Piggly Wiggly and get something for her neighbor instead.

The image of Hazel was so vivid in her mind that she could have sworn she caught a whiff of magnolia in the air. She had mixed emotions where Hazel was concerned. The fact that Hazel was always watching everything she did was a constant irritant, but a part of her felt sorry for her neighbor. From what Sydney could tell, the woman had very few, if any, visitors. All she had was her cat to keep her company.

She was hoping that if she introduced herself then maybe Hazel would be less suspicious. *At least I will have done my part.* There was another reason too. Since the incident with the little Nolan girl, she'd been unable to get that family out her mind. She wanted to help them but wasn't sure how. However, she could do something nice for Hazel Finch. And she could do it today.

Forty minutes later, Sydney stood on Hazel's porch, balancing the plate of Piggly Wiggly's finest deli cookies in one hand while reaching for the doorbell with the other. The main door was open, but the glass storm door closed. She peered inside, feeling more like a Peeping Tom than a concerned neighbor. The room was dark, but she caught a glimpse of a tweed recliner. She was about to place the cookies on the door mat when she saw Hazel peeping around the corner. It was an awkward situation. Her hand seemed to have a mind of its own as it went up to wave at Hazel. There she stood with a silly grin on her face.

"I just wanted to say hello," Sydney said, hoping her voice would carry through the glass door. "I brought you some cookies. I'll just put them here." She jumped. Something furry rubbed against her ankle. She looked down to see Hazel's orange cat, purring like a motor.

That was all the encouragement Hazel needed. She walked to the door and opened it, bending down to retrieve the cat. "Dixie, where've you been you naughty girl? Mama's been lookin' for you, yes she has." Hazel brought the cat up to her cheek and folded into it like a soft blanket.

For a second Sydney feared she would turn and go back into her house without so much as speaking. Instead, Hazel reached for the plate of cookies, a smile curving her ample cheeks. Still holding the cat, she brought the plate, Saran Wrap and all, to her nose and inhaled. "I just love chocolate chip cookies."

Sydney suppressed a smile. She could picture Hazel scarfing down the cookies in one big gulp.

Hazel turned to go inside and looked back over her shoulder. "Well, aren't you coming?"

"Um...yes, of course."

Hazel put Dixie on the couch and dug into the plate of cookies. Sydney realized right away that she couldn't depend on Hazel to follow the rules of etiquette and invite her to have a seat, so she sat down on the couch next to Dixie. The living room was stuffed with a hodgepodge of furniture, ranging from fine antiques to yard sale junk. It was amazing how someone could cram so many things into one room. A large hanging basket filled with plastic ivy and pink silk hibiscus flowers took up the bulk of the picture window. Tall artificial palm trees stood like toy soldiers in each corner of the room. A decorative fan splattered with a variety of tropical flowers hung on the wall behind the couch.

She heard the canary before she saw it. The bright yellow bird was perched inside its cage, chirping happily. Sydney smiled. The bird was the crowning touch to the room. She looked at the French provincial couch with its jade green and cream brocade pattern sitting next to the raggedy tweed recliner. Why not have a cat and a canary? Somehow, it just fit.

The magnolia scent was tempered with the smell of cats, birds, and mildew. A picture in a flimsy metal frame caught Sydney's attention. She recognized Hazel right away in her muu muu. This one was white and flowing in the wind. She had her arm tightly clasped around the waist of a man who looked to be about her same age. He was frail in comparison to her bulky frame. His jeans were rolled up at the ankles, revealing sunburned bare feet. They were both smiling.

"Is that your brother?"

Hazel stopped mid bite, her mouth full. "Harvey? No, Harvey's my husband."

"Oh, does Harvey live nearby?"

"Yeah, he lives here."

Sydney's eyes grew wide. She'd never seen anyone else and had been so sure that Hazel lived alone. She chose her next words carefully. "Where's Harvey now? Is he working out of town?"

Hazel laughed. "Harvey?"

Sydney nodded.

"Nope, he'll be home in a few minutes. He just went to the store."

Sydney was at a loss for words. How could she have missed him? She looked around the room, her eyes scouring it for any sign of a male presence.

Hazel took a bite of her cookie. "I can't wait for you to meet Harvey. He's so funny. He keeps me laughing all the time."

The door bell rang.

"There's Harvey now." Hazel jumped up like a kid on Christmas morning and ran to the door. "Oh, it's just you." Her shoulders slumped and she walked back and plopped down on her recliner. She looked at Sydney. "It's just Louellen."

Louellen? Sydney looked toward the door. Was Hazel talking about the same Louellen from the mill?

Louellen looked as surprised to see Sydney as Sydney was to see her. She was immaculately dressed in a tan cardigan sweater and matching tailored slacks. Her salt and pepper hair was pulled up in a neat French twist.

"I thought you were Harvey," Hazel said.

Louellen ignored the comment and directed her attention to Sydney. "I didn't realize that you knew my sister."

Sister? Louellen was Hazel's sister? The two were as different as night and day. Tess Lambert had told her that Hazel's brother had worked at the mill at one time. She must've meant Hazel's sister. "I'm Hazel's next door neighbor."

"Where's Harvey? He should've been back ten minutes ago." Hazel's arms were crossed tightly over her chest, and her face was drawn in a frown with her lips forming a pout. "He knows I need my Mayfield milk. I don't like those other kinds. Just Mayfield with my Cheerios."

Louellen's eyes darted to Sydney. She looked embarrassed. She walked over and sat on the arm of the chair next to Hazel. Her voice became soothing and she stroked Hazel's silver hair and patted her back. "Sis, I just brought you a gallon of milk yesterday."

Hazel's bottom lip jutted out. "It wasn't Mayfield. I gave it to Dixie, and she wouldn't even drink it so I poured it down the sink. Anyway, it doesn't matter. Harvey went to get some more."

Sydney could tell how uncomfortable her presence was making Louellen. She felt like an intruder and knew it was time to leave. She stood. "I need to be going."

"But you haven't met Harvey yet!"

"Sis, Sydney can meet Harvey some other time."

"That's a good idea," Sydney said, making her way to the door.

Louellen followed her. "Thank you for visiting Hazel."

* * * * *

Sydney reached for a pack of orange herbal tea, hoping it would do the trick to calm her nerves. Her visit with Hazel was not at all what she'd expected. A hot blanket of shame covered her when she thought about all the times she'd resented Hazel for watching her. Seeing Louellen had been a shock too. Never in a million years would she have connected the two sisters. Even after seeing them together, it was still hard to believe.

The knocking at her front door sent her rushing to open it.

"Louellen, is everything all right?"

"Yes, I just want to talk to you a minute about Hazel." Louellen looked past Sydney and through the open door. "Do you mind if I come in?"

Sydney ran her fingers through her hair. "No, not at all. Please, have a seat. Here, let me move these clothes out of the way." She grabbed an armful of clean clothes that still needed to be folded. "I'm going to put these in the bedroom. I'll be right back. Can I get you a cup of herbal tea?"

"No, I can't stay long."

Louellen was fidgeting with her hands and started talking before Sydney had a chance to sit down. "I just want to explain about Hazel."

"You don't owe me any explanation."

"I think I do. If you know what happened to her, it will be easier for you to understand why she acts the way she does."

Sydney scooted to the edge of her seat.

"Hazel is six years younger than me. She was always a little different and naïve. Mother was always worried that she would get taken advantage of. I'm afraid we all went a little overboard trying to protect her." Her eyes looked distant. She paused for a moment and then continued. "Anyway, Hazel never dated much and was a loner. She has always liked animals more than people. We didn't think twice when she told us that she wanted to take an online Spanish class. Before we knew it, she and Harvey, her instructor, were instant messaging each other several times a day. We were all shocked when Hazel announced that she was getting married to a man none of us had ever met. Then she told us they were moving to Hawaii." Louellen shook her head. "Looking back, I can't say that I blame Hazel. I think she was searching for a sliver of happiness, and she found it for a while. Everything would've probably been okay if Harvey hadn't been killed in an automobile accident. He was going to the grocery store for Hazel."

Sydney nodded. "It all makes perfect sense now. I'm so sorry."

Louellen's eyes grew soft. "Me too. Sometimes Hazel seems normal and then other times—like today— she's in another world. She relives that day over and over again. I've tried to tell her that Harvey's gone, but that only makes it worse."

She thought of her neighbor and grew misty-eyed. Here they were, two strangers, living side by side, both consumed by memories. Given a different set of circumstances, she could have been Hazel.

*   *   *   *   *

"Ms. Lassiter?" The male voice came over the receiver.

"Yes."

"This is Timothy McWhorter. I work up at the Winchester outlying woodlands site. You haven't met me yet, but I need to talk to you. I need you to come up here now. I think you'll be interested in what I have to show you."

Sydney looked at her watch—*4:15.* "Timothy, it's late. Is it something urgent? Does it have something to do with safety? Are you hurt?"

"Yes ma'am, I mean no ma'am. I ain't hurt, but it does have something to do with safety. They're doing some dangerous stuff up here, but I don't want to talk about it over the phone. I just need for you to come."

She thought about Joe Slaton, the outlying woodlands manager. Sydney had only met him once in the conference room on her first day. She had an appointment to visit there next week. "Have you spoken to Mr. Slaton about this?"

"No ma'am, he's out of town."

Sydney considered her options. It was at least a forty-five minute drive, and now that the time had changed, it was getting dark as early as 6:00. "Can this wait until tomorrow?"

"No ma'am. It's urgent."

"Okay, I'll be there as soon as I can, but I will be bringing Sean O'Conner with me so he can assess the situation too."

She disconnected the call and then dialed Sean's cell number. If there was a problem, it would be better to get him on her side from the very beginning. And she didn't feel comfortable going out there late in the evening by herself. Sean's line rang and then she got his voice mail. She left a message, telling him where she was going.

*   *   *   *   *

Sydney drove down the narrow winding road. The subtle smoke of dusk settled in, making the trees on the sides loom high and smothering. When she reached the tiny outlying woodlands shack, it looked deserted. It was still light enough to see, but she reached in her glove box and retrieved her flashlight just in case.

"Hello, is anybody here?" Her voice sounded hollow as it echoed through the trees. She looked around at the stacks of logs and then in the shack's open door. A cracking noise from behind the shack caused her to jump. She shined her flashlight into the woods. No sign of life.

"Timothy, are you here?"

No reply. Tension crawled up her neck, reminding her that she was alone in a remote area. Was this some kind of sick joke or antic to scare her? Panic rippled up her spine. Was it her imagination or was someone moving in the woods? The little voice in her mind became a shrill warning.

Run, Sydney! Run while you still can.

"Deceit is in the heart of them that imagine evil."
—Proverbs 12:20

chapter twenty-six

He waited until dark before parking his car behind the garden and feed store, a couple of blocks from her house. All he had to do was follow the railroad tracks. His pace quickened the closer he got to Sydney's. The lights were out in the house. *Good.* A dog barked in the distance.

His hands worked expertly to open her back gate where he made his way to the patio. Opening the French door was a cinch, and then he took a step back. He cursed when a flowerpot came crashing around his feet. He waited for a second, half expecting to hear a siren or an alarm. There was no sound except the steady pounding in his chest. He entered the house and turned on his small flashlight. Several folders were scattered on the dining room table. He almost stopped to examine them and then changed his mind. Last time she'd come home and surprised him. He'd get what he came for this time. He made his way to the desk. An unfinished letter lay on top, along with a stack of bills, ready to be mailed. He tugged at the locked drawer and smiled. It would be easy to pry open.

The shrill ringing of the phone startled him. He listened to the message. "Hey Sydney, it's me, Ginger. Where are you? Call me back."

A few more precious minutes. That's all he would need.

"Faithful are the wounds of a friend; but the kisses of an enemy are deceitful."
—Proverbs 27:6

chapter twenty-seven

Sydney's mind said *run*, but her feet stood rooted to the ground. Her skin crawled like living ants. She strained to hear. There it was again—the rustling in the woods. The empty space around her loomed large and she anticipated an attack from any direction. Her pace quickened to a trot, and it was all she could to keep from breaking into a sprint to get to the jeep.

She fumbled with her keys. The second it took to unlock the door seemed like an eternity. She opened the door and plunged into the safety of the vehicle.

Had someone been in the woods or was she jumping at her own shadow, afraid of the boogey man? One thing was for sure, she wasn't going to hang around to find out.

She drove out of the woodlands and glanced at her phone. She had one message. It was Sean, explaining that he'd been at the gym and had left his phone in his locker. Why was she not surprised?

*　*　*　*　*

"Ms. Lassiter, Ms. Lassiter." The police officer repeated Sydney's name louder, as if he were speaking to a child. "Do you know what's missing?"

Yes, I know what's missing—my most prized possession! She waited for the officer to react to her statement and then realized that she'd not said anything, only thought it.

The officer's brown hair was cropped close to his head. So close that Sydney could see his scalp when he bent his head to study his pad. He was young, barely past his teens, and still wet behind the ears, looking more like a Boy Scout than a police officer. He cleared his throat. "What did you say is missing ma'am?"

She looked at his exasperated expression. He repeated the question again, this time louder. "What— is—missing?"

The words exploded from her mouth. "I don't know! Officer, I'm not sure what all is missing right now. As you can see, this has been a shock for me," she said, adopting the same smug tone she'd heard Judith use.

"Just tell me again what happened."

Sydney sighed, not trying to mask her frustration. "I've already told you." She ran her fingers through her hair, hating the way it felt dirty and stringy. "I came home from work later than usual because I had to go and check on a problem. The front door was locked, and everything looked fine from the outside. When I went inside, I noticed that the middle drawer of my desk had been tampered with. My things were all shuffled around."

"Shuffled around? How?"

She could feel the fingers of hysteria clawing the edges of her mind. "Things were moved. I keep everything in order."

He pushed up his glasses and gave a quirky smile. "Are you sure?"

Her eyes met his in defiance. "I know when my things have been moved."

"Tell me about the desk drawer. How do you know for sure that it has been tampered with?"

"Because it was locked and now it's open."

He nodded and scribbled on his pad. His glasses slipped again, but this time he left them there and peered over them. "Then what happened?"

"I saw the broken pot and realized that someone had forced his way in through the patio door."

"His way?"

Sydney's face was a blank. "What?"

"You said *his way in*. Why did you say that?" A hysterical laugh forced its way up her throat, and she swallowed it down. "His, her—I don't know."

"Is there anything else you can tell me?"

Sydney looked him straight in the eye. "No."

The officer studied her for a moment with furrowed brows. He closed his pad and stood. "Ms. Lassiter, if you think of anything else..." He left the sentence hanging and handed her his card. "You will have to come down to the station tomorrow and fill out some paperwork." He looked at her strained expression. "Is there anyone we should call?"

"No!" She softened the outburst with a forced smile. "I'll be fine."

"In that case, I'll see you tomorrow."

Sydney nodded and locked the door behind him. She looked around the room of the cozy home she'd grown to love. Now everything was colored with fear. Her gaze went to the large bay window, one of the features that made her choose this place. Her blinds were pulled up, the huge black squares of night staring menacingly through the panes.

She went around the room and pulled down the blinds, then ran a tired hand through her hair and went to the phone. Her fingers dialed his number almost by instinct. She let it ring at least a dozen times. No answer. Tears boiled over and she slammed down the phone.

Sydney sat on the couch and tried to control her shaking body as the realization of the night's events soaked like rubbing alcohol into an open cut. This was no random break in. Someone knew exactly what they wanted and had taken it. Avery's journal and the articles were gone. Any clues she might have found were lost. She shivered as a more terrifying thought pierced her mind. Someone knew who she was.

The phone rang. Kendall's voice came over the line.
"Sydney, have you been trying to call? What's wrong?"
"My house got broken into tonight."
"What? Are you all right?"
A lump formed in the back of Sydney's throat. The
compassion in his voice made her wish he was here.
"It happened while I was at work."
"I'm on my way."

* * * * *

"What happened to you?"
Sydney looked up as Sean barged into her office.
"What're you talking about?"
He pointed, then sat in a chair in front of her desk.
"You've got dark circles under your eyes, like you haven't
slept in a month."
"Well, if you must know, my house was broken into
last night." She watched his face for a reaction. At this
point, she wasn't sure who to trust. She was relieved to
see genuine concern in his eyes.
"Syd, are you all right? Were you there?"
"No, it happened while I was at the outlying
woodlands on a wild goose chase."
"I got your call. What was that all about?"
"I'm not sure. Timothy McWhorter called me
yesterday and said there was a dangerous situation I
needed to check on."
His eyes narrowed. "What kind of situation?"
"I'm not sure. He wouldn't tell me over the phone."
"Why didn't you call Joe Slaton?"
"He was out of town."
Sean shook his head. "No he wasn't. I spoke to him
yesterday afternoon."
"What?" She thought back to the phone call. Like
a fool, she believed every word the man had told her and
hadn't even bothered to validate anything. Then again,
why would she? She couldn't possibly know it was all a
ruse.

"Sydney, Timothy McWhorter hasn't worked for Chamberland for several months."

The air left her lungs. She shook her head so hard that hair slung in her mouth. "No, that's not possible. He called me yesterday."

Sean's eyes met hers. "I don't doubt that someone called you, but I can assure you it wasn't Timothy McWhorter." He studied her face, which was growing paler by the minute. "What was stolen?"

"Huh?" Sean's voice cut through her thoughts. "Oh, nothing."

He raised an eyebrow. "Nothing at all?"

She nodded.

"Let me get this straight. Someone called you from the woodlands, and you went out there. And while you were gone, your house got broken into?"

"I know it sounds crazy, but that's what happened."

"And nothing was stolen?"

Her eyes met his in a challenge. "That's right."

"Syd, one of these days you're going to have to learn to trust me."

She studied the enigmatic expression on his face. What was she seeing? Compassion? Mockery? It was impossible to tell.

"Trust, Mr. O'Conner, is something that has to be earned."

* * * * *

The day's events left Sydney emotionally drained. She pulled into her driveway and got out of the jeep. Hazel's perfume floated through the air as welcoming as a loaf of freshly baked bread. Louellen's explanation about Hazel had deeply touched Sydney, and she wanted to befriend her. She spotted her standing by the edge of her flower bed dressed in a sky blue muu muu. Dixie was draped like a blanket across her arm.

Sydney waved. "Hello, Hazel."

Hazel stopped petting her cat and looked sternly at Sydney. "Hazel can't warn Sydney."

Fear returned with a vengeance, leaving Sydney's mouth dry. "Warn me about what?" Her mind reeled. Hazel had undoubtedly seen the police car last night. Was it possible that she'd also seen something else?

"Hazel," Sydney said, keeping her voice gentle. "Did you see someone at my house last night?"

"Louellen said not to meddle in other people's business."

Sydney swallowed hard. "No, Hazel. You're not meddling. If you saw someone, I need to know."

Hazel backed away, shaking her head. "No, no, no. I'm not supposed to cause trouble."

She was still muttering as she disappeared around the back of the house.

* * * * *

"What time are you leaving today?"

Sydney looked up from her desk to see Sean enter the room. "In about five minutes. I'm just going over the OSHA report so I'll have everything ready when Jake comes tomorrow." Sydney took a deep breath and let it out slowly. It seemed that everyone in the sawmill was breathing a little easier ever since they'd passed their most recent inspection. Everyone, that is, except her. She'd been in a state of constant turmoil ever since Avery's journal had been stolen.

"What time is the meeting?"

"I think he's coming at ten." Jake Roberts had scheduled a follow-up meeting with Sydney and Sean to go over the OSHA report. Sydney wanted to make sure she had all her ducks in a row before tomorrow.

Sean leaned against the doorframe and studied her face. "Are you doing okay, Syd? You look a little edgy."

Edgy? That was the understatement of the year. No, I'm not okay, she wanted to scream. Her whole world was falling apart. What little security she finally managed to gain was snatched away. Someone broke into her house, invaded her privacy, and caused her to be afraid of her own shadow. She only got about two hours of sleep the night before because she was too busy jumping every time she heard the slightest noise—the floor creaking, the rumble of the ice machine. That's all it took to send her scurrying like a mouse under the covers. She tucked a strand of hair behind her ear. "I'm fine," she said, looking down at the paperwork on her desk.

"Good, I'm glad to hear it."

It was all Sydney could do to not smirk at his comment. Lip service, that's all he was. He wasn't concerned about her. He was too busy thinking about Sean.

He looked at his watch. "I'll meet you by your jeep in about five minutes."

Her head shot up. "What?"

"Didn't you say that you needed five more minutes to finish up?"

"Well, yes but—"

"I need your help with something."

She shook her head. "Okay, whatever."

Five minutes later she found Sean leaning against her jeep. She didn't bother to hide the annoyed expression that was twisting its way over her face. "All right. I'm here. What do you need?"

He seemed oblivious to her dark mood and instead went to the passenger side of his truck, unlocked the door, and held it open for her. "Let's go in mine."

Her eyebrow arched. "Where?"

A smile softened his chiseled jaw. "You'll see."

Her briefcase felt heavy in her hand. "Sean, I'm really tired. I don't think—"

He took her briefcase and ushered her in his truck. "It won't take long. I promise."

They drove in silence out of the sawmill. Sean inserted a CD into the player. "Do you like Harry Connick, Jr.?"

Sydney nodded, all the while trying to figure out what he was up to. She stole a glance at him. He had one hand on the wheel, and the other resting on the console, dangerously close to her hand. She looked at his long lean fingers and moved her hand away from his to her lap. She waited for him to speak first. When it became apparent that he had no intention of doing so, she broke the ice.

"Where are we going?"

"You'll see."

A dull headache was pounding across the bridge of her nose. She didn't have time to play this juvenile game. "Where are we going?" she asked again. This time her voice was firm.

He reached and patted her hand. "Lean back. Relax. We'll be there in a few minutes."

She smirked. "It's not like I have a choice." It was just like him to keep her guessing. He always had to have the upper hand.

He turned up the music and began humming under his breath. Sydney leaned back and looked out her window. They were crossing over the bridge that led out of Stoney Creek. The Tennessee River sparkled like a million diamonds in the afternoon sun, and the birds opened their wings like miniature gliders and soared lazily over it like they had all the time in the world. At that moment she would have given anything to be one of them.

A few minutes later, they arrived at their destination. "We're here."

Sydney wrinkled her nose. "The Riverton Catfish House? You're taking me here?"

A crooked smile curved on his lips, and she wondered if he'd intentionally smiled that way to send her heart fluttering. "Yep, the best catfish in three counties. Or so I've heard."

She shook her head and reached for her door. This guy was unbelievable.

"Don't you touch that." He jumped out and came around to open it. She was reminded of how disappointed she'd been when Kendall didn't open the door for her. A thundercloud of irritation clouded her and she told herself that it didn't matter. Kendall was so beyond Sean in other ways. Opening a door. How inconsequential was that?

The Riverton Catfish Place was a house converted into a restaurant. Even though it was one big open expanse, a musty smell permeated the caramel-colored shag carpet in the foyer. And if Sydney looked close enough, she was sure to see a thin layer of dust covering the mounted shark hanging on the wall. A predominately pink picture of spring flowers in a vase hung next to a black and white photograph of a lighthouse, and Sydney could imagine the owners scouring their homes to find enough artwork and knick knacks to adorn the walls.

The food, however, made up for the lack of ambience. They sat in their metal diner-style chairs, the seats covered in black vinyl, and feasted on fried catfish filets. The fish was light and tender and just greasy enough to melt in your mouth. *Comfort food.*

Sydney leaned back in her chair as the young waitress approached the table. The freckled-faced girl, with her cherry hair pulled in a tight pony tail, couldn't have been older than fourteen. She was probably a member of the family.

"Would you like some dessert?"

"I don't think so." She'd stuffed herself to the point that her stomach was hurting. A phrase that Avery used to say flashed in her mind. He'd lean back and pat his belly. "I've eaten so much that you're gonna need a wheelbarrow to tote me out of here." Sydney smiled to herself and pictured what Sean's expression would be if she said that.

"What? No dessert?" Sean made a face and then looked at the waitress. "We'll each have a piece of buttermilk pie." His eyes met Sydney's. "Unless you want to share?"

There was an intimacy in his tone that caused Sydney's eyes to widen. Her face flamed. "No, I don't want to share." She was about to reiterate to the waitress that she didn't want dessert but Sean didn't give her a chance.

"Two desserts it is."

They watched the waitress flutter away.

"Why did you do that?"

"Do what?"

"I don't want dessert."

Sean leaned back in his chair. "Of course you do. You just don't know it yet."

Her eyes narrowed, causing a smile to tug at the corners of Sean's mouth. Why did she get the feeling they were talking about more than just dessert? Was he hitting on her? He was all Dr. Jekyll now. The question was when would Mr. Hyde return?

Sydney looked him square in the eyes. "Well aren't you just peaches and cream today."

"What do you mean? I'm always nice."

She folded her arms across her chest. "Humph."

"Come on Syd, you can't come here and not get the buttermilk pie."

The waitress returned. "That's right," she said, placing the pieces of pie in front of them. "We're famous for our buttermilk pie."

Sydney took a bite and let it slip like velvet on her tongue. She had to admit that it was delicious. She looked up to see Sean studying her reaction.

"See, I told you."

"I only wish the company was as good as the pie."

His hearty laughter broke the tension, and she found herself laughing too.

"So why did you take me to dinner?"

"If you'll remember, I tried to take you after the football game, but you turned me down. I figured if I told you my intentions tonight, you wouldn't come with me."

"You're right."

He chuckled.

She studied his eyes, her face a question, letting him know he wasn't going to get off that easily. "Well?"

He grew serious. "We've all been under so much stress with the OSHA inspection. You looked so keyed up this afternoon that I figured you could use a little R and R." He leaned back in his seat. "Right?"

She followed suit and leaned back in her chair. "Yeah, it has been stressful lately. I'm just glad the inspection's over with. Maybe now I can get to some of the things I've been keeping on the back burner."

He took the last bite of his pie. "Speaking of which, how's that report of yours coming along? The one establishing the ten-year accident trend."

She couldn't answer right away because she was too busy choking on a bite of pie. She should have known he would ask her about that. The man had a memory like an elephant. *He knows...he knows the accident report was a ruse to find out what happened to Avery. But how? How could he know?* She fought to keep her voice even. "I haven't really pursued that any further. I mean—it's just that I've had too much to do."

"I see."

They're eyes met, hers fire and his ice. *What do you see?* She wanted to scream. *Tell me what you see!* "How's Kendall?"

"Fine."

Sean took his straw and twirled the ice in his glass before lifting it to his lips. The liquid swirled into a tornado. He gulped it down. "I figure he's hoping to make it to state playoffs this year."

She was still mulling over the accident reports. Her reply was automatic. "Yeah, I guess."

"Well, from what I hear around town, it's in his best interest to win state. He's come close a few times—but no prize. In a town like Stoney Creek, winning guarantees job security."

This caught her full attention. "Is that right? I wouldn't worry too much about Kendall if I were you."

She thought she saw his jaw muscle work but couldn't be sure. "Believe me, it's not Kendall I'm worried about."

"Then who?" She changed the subject before he could respond. "Back to your comment about football. What makes you the expert? You know, it's awfully easy to sit back and take cheap shots at Kendall when you don't know the first thing about it."

He laughed. "Do you think lover boy's the only one who played football? It just so happens that I was the starting quarterback for my high school football team."

She raised an eyebrow. "Oh really? Where did you say you went to high school?"

"Huh?"

"High School?"

"Oh, McCullough High."

"Fascinating."

He started to respond but was interrupted by the waitress bringing their bill. Sean handed her his credit card, and they watched her walk away.

"You know, there's something I still don't get."

"Oh yeah? What's that?"

"You and Kendall."

She rolled her eyes. How many times were they going to keep having the same conversation? "Why do you find it so hard to believe that Kendall and I could be attracted to each other?"

He was quick to answer. "You misunderstand me. I'm not saying that. I can see why Kendall's attracted to you. He'd have to be blind not to be."

His compliment caught her off guard. Color rose in her cheeks, and she hoped it wasn't blaring like a neon sign.

"I just don't understand what you see in him."

"I—"

He held up his hand. "I'm not finished yet. I mean, look at you. Here you are, this beautiful, wealthy, high society, big city girl, and he's a...a..."

"A what?" Her face was beet red.

"All right. You want me to say it? I'll say it. He's a hick."

"What's the matter with you? What is it with you and Kendall? First you act like you barely know him, and the next minute I see you having an in-depth conversation with him." Her words came out in angry bits like she'd chewed them up and spit them out. "And another thing, what makes you think I'm rich? You don't know anything about me."

"I know a lot more than you think."

Her face paled. She stood and slammed her napkin on the table. "I'm going to the restroom. I'll meet you at the truck."

They rode in thick silence until Sean spoke up. "Look Syd, I apologize for upsetting you."

Silence.

"My intention tonight was to mend some fences, not to make things worse between us."

She still didn't answer.

"I'm going to say one more thing about Kendall, and then I promise I won't mention it again."

She turned to look at him.

"Kendall's a small-town boy who's still basking in his glory days. He doesn't care about you. Not really. You're just a trophy to him."

A smirk escaped her lips.

"And putting all that aside, he just doesn't seem like your type."

"Oh yeah, and just who is my type?"

It was his turn to remain silent.

"Are you my type, Sean O'Conner? Is that what you're saying?"

He shifted in his seat. "Well I'm not saying that, but you have to admit, you can do a heck of a lot better than him."

Her arms were folded like a vice over her chest. She turned away from him to stare out the window.

"You might as well get comfortable."

She jerked her head back at him. "What?"

"I refuse to take you home angry. So you might as well get comfortable because I'm going to keep driving until you're in a better mood."

His comment was so out of place that it struck her as funny. She laughed despite herself. He laughed too, and the tension between them eased. Sean turned up the music.

Sydney knew she should have remained angry, but it took too much energy. Sean's opinion of Kendall didn't matter anyway. What mattered was how she felt. What did she feel? She brushed the thought aside and let her worries get lost in the gentle rhythm of the song.

It was dark by the time Sean pulled into her driveway. Sydney smiled in spite of herself when she saw the lace curtain on Hazel's window move.

Sean noticed it too. His eyebrow arched. "Your neighbor keeps close tabs on you, doesn't she?"

"You'd just have to know Hazel. She's harmless." Sydney reached for the door handle. "Well," she chuckled, "it's been interesting."

He reached and caught hold of her arm. The air was electric. His face moved a mere inch from hers. "Don't touch that door," he said, his voice just husky enough to send a shiver of anticipation racing down her spine.

Like a fly caught in a spider's snare, powerless to resist, she sat glued to her seat as his lips met hers and melted through to her knees like sweet poison. She opened her eyes and moved away from him. If he was as affected by the kiss as she was, he didn't show it. A pleased expression came over his face. "I'll bet Kendall never kissed you like that."

Her hand came up and gave a satisfying *whack* when it struck his face. "I've been wanting to do that for a long time."

She could almost hear Hazel cheering when she got out of the truck and slammed the door.

"A soft answer turneth away wrath: but grievous words stir up anger."
—Proverbs 15:1

chapter twenty-eight

When Sydney arrived at the sawmill the next morning, Barb met her at the door, holding a cup of coffee and wearing a tight sweater and a smug expression. "Sean and Mr. Roberts are already in the conference room. They were wondering why you're late!" she said then took a sip of coffee.

The first comment that ran through Sydney's mind was, Well don't get too worked up over it or you'll pop the buttons off that sweater. But she was trying to do better so she bit her tongue and said instead, "Barb, blue is a great color for you. You should wear it more often."

Barb's eyes widened, and she looked down at her sweater. Sydney breezed past her.

"Good morning." Jake smiled and offered his hand to Sydney as he peered over his tiny glasses. It was the first time Sydney had seen him wearing anything other than a plaid shirt and jeans. Were it not for his potbelly protruding over his belt, he might have looked attractive in his black shirt and corduroy slacks.

"Good morning," she said, noticing that Sean's appearance was impeccable as usual. Her eyes were drawn to his cheek, where she expected to see a blotch. No trace.

"Sean was just going over the report."

"Great."

"First of all, I'd like to commend you and Sean on the progress you've made at the mill. It's remarkable what you've been able to accomplish in a short period of time. According to the report, everything seems to be in good order. We just have to be sure to keep it that way. Have you come up with a safety incentive program for the workers?"

Before Sydney could respond, Sean broke in. "Sydney and I are in the process of finalizing that now that the OSHA inspection is over. Right, Syd?"

Jake looked back and forth at the two of them.

Sydney nodded. She'd been so busy investigating her father's death that she'd not thought beyond the inspection, had not even considered instituting an incentive program. Rescued by Sean again.

Sydney followed Sean's lead. "That's right, Jake. We've been talking about a quarterly incentive program where the guys will get a bonus if they go without an accident for a certain number of days."

"Good. I think that's what we need to keep people alert."

"Okay. I think we're ready to take Jake on a tour of the mill and show him the improvements." Sean handed Sydney and Jake a hard hat and ushered them toward the door. Sydney turned and mouthed *thank you* to Sean behind Jake's back.

He patted his jaw. "Don't mention it."

The inspection progressed through the mill where Sean directed Jake's attention to the men on the green chain, wearing their hard hats, safety shoes, and goggles. He then pointed out the various pieces of equipment where guards had been installed.

Jake turned to Sydney. "Well, young lady, it looks like you've done an excellent job." Before Jake could continue, the sound of a siren blasted through the mill. Several workers rushed past them.

"What in the tarnation is that?" Jake asked, looking first at Sean and then at Sydney.

"There's been an accident!" Sean thrust his clipboard at Sydney and ran in the direction of the other men. Sydney forgot about Jake Roberts and ran to catch up. Sydney and Sean looked at each other in shock. This couldn't be happening. Not now!

"What's going on?" Sean pushed his way through the crowd of workers. Sydney saw Jerrold Melton and Clyde Filmore tangled in a fight. Jerrold had a stream of blood running from his nose. Several of the men were hollering and urging them on.

"Stop it!" Sean broke in between them. "I said stop it right now!" He grabbed Jerrold around the neck and jerked him off Clyde. Then Buck Gibson appeared from nowhere and grabbed Clyde and held him back. Both men cursed each other. Sydney was startled by their savage expressions and the blue veins popping out on their necks. She was jolted back to the cockfight, not seeing the two men, but blood-crazed roosters being held by their handlers, ready to tear each other apart.

"Shut up and tell me what's going on!" Sean said.

Jerrold's voice was raw. "He switched on the power while I was lubricating the chain and pretty near kilt me. That's what's going on! If it hadn't of caught my shirt..." Jerrold held up his arm to show that part of his sleeve was ripped out of his shirt. "That would've been my arm!"

Clyde went wild, his arms flailing to get at Jerrold as Buck held him back. "You sorry son of a gun! You didn't have that piece of equipment tagged out, and you know it! There's no way I could've knew you were working on that chain."

"How bad are you hurt, Jerrold?"

"I'm not hurt, Mr. O'Conner, I jest got caught because of that sorry—"

"That's enough!" Sean shouted. "Jerrold, you didn't put up a lockout sign on the switch when you started lubricating the chain, and Clyde flipped it. You better be glad the only thing caught was your sleeve."

Sydney looked at Clyde and Jerrold. She wondered if Sean was thinking the same thing that she was. There was more to this than someone forgetting to tag out.

Jake Roberts cleared his throat and stepped forward, shoving his clipboard at Sean. "What kind of circus are you running around here? Well, this is just peachy, ain't it Ms. Lassiter? Exactly what I deserve for sending a woman to do a man's job."

The way her name rolled off Jake's tongue made Sydney feel dirty. Her head was reeling. According to Jake Roberts, her job performance had gone from excellent to substandard in the span of three swift minutes. All she could think about was getting out of the sawmill.

"Wait one minute." The sound of Sean's voice made her turn just in time to see Sean take hold of Jake's shoulder and swing him around to face him. For a moment she thought Sean was going to hit him. "Syd has done an excellent job. She had no more control over what happened here today than you or me. This was strictly human error."

"Well then," Jake said, jerking free from Sean's grasp, "maybe you're not doing your job!"

Sydney rushed to his defense, the confidence in her voice surprising her. "Sean has gone over that lockout procedure in every safety meeting we've had. This is not his fault!"

Jake squared his shoulders. "Then whose fault is it? Maybe you two have been too busy taking care of each other to take care of business at the mill. It's a miracle that we made it through the OSHA inspection." He spit out the words before marching out of the mill.

Sydney grabbed Sean's arm as he started after Jake. "Sean, it's not worth losing your job over. Just let it go."

"Ye shall know them by their fruits..."
—Matthew 7:16

chapter twenty-nine

"I can't believe you're here." Sydney's eyes smiled over her cup of herbal tea. She watched Ginger thumb through the collection of videos and DVDs. Ginger called her a week ago to let her know that she would be coming to visit while Mark was out of town.

Ginger's shiny hair bounced on her shoulders. Her red knit shirt accentuated her ample bosom and tiny waist. She was always complaining about having a size ten top and a size six bottom. If only the rest of us could be so lucky, Sydney thought.

"Let me see what we have here," Ginger said. *"The Pelican Brief, The Fugitive, The Count of Monte Cristo.* Hmmm, wonder if there's a clue in these titles."

"Oh shut up and pick something."

Ginger ignored Sydney's remark and pretended to take stock of Sydney's movie inventory. "I enjoyed meeting Kendall and Sean."

"Yeah, they were on their best behavior for you."

"Syd, can I ask you a question?" Ginger turned to face Sydney.

"Sure."

"Why are you eating hamburger when you could have steak?"

"What are you talking about?" Sydney put down her cup of herbal tea and looked at Ginger.

"Don't get me wrong. Kendall's a cute guy, but he doesn't hold a candle to Sean. That guy is drop-dead gorgeous. You guys just look like you were meant for each other."

"So did Adam and I, remember? And besides, eating steak all the time can get a little too rich, if you know what I mean. And so what if Sean is...good looking?" She almost said *gorgeous* but couldn't bring herself to say it. That would be giving him too much credit. "When did looks become the only determining factor?"

Ginger raised an eyebrow and Sydney sought for the words to explain how she felt.

"Look, I know Kendall isn't as handsome as Sean." It was the first time she'd admitted it. "But he has so many other wonderful qualities."

"Such as?"

"He's sweet."

Ginger wrinkled her nose, and Sydney cringed when that tale-tell eyebrow of hers raised.

"And honest." Sydney inserted before Ginger could say anything else. "Did I ever tell you about the time he lectured me about cheating?"

"I must've missed that one," Ginger said dryly.

"I was in junior high. Emma, Kendall's younger sister, and I were best friends. I spent more weekends at her house than my own." Sydney's voice became nostalgic. "Anyway, Emma and I had this math teacher. Mrs. Drucker." Sydney spat out the name like it left a nasty taste in her mouth. "All the students dreaded her tests. They were long and tedious, and everyone knew that she used the same tests over and over. Somehow Emma got a hold of an old test that had all the answers. We were in her room making a cheat sheet when Kendall saw us."

*　　*　　*　　*　　*

Cindy's eyes turned to saucers when she saw what Emma was holding. "Where'd you get that?"

"Luke Holcomb gave it to me."

"But we can't."

280

"Oh, yes we can." Emma was sitting on her bed with her legs crossed Indian style. "Aren't you sick of getting C's?"

"Well, yeah but—"

"Don't be a ninny." She reached for a sheet of paper and turned over on her stomach. "Come on. I need some help to make sure it's right."

They were so intent that they didn't hear Kendall enter the room. By the time Cindy felt his presence over her shoulder, it was too late.

"What ya got there?"

Emma jumped guiltily and moved to cover the paper, but he was faster.

It only took one look to know what they were doing. He glared at Emma. "Where'd you get this?"

She reached for it, her eyes sparking with anger. "It's none of your business. Give it back!"

"I most certainly will not! I can't believe the two of y'all would do such a thing." Cindy wished she could crawl under the bed. Anything to escape this humiliation, especially from her idol.

"Are you going to tell Mom and Dad?" Emma's voice sounded small.

Kendall shook his head in disgust. "I oughta." He thrust the paper at Emma. "I'm not gonna look over your shoulder every minute to make sure you're doing the right thing. You'll have to let your own conscience be your guide." He turned and left the room.

* * * * *

Ginger had gotten caught up in the story and was hanging on every word. "What did you do? Did you go ahead and cheat?"

Sydney smiled. "Emma did."

Ginger's eyes widened. "Really?"

"Uh-huh."

"How about you?"

Sydney laughed. "No, I didn't cheat, not then or any other time. How could I? Every time I even so much as thought about cheating, a picture of Kendall, with his scathing eyes, would cross my mind. It was enough to keep me on the straight and narrow."

Ginger chuckled and then grew serious. "It must be hard to pretend that you don't know any of these people."

"You have no idea."

"Do you think any of them recognize you?"

Sydney thought for a moment and then shook her head. "No, I don't think so. I look so different now."

Ginger turned her attention to the movies. "Let's watch this one."

"Okay, I'll go and make us some popcorn."

Ginger moved to put the movie in the player but stopped. She went to the bookcase instead. "Where did you get this?"

"Get what?"

"This." Ginger held out her hand to show Sydney what she was holding.

"Do you remember when I told you about the two men getting into a fight over the lockout procedure?"

Ginger nodded.

"Afterwards, when I was going over the area with a fine toothed comb, I found this. It was on the ground beside the machinery, buried in sawdust."

Ginger's voice grew preachy like she was scolding an errant child. "Do you not have any idea what this is?"

"No, I don't. What is it?"

"It's an apparatus used for taking drugs."

Sydney's eyes flew open wide. "What?"

"People use this to take meth."

Hot prickles pelted Sydney. She forgot all about making popcorn and took the device from Ginger and sat down on the couch to examine it. She thought back to the day of the fight and how the men were filled with such violent rage. Her mouth went dry as it all came together. All of the accidents at the mill had been caused by human error. If the men were on drugs...Her mind pondered the possibility. "This could be what's going on at the mill. This could explain the accidents."

Ginger frowned. "This could also be dangerous. Who's in charge of drug testing at the mill?"

Sydney thought for a moment and frowned. "Who do you think? Sean O'Conner."

*   *   *   *   *

Sydney brought the drug apparatus to his office at the end of the day. She plopped it on his desk.

"You wanna explain this?"

His eyes narrowed. "What're you talking about?"

"I found this on the ground next to where Clyde and Jerrold were having their fight. You and I both know it can only mean one thing. They were high on drugs. That's why they were acting so irrational." She clenched her fist. "I'd bet my life on it."

She leaned over his desk and looked him straight in the eyes. "Sean, is this what has been going on at the mill all along? Is this why we've been having all those random accidents? You have to tell me the truth." Her face was hard but her eyes revealed pain and betrayal.

Sean leaned back in his chair. "Have a seat, Syd. And close the door first, will you?" He waited for her to sit down, his mind going a million miles a minute, mulling over the situation so he could come up with the right words to diffuse this thing. He propped his elbows on the arms of his chair and pressed his fingertips together.

"You wanna start from the beginning?"

She took a deep breath. "Like I told you, I found this in the sawmill. It was lying on the ground, right next to where Clyde and Jerrold had that big blow up."

He nodded. "Uh-huh. That was last week. Why are you just now bringing this in?"

"I didn't know what it was at first. I shoved it in my pocket. I left it lying on my bookshelf at home."

His eyebrow lifted, and she became flustered.

"When Ginger came for a visit. Remember my friend Ginger? The one I introduced you to?"

"I remember."

"Well, Ginger saw it and asked me where I got it. She told me that it was a device used for taking meth."

"And how did Ginger know what it was?"

"Ginger's husband is a police officer."

"Oh, I see."

"Do you?" Her voice became louder. "Do you really understand what this means? I've been busting my tail, trying to get all the safety issues cleared up, and all the while those lug heads in the mill have been high on drugs. It all makes sense now."

"Just a minute. Don't you think you're jumping the gun here?"

Her brazen eyes met his. "Am I?"

He picked up the drug apparatus. "First of all, you should've never taken this home."

"I already told you why I—"

"That's not good enough, Syd."

"What do you mean?"

"Well, if you'd brought this to my attention last week, then I could've confronted the men. Now, there's not much I can do except keep my eye on them."

"You could test them for drug use."

"On what grounds?"

"I just gave you a good reason."

"It's a little late in the game for that, don't you think? If I pull Clyde and Jerrold in here and demand that they go through testing, they'd start yelling discrimination so fast my head would spin." He shook his head. "I've got enough to worry about without adding that to the list."

She stood. "I've always known you were a stubborn mule, Sean O'Conner, but I never pegged you for stupid. I just can't believe you're not even going to check into this."

"Whoa, hold your horses. I never said that. If there's drug use going on in my mill, I guarantee that I'll get to the bottom of it." She stood and he had a strong urge to sweep her up in his arms and get her as far away from Stoney Creek as possible.

"Let's hope for both our sakes that you do." She went to the door. Her hand reached for the knob.

"Sydney."

She turned back to face him.

His eyes met hers. "Can you just trust me? That's all I'm asking for."

"What are you talking about?"

He shook his head. "Never mind."

"One more question."

"Yes?"

"Are random drug checks being done on a regular basis?"

"Of course."

"Who's in charge of it?"

"I am."

"And the tests have been coming up clean?"

"So far."

"I just wanted to hear you say it." She opened the door and left the room.

*   *   *   *   *

Ginger dipped a spoon in the peanut butter jar and pulled out a tablespoon-size portion and slathered it on her apple. She plopped down on the sofa and kicked off her shoes, sending them sprawling across the room. She gnawed away at the apple with her front teeth.

"You look like a beaver when you do that."

She stopped and looked up at Mark. "Oh, sorry."

"No, I like it."

She wrinkled her nose. "Really?"

"Yeah, you're comfortable in your own skin."

"Thanks." She loved that about Mark. How he would compliment her on the most ordinary of things.

She took another bite of her apple. "You know what? I had a great time at Syndey's, but it sure is good to be home."

He sat down next to her and scooted close. He kept his face serious, but his eyes danced with mischief. "I'm glad to hear you say that because I was beginning to wonder. I know how close you and Sydney are, and I was afraid I might have to catch a flight and drag you home."

She held the apple out from her mouth and then poked him in the ribs with her free elbow. "Oh Mark, you know better than that." She snuggled into the curve of his shoulder as he draped his arm around her. She held up her apple. "Wanna bite?"

"No thanks."

She shrugged and then took another plug out of the apple. "Mark, you wouldn't have recognized her."

His face contorted in a mock surprise. "Don't tell me: she cut off her hair and dyed it red."

Ginger rolled her eyes, even though she wasn't really annoyed. She loved it when Mark teased her. "Seriously, she's changed."

"How so?"

"Well for one thing, everything wasn't all about her. There's this crazy neighbor who dresses like a *Hawaii gone bad commercial*. Sydney looks after her. She insisted that we take Hazel—" Ginger looked at Mark, "that's the lady's name. Anyway, Sydney takes her a plate of cookies at least once a week. And then there's Stella." She caught herself. "This other lady that Sydney's grown really close to." She almost said *Sydney's grandmother* and then caught herself. Ginger shook her head. "It's obvious that she cares about these people. She didn't seem so caught up in herself."

"That's fantastic. How's the boyfriend situation? Who's the man of the hour?"

"There are two of them in the picture right now."

"Only two?" This earned him another jab in the ribs.

"That's not fair." Ginger wrinkled her nose. "I met both of them and was surprised that Sydney was leaning toward Kendall, the coach. Kendall looks like an all-American boy. He's nice but shy. Sean, the other one, seems like more her type. He's outgoing and handsome as the devil."

Mark moved his arm from her shoulder and encircled her neck in a choke hold. "Hey now." He let go.

She laughed and then batted her eyelashes before turning and looking into his eyes. "Well not as handsome as you. No one's that handsome." Ginger grew serious. "I liked Sean better at first. Now, after the drug thing, I'm not so sure."

Mark's eyes grew wary. "Drug thing?"

Ginger told him how Sydney found the meth apparatus at the sawmill and how Sean was in charge of the random drug testing. She watched Mark intently, knowing that the police officer in him would analyze every detail. After a moment he spoke. "Just because this guy, Sean, does the random drug testing for the mill doesn't mean he's involved."

Ginger's face relaxed. "Well, that's what I told Sydney, but for some reason she jumped to the conclusion that he was guilty."

Mark shook his head. "Meth is some dirty stuff. Unfortunately, it's everywhere now. We deal with it all the time—even have a special unit that goes around disassembling meth labs." He thought for a moment. "I could run a check on him."

"I wish you would." Ginger had already told Sydney that she would ask him. Mark had access to a system at work and could find out about anyone, providing that he had the person's first and last name and either the date of birth or social security number.

"I'll need his—"

Ginger jumped up from the sofa and practically leapt to her purse. She reached in and pulled out a slip of paper and waved it in the air like a prize trophy. "I already have his date of birth."

Mark reached for the paper and scanned the information. "Is there anything else you can tell me about him?"

Ginger thought for a moment. "Sydney said he was the starting quarterback for his high school football team. Does that help?"

"Sure, if I knew the name of the school."

Ginger nodded and then reached for the phone. "I'll call Sydney."

"Ask her if she knows where he went to college."

A few minutes later Ginger hung up the phone. "He went to McCullough High School. It's in a town called The Woodlands on the north side of Houston. Sydney didn't know which college he attended."

Mark shrugged. "That's okay. I'm sure I'll be able to pull it up when I plug his name into the system." He studied the paper he was holding. "McCullough High. The Woodlands. Why does that sound familiar?" His brows knitted. "Do you remember Dustin Akin?"

"I'm not sure."

"He graduated from the academy with me. He's from The Woodlands, and I believe he went to that same high school."

Ginger broke into a smile. Mark's knack for remembering details never ceased to amaze her. He was always spouting off tidbits of information about people. "It's a small world, especially among police officers."

Mark shook his head and laughed. He held up the paper. "All this readily available information. Why do I get the feeling that I've been set up?"

She batted her eyelashes. "Would I do that?"

He raised an eyebrow. "Most definitely."

A mischievous smile crept across her mouth as she sat down beside him and gave him a long kiss that left them both a little breathless. He drew back and put his arm around her. She reached for his hand and intertwined her fingers with his. "Thanks for running the check. I worry about Sydney sometimes."

He nodded. "She needs to be careful. If some of those people at the mill are taking drugs..." He let the sentence lag. "When people get involved in that, there's no telling what they might do."

Mark's words felt more like an omen than an opinion. Ginger had never told Mark the real reason Sydney was in Stoney Creek. She had wanted to several times but had given Sydney her word that she wouldn't. "Sydney's smart. She'll be careful." Even as she spoke the words, she hoped that would be the case.

* * * * *

Sydney put the bag of groceries on the counter and took out a container of chocolate chip cookies. She smiled as she remembered her first visit to Hazel's house. She pictured Hazel's eager expression when she devoured the entire plate of cookies.

She made her way over to Hazel's with the cookies, her step so light that she resisted the impulse to skip. Stella was right. Serving other people was therapeutic—just what she needed to escape her own problems. It felt especially good to do things for Hazel because she was so appreciative of the smallest gesture. The familiar fragrance of magnolias floated through the air like tender notes of music when Sydney approached the house.

"Giv'er back! I want to hold the cat. You're gonna hurt him!"

Sydney strained to hear the conversation taking place behind Hazel's house.

"No, I'm first. Wally, you said I could be first. Giv'er here! Louellen was first last time. I'm telling Mama!"

Sydney stopped dead in her tracks. Was that Hazel's voice? It sounded like a child's.

"Just because you're my big brother doesn't mean you get to pick who's first every time. And besides, I know what you'll do. I saw you put that kitten in Mamma's pillow case with a rock. You'll throw my cat in the creek just like you did that kitten." Her voice crescendoed. "I won't let you drown my cat. You're mean, Wally. Everybody thinks you're nice, but you're mean!"

Sydney peeked around the corner of the house. Even though she knew better, she halfway expected to see

Hazel talking to two children. Instead, she saw Hazel sitting on the steps with Dixie lying across her lap. Her hands were waving through the air as she spoke to her imaginary companions.

"Even in laughter the heart is sorrowful."
—Proverbs 14:13

chapter thirty

Sydney walked past Barb's desk and reached in her cubicle to retrieve her mail. She leafed through her mail and then stopped. "Barb, why was this catalog put in my box?"

Barb looked at what Sydney was holding. "Oh that. Talley Equipment has been sending us safety equipment catalogs for years." She shrugged. "I just thought you might like to look at it."

"Thanks. I'll do that. But, it's addressed to Lewis Jackson."

"Yeah, Lewis used to work here a long time ago. He was one of our foremen. You'd think the people sending out that catalog would have enough sense to update their list. Lewis hasn't worked here for over ten years."

The name rang a bell. Lewis: why did that name sound so familiar? Then it hit her. Avery mentioned Lewis in his journal. He was the foreman who had dismissed the logger's claims that they were being shorted on their loads. Avery had written that just before he wrote about the incident with the tumbling logs that almost killed him. She had asked Louellen about Lewis the same time she had asked her about Cecil Prichard. She remembered that Louellen had acted funny when she had asked about Lewis. Now she wondered. Could this be the same Lewis? She had assumed that Lewis was the man's last name, not his first.

Sydney looked up and realized that Barb was studying her. "I believe this is the same man I asked Louellen about. She told me he was dead. Do you know how he died?"

Barb's eyes went wide and then she doubled over in laughter.

"What's so funny?"

"Dead my foot. Lewis is no more dead than you or me. He owns a sporting goods store over in Glendale."

Sydney shook her head. "Maybe Louellen was talking about a different Lewis."

Barb reached for a tissue and dabbed the corners of her eyes. "I doubt it."

"Well, then why did she tell me that?"

"Because Lewis Jackson's her ex husband, that's why. She hates his guts."

*   *   *   *   *

Lewis Jackson's sporting goods store was located just off the town square in Glendale. Sydney parked her jeep in front of the store. A bell rang when she opened the door, announcing her arrival. A deep baritone voice sounded from the back of the store. "I'll be with you in a moment."

The wooden floor creaked under Sydney's feet. The mingled smells of leather and vinyl seeped into her system. It was like one of those old dime stores, except instead of candy she saw an assortment of brightly colored sweatshirts and T-shirts, all bearing the logos of state universities. Tables were piled high with sporting accessories. One wall was covered with tennis and racquetball rackets. The other displayed football helmets, baseball caps, and bats.

She heard the same male voice again and then a woman's voice coming from the back of the store. Sydney eased her way in that direction to see if she could get a look at the man. Hopefully he would turn out to be Lewis Jackson. She saw the woman first. She was in her late thirties and was trim with a dark tan, despite the cool weather. *Fake and bake in the tanning bed* Ginger would say. Her medium brown hair was stylishly cut so that it wisped around her chin. A small boy tugged at the young woman's leg, vying for her attention. At first she was oblivious to the boy, but after a few tugs, she relented and bent over to talk to him.

Sydney turned her gaze to the man and realized he had already seen her. He was looking her over while continuing his conversation with the other woman. The woman turned to see what had caught his attention.

Sydney pretended to take interest in a set of golf clubs.

The man made his way up to the front of the store with the woman and her child following. "Grace, it'll take about two weeks for those clubs to arrive. I'll call you when they come."

"Remember, Lewis, if Henry calls, you don't know a thing. I want this to be a surprise."

Lewis chuckled. "Don't worry about that. I'm not the one who let it slip last time. You were."

The woman looked sheepish and made a motion like she was zipping her lips. "No slip-ups this time. Call me," she mouthed then walked out the door.

He winked.

Sydney had positioned herself behind a clothes rack so she could watch the exchange. She'd asked herself a million times why Louellen had told her that Lewis was dead. Maybe it was all as simple as Barb had made it out to be. Maybe Louellen hated his guts so much that she considered him dead. But why did she lie? Was there more to it? Was she protecting someone? Who? Lewis? Herself?

Lewis Jackson was in his mid sixties and very attractive. His southern drawl was so cultured that the words rolled out like a ballad. His crisp polo shirt and gray slacks seemed to be an extension of his athletic frame. His silver hair and steel gray eyes complemented his tanned skin and white teeth. He looked like he walked straight out of a golfing magazine. It wasn't hard to see why the woman in the store was hanging on his every word. He was a picture of southern grace.

"Can I help you?" Lewis walked toward Sydney, giving her a friendly smile as he approached. She wasn't prepared for those shameless eyes that raked her over from head to toe. Yes, he was certainly a ladies' man. His eyes, his walk, everything about him sent a clear message that he was on the make, and at the moment, she just happened to be his closest target. Her cheeks burned.

Should she pretend to be a customer or get straight to the point? "Yes. My name is Sydney Lassiter, and I'm a consultant for Chamberland Sawmill. I'd like to ask you a few questions."

Lewis' smile remained on his face, but his eyes went cold. Or was she so convinced of his guilt that she imagined it? He glanced at his watch, and she had the feeling he was contemplating whether or not to talk to her. "Sydney," he said, "I'll be glad to talk to you if you'll give me a minute to close up, and then we'll go back to my office."

* * * * *

"Miss or Mrs?" Lewis asked. He motioned to a seat directly across from his desk.

He wasn't missing any tricks. "Miss."

"What can I do for you, Miss Lassiter?"

Sydney retrieved a small notebook from her purse and cleared her throat. "I understand that you worked as a foreman at the sawmill a few years ago."

"That's right. I've been gone from there for about eight or nine years." Lewis reached in his pocket and pulled out a stick of gum. "Want one?"

"No thanks."

He removed the wrapper and folded the stick into a neat square before placing it in his mouth.

"I'm investigating some accidents at the mill and

wondered if you could tell me what kind of accidents happened when you were there."

Lewis shifted in his chair and crossed his legs. "Miss Lassiter, I don't see how anything that happened at the mill that long ago could have anything to do with what's happening now. Besides, I can't think of anything unusual that happened while I was there. There were always the run-of-the-mill accidents, like cut fingers, sawdust in people's eyes. That sort of thing."

Sydney studied Lewis' face. She wasn't making any progress. She swallowed hard and decided to plunge in. "Do you remember Buford Phillips' death, Mr. Jackson? Didn't that happen while you were there? Wasn't that an unusual occurrence?"

She watched his eyes. He was startled by her question, though he fought hard not to show it. For a split second, she saw something. What was it? Fear? Anger?

"I hate to speak evil of the dead, but Buford Phillips was a drunk. I think it was pretty much established at the time of the accident that it was his fault."

"Oh, I see." Sydney looked down at her notes. "Can you tell me of any other unusual accidents during that time that come to your mind? For instance, in the lumber yard or maybe in the log yard with some of the trucks?"

"No, I don't think so."

Her eyes met his. "Did you know Avery McClain?"

The air seemed to stand still. "Yes."

"Do you not remember an incident where a chain broke and logs rolled off and almost killed him?"

Lewis' face went white. Sydney looked down and pretended to check her notes. "No, I'm mistaken. The chain didn't break." Her eyes lifted and met his in a direct challenge. "It was cut."

"I don't know what you're talking about. Who gave you that information?" His face was flushed and his eyes narrowed.

"I read it in some of the old files."

"No you didn't. You're lying. Who are you, and why are you really here? You're fishing for information."

Her heart began to pound. "Why did you leave the sawmill, Mr. Jackson?"

"That's none of your business."

"When the loggers came to you, complaining about being shorted on their loads, why did you ignore them? Why didn't you do something?"

Lewis' face went black. "I don't know who you are or what you think you're doing, but it's time for you to leave."

"What are you hiding, Mr. Jackson? Avery McClain was killed in an explosion. Do you know anything about that?"

He jumped up so fast that for a moment she feared he would attack her. "You've got about two seconds to get out of my store."

She stood. Without another word she turned on her heel and left.

*   *   *   *   *

Lewis watched her get into the jeep and drive away. He picked up the phone. "I know we agreed not to talk, but Sydney Lassiter was just here. Something has to be done."

*   *   *   *   *

It took a good ten minutes for Sydney's pulse to return to normal. As she drove back to Stoney Creek, she replayed her conversation with Lewis. He was guilty. She was sure of it. Or at the very least, he knew something about Avery's death. She hadn't intended to question him about Avery. In her anger the words had slipped out. Lewis' words seared her mind. *Who are you? Why are you really here?* Hers was a precarious situation. She wanted to find the answers she so desperately needed, but she aroused suspicion every time she asked those crucial questions.

Lewis was angry. Angry enough to start snooping around in her business? Why had she been so careless? If only she'd not gotten so incensed. Maybe then she could have questioned him in a less confrontational way. She shook her head and slung her hair back out of her face. She was tired of second-guessing herself. Tired of all the headaches at the mill and tired of being sick and tired. So what if Lewis was suspicious? So what? It didn't make any difference. Someone broke into her home and stole Avery's journal. Anyone reading that journal could put two and two together to figure out who she was. It was only a matter of time.

* * * * *

Sydney picked up one of the huge floral pillows and examined it. She gave it a squeeze and a clip from a Charmin commercial flashed in her mind. *Don't squeeze the Charmin.* "Are these pillows new?"

Stella's voice drifted from the kitchen. "Yes, I thought the living room could use some color."

"They look nice." Sydney placed it behind her back and tucked her feet under her legs. Stella's home was becoming more and more of a refuge. She snuggled in the corner of the sofa and watched Stella enter the room, carrying a tray of lemonade and cookies. She rose. "Here, let me help you."

"No, you just relax."

Stella sat down in the love seat and Sydney noticed that there were shadows under her eyes. The tiny lines etched around her eyes looked deeper than she remembered. Sydney wondered how much stress her return to Stoney Creek had caused Stella. Guilt surfaced. This was the first time she'd ever even thought about it.

"Here you are." Stella handed Sydney a tall tumbler of lemonade.

"Stella, I love you," Sydney blurted.

Stella looked taken back, but pleased nonetheless.

"Well, I love you too, hon. I've been worried about you."
Stella reached and patted Sydney's hand.

"I don't want you worrying about me. Everything
will be fine." Sydney sipped the lemonade. Her mind
clicked over the events of the past few days. She told
Stella that she suspected drug use at the mill, and she
told her about the visit to Lewis Jackson. Now she
second-guessed herself for doing so. She had no right to
burden Stella with her problems.

Sydney looked up and realized that Stella was
studying her with those perceptive eyes.

"Sydney, I know we've been over this before, and I
hope you don't think I'm nagging, but I want you to try
to put this whole thing about Avery behind you."

Sydney didn't answer right away. She broke her eyes
away from Stella's and stared at some unseen spot on
the rug. "You're probably right," she finally said. "It's
all one big dead end anyway."

"Have you been to the cemetery yet?"

Sydney's head jerked up. "The cemetery?"

"To visit your parents' grave."

Any reply Sydney could have mustered stuck like
cement on her tongue, but her mind moved a million
miles an hour. How could she put into words how she
felt? Visiting them would make it all seem so...final.
"No, um, I haven't done that yet." She cleared her throat.
"I don't think I'm ready to do that, but I did visit the old
home place when I first got to town." Sydney placed the
tumbler on the coffee table and rose from the couch. She
walked over to the double French doors and stood with
her back facing Stella. After a few moments of silence,
she continued in a low voice, almost as if she were talking
to herself.

"When I went to see my...the house, well, thank
goodness, there was no one home, so I walked around
outside. There's still a swing on the porch. I sat down in
it." She paused. "Then I saw a rocking chair in the far
corner of the porch. It was in the same spot where Mom
used to sit and watch me swing." Sydney turned to face
Stella. "I sat in the swing for a few minutes and closed

my eyes. I could hear Mom and Dad laughing the way they used to before she got sick."

Stella came up from behind her and opened the French doors. "Let's sit on the patio."

The metal scraping the brick seemed loud to Sydney as she pulled out a patio chair. The crisp autumn air splashed their faces and they sat in silence, watching the setting sun start its descent below the horizon.

Stella was the first to speak. "It's such a beautiful sunset."

"Uh-huh."

"This is one of my favorite times of the day."

Sydney's response was automatic. "Oh," and then, "yeah, it's nice out here."

"If you'll wait a few seconds...there. Look at that."

Sydney looked to where Stella was pointing.

"When the sun sets just right..." She stopped speaking until Sydney looked up and met her eyes. "When the sun hits the clouds just right, they burst with color, looking like puffy swirls of pink and blue cotton candy."

"That's exactly what Mom used to say!" It took her all of a second to realize that Stella was aware of that fact. "A cotton candy sky—that's what she used to call it."

Sydney's eyes grew misty and they lifted to the horizon. "We used to lie on our backs in the cool grass and watch the sunset together. Mom would reach and pluck it right out of the sky. She'd pop it in her mouth and then hand me a piece. Her description was so vivid that I swear I actually tasted the sugar melt in my mouth."

"I remember."

Tears pooled in Sydney's eyes before making their way down her cheeks. She shook her head and used her sleeve to wipe them away. "Dad used to say that Mom saw the world through rose-colored glasses. After she was gone...well, I'm afraid I've never been able to look at another sunset and see that much color again."

"Our parents lend us their glasses, and as a child, that's how we see ourselves—through those glasses. You're lucky to have had Susan's, even for a little while."

"You make it sound so easy."

Stella cocked her head. "Do I?" She thought for a moment. "No, I don't think it's easy. Life is a hard road, most of it uphill I must say. But I do know one thing. All of the trials we go through make us stronger. We hate them, pray for their removal, but in the end, they often turn out to be our greatest blessings. I don't ask the Lord to remove my mountains anymore. I just ask for help climbing them. Out of the greatest tragedy comes the greatest personal victory." Stella looked at Sydney. "Are you listening to anything I'm saying?"

Sydney ran her hands through her hair. Her voice was tired, defeated. "Yeah, I hear you."

"Do you think for one minute that Susan wasn't hurting?"

Sydney's eyes took on a wounded expression.

"Toward the end, Susan was in a great deal of pain most of the time. I imagine it hurt her to know that she wouldn't be able to grow old with Avery." Stella's voice grew soft when a tear trickled down Sydney's cheek. "That she wouldn't live to see you grow up. She always looked for the cotton candy in every sky. It might've been hard to find at times, but it was there nevertheless."

Sydney clenched her fist. Her tears were falling faster now. "I just don't understand why everything has to be so hard."

Stella reached for her arm. "I don't know." She patted Sydney's hand. "Honey, I just don't know. But I do know that the Lord doesn't expect us to go it alone. He's always there for us. He's standing there with His arms wide open, just waiting for us to turn to Him. He can give you peace, even in the midst of your affliction." Stella's eyes took on a faraway look. "One of my favorite Bible verses is found in John 14:27. 'Peace I leave with you, my peace I give unto you: not as the world giveth, give I unto you. Let not your heart be troubled, neither let it be afraid.'"

Sydney's mind was on fire. There were so many emotions churning inside that she didn't know that to think. She wanted to believe Stella. She wanted to believe that everything would be okay. She wanted to believe...and yet there was the hideous doubt. That black mist of doubt that was so thick and deep she could never see her way through it.

"Honey, the only way you're going to find any peace is to put closure on this whole thing. I want you to promise me that you'll go to the cemetery. Maybe then you'll be able to get on with your life."

Sydney wiped her eyes with the back of her hand. Her nose was stuffy and her head felt as heavy as lead. A dull headache was throbbing across the bridge of her nose. "Okay, I promise. I'll try."

*   *   *   *   *

Sydney pulled out of Stella's driveway and took a deep breath. Stella was right: it was time for her get on with her life and put the past behind her. She intended to do just that...as soon as she found out what happened to Avery. She glanced up. The sky that was pink and blue just thirty minutes ago was turning a smoldering gray. A storm was moving in. She'd always been amazed at how fast a weather front could move in and out of the plains of Texas, but it rarely happened so quickly here. She rolled down her window, enjoying the energy that was building. She came to the edge of the mountain, just before the road started sloping down, and her eyes rested on a familiar building, The Jam Session. The restaurant was appropriately named because it offered live entertainment every evening. The Jam Session was a gathering place for amateur singers and wannabe entertainers. She remembered the times when she and her parents would drop by to grab a quick sandwich before going to a ballgame. Before she could second-guess herself, she pulled into the crowded parking lot. At the very least, it would provide a diversion from her problems.

Sydney smiled as she listened to the conversation of a middle-aged couple walking in front of her toward the restaurant. "Where did all these dadburn people

come from?" the man said. "You can't never find no
parking place here no more."

The woman looked over at him with a grimace on
her face and pointed to a dark spot on the pavement.
"That oil spill smells, and the grease they cook with
makes me sick. Why can't we go get something to eat
someplace nice for onced?"

"Cause I want to see the talents contest, that's why."

A talent contest? Sydney couldn't remember ever
going to a talent show at The Jam Session. Should be
interesting.

The man holding the microphone looked up when
the couple entered with Sydney following close behind.
"Come on in," he yelled. The couple made their way to
an empty table at the back of the room, and Sydney
moved in the opposite direction to a small table in the
corner near the kitchen.

"The fun's just beginning," the announcer said.
"Our first contestant is a pretty lil' thang. She's gonna
do a cloggin' number called *Born to Boogie*."

The music rolled on, and the energetic brunette
clogged while the crowd roared and clapped. Sydney
looked around the room. It was just as she remembered
it. The crowd was made up of mostly country people from
the surrounding area. Or good ol' salt of the earth folks,
as she'd heard Avery say. Many of the older men wore
overalls, and she counted at least three silver-haired
women in the audience whose hair was swept up in large
buns. Every three days or so, these women would go to
the hairdresser to have their hair set. *Set* was an
appropriate word because once set, like cement, there
was no moving it. Nostalgia swept over her, and she
couldn't be sure but thought she experienced a vague
sense of familiarity when she looked at the faces. The
majority of the younger women still had the eighties
hair style. The one where the bangs were so tall they
could almost stand up and walk by themselves. The men
donned faded jeans and cowboy boots. She scanned their
faces, wondering if any of them worked at the sawmill.

"Can I get you something to eat or drink?"

Sydney looked up to see a skinny waitress standing beside her, practically yelling over the music.

"Yes, I'll have a Sprite."

The announcer was on the stage again, thanking the girl for her performance. "Next, we have Larry Joe. Now y'all give 'im a big round of applause. He ain't no feriner to these parts. He's from right here on the mount'n."

The crowd clapped louder.

"Where's Judy? She's a bustin' a gut to get to sing instead of doing her job," an angry male voice yelled from the kitchen.

"I said I'm fixin' to come and help, and I meant it," the skinny waitress said as she smoothed her apron and took her time sauntering back toward the kitchen.

A smile spread over Sydney's face. No, things hadn't changed much.

It was dark when Sydney stepped out of the restaurant. A taste of rain was in the misty air. She'd stayed longer than she'd intended, but it was worth it. She'd actually enjoyed herself. The parking lot had been so packed when she first arrived that she'd been forced to park at the far end. All thoughts of her pleasant evening vanished when she felt the familiar fears return. It was that same feeling of being watched that ripped away her confidence and stripped her to the core. Why did she always feel that way? Was she losing her mind? The hair on the back of her neck stood and she glanced around the parking lot. All the vehicles were empty except one, a beat up gray Chevy. A man was sitting in the truck. Was that who was watching her? She quickened her pace to get to the jeep. She could still hear the music and the crowd inside as she climbed in. In the safety of her jeep, it was easier to laugh at her paranoia before heading off the mountain. The man in the Chevy was probably waiting for someone inside. The mist turned to rain, and she got caught up in the rhythm of the wipers, listening to them wick away the drops that were spilling on her windshield.

The lights came up behind her so suddenly that they

seemed to appear out of thin air. She glanced in her rearview mirror. The lights were getting closer. She pushed the accelerator. A few more miles would put her at the foot of the mountain and closer to town. The lights were directly behind her now, and whoever it was had left them on bright. She willed herself to remain calm and wished that there were two lanes going down the mountain instead of one. Maybe then this bozo could pass her instead of tailgating. She sped up even more, hoping to distance herself. Her stomach dropped. The lights stayed right on her tail.

She looked in her rearview mirror, trying to see what kind of vehicle it was. It was hard to tell for sure but it looked like a pickup truck. She turned her attention to the road ahead. Her jeep lurched, and the pavement slipped out from under her. She was hydroplaning! She fought the urge to slam on her brakes and eased her foot off the accelerator. She fought to keep the wheel straight. Panic ripped through her when the truck jarred her jeep. It had bumped into her! She gripped the steering wheel, her body stiff. Before she could question whether the hit was accidental, it hit her again, this time sending the back of her jeep sliding sideways.

"Get off my bumper!" she yelled, as if the person behind the two menacing headlights could hear her. She forgot about the wet pavement and sped faster and faster down the curvy road, trying to get away from the truck that stuck to her like a magnet.

Lightning flashed overhead, and the steady drizzle turned into sheets of rain that pelted like golf balls. Sydney's heart beat so fast that she thought it would jump out of her chest. Her temples throbbed in sequence. She thought her back wheels would surely go off the road with every swerve that she made. Then it happened. The vehicle raced around, cutting so close in front of her that she ran off into the shoulder of the road. She could see the tail lights as it sped away into the darkness.

Sydney's whole body was trembling. She would never know for sure but thought it was the same beat-up Chevy she'd seen at The Jam Session.

"The lip of truth shall be established forever:
but a lying tongue is but for a moment."
—Proverbs 12:19

chapter thirty-one

Sydney stared past the mountain of paperwork on her desk. She had a ton of work to do and hadn't been able to concentrate on any of it. Last night's incident was still too fresh on her mind, and she kept seeing the tail lights of the beat-up Chevy racing off in the rain. She'd almost called the police but decided against it. What good would it do? She'd called them after Avery's journal was stolen, and all they did was put her through the third degree, making her feel like she was the one to blame—or worse: crazy. She conjured up a picture of the young officer with the pasty face and crew cut. She could hear him now. There would be a hint of condescension in his voice and a look of pity in his eyes. "Let me get this straight, Miss Lassiter. Are you telling me that a truck nudged your bumper and caused you to run off the road? Are you sure you didn't just run off the road on your own? After all, it was raining pretty hard last night and you were going awfully fast down the mountain." She shook her head and massaged her neck. No, she wouldn't call the police.

She turned her chair toward the window. The mishmash of fall colors outside would have been a feast for the eyes on another occasion. She watched a gust of wind send a pile of leaves spiraling in the air. Spiraling. That's what her thoughts were doing. Who had been driving that truck? And why? Why did he race around her? Whoever it was was toying with her. Otherwise, he would have stuck around long enough to try and cause her to have a serious accident. She shuddered. Or a fatal accident. There were so many unanswered questions. Was this attack initiated by Lewis? Or did it have to do with her suspicion of drug use at the mill? Maybe she was being attacked by the person who stole the journal. She was a blind sitting duck.

The ringing of her phone brought her to the present. Barb's voice sounded in the speaker. "Sydney, Louellen's on line one."

"Thanks, Barb." Sydney reached for the phone. "Hello?"

"Sydney, I'm sorry to bother you."

"What can I do for you?"

"It's about Hazel."

Sydney straightened in her chair. "Is she all right?"

"Her cat has climbed up in a tree, and we can't get it to come down. She keeps saying, 'Call Sydney. She'll know what to do.'"

Sydney rubbed her forehead. "Have you tried opening a can of tuna and putting it at the bottom of the tree?"

"Would you believe? We have. We've tried everything short of calling the fire department."

Sydney glanced at her watch—4:30. "Okay, I'll be there in a few minutes."

"Thanks so much."

The first thing Sydney saw when she pulled in her driveway was Hazel, wringing her hands. She hopped out of the jeep. "I'll be right over," she said to Louellen. "Let me put on a pair of sweats."

When Sydney came out, Hazel was walking circles around the tree. "Sydney will know what to do. She can get Dixie down," she kept repeating. When she saw Sydney coming across the yard, she ran and threw her arms around her. "Please get Dixie down for me, Sydney."

Sydney smiled, trying to release herself from the tight embrace. "It's going to be okay. I promise. I'll get her."

"I'm sorry we don't have a ladder," Louellen said, managing a weak smile, but her eyes were strained and Sydney guessed she was at her wits end.

Sydney grabbed the lowest branch and heaved herself up. "Not a problem." She nimbly climbed higher toward Dixie. "Here kitty, kitty. Come here, Dixie."

Dixie was hunkered down on the very edge of one of the top branches and had no intention of moving. From the looks of her, holding on for dear life, she figured Dixie was as terrified at the situation as Hazel was. She'd have to climb to the very top to retrieve her.

A few minutes later, Sydney descended from the tree and handed Hazel her cat. She watched Hazel bury her nose in the Dixie's orange fur, hugging her like she was a long-lost family member. Maybe she hadn't accomplished what she wanted to by coming to Stoney Creek, but she'd definitely made a difference in Hazel's life.

Louellen touched Sydney's arm. "Thank you so much."

Sydney smiled. "You're welcome," she said, surprised by the emotion that was forming a lump in her throat.

Louellen took charge. "Hazel, let's get you and Dixie inside so y'all can take a nap. Sydney, won't you come in and have something to drink?"

Sydney shrugged. "Sure."

It didn't take long for Louellen to get Hazel settled down. Afterwards, Sydney and Louellen sat in the living room. All the while Sydney tried to figure out how to broach the subject of Lewis Jackson. She liked Louellen and dreaded the reaction that her questions were sure to generate.

"You're quite the climber."

Sydney laughed. "Yes, it's a hobby of mine."

"Well, it certainly came in handy today. Thank you again."

"You're welcome."

Louellen's soft, cultured voice had a musical quality about it that was as soothing as a lullaby. "Hazel has grown attached to you, Sydney. She loves having you next door."

"The feeling's mutual." Sydney cleared her throat and placed her glass of ice water on a nearby table. "I went to the sporting goods store in Glendale the other day and ran into someone you know."

"Oh?"

Sydney cringed as she watched Louellen's eyes grow wary. "Lewis Jackson."

Except for the slight tremor in her hand when she raised the glass of water to her lips, Louellen remained the picture of composure.

"I didn't realize that you had an ex husband."

"Yes."

Louellen's short answers weren't going to make this easy. "I thought you told me that Lewis Jackson was dead."

"I'm...um, I'm not sure what you mean."

Sydney's eyes caught Louellen's and held them. "Remember the day I asked Barb about Cecil Prichard?" Sydney waited for Louellen to acknowledge her comment by at least nodding. When she didn't, Sydney continued. "Anyway, I asked Barb how to get in touch with Cecil Prichard, and you told me. That's when I asked you about Lewis. You told me he was dead."

"Did I? I don't remember saying that."

Sydney tried to keep her voice kind. "Yes, you did. Why?"

Louellen shifted in her seat. "Well, if I told you that—which I don't know why I would've—I apologize."

"Are you and Lewis on good terms?"

"Well, no..." She looked like she was about to say more but stopped. "Why are you asking me questions about Lewis? To come to think of it, why were you asking about Cecil Prichard?"

It was time to give the pat answer that no one really believed. "I'm compiling an accident trend report—"

Hazel burst into the room.

"Don't say a word, Sydney! Eyes are watching. Eyes are always watching...waiting."

A shudder slithered down Sydney's spine. Louellen jumped to her feet. "Hazel, what in the world are you talking about?" She reached for Hazel's arm, but Hazel jerked away.

"Ask Sydney." She looked at Sydney. "You know, don't you?"

Louellen looked at Sydney for an explanation, but Sydney was too shocked to do anything but nod. Louellen took Hazel by the arm again. This time she didn't protest. "Let's get you in the bed." She looked at Sydney. "I'm so sorry about Hazel's outburst. There's no telling what triggered it."

By this time, Sydney had collected her wits enough to formulate some questions. She looked at Hazel. "Whose eyes are watching? Tell me who you think it is."

Hazel's eyes darted back and forth between Louellen and Sydney. Before she could answer, Louellen intervened. "I believe Hazel's had enough excitement for one day."

Sydney's eyes met Louellen's for one long moment, and Sydney wasn't sure if Louellen was trying to protect Hazel or herself.

"Hazel's fine now. We'll see you later, Sydney."

* * * * *

A good hard jog would have been just the medicine to ease the tension from Sydney's stressful day, but when she plopped down on the couch to put on her tennis shoes, she decided that a nap was more enticing. She was weary to the bone. Her blinking answering machine caught her attention. She had two messages, and the first one was from Kendall.

"Hey, hon, it's me." She smiled. Kendall's voice was like a warm blanket. "Just wondering if you have any plans for Saturday. Don't make any. Give me a call when you get a chance." Spending a day with Kendall was just the tonic she needed. He didn't treat her like an outsider or expect anything from her that she couldn't give. Her relationship with Kendall was...she struggled to find the right word...comfortable.

The second message was from Ginger. "Hey Syd. I've got some good news. All of Sean's paperwork came back clean." She laughed. "You can rest assured that he doesn't have a criminal record. He's as clean as a whistle. By the way, according to Mark, he had a 4.0 average in college. Looks and brains! What a combination! Oh, another thing, Mark hasn't been able to get in touch with Dustin Akin, his buddy who attended Sean's high school. He has been out of town. Anyway, I'm sure that'll check out too, but I'll let you know. Be safe and call me."

Sydney deleted the message and sank into the couch. *A 4.0.* She wasn't surprised. Nothing about Sean O'Conner surprised her. Sean was fire and Kendall was comfort. Which one did she want? Comfort. *I want comfort,* she repeated and drifted off to sleep.

* * * * *

When Sydney awoke from her nap, two things hit her at once: the darkness outside and her growling stomach. She sat up on the sofa and let her mind slowly adjust to the world of the living. She must've been more tired than she thought. She looked at her clock—10:30 PM—just enough time to make a quick run to Jacks before they closed at eleven. Any other night she might be tempted to eat a bowl of cereal and go to bed and sleep until morning, but she had some work to catch up on. With one hand on the back of her neck massaging it, she stood and looked around for her briefcase. She'd been in such a hurry to get to Hazel that she'd probably left it in the jeep.

A couple of clicks to the remote on her key chain, and the back door of the jeep popped open. She reached to retrieve her briefcase, but it wasn't there. Her heart skipped a beat when she realized what she'd done. In her haste to get out of the office, she'd left it. How could she have been so careless? Since her arrival in Stoney Creek, she'd kept a meticulous record of her ongoing investigation into Avery's death. She'd recorded all of the visits that she'd made. She'd even gone so far as to include her suspicion of drug use at the mill and how it could have been the cause of some of the accidents. Eventually, she hoped to compile enough evidence to convince Walter that Avery's death was not an accident.

She ran back inside to get her purse, all thoughts of going to Jacks now forgotten. She was going to have to go to the office and get her briefcase. She couldn't run the risk of Sean or someone else getting to work before her and snooping around in her notes. Besides, the only way she would get a wink of sleep was to have the briefcase back safely in her possession.

As she drove to the sawmill, the incident with the pickup truck kept running through her mind. She looked in her rearview mirror to make sure she wasn't being followed. The road behind her was empty. Going to the sawmill by herself was probably not the wisest thing to do, but there was no other choice. Thank goodness Sean had given all the office employees a key to the building.

When she arrived at the mill, she was struck by the stillness of it. Normally, second shift would be operating, but not this week. Orders had been slow enough to prompt Sean to run only first shift. In a couple more hours, the filers would arrive to get the saws ready for the next day.

Fog was settling in the air, its invisible tentacles encircled the building and seeped dampness into the earth. She shivered and glanced up at the soft beaming haloes illuminating from the security lights on the building. It took her a minute to get the door unlocked. She stepped in and locked the door behind her. She looked around. What if she wasn't alone? What if someone followed her here? She shook off the negative thoughts and walked briskly to her office. Her briefcase was in the corner, right where she'd left it. She bent to retrieve it when lights from outside caught her attention. She stole to the window and peered out. Two trucks were leaving the premises, their headlights casting long cylindrical columns against the fog, looking like four gigantic flashlights all moving in a fluid motion.

She strained against the darkness to read her wall clock. It was now 10:45 PM. Why would trucks be leaving the mill at this time of the night? She left her office and went to the front door, all the while thinking that Sean O'Conner had better have a good explanation. As it turned out, she didn't have to wait long to ask him. She opened the door, and there he stood.

His presence took her so off guard that it sent shakes down to her knees. "Sean!"

He looked as shaken as she felt. "Sydney! What are you doing here?"

"I forgot my briefcase."

He glanced down to see her holding it. "Oh."

Her eyes grew speculative. "A more appropriate question is what are you doing here this time of the night, and where are those trucks going?"

"What're you talking about?" Before she could respond to his question, he pointed to her briefcase. "What kind of top-secret information are you carrying in that thing anyway?"

Her hand tightened around the handle. "What do you mean?"

"Well, whatever it is must be pretty important to send you rushing back here to get it in the middle of the night."

Her heart began to pound, sending a sickening clammy feeling down to her stomach. She tried to laugh, but it came out more like a choked chuckle. "My, my, Mr. O'Conner, you do have a vivid imagination. I just needed to get some work done. That's all."

He studied her face. "One of these days you're going to have to learn to trust me, Syd."

"What're you talking about?"

"I think you know."

"No, I don't have a clue. Stop playing games with me—" She stopped mid sentence. He was diverting her attention away from the trucks. "Why are you shipping lumber out this time of the night? You're not running second shift this week. Besides that, trucks don't go out at night. The whole place looked deserted when I got here, and then I saw those trucks."

His only answer was a shrug. He was standing in the doorway. She took a step toward him, her eyes glaring into his, willing him to tell her the truth. "Well?" She had him, and they both knew it.

"I had a rush order to come through this afternoon."

"Oh, really? Who?"

"That's not your concern. Sydney, I have a mill to run. If I decide to ship something out at night, it's my business. Not yours. I'm the mill manager, and you're the safety consultant. Safety is your only responsibility."

His comment stung, but she was determined to not let him know how much. "Point well taken. Now, if you'll excuse me, I'll be on my way."

His frame took up the bulk of the doorway, and he stayed where he was, blocking her way out. She clenched her teeth. "Get out of my way."

He chuckled. "Gladly. Allow me to escort you to your jeep."

She pushed past him. "Don't bother."

He tugged on her arm, and she turned to face him. Her face was flushed.

He still had her by the wrist. "Look Syd, I didn't mean—"

She jerked her arm away from his grasp. "I've had a rough day. I don't want to argue with you any longer. I'm going home to get some sleep."

"I'm sorry. I didn't mean to sound so...so—"

"Heartless? Mean? Hateful?"

A smile stole across his face. "Yeah, I guess that's what I was trying to say."

His smile caught hers and tugged at the corners of her lips. She softened.

He reached for her hand again as if it was the most natural of gestures. "We do have a fiery relationship, Syd."

Instantly, she was jolted back to Ginger's call and the thoughts it had prompted. Fire, that's what Sean was. Color warmed her cheeks. Ginger had given Sean a clean report and, despite their differences, Sean had always been fair with her. Why was she always so quick to assume that he was guilty?

Sean didn't seem to notice the turmoil going on in her mind. He was too busy looking at her disheveled hair. She had it pulled up in a pony tail, and half of it had fallen out of the holder. He reached and pushed back a strand. His nearness was magnetic, and she felt the familiar attraction swell like an unquenchable flame.

"Look at you. Your sweats have black streaks all over them. What have you been doing?"

"Climbing a tree."

He laughed. "I don't doubt it."

He leaned down, and for a moment she thought he was going to kiss her. This sent a quiver of eagerness racing down her back. She was annoyed at the disappointment she felt when he stepped back and squeezed her hand and then let it go. "I'd better let you get home." He raised an eyebrow. "Unless you'd like to go out for a late dinner?"

"At eleven o'clock at night? I don't think so."

"Come on, Syd. We could drive over to Glendale and get some Krystals. They're open all night."

Krystals was a fast food restaurant that was famous for their little square hamburgers about the size of the palm of the hand. "Don't tempt me. I like Krystals."

"We could have a Krystal eating contest."

Sydney wrinkled her nose. "No thanks. I'm a little leery about going to dinner with you after our last experience. I don't want to get mauled again in the car afterwards."

He laughed and patted his jaw. "If I'm remembering correctly, I don't think you have any problem defending yourself. Just ask my tender cheek."

She shook her head and turned to go down the steps toward her jeep. "You're impossible. I'll see you tomorrow." She stopped.

Sean came up behind her. "What's wrong?"

Parked beside her jeep was the old gray beat-up Chevy pickup she'd seen at The Jam Session, the one she suspected of running her off the road. Her knees went weak, and she struggled to keep the quiver out of her voice when she spoke. "Sean, where's your truck?" She turned to face him.

"Syd, you're trembling all over."

"Why are you driving this truck?"

"It belongs to the mill. Buck or one of the other guys usually drives it. My truck went belly up this morning so I borrowed this one until I can get mine fixed."

Her head started spinning wildly, making her feel like she was on an out of control merry-go-round. She took a step back from him and then turned to get in her jeep. Sean took her arm to steady her. "Syd, what is it?"

"Nothing. I'm just tired."

"Do you need me to drive you home?"

"No!" The word exploded out of her mouth. "No," she said again, trying to keep her voice even. She gave him a weak smile. "I'll be all right. I just need to go home and get some rest."

*   *   *   *   *

Unfortunately, rest was the one thing that wouldn't come. Sydney tossed and turned all night, wondering if it was indeed the same truck she'd seen at The Jam Session. Who had been driving it? Sean? She shook her head. Surely not. He seemed genuinely surprised at her shock. If it had been Sean, he would have anticipated her reaction, wouldn't he? Maybe he was a good enough actor to be convincing. But why? Why would Sean run her off the road? What could he possibly have to do with Avery's death? He was an outsider. He'd taken up for her when Jake accused her of being negligent on safety issues. If Sean hadn't rushed to her defense, Jake would have probably fired her. Sean could have gotten rid of her that way. He didn't need to run her off the road. She thought of something else. She'd found the device used to take meth after the incident with Jake and then confronted Sean about drug testing. Was that it? Was he trying to cover something up? No, she couldn't believe that it had been Sean.

Perhaps Sean was telling the truth. If he'd gotten the truck this morning, then someone else had been driving it last night. Who? Buck? She shivered, picturing Buck's cold, fathomless eyes. Yes, it could have been Buck. She remembered the kiln accident. Buck placed the blame on her. Buck hated her. Then there was Lewis Jackson...

Time was ticking down. Whoever it was would come after her again, and next time he might do more than push her off the road. Next time he would come gunning for her for real.

"Keep thy heart with all diligence; for out of it are the issues of life."
—Proverbs 4:23

chapter thirty-two

When Jarilyn called the next day to invite Sydney to an early dinner and to accompany her to Friday night's football game, Sydney accepted the invitation with open arms. She hoped that dinner with a friend would help restore an element of sanity to her life. Sydney and Jarilyn's friendship had been a gradual process, deepening a little more every time they were together. Jarilyn had opened up to Sydney, telling her how Reggie's father had deserted her a few months after he found out she was pregnant. She confided the struggles she had faced raising Reggie on her own. "I've lain awake many a night just praying that everything would be okay, and somehow it usually is," Jarilyn said.

Sydney divulged as little as possible about her own life. The easiest thing to do was to tell basic facts, leaving out the details. She told Jarilyn about growing up in Ft. Worth with her aunt after her parents died. There had been a few occasions when she had fought the impulse to bare her soul to Jarilyn. She knew that was impossible and left it at that.

They agreed to meet at a Mexican restaurant in Glendale. As usual, Sydney's Friday had been hectic. She'd planned on getting off work a few minutes early to give herself plenty of extra time to get to Glendale, but it didn't work out that way. Sean called a last-minute staff meeting that didn't end until 5:15. When she pulled into the parking lot of the restaurant, she was ten minutes late.

She rushed in and made her way to the table where Jarilyn was sitting. A small lantern hanging on the wall reflected an amber light on Jarilyn's chocolate skin, adding a touch of mystery to her striking features. Sydney sat down in the booth and her heart warmed when Jarilyn reached across the table and patted her hand. She had once heard that friends were like precious jewels to be cherished, and she had certainly found a jewel in Jarilyn.

"It's so good to see you, Sydney."

"I'm sorry I'm running late."

"That's okay. I just got here a few minutes ago. Fridays are always a madhouse at the bank."

Sydney chuckled. "Sounds like we had a similar day."

"What do you think about the game tonight?" Sydney picked up the menu with one hand and retrieved a chip with the other. She dipped it in salsa and popped it in her mouth. The chip was a little stale. She couldn't help but think about the Blue Mesa, one of her favorite Mexican restaurants in Ft. Worth. Some of Blue Mesa's sweet potato chips and chipotle salsa would be good right now. This little restaurant, sandwiched in a strip mall with its generic menus and glass vases of plastic flowers, couldn't hold a candle to the posh décor of the Blue Mesa. The mom and pop restaurants so prevalent in the South had their own appeal, but sometimes she missed the wide variety of restaurants in Ft. Worth.

"Reggie says we have our work cut out for us, but Coach Fletcher believes we have a good chance of winning."

"I sure hope so," Sydney said in between bites. "What're you going to have?"

"I'm thinking about getting a taco salad."

"That sounds good."

Jarilyn studied Sydney's face for a minute. "I'm so glad he has someone like you."

"Who?"

"Kendall." Jarilyn laughed and laid the menu on the table.

Sydney's eyes widened. Jarilyn had made a similar remark on the first day they met at football practice. Sydney had been tempted to ask her about it, but couldn't figure out how to phrase the question. "What do you mean?"

Jarilyn's face grew serious. "Sydney, I can't begin to explain how much Kendall means to Reggie and me. He's been like a brother and a father to Reggie—all rolled in one. He's a wonderful role model. Sometimes I think he's Reggie's salvation. I shudder when I think about all the things Reggie could be doing other than playing football. I want the best for Kendall, and I think you're the best—not like that other woman he was dating."

"What woman was that?" Sydney pretended to read the menu to avoid making eye contact.

"That Jessica woman. She dropped him like a hot potato the minute that fancy friend of yours came to town. Kendall took it pretty hard, too. He was just another notch on her belt. But this time I think she's met her match. From what I hear, that guy's a player like Jessica. He dates lots of pretty women."

Sydney's face grew warm. Even though Jarilyn wasn't saying as much, Sydney knew she was remembering the time Sean sat with her during one of the football games. Was this Jarilyn's way of warning her about Sean?

"All I've got to say is that Jessica may be in for a big upset with this one, and it would serve her right."

Sydney put down the menu and tried to erase the images of Sean with Jessica and then Kendall with Jessica that were flip-flopping back and forth like a yoyo. "We'd better order or we'll be late for the game."

*　*　*　*　*

"Close your eyes. We're almost there."

Sydney raised an eyebrow at Kendall and shook her head. "The last time I closed my eyes, we ended up out in the middle of nowhere at a rooster fight."

"Please, just close your eyes."

Sydney sighed. "Okay." Ever since Kendall had picked her up this afternoon, he'd been secretive about their destination. When she prodded him, he gave her his famous boyish grin, the one that melted her heart.

"Okay, we're here. You can open them now."

She smiled at the open excitement in Kendall's voice. It was hard to believe this was the same man whose face had been as hard as flint as he led his team to victory the night before. Kendall was an enigma with more layers than an onion, and she wondered if she would ever be able to fully understand him.

Sydney opened her eyes and then widened them in surprise. Tall pine trees surrounded a log cabin overlooking a scenic part of the Tennessee River. The sparkling blue water was framed by rolling mountains in the distance. A thick carpet of pine needles cushioned her step when she got out of the truck.

"Who lives here?"

"I do when I'm not staying at the house with Emma and Mom." There was a touch of pride in his voice.

"Kendall—wow! This is incredible. When did you buy it?"

Kendall looked down at the ground. "I built it myself with one of those pre-fab kits, but I've put a lot of extras into it. Come on inside and I'll show you around." He took her hand and led her up the steps.

When they reached the door, he surprised her by giving her a long kiss that melted through her like warm chocolate. "Welcome to my own little part of heaven," he said, opening the door.

"That it is," she said, mostly to herself as she stepped inside. The floor was covered with wide cherry planks. A stacked stone fireplace took up the bulk of one wall. Sydney walked over and ran her fingers over the grainy hearth that had been formed from a split log. It was definitely a man's place, complete with a deer head mounted over the mantel and rifles propped in the corner, but it had a cozy feel about it too. Pillows with a woven Indian design of rich, vibrant colors were heaped haphazardly on the dark leather sofa and chairs.

Kendall came up behind her and encircled his arms around her waist. His lips brushed against her neck, sending a thousand tiny shivers rippling down her spine. "Why don't you relax, and I'll bring in some wood and make us a fire."

"Sounds good to me."

A few minutes later, Sydney and Kendall settled down on the sofa. She snuggled close to him and watched the flames lick hungrily at the logs, their movement reflecting colors of yellow, blue, and red on the polished wooden floor. Kendall was full of surprises. When he had told her he wanted to show her something, she had no idea he was taking her to a log cabin on the lake. A cabin he had practically built single-handedly. It felt right to be here in this setting with Kendall. It helped take her mind off of her problems—and off of Sean.

He looked over at her and grinned. "What's going through that pretty head of yours?"

There was no way she was going to tell him that she had been thinking about Sean. "Oh, I was just thinking how relaxed I feel."

"Well, don't get too comfortable. I'm hungry." Kendall laughed and started tickling her.

"Kendall, stop," she begged as she tried to get away from him. Before she could make her escape, he pulled her closer and covered her lips with his. A feeling of deep affection and security flooded her. Reluctantly, he released her. "Okay, I'll let you go if you promise to get the food ready while I stoke the fire and bring in a couple more logs."

"It's a deal."

Sydney took stock of the well-furnished kitchen. A few minutes later she had their plates piled with the barbecue they had picked up on the way out of town. She rummaged through the cabinets and found some packs of hot chocolate and a bag of potato chips. She reached for the kettle on the stove and filled it with water and then placed it on the burner.

Kendall came up behind her and grabbed her around the waist. He pulled her close and buried his nose in her neck.

"I thought you said you were hungry." Sydney laughed and untangled his arms.

"It's spittin' snow outside," he said, releasing her and grabbing a handful of chips.

"You're kidding. This early in the fall?"

"If you don't believe me come and look."

She moved to the window and looked out at the flurrying snow. The scene outside made her glad that she was in the warmth of the cozy cabin with Kendall.

After they finished dinner, Sydney looked at her watch. "You know, we've got to get back to town. I have a lot to do before I go to work on Monday."

"You worry too much. Just relax and enjoy yourself. You'll have plenty of time tomorrow to work, and besides, they were running that mill long before you got there." She'd heard that before. She changed the course of the conversation as she began clearing the table. "Kendall, this cabin—it's so fantastic. I'm surprised you don't live here all the time."

He shrugged. "I've considered it, but it's out of the way. I like being close to the school, and I enjoy the company of Mom and Emma."

"I can't believe I've known you all this time and didn't realize you had this cabin."

"There are only a few people who know about this place."

"I saw a four-wheeler parked outside, and then there's the fishing boat in the shed. Does all of that belong to you?"

He smiled and got up from the table. "Yes, all of that belongs to me. I come up here whenever I get a chance. I like my privacy, that's all."

Kendall came around the table and took the plate out of Sydney's hand. His lips brushed the side of her face.

"We've got to go," she whispered.

"Okay, if we really have to. I'll put out the fire if you'll take care of the kitchen."

* * * * *

Sydney hummed while cleaning the kitchen. It felt so right to be here. So comfortable. "Where are the trash bags?" she yelled, but there was no answer. After waiting for a couple of minutes, she decided to search for them herself. She looked through all the cabinets and came up empty-handed. That's when she saw the door off the kitchen. It was a laundry room with deep cabinets above the washer and dryer. She opened the first cabinet and saw only cleaning supplies and several bottles of iodine—no plastic bags. She proceeded to the next cabinet and found the garbage bags. The box was beside two other large boxes—no, not boxes, but cases of...allergy medicine? Why would Kendall need two whole cases of allergy medicine? Each case looked like it contained at least fifty boxes of medicine. And what was this? There was something pushed back behind one of the boxes. She reached and pulled out a framed picture of Kendall and Jessica. The picture, taken in front of the cabin, had obviously been taken by Kendall. Part of his arm had been caught in the picture, like he'd been holding the camera at arm's length. He and Jessica had their heads together, and Kendall looked so...She couldn't even bring herself to think it, but it was there. There was no denying it. The look on Kendall's face was one of perfect contentment. Jarilyn's words seared her mind. Jessica had been here with Kendall. She'd dumped Kendall for Sean. Did Kendall still have feelings for her? She thought back to the night they'd gone to Jessica's house for dinner and remembered the warmth that came into Kendall's voice when he talked about how well she could cook. Jessica and Kendall...Jessica and Sean. It was too much to take.

"What are you doing in here?"

She jumped as Kendall came in the door. His eyes

flickered first to the open cabinet and then to the picture in her hand. What was it about his eyes? There were always so warm and expressive. Now they were cold hard marbles and all she could see in them was her own startled reflection, cowering back. A chill came over her. She looked down at the picture that now felt as heavy as lead in her hand.

"I was looking for the garbage bags. I didn't mean to snoop. I accidentally came across...Kendall, I didn't know that you have allergies."

Kendall's face remained unreadable. She felt very small, standing there holding the picture, and then her anger took over. She thrust the picture in his hands, grabbed a garbage bag, and brushed past him. Kendall had invited her here. She'd stumbled upon the picture accidentally. She had no reason to feel ashamed.

Sydney went back to the kitchen and started shoving the remains of dinner into the garbage bag. Kendall followed her. He watched for a second and then reached and took the bag from her. He looked directly in her face. "I'm sorry you had to come across that picture. I would've told you about Jessica. It's just that—um, well, I didn't think it was that important. That's all in the past—over now." He reached and touched a strand of her hair. "You have to know how I feel about you."

She stood staring at him while his eyes pleaded with hers for understanding. "I'm sorry I reacted that way," she said. "It was that look in your eyes. You acted so furious when you came through the door, like I'd done something terrible. I couldn't understand why you would react that way unless you still..." The words got caught in her throat, and she forced them out. "Unless you still have feelings for her."

Kendall leaned back against the cabinet. Splotches of red were forming on his neck and moving up to his face. Her candor was obviously making him uncomfortable. "I guess I'll always have a special feeling for Jess."

Sydney's throat went as dry as sandpaper.

"She's been a part of my life for so long..." He paused to find the right words. "Jess and I were engaged. Two months before our wedding, she broke it off."

Sydney's heart sank. What had Jessica said? The mocking words tore through her mind with brutal force. "I broke Kendall's heart."

"It wasn't until you came along that I even felt attracted to anyone else. Now I hardly even think of her anymore."

Hardly? What was that supposed to mean? She looked up and realized that he was smiling tenderly at her. She forced herself to smile back.

"Let's just take things one step at a time," he was saying. "Give it some time. See what happens."

Wasn't she just congratulating herself on being able to put Sean out of her mind for a few hours? How could she fault Kendall for harboring past feelings for Jessica? She nodded.

"That's my girl." He took her in his arms.

But for her the matter wasn't settled—not by a long shot.

* * * * *

The idea for the Helping Hands Organization didn't come to Sydney all at once. Like bits and pieces of an almost forgotten dream, the fragments shifted in the kaleidoscope of her mind until suddenly, it all became clear. No doubt the late-night talks with Stella had been part of the catalyst that prompted her decision. But that wasn't all. It was more than that. It was her past and present all welded together—a way to help ease that sinister shadow of guilt that was always right on her heels, the one she never could outrun. No matter where she went or what she did, it was always there. She could have traveled to the end of the earth and back and it wouldn't have made a bit of difference, for how could she escape herself?

At night in her dreams, she was on the boat,

checking the bilge. No matter how hard she tried, she could never plug up the leaks. Some nights she would wake up, choking on the toxic poisons that were filling the cabin of the boat. Other nights it was the searing heat from the explosion that jarred her awake, leaving her lying on her bed, gasping for air like a limp fish discarded on dry land.

Maybe there was nothing on earth strong enough to erase the hurt of the past, but as long as there was breath in her lungs, she had to continue to try. If she could help others, then just maybe she could find a shred of hope for herself. When the idea for Helping Hands came, it was like a ray of fresh sunlight that dissipated the gloom. She was so excited that she wanted to share it with someone. She told Stella and Ginger first. Stella was pleased and offered her help. Ginger was surprised and had a slew of questions about the particulars. Sydney tried to share her plan with Kendall, but he was too preoccupied with football to pay much attention, so she dropped it.

She almost talked to Sean about it but changed her mind at the last minute. The crux of the matter was that Sean would have probably really listened and talked to her about it. A vague fear was beginning to form in the back of Sydney's mind, and she kept hearing Sean's remark about Kendall wanting a trophy girlfriend. She and Kendall never talked about anything of substance. Whenever she tried to take their conversation to a more serious level, Kendall either clammed up or changed the subject. Sean, on the other hand, was very easy to talk to—too easy. She knew that any relationship with Sean would end up like her relationship with Adam—a dead end. Why then was she still so attracted to him? Sometimes it seemed that all Sean had to do was look at her to know what she was thinking. Kendall was the one she wanted to build a relationship with. There were so many things she admired about Kendall—his goodness, his integrity. How come Kendall didn't understand her any more than she understood him?

All of these thoughts kept running through Sydney's mind as she drove to Tuesday Phillips' house. Sydney had called Tuesday and told her about the idea for Helping Hands. "It's really a simple concept," she said. "I want to start an organization that helps people in the community. We can start by providing the basics like food and clothing. I would like to get donations from private individuals to help fund it." She didn't mention the fact that she had enough of her own money to buy a building and get the organization off the ground ten times over.

Tuesday was quiet for a moment. "I want to help," she finally said.

A smile tugged at the corners of Sydney's lips. "I was hoping you'd say that because I'd like for you to help run it."

There was a gasp on the other side of the phone and then a chuckle. "Tell me what you have in mind."

"I thought we'd start by helping the Nolan family."

Tuesday was waiting on her front porch when Sydney pulled into the driveway. When she got in the jeep, Tuesday reached in her purse and retrieved slips of paper with the children's sizes scrawled on them. "Are you ready to do some shopping?"

Sydney smiled. "No time like the present."

*   *   *   *   *

A few hours later, Sydney and Tuesday pulled up in front of the Nolan's trailer with their goods. The weather had turned unseasonably warm for fall, making Sydney regret her decision to wear a sweater. They had debated about whether or not they should drop off the clothes anonymously or deliver them in person. They decided on the latter. Sydney got of the jeep and a knot formed in her stomach. The rusty blue trailer was braced up on concrete blocks that looked about as flimsy as toothpicks. Someone had attempted to attach an aluminum piece of underpinning around the bottom, but had given up halfway through the task. The piece that was still hanging was bent up on one side, reminding Sydney of a metal can that had been chewed open with a can opener. A layer of brown leaves covered the yard that was littered with a junk car, bicycles, and toys. An overall sense of decay pervaded the place, and Sydney wondered how much longer the old trailer would hold together. She glanced at her companion. Tuesday looked tired from all the shopping, but her chin was set with determination. "I'm tellin' you, this little family needs all the help they can get. It's a sad situation."

"Yes, it is," Sydney agreed grimly.

Sydney and Tuesday went around the back of the jeep to retrieve the clothes and toys they'd placed in cardboard boxes.

"Maybe we should've called them first to let them know we're coming."

Tuesday shook her head. "No, it'll be all right." She approached the door with Sydney following close behind. It took a couple of knocks to get a response. Finally, one of the girls opened the door. When she saw Tuesday and Sydney, she gave them a shy smile, then turned and yelled into the house.

"Mama, Sister Phillips is here."

This news caused an explosion of activity to erupt in the house as the younger ones started running around the living room and jumping on and off the furniture.

"Tell her to come on in. I'll be right there," yelled a voice from the back.

Not surprisingly, the inside of the house was the perfect match to the outside with its shabby furniture crowded into the small room. The trailer would have been a cramped living quarter for a family of three or four, much less a family of seven. Two metal butterflies were hanging on the wall, surrounded by varying sizes of family photos. Lace curtains, yellow with age, were half hanging on the windows.

"Look," one of the younger boys said, his eyes shining with excitement, "they brought us presents."

The children gathered around while Tuesday dispersed gifts.

Patsy Nolan came into the room. She looked at Sydney's designer sweater and jeans. They were a stark contrast to Patsy's baggy sweat pants and stained T-shirt. When Patsy reached and pushed back a strand of her dark hair that was streaked with gray, Sydney had the urge to jump up and throw her arms around the woman. The last thing she wanted was for Patsy to be ashamed. *I may look all put together on the outside, Sydney thought, but goodness knows I've got enough problems within to make up for it.*

Tuesday did the introductions. "Patsy, this is a good friend of mine, Sydney Lassiter. She goes to church with us."

Patsy's face colored and she looked at the floor. "I don't get out to church much no more 'cause of work."

Tuesday nodded in understanding.

Patsy extended her hand and smiled tentatively. "It's nice to meet you, Sydney." She looked at Tuesday and motioned at the boxes. It might have been Christmas morning in the small home as the children searched through the items, their faces beaming. Patsy sat down on the sofa. "These clothes and toys—well, how nice...I just don't think I can accept."

Tuesday interrupted her. "Nonsense. Well, of course you can, honey. You shore can." The words were spoken with such complete authority that it would have been impossible for Patsy to refuse. Tuesday reached and patted Patsy's hand.

In that moment Sydney knew for a certainty that forming Helping Hands was the right thing to do. She also knew that Tuesday Phillips was indeed the perfect person to run it.

"All of this stuff...there's so much. I don't know how I can possibly thank you."

"Don't thank me. I didn't do it. Sydney did," Tuesday said.

Sydney's face turned as red as her sweater.

"Thank you," Patsy said. Her eyes met Sydney's.

"You're welcome," Sydney said.

A thought struck Sydney. Where was the oldest daughter? The one who asked to take home the peanut butter and jelly sandwiches? She wasn't among the children. No sooner had the thought crossed her mind than she looked up to see the girl standing in the doorway, watching her happy siblings. Sydney smiled, and she smiled back shyly. Sydney motioned for her to come and sit down beside her.

"What's your name?"

"Brenda," the girl said so softly that Sydney had to strain to hear her.

"Brenda, I'm Sydney. Let's see, I believe there's something here for you too." She bent over one of the boxes and retrieved a turtleneck sweater and pair of jeans.

Brenda didn't say anything at first. She just held the clothes in her lap and rubbed her hand over the sweater. Then, to Sydney's surprise, Brenda hugged her. That's when something totally unexpected happened. A warm feeling of peace flooded over Sydney, and she marveled at it. Peace. It was the one thing she sought after the most—the thing that always eluded her. And here it was, a gift straight out of the blue when she least expected it.

*   *   *   *   *

Patsy and the children stood by the front door and waved goodbye to Sydney and Tuesday. Looking at the family, huddled on the porch of the trailer, Sydney thought again how unfair it was that she had everything and these people had nothing. But as she and Tuesday drove away, Sydney saw Patsy hug Brenda. Brenda rewarded her mother with a brilliant smile that showed so much love, it filled Sydney with a bittersweet longing, and she knew that it was really the opposite. The Nolan family was the one that had everything because they had what mattered. They had each other, and all the money in the world couldn't buy that.

Sydney and Tuesday drove in silence until Tuesday spoke. "You done a good thing here tonight."

"I'm just glad I could be of some help."

"Oh, you were. That's for shore. You know, there are some people in this world who say that money cain't buy happiness."

It was like Tuesday had read her mind. "That's for sure."

"I said that's what some people say. I didn't say I agree."

Where was this conversation going?

"Well if you ask me, I say those people who believe money don't buy happiness just don't know where to shop. Look at the happiness you brung that family tonight. It just goes to prove that money can be very useful...in the right hands."

"Yes, I suppose you're right."

"Absolutely."

* * * * *

They drove in silence again and Tuesday began chewing her lip. "I've been thinking about that first time you came to visit me and the questions you were asking."

Sydney was silent for a moment. "Yes?"

"Well somethin's been gnawing at me." Tuesday paused and shifted in her seat. "Well, I ain't quite shore how to tell you this 'cause I don't wanna sound crazy."

"Just tell me."

"All right it's like this. Ever since I first met you, I had this feeling, like you're in danger."

Sydney's eyes went round. "What kind of danger?"

Tuesday blew out a breath. "That's just it. I don't know. I keep trying to figure it out. It's just a feeling. That's all."

"You told me that Buford was mixed up with some shady men at the mill. Do you remember a man by the name of Lewis Jackson?"

"That name don't ring no bell. I'm sorry. It's been too long." She stared out the window into the blackness. "There is something else."

"What?"

Tuesday began turning her wedding band on her finger. "I probably shouldn't even say nothing 'cause I don't know exactly. What I mean is that the other night I dreamed about that tune that one of the men was always whistling—like to have drove Buford crazy."

"Which man? What song?"

Tuesday scratched her head. "I can't remember. Oh, I shouldn't have said nothing about it. It's probably nothing." She paused. "It's caught on the edge of my mind, and I just can't get my hands on it."

"If it comes to you, will you tell me?"

"Sure. Look Sydney, I don't know why you're so concerned about the past, but I know there's a lot more to all this than you're telling me. Am I right?"

Sydney's silence was a confirmation.

"Anyways, I guess you have your reasons for keeping quiet, but I feel impressed to tell you that whatever it is you're running from, you're gonna have to face it sooner or later. That's the only way you're gonna be able to go on."

The truth of Tuesday's words hit Sydney like a landslide. It was almost exactly what Stella had told her. But how could Tuesday have known?

"I know what you're thinking: that I'm rattling on like a crazy woman. Maybe I am, and maybe I don't know what I'm talking about. It's just a gut feeling I have. That's all."

Peace vanished when the all-too-familiar sick dread settled over her. She swallowed hard. "My life is just really complicated. I have all these different things pulling at me, and I'm not sure which direction to take."

"You have to listen to your heart."

Weren't those almost the exact words Ginger and Stella had used? Sydney tried to keep her voice even. "What do you mean?"

"Well, I'd say you done a pretty good job of listening to your heart today."

Sydney had never thought about it that way. She'd always associated listening to her heart with getting to the bottom of Avery's death. But she'd listened to that inner voice when it prompted her to help and had felt peace. Was it possible that the same feeling that had prompted her to help the Nolans and Hazel was the same one that kept urging her to get to the bottom of Avery's death?

"You have to learn to shut out all them outside voices that are coming at you and go to that inner place inside your heart." Tuesday balled up her fist and placed it over the center of her chest. She paused. "If you'll learn to listen, and I mean if you'll learn to *really* listen, you won't never go wrong."

Sydney thought about this for a moment. Tuesday's words were coming at her so fast that she couldn't sort through it all right now. She was filing each word away so she could ponder over them at her own pace.

"Just promise me you'll be careful."

Sydney looked at her. "What?"

"Whatever it is you're dealing with is very serious. Please be careful."

"I will." Sydney paused. "And will you please promise me that if you remember anything you'll let me know?"

"I give you my word on it."

*   *   *   *   *

Sleep didn't come easy for Sydney that night. In the blackness of night, her fears rose to a fevered pitch, and she was helpless against them. She kept thinking about Tuesday's warning and the truck that ran her off the road. Tuesday was right. Danger was so close that she could feel its sick tentacles twisting in so tight that she felt like she would smother. Tuesday's advice to face the fear and stop running was almost word for word what Stella told her. The cemetery loomed like a dagger, hanging by a silk thread. She had to visit the cemetery and look those graves straight in the eye so she could put it all behind her. There was no getting around it.

Tomorrow—I'll go tomorrow, she promised herself. She buried her head in her pillow and tried to get some sleep.

"My heart panteth, my strength faileth me;
As far as the light of mine eyes, it also is gone from me."
—Psalm 38:10

chapter thirty-three

Sydney had visited the cemetery for years in her mind. She gripped the steering wheel, barely aware of the dampness that oozed from the palms of her hands. She was thankful for her five-speed as she shifted to a lower gear while driving up the steep winding road. The weather was warm—too warm for the time of year. It was stuffy in the jeep, and she rolled down the window. There was an uncanny calm in the air, almost like the sky was holding its breath. The calm before the storm. Dark clouds were gathering overhead, letting her know she didn't have much time before the bottom fell out.

Half a mile off the main road, the cemetery came into full view, perched on the hill, just as she remembered. She stopped in front of the old rusted sign that read *New Prospect Cemetery*. Any other time she might've found it amusing. Why in the world would anyone name a cemetery *New Prospect*?

Huge magnolia trees stood as sentinels for the hundreds of tombstones dotting the landscape. Sprigs of artificial flowers threaded a crazy quilt pattern over the graves. Five or six graves were surrounded by wooden fences. A heap of old discarded flowers lay at the edge of the cemetery.

Sydney parked the jeep in the vicinity she remembered. She reached for the flowers that would be her small tribute to her parents. A dozen yellow roses for Susan and a single red rose for Avery.

She walked among the tombstones, trying to avoid stepping on any of the graves. She'd been afraid of cemeteries when she was a young child. When she'd thought of cemeteries, she pictured the ghosts and goblins of Halloween that rested under the black tombstones labeled R.I.P. They lurked there, waiting to spring back to life at the first light of the full moon. She'd been so young and innocent, so unprepared for what lay ahead. She couldn't possibly have imagined then that her beloved parents would be among the buried dead. Now she would give anything if they would suddenly spring back to life.

Images of her last visit to this cemetery floated in her mind like actors across a stage. It had been a beautiful sunny day. She could hear Judith, urging Avery to get into the car. The passage of time had been a buffer to the pain. Here, in this place, time reversed itself. She might have been sixteen all over again.

The roar of thunder jolted her and propelled her feet forward. It was getting dark fast, and she would have to hurry before the approaching storm made it impossible to find their graves.

She walked to the location she remembered and hunted for their names but couldn't find them. Where were they? The trees seemed to come alive. The heavy branches swayed and twisted in the air that was building momentum by the minute. She picked her way through the headstones, desperately searching to find them. A few minutes later, she stopped, realizing that she'd made a full circle, and they were nowhere to be found. She looked up at the clouds and felt the first drops of rain. She surveyed the cemetery again, and then she spotted them, a mere four feet from where she'd first begun her search. She had walked right past them.

There was one large tombstone for the both of them. On one side were the words Avery McClain, Beloved Husband and Father. On the other side of the tombstone was written Susan McClain, Beloved Wife and Mother. Across the bottom was an inscription. "Earth holds no sorrows that cannot be healed in Heaven."

Tears fell down her face, matching the heavy drops of rain that were now pouring like a waterfall from the sky. She carefully placed the flowers on their graves. Never before had she felt so completely and totally alone. Susan's face flashed in her mind. She saw it transform right before her very eyes from vibrant to a sickly pallor of death. Then the explosion, its searing heat, destroying everything in its wake. Pain, the dreaded familiar pain, throbbed in her thigh and she saw Avery. It was too much. Her grief rose from the shadows and became a living thing that was so terrible in its majesty that she feared it would devour her very soul. She cried out in anguish, the emptiness enveloping her like a shroud. The hollow echo of the wind rushing through the trees was her only answer. She saw herself returning home to an empty house after her mother's funeral, remembered the terrible loss of losing her dad and not being able to attend his funeral, felt again the pain of not being able to return home after the accident.

She fell to the earth and wept. A voice penetrated through the blackness in her mind. It rose like a gentle wave, enveloping the pain. Ginger's words: "You never have to be alone again. The Lord will always be there for you."

She clung to those words and knelt between her parents' graves, ignoring the rain soaking her clothes. Her anguished prayer spiraled to heaven. "Please Lord, where are you now? Be with me now. I need—"

Lightning split a nearby tree. She jumped to her feet and ran toward the jeep, her feet making a soft suction in the wet earth. Her body trembled. Somehow she managed to get in and start the engine. Rain was coming down so hard that she had to inch her way to the main road. Branches were scattered everywhere. Sydney strained to see the meager path that her headlights were creating. She could barely make out the road up ahead. It was like none of this was real. Her body was going through the motions while her mind was caught in some black tunnel.

"Stop!" A man was standing in the middle of the road, waving his arms. Sydney hit her breaks and skidded a few feet. A flash of lightning lit the sky, and she noticed that a power line had fallen behind where the man was standing.

He walked over to the jeep. "What are you doing here?"

It took her a minute to convince herself that he was real and not some figment of her messed up mind. "Kendall?"

"Sydney, what are you doing?"

"I was taking a drive and got caught in the storm." She was thankful that she was soaked from head to toe so that Kendall wouldn't be able to tell she'd been crying.

"How did you get so wet?"

"What has happened?" Sydney asked, ignoring his remark.

"A tornado touched down, and the volunteer firefighters have been called in to help." Kendall's eyes studied her face. "Are you all right?"

"Yes, I'm okay. Was anyone hurt?"

"Part of the roof blew off the Malone place, and Betty got cut on her leg, but she's going to be okay. I don't think anyone was seriously hurt."

"That's good to hear."

Kendall was still studying her.

"Are the roads passable? Can I get home?"

"Yeah, you'll have to take a detour." He pointed. "If you take a left on Cooper, it'll take you back to the main road."

"Good, it's been a long day."

He put his hand on her arm. "Sydney, what's going on?"

She shook her head. "I'm okay. Just tired." She gave him a weak smile. "Call me when you get home."

"Of course." He leaned in and cupped her chin with his hand. He searched her face with those soft eyes of his until she felt like she would melt. He moved his hand under her hair to encircle the nape of her neck. Ever so softly, his lips came to hers. The tenderness in his touch was almost overwhelming. After a moment he pulled away and brushed a strand of hair from her face. "I won't ask you any questions until you're ready to answer them. Okay?"

She nodded, not quite ready to let go of the warmth they shared. He was here, right when she'd needed someone the most. He couldn't begin to understand what that meant to her.

"We'll talk when you're ready."

She smiled. "Okay."

"It's a rough night, and I've got to help or I would go with you right now to make sure you get home safe and sound. Promise you'll be careful?"

"I will."

* * * * *

Kendall watched Sydney drive away. He noticed her tires were caked with mud. The road she came out of was a dead end, leading to only one place: the cemetery. In two swift strides he walked to the company of fire fighters. "Guys, I'll be back in a few minutes. I need to take a look at something."

Kendall scoured the cemetery with his flashlight. No signs of life—only the grotesque shadows of wet tombstones. Was this where she'd come from? He searched until he found what he was looking for—the muddy tracks where she had parked her jeep. He followed the soft indention of footprints until he stood in the exact spot Sydney had stood earlier. There in front of him were two graves. He looked down at the fresh flowers, falling limp in the rain. On the tombstone was the inscription "Earth holds no sorrows that cannot be healed in Heaven." For a moment he forgot about Sydney and thought about his own dad who was buried a mere hundred yards from where he stood.

"As vinegar to the teeth, and as smoke to the eyes,
So is the sluggard to them that send him."
—Proverbs 10:26

chapter thirty-four

The storm from the night before left a steady drizzle in its wake. Sydney didn't mind the rain. Its steady rhythm acted as a cleansing agent that eased the hurt from the previous day. Going to the cemetery had been one of the hardest things she'd ever done, but she'd come away with a small victory. She'd faced it and survived.

Kendall called to check on her just as he said he would. She'd been afraid that he would press her but he didn't. He seemed to understand that she needed her space. The mere sound of his voice was the perfect salve for her raw nerves. So much so that after their conversation, she went to bed and slept soundly for the first time in weeks.

It was so dark and foggy when she left her house this morning that she felt like she was leaving for work in the middle of the night. She pulled into the sawmill and opened the door of her jeep, struggling against the rain to open her umbrella. She grabbed her purse and briefcase and pulled her pale blue raincoat tightly around her. The coat and matching umbrella had been gifts from Judith. The raincoat wasn't her style, and it had taken a few months before she decided she liked it enough to wear. She was grateful to have it today.

The office would not be open for another hour. She'd arrived early to get a head start on her day. She frowned when she saw Sean's truck. She was hoping to get there before him. He got to work so early that she'd only managed to beat him twice. It gave her great pleasure to see him so aggravated over it. Too bad she hadn't beaten him today.

She huddled under the protectiveness of the umbrella while walking to the office. She ascended the stairs and opened the door leading to the screen porch. A dark figure stepped out of the shadows. At first she assumed it was one of the sawmill workers who had forgotten either his earplugs or hard hat, but then she didn't recognize him.

"Good morning. May I help you?" she asked, getting a closer look at the man. He was wearing overalls, and his long stringy hair was matted to his head, partially covering his unshaved face.

Rather than answering, the man smiled, revealing a huge gap between his two front teeth. Sydney gasped when she saw the glint of metal and realized he was holding a switch-blade knife. He was using it to clean his fingernails.

The man took another step in her direction, blocking her entrance into the office. She took a step back and lifted her umbrella and pointed the metal end toward him.

"What do you want?"

He loomed even closer and pointed the knife in her direction. "I want you to stop meddlin'. That's what I want. You need to go back to where you come from. Your guard dog won't be around forever to protect you."

The man pushed past her and darted down the steps and into the darkness.

*   *   *   *   *

Sydney's hands shook uncontrollably and she fumbled to open the door. After she managed to get inside, she dropped her briefcase on her office floor and headed to the restroom. Her stomach turned summersaults.

Guard dog? What did the man mean by that? What guard dog? Was there someone looking out for her that she didn't know about? Was it Walter?

She didn't know how much time had lapsed before she heard someone in the hall.

"Syd, is that you in there? Are you all right?" Sean's voice boomed from the other side of the door.

"Yeah, I'm in here. I'll be out in a minute." Sydney splashed cold water on her face and blotted it dry.

Sean was waiting for her when she came out. "You're white as a sheet. What's wrong? Are you sick?"

Sydney shook her head and walked past him to her office where she sat down behind her desk. Her stomach was still lurching, but it was more than nausea. It was a gut-wrenching feeling that cut clear to the bone.

Sean sat in one the chairs in front of her desk. He studied her face. "What's going on?"

His eyes met hers and held them until she looked away. What good would it do to tell Sean? What good would it do to call the police? She couldn't tell them about Avery. She couldn't tell them who she really was.

Sean closed the door. "Syd, something happened to you, and I need to know what it was."

She had to tell somebody. "I was threatened this morning on the porch outside the office by a man holding a switch blade." Her explanation sounded flat and emotionless.

"What?" He came out of his chair and went around her desk and stood beside her. "By who?"

She pushed her hair away from her face. "I don't know. I've never seen him before."

"What did he look like?"

"He was a big man with stringy hair and a gap between his teeth."

"What was he wearing?"

"Overalls."

"He had a knife?"

She closed her eyes and shook her head. "He was using it to clean his fingernails."

"What did he say?"

"He told me to stop meddling and that I should go back to where I came from." She bit her lip. "He also told me that my guard dog wouldn't be around forever to protect me."

Sean's face went black at that last part. He shook his head. "This is incredible. It doesn't make any sense."

Sydney couldn't believe what she was hearing. "Are you saying you don't believe me?"

"It's not that. I just can't believe that it happened. That's all I'm saying."

"Well, believe it!"

He knelt beside her. Any other time his close proximity would have been disconcerting, but under the current circumstance, she was oblivious. "Look Syd, I promise you, I'll get to the bottom of this." His handsome face was a mixture of compassion and concern, causing tears to well in her eyes and trickle down her cheeks. Ever so softly, he touched her cheek and brushed away a tear. Before she realized what was happening, his lips met hers in a tender kiss.

Without another word, he stood and left her office.

* * * * *

Sean tore through the mill, searching for Buck Gibson. Even though it was not yet 8:00 AM, he guessed that Buck would be lurking in the background so he could admire his handiwork from a distance. He found him in the lumber yard.

A nervous smile twitched on Buck's lips when he saw Sean coming toward him. "It's a little early for you to be out here in the lumber yard, ain't it boss?"

Sean grabbed Buck's shirt and shoved him against a stack of lumber, pitting his face a mere inch from Buck's.

"Just what do you think you're doing?"

"I don't know what you're talkin' about," Buck said, but he wouldn't look Sean in the eye.

"Who was it? Who did you get to threaten Sydney?"

"That ain't important."

"I'll be the judge of that." Sean gripped Buck's shirt even tighter. "You know better than to do something like that without asking me first."

"Well that's just the thang. My orders came from higher up. It seems that you ain't the one in control 'round here no more."

Buck's voice turned quiet. "I warned you not to get soft on her. This time my orders were just to scare her. Next time..." He paused. "Next time, who knows what my orders'll be."

* * * * *

Sydney threw her jacket across the back of the chair and headed for the kitchen. "How about some popcorn?"

"That sounds great," Kendall said. He sat down and stretched his legs on the oversized ottoman.

When she'd talked to Kendall on the phone earlier today, he'd invited her to the bonfire and suggested that they go to her house and watch a movie afterwards. This surprised her because Kendall was usually too caught up in football to do anything during the week.

The bonfire had been a spectacle. Dover was one of Stoney Creek's biggest rivals, and the entire town, it seemed, came out to show their support. The cheerleaders lead the hyper crowd of spectators and football players in roaring chants while the band played The Eye of the Tiger. The pinnacle of the evening came when Kendall stood up and delivered his pep speech.

Sydney admitted that a part of her enjoyed the notoriety she received from the town's folk—an honor bestowed on her for the sole reason that she was Kendall's girlfriend. She had to make sure she was falling for the real Kendall and not the legendary coach. But in Stoney Creek where football was life, separating the two was proving to be a difficult task. She shook her head. For once she was going to enjoy a nice cozy evening with

Kendall without analyzing it to death. After her eventful week, she could use some down time. She wouldn't think about the cemetery or the man on the porch. She would concentrate on Kendall. It would do her some good to take a break from the problems.

She watched the kernels of corn in the bottom of her skillet transform into white blossoms. The buttery smell made her mouth water. She couldn't cook a lot of things, but she sure knew how to make popcorn the old fashioned way. She accidentally touched the side of the hot skillet.

"Ouch!"

"Are you okay?"

"Yes, I'm fine," she said, sucking on her finger.

A few seconds later, armed with a big bowl of popcorn, she plopped down on the sofa beside Kendall. "How's the team shaping up?"

"Pretty good." He placed the folded paper he had been studying in his pocket.

Sydney motioned. "What was that?"

Before answering, Kendall stuffed a handful of popcorn into his mouth.

"I was just going over some plays for tomorrow night's game. We need a win over Dover so we can have a shot at the divisional playoff."

"I'm sure you'll win."

"Yeah, I sure hope so."

Sydney sat back on the couch. "I didn't have time to pick up a movie this afternoon. We'll have to watch one I already have. I hope that's okay. I have a pretty good selection to choose from."

"Huh?"

Sydney shook her head. He was not hearing a word she was saying. She always felt like she was competing with football for Kendall's attention. Would it hurt him to think about her just once? "What do you want to watch?"

Kendall sat up and scooted to the edge of the couch. "I'm sorry hon. I know we planned to watch a movie tonight, but I'm beat. I think I'll just go on home."

"Do you feel okay?"

"Yeah, I'm fine. Just tired." He gave her a peck on the check before getting up and making his way to the door.

"I'll see you at the game tomorrow night?"

Sydney nodded.

"Good." He smiled. It was a picture of boyish innocence, and she felt herself soften.

"Good luck tomorrow night. I'll keep my fingers crossed," she said as he closed the door.

She shook her head. So much for rest and relaxation. Another perplexing evening with Kendall Fletcher. And they say women are moody.

*   *   *   *   *

Walter looked at his watch. He'd have to hurry to meet Maurene on time. She had gone shopping and planned to meet him at the game. He looked up at the sky. He hoped the rain would hold off until after the game, but no such luck. The first sprinkle fell on his arm as he locked the front door and walked down the path toward his car. A crunching sound stopped him in his tracks. He strained his ears and heard it again. It sounded like footsteps. "Who's there?"

No answer.

He turned in the direction of the noise and peered into the darkness. "Show yourself! What do you want?"

He got in his car just as the rain broke through the clouds. He tried to put his key in the ignition but it wouldn't go. He looked down and realized he was using the wrong key. He looked toward the woods. All he could see were sheets of rain.

"The fining pot is for silver, and the furnace for gold: but the Lord trieth the hearts."
—Proverbs 17:3

chapter thirty-five

Kendall paced back and forth on the sideline, clapping his hands. Stoney Creek won the toss and chose to defer to the second half. The cold rain continued to fall. He looked up at the crowd in the direction of where his mom, Emma, Jarilyn, and Sydney usually sat. He hoped to get a glimpse of them, but the crowd was now a collage of colorful hats and raincoats, making it impossible to pick them out.

Threats had been floating back and forth between the field houses of Dover and Stoney Creek all week long. The last thing Dover sent was a hand-drawn picture of a football jersey being burned. The jersey had Reggie's number on it. The animosity between the two teams was more than simple rivalry. Dover's head coach, Ben Howard, hated him, and in a way, he didn't blame him.

Ben had been the head football coach at Stoney Creek when Kendall graduated from college. He had taken Kendall under his wing and mentored him. Before long, Kendall became his assistant coach and closest friend. That's when the losing streak began. One thing Stoney Creek would never tolerate was a losing football team. Ben knew that. He knew the stakes. The pressure was rough. Kendall felt it too—the overall pressure to win at all costs. Coach Howard had been asked to resign, and after a few carefully placed words in the right places from Walter, Kendall was made head coach. Lucky for

Howard, he was snatched up almost immediately by Dover as their head coach.

Kendall turned his attention to the game and urged his kickoff team onto the field as they slapped and butted each other, pumping up their adrenalin. Travis Riddle, the big offensive tackle and co-captain of the team, pointed a finger and shook his fist while yelling expletives at Dover's co-captain, the same player he had just shaken hands with a few minutes earlier.

The scoreboard was hard to see through the sheets of rain. Only forty-eight minutes of football, and that scoreboard would show that Stoney Creek had the right to the division playoff and a shot at the state championship. He could almost taste it!

During the past week, Kendall and his players had studied Dover's scouting report. Their quarterback was pretty good and had a decent arm, but their offensive line was weak and didn't appear to have the strength to stop Jerry Walker, Stoney Creek's big fast lineman. Dover had only one good pass receiver, and Kendall had worked out a defense that would double-team him in passing situations.

The clock ticked on. The defensive team raced onto the field after a poor Dover return, and sure enough, it was three downs and out to give Stoney Creek the ball on Dover's forty-five yard line after the punt. The crowd went wild. It only took six plays for their first touchdown.

* * * * *

Sydney watched the game with her hand on top of her head to keep her hat from dashing off with every gust of wind. When the rain began, Jarilyn had joined Jessica, Emma, and Mrs. Fletcher under the roof of the concession stand. They were the smart ones. She shivered and snuggled down deeper into her oversized poncho. At any rate, she'd rather sit in the rain than put up with Jessica for the whole game.

"Do you have room in there for me?"

Sydney looked up to see Sean smiling down at her. The tiny droplets of water on his dark hair only intensified his attractiveness and shot an arrow of warmth right to her heart. "Of course not, but you can have a seat." She moved the wet program from the bleacher. "What's the matter? You couldn't find Jessica?"

"Skip the sarcasm, Syd. I decided I'd rather sit up here with you in the rain watching this lopsided game. It's the beginning of the third quarter, and we're up twenty-four to six. We could leave and go get something to eat."

"No, I want to see all of the game," she said, not acknowledging how much she appreciated his remark about sitting with her in the rain, even though she doubted that he really meant it. She was also grateful for his warmth and protection from the wind.

"Why am I not surprised?" he said, leafing through the wet program. After a few minutes, he chuckled.

"What's so funny?"

"Only in Stoney Creek."

"What?" The condescension in his voice pricked at her. It didn't matter that she sometimes balked at the peculiarity of the town. She could do that because she was from here. She wasn't about to sit quietly while an outsider took pot shots at her town.

"Look at this advertisement." He held the program up so she could see as he read aloud. "Dempsey Funeral Home—We're the last ones to let you down."

Sydney laughed despite herself. "That's almost as bad as a sign I saw on a church the other day. It said: 'Wal-mart is not the only saving place.'"

Sean chuckled and shook his head. "I must admit that small towns do have their share of charms."

"Such as?"

"Moon Pies, Krystals, fried catfish." He looked at her. "The company of a beautiful woman."

Her face warmed despite the cold.

"Where else could I spend a Friday night, sitting on cold bleachers in the pouring rain, watching a game that was over in the first half?"

"This is changing the subject, but were you able to find out anything about the man who threatened me?"

Sean cleared his throat, his eyes not meeting hers. "No, I'm sorry. I questioned everybody at the mill. No one knew a thing about it. I'm beginning to wonder if the incident wasn't some sort of fluke."

Sydney looked away so he wouldn't see her disappointment. "If you find out anything, will you let me know?"

"I certainly will." Sean looked past her. "Syd, do you know that woman who's sitting in the middle section of the bleachers? She's wearing a red sweater."

Sydney turned to look. Her insides knotted when she saw Maurene and Walter. Surely they couldn't be who Sean was referring to. A shiver ran up Sydney's spine when Maurene's eyes caught hers and held them for a moment. Maurene's eyes had that same expression they had at Walter's when Sydney saw her standing at the top of the stairs.

Sydney turned back around. "Who?"

"What do you mean *who*? That bleached blonde with the beady eyes. Didn't you see her staring at you?"

Sydney pulled her poncho tighter around her. "I don't recognize her. There are hundreds of people sitting on the bleachers. She could've been looking past me to someone else. I was probably in her line of direction. That's all."

"You and I both know that woman was staring at you."

Sydney threw up her hands. "What difference does it make?"

Sean's eyes met hers, but this time she wasn't going to offer him a thing. "Okay," he finally said. "We'll play this thing your way."

They watched the game in silence. Kendall rotated his second offensive team players in and out during the last five minutes of the third quarter. Dover scored another touchdown, but not before Stoney Creek scored two more.

* * * * *

The rain turned to drizzle at the start of the fourth quarter, and Kendall huddled with his first team. "I'm going to put you guys back in. Reggie has a shot at breaking the division record in pass completions, passing yardage, and touchdowns. Just don't let up. That's when you get hurt—when you're goofing off. If any of you get tired, just pat your hand on the top of your helmet, and we'll give you a break."

"All right!" The team gave each other high fives. With only two minutes left in the game, Travis Riddle patted his helmet for the second string tackle to replace him.

* * * * *

A few seconds later, Sydney watched the unthinkable happen. Dover's defensive linebacker blitzed past Stoney Creek's substitute lineman. Reggie dropped back in the pocket and found his receiver open. Oblivious to the charging linebacker to his left, he planted his feet to pass.

The crowd moaned in unison when Reggie hit the ground. A hush fell over the stadium. Reggie lay motionless on the field. A dull, sick feeling filled Sydney's stomach as she watched Kendall and the other coaches run onto the field. Her first thought was for Jarilyn.

"The quarterback is hurt," the voice boomed over the speakers. "Folks, this could be bad news for Stoney Creek. It looks like a shoulder injury. They're carrying him off the field."

"I've got to find Jarilyn," Sydney said. She jumped up and started down the bleachers and then stopped dead in her tracks. Her mind couldn't believe what her eyes were seeing. Kendall was running across the field toward Coach Howard. His face was furious, and Sydney thought could see the veins on the sides of his neck sticking out like ropes. When he stopped, Kendall's face was only a fraction of an inch from Coach Howard's, and it looked like Coach Howard was laughing at what Kendall was saying. Kendall struck the side of Coach Howard's head. A second later all pandemonium broke loose when the players, followed by the crowd, exploded onto the field to join the brawl. Sydney stood and watched Kendall and Coach Howard exchange blows.

Sean came up behind Sydney, took her elbow and guided her down the bleachers as police officers ran onto the field. They watched one policeman escort Kendall off.

"Is he under arrest?" Sydney asked, not expecting an answer.

"I don't know." Sean's voice was void of emotion. "Right now we need to find Jarilyn and make sure Reggie's okay."

"You're right."

Sean and Sydney reached the field the same time as Jarilyn. She looked like she could faint.

"Jarilyn, it's going to be all right," Sydney said. The words rang hollow in her ears as she put her arm around Jarilyn's shoulder.

An ambulance pulled up to where Reggie was lying by the time Sean and Sydney got Jarilyn calmed down. "Are you all right baby?" Jarilyn patted Reggie's face.

Reggie grimaced but didn't open his eyes.

"Ma'am, he's going to be all right," the ambulance driver said.

Sydney looked up just in time to see Kendall jogging back onto the field toward them. A dark mark ran below his left eye and down his cheek.

"It's okay. I can take care of things from here." Kendall helped the driver get Reggie situated. "Jarilyn, you can ride with me to the hospital," he said in a low voice. He looked over at Sydney and Sean, standing there—together. His eyes met Sydney's. He walked over to her and kissed her on the cheek.

"I'm sorry about what happened tonight," Kendall said, "but I couldn't let Howard get away with that. He sent his linebacker in to take Reggie out."

Sydney frowned. "Are you sure it was intentional?" He scowled. "Yeah, I'm sure." He paused. "Look, I'll call you as soon as I know something."

Sean cleared his throat as the ambulance drove away. "He's quite the hero, isn't he? He probably just cost Stoney Creek an opportunity to play in the state playoffs and all he can say is 'I couldn't let Howard get away with that.'"

Blood rushed to Sydney's face. "I don't think that's fair, Sean O'Conner. Kendall's been through so much today. When he should be out celebrating with his team over their win tonight, he's on his way to the hospital with his most valuable player. I think you could be a little more compassionate!"

She looked Sean straight in the eye. "Why do you hate Kendall? Is it because he's everything you're not? Is that it?"

Sean rocked back. "Yeah, that's it. It looks like you've got it all figured out." He turned and left her standing alone on the field.

*"I will not be afraid of ten thousands of people, that have set
themselves against me round about."*
—*Psalms 3:6*

chapter thirty-six

Kendall insisted that the ambulance take Reggie
to Glendale because they had a better medical facility
than Stoney Creek. He paced back and forth across the
waiting room in much the same manner he had on the
sidelines of the football game. Every few minutes he
stole a glance at Jarilyn, who was sitting in one of the
chairs. The lines around her eyes and mouth seemed to
grow deeper with each passing moment. The more he
looked at her, the angrier he became. Oh how he'd like
to get his hands on Coach Howard—to finish what he'd
started earlier when he'd charged across the field. It was
one thing for Ben to come after him, but to injure his
star player—now that was unthinkable. Reggie was one
of his. His prodigy. He'd taken him under his wing,
watched him excel, and then there was Jarilyn. Kendall
knew how much she and Reggie had been counting on a
scholarship. Now with one bad hit, all of those hopes
could be gone.

* * * * *

"Are you Reggie's mother?" The voice jerked
Kendall back to reality. He looked at the woman
standing in front of Jarilyn. At first he thought the
woman was a nurse, and then he realized she was the
doctor.

357

"Yes, I'm Reggie's mother," Jarilyn said.

The doctor cleared her throat. "Reggie has suffered a shoulder separation, but he'll be all right. It's just going to take some time to heal."

"How much time?" Kendall asked, looking at Jarilyn. They were both wanting to know the same thing. When could Reggie play again?

"Well, some of that'll depend on Reggie. I'd say two months at best and four at worst."

Jarilyn was the first to find her voice. "Will he be able to finish playing this season?"

The doctor shook her head. "I wouldn't recommend it. If Reggie were to get hit again in the shoulder," she looked from Kendall to Jarilyn, "his injury could become permanent."

Jarilyn's body swayed to one side. Kendall rushed to her side and put his arm around her shoulder. "It'll be all right. We'll figure this thing out."

* * * * *

Mrs. Fletcher reached in the dryer and grabbed an armful of clothes and dropped them into the basket to be folded. She could hear the sound of Emma's music over the hum of the washing machine. The shrill ringing of the phone sent her rushing into the living room. Maybe this was the call they'd been waiting for, the call that would let them know if Stoney Creek would be allowed to participate in the division playoffs. After Friday night's fiasco with Dover, things weren't looking promising. The Alabama High School Activities Association would reach a decision today.

Kendall wasn't even going to answer it. He was waiting for her to get it. She reached for the receiver, all the while her eyes were on Kendall. He was sitting at the desk with his forehead in his hand. Even from an angle, she could tell that his jaw was tight.

She picked up the receiver and felt a momentary letdown when she realized it was a sales call. "No. Thank you. I'm not interested." The sour taste of panic rose in her throat and she saw an image of J. W. the night he died. He sat in that same spot with his forehead in his hand just before he told her that he was going to clean his guns.

"Kendall, you look so tired. It may be a while before we hear anything. Why don't you go and lay down?"

"No, I won't be able to rest until I hear something. I'm too worried about what's going to happen with the team. We've worked so hard and come so far. It just seems so unfair to have it all end now."

"What's the doctor saying about Reggie? Will he be able to play?"

Kendall ran a hand through his hair. "It doesn't look like it." He took a deep breath. "At this point, it might not even matter." He shook his head. "I've coached most of these guys since their freshman year, and now they're seniors. This is their chance at the state championship."

"Kendall, I know you're upset, but it is just a game."

"Well, it's not to my boys. It could mean scholarships and college educations."

Gail studied her son's face for a moment. "Are you sure this is about those boys or is it about you?"

Kendall looked startled. Gail's voice became soft. "Honey, I know what kind of pressure you're under to win, and I also know what it feels like to live in a fishbowl."

"Do you? Does anybody really know how I feel?"

"Are you sure this is just about football?"

Kendall stood. "Well of course it's about football. What else is there?"

The phone rang again and Kendall's eyes met his mother's. She went to answer it.

"Hello?"

She handed him the phone. "It's Walter. He said the association reached their decision."

Gail held her breath as she watched Kendall's expression. Then she saw the smile break out over his face. A few minutes later he hung up the phone and grabbed her and began dancing around the room.

"Well, Mama, Walter did it again. I don't know how he managed it, but somehow he did. It looks like Stoney Creek'll be playing in the division playoffs."

*"And David said to Saul, Let no man's heart fail because of him;
thy servant will go and fight with this Philistine."*
—*1 Samuel 17:32*

chapter thirty-seven

Without a doubt, Reggie's injury had been a debilitating blow to Stoney Creek. Still, Kendall and his team managed to win the first round of the division playoffs by a hair. The question was: Could they win the second round without Reggie?

*   *   *   *   *

Any other time, the tantalizing smells of hotdogs, popcorn, and hot chocolate would have tempted Sydney as she walked past the concession stand, but not tonight. Her stomach was tied in knots. She knew how much this game meant to Kendall and the Stoney Creek players, especially Reggie. His football injury was rotten luck. He deserved better. She pulled her fleece-lined jacket closer around her and watched the frosty vapors of her breath dissipate in the cold November wind.

The bleachers were filled with devoted fans. In the eyes of Stoney Creek, few things compared to this.

Sydney searched the bleachers for Jarilyn. She and Jarilyn had ridden to the game together. She'd gone to the restroom while Jarilyn saved their seats.

"Hey Sydney! We're up here." Sydney looked up to see Jarilyn sitting with Emma, Chuck, and Jessica. Oh great, Jessica again. It always came down to Jessica. Sydney nodded at them and mounted the bleachers.

Just when Jessica opened her mouth to speak, the band entered the stadium and drowned out her voice. Their shining metal instruments gleamed under the lights. Sydney couldn't help but notice how young they looked. Then the crowd jumped to its feet and yelled as the Stoney Creek football players and coaches ran onto the field. She watched Kendall's short, jerky movements.

Jariiyn's voice caught Sydney's attention. "Coach Fletcher's letting Reggie dress out tonight."

"I'm glad," Sydney said, knowing that Jarilyn was hoping against all odds that he would be allowed to play, even though they both knew better. Kendall would never risk injuring Reggie permanently.

Without thinking, Sydney scanned the crowd, looking for Sean. She wondered if he would come tonight.

Sydney's emotions soared and dropped like a roller coaster as Stoney Creek and Bloomingdale went back and forth, scoring touchdowns and extra points. The score was tied 14 to 14, and then Bloomingdale kicked a field goal. After the kickoff, Sydney looked at the scoreboard. Bloomingdale 17 and Stoney Creek 14. Stoney Creek returned the kickoff to Bloomingdale's 35 yard line. It was fourth down and three to go with only 15 seconds left on the clock. She watched the Stoney Creek players line up. Then Stoney Creek called for a timeout, and the players ran back to the huddle.

*   *   *   *   *

Sydney watched Reggie walk over to Kendall. Reggie pointed to the scoreboard and then to the field. Kendall shook his head and Reggie threw up his hands. Kendall put his hand on Reggie's shoulder and they spoke a few more words to each other. It was doubtful the team could win without Reggie. "For goodness sake, please don't let him go in if he's not ready," she said under her breath.

"What did you say?" Jarilyn asked.

Sydney motioned to the field. "I think Reggie's begging Kendall to put him in."

Jarilyn put her gloved hand to her mouth and waited. Sydney touched her on the arm. "You can't let Kendall put him in. What if he gets hurt worse?" Jarilyn's eyes met Sydney's, and then she looked away. "I have complete confidence in Coach Fletcher."

* * * * *

The announcer yelled over the speaker. "Folks, Reggie Kelly, Stoney Creek's star quarterback, is coming into the game." Sydney watched Reggie line up behind Number 56, Jonathan Mark, Stoney Creek's center. Looking at him now, it was hard to believe that he was injured. He looked focused and confident, as if he could command the universe. The center snapped the ball to him. He faked it off to Robert Edwards, number 41. Then he passed it off to his wide receiver. The crowd was on its feet. The wide receiver made a lateral to the tailback, Chad Hopkins, who ran into the end zone for a touchdown. Stoney Creek had won the second round of the divisional playoffs. The crowd went wild and the players hoisted Reggie on their shoulders and carried him around the field.

The buzzer rang. The roar of the crowd was deafening.

Jarilyn was screaming and hugging Sydney. "We won! We won! I can't believe we won."

"I know," Sydney exclaimed. They walked down the bleachers with the crowd.

* * * * *

By the time they reached the field, Kendall was surrounded by people.

"I'm going to find Reggie," Jarilyn said. "I'll meet you at the car."

"That sounds good." Sydney began pushing her way through the crowd to get to Kendall.

Kendall looked through the crowd at Sydney. His face was radiant. The broad grin that split his face when he saw her hit her with enough force to send a tingle shooting through her body. They might've been the only two people on the field. "We won," he called out to her. "Can you believe it? We won!"

She tried to make her way to his side. "I know."

The next event seemed to happen in slow motion. Sydney watched Jessica emerge from the mass of people. Before Kendall could reach Sydney, Jessica stepped in front of him and threw her arms around his neck and gave him a full kiss on the mouth. This brought a few wolf calls from the crowd.

"Congratulations champ," Jessica said.

Kendall tried to untangle himself from Jessica's grasp. His face was red. "Thanks Jess," he said a little breathlessly.

Jessica turned and looked at Sydney before sauntering off in the crowd.

"Looks like you've got some competition."

"What?" Sydney slung around to see Sean standing beside her.

"It looks like you're not the only one standing in line to give lover boy a congratulatory kiss."

"Oh why don't you just drop dead!"

Sean chuckled. "It was just a simple observation. And by the way, he'd have to be a fool to go after Jessica when he can have you. Then again, he's not exactly the smartest guy on the block."

Sydney ignored Sean and moved toward Kendall. When she reached him, he leaned down and gave her a peck on the cheek. Any other time Sydney wouldn't have thought twice about it, but after witnessing Jessica's mauling, she felt like Kendall was kissing his sister rather than his girlfriend. "Hey hon, I'm sorry you had to see that. I don't know what got into Jessica."

A tight smile formed on her lips. "Congratulations."

Before she could say anything else, someone tapped Kendall on the shoulder. "Coach, can you gather your team on the sideline? I want to get a picture for the paper."

"Sure."

Kendall turned back toward her. "I'll call you tomorrow."

Sydney didn't answer.

* * * * *

The shrill ringing of the phone jarred Sydney awake. She raised and looked at her clock—*6:15* AM. Who would be calling this early in the morning?

"Hello?" Her voice was still coated with sleep.

"Hey, it's me."

There was a long pause.

"Kendall?"

"Something terrible has happened."

Sydney was now wide awake. She sat up in her bed. "Kendall, what's wrong?"

"It's Reggie. He was involved in an accident last night."

"Is he okay?"

There was silence for a few moments.

"He's dead."

"No! It can't be true! What happened?"

"He was out celebrating last night with some of the guys, and he fell off a bridge and broke his neck."

She tried to collect her thoughts. "What can I do to help?"

"I'm going over to Jarilyn's to pay my respects, and I want—need—you to come with me."

"I'll get dressed right now and meet you at your house." She stumbled out of bed and began rummaging through her pile of clothes to find something to wear.

"Sydney?"

"Yes?"

"Hurry."

"Attend unto my cry; for I am brought very low: deliver me
from my persecutors;
for they are stronger than I."
—*Psalms 142:6*

chapter thirty-eight

Kendall must have seen Sydney drive up the long driveway because when she pulled up, he darted out the door and got in her jeep. His eyes were red and blotchy.

She leaned over and hugged him. "I'm so sorry."

He nodded. "I know."

It hurt to look at him, and for the first time since she'd heard the news, tears formed in her eyes.

They drove to Jarilyn's house in silence. A thousand thoughts tumbled in her mind. She wanted to ask Kendall more questions about how Reggie was killed but could tell that he was in no condition for it.

*　　*　　*　　*　　*

A cold dread settled over Sydney when they arrived at Jarilyn's house, even worse than when Sydney first heard the news. Maybe bombarding Jarilyn wasn't such a great idea. A Cadillac bearing Tennessee license plates was parked in the driveway, and Sydney remembered that

Jarilyn had an older sister who lived in Knoxville. Considering that Knoxville was a good three hours away, Sydney guessed that Jarilyn's sister must have left in the early hours of the morning to be with Jarilyn.

Kendall moved to get out of the jeep and Sydney caught his arm. "Are you sure this is a good idea? I mean, maybe Jarilyn needs her space right now."

"I have to go in and talk to her."

"Okay."

Jarilyn's sister answered the door on the first knock, and Sydney could immediately see the familial resemblance between the two sisters.

"May I help you?"

"I'm Kendall Fletcher, Reggie's football coach." His voice dribbled off. "I mean...I was Reggie's football coach."

The stately lady nodded in understanding and then extended her hand. "My name is Serena. It's a pleasure to meet you. Jarilyn thinks the world of you."

Sydney marveled at how composed Jarilyn's sister was under the circumstances. "My name is Sydney Lassiter."

Serena acknowledged Sydney's comment with a solemn nod. "Please come inside and have a seat in the living room."

They followed Serena down the hall and Kendall spoke. "I need to speak to Jarilyn."

Serena answered, "I'm not sure she's ready for that yet."

"Please, tell her that I'm here."

Serena looked at him for a moment with her dark eyes. "Okay. I'll be right back."

A few minutes later, she returned with Jarilyn. Sydney had to fight back the tears. Serena helped her to a recliner across from the sofa. "I appreciate y'all comin'."

Kendall knelt beside her and cupped his hands around hers. "I wish there was something I could say...I'm so sorry."

She began to sob. "I know."

Sydney's eyes burned as she watched the tender emotion between these people who meant so much to each other and to her.

"Is there anything I can do?" he asked.

Jarilyn raised her head from the tissue and looked Kendall straight in the eye. "Yes, you can find out who gave Reggie those drugs."

* * * * *

By the time Kendall and Sydney got back to his house, she could tell that he was ready to talk. They sat in her jeep, and she listened patiently while bits and pieces of his pent-up emotions started coming out.

"I've known Reggie since he was in junior high." He turned and stared out the passenger window.

The minutes seemed to hang suspended in the air. Sydney waited for him to continue. She was tempted to press him but had learned that there was no rushing Kendall. He would have to let it out in his own time, on his terms.

Kendall rubbed his hand through his hair. "It's just so hard to believe." He clenched his fist. "How could he have been so stupid?" Kendall hit the dashboard.

Sydney flinched. The anger had surfaced so quickly and without warning. Sometimes he was like two different people. Then again...She shook her head, remembering her hysterical outburst at the hospital when she realized the doctor had made her look just like Judith. Grief could do strange things to people.

"I can't believe that Reggie did this to me. He knew how much I needed him."

Sydney shook her head, not sure that she'd heard him right. "What?"

"He knew better than to mess with that stuff. He's seen what it can do to people."

"Kendall, Reggie didn't do this to you personally. It's just a tragic accident."

Even as she spoke the words, it didn't seem real. An image of Reggie standing tall on that first day she'd met him after practice flashed in her mind. His confident smile, the pride in Jarilyn's eyes. "It's just so hard to believe," she finally said. "He seemed so clean-cut—the all-American guy. How long had he been on drugs?"

Kendall shook his head. He looked defeated and tired. "I guess we'll never know for sure. The guys who were with him when he died came up clean. They'd been drinking but no drugs. One of them said that Reggie took a hit before the game so he wouldn't feel the pain in his shoulder." His voice broke. "And I let him play. He must've known that when push came to shove, I'd break down and let him play." He stared off in the distance. "I wanted it so bad…and so did he."

"What's going to happen to Jarilyn? He was her life."

The faint lines around Kendall's eyes seemed deeper, sadder. His voice sounded hollow and lost. "What happens to any of us when we lose someone we love that much?"

"Yeah, what happens to me and to you?" she said softly.

"I was the first person to find him," he said quietly as he looked out the window again.

"Who? Reggie?"

He turned to face her. "My dad. I was the first to find him. I got home from practice early that afternoon and went looking for him." He paused. "I found him in the garage."

Sydney's eyes grew moist. "I'm so sorry."

"It's my fault."

She touched him on the arm. "How could it be your fault?"

"I should've known what was going on with my own player. Maybe then I could've prevented it."

Kendall was talking about Reggie, but there was more to it than that. Sydney knew he was referring to his father. He was feeling guilty about his death. *Oh,*

Kendall you can't keep carrying around this guilt. You're destroying yourself over something that you had no control over. "Kendall, you couldn't control Reggie any more than you can control your other players. People make their own decisions."

Sydney stopped short. Wait a minute. Is that what she'd been doing? It seemed so clear when she was analyzing Kendall's situation, so much clearer than her own. She could look at it from a distance, with less emotion. Did someone murder Avery or had she been trying to create some phantom ghost to relieve her guilt? She shook her head, knowing that the question would continue to haunt her until she discovered the truth.

Kendall put his head in his hands.

She rubbed his back. "It's okay. It's gonna be okay."

He raised his head. "Will you just hold me?"

She put her arms around him and held him tight. It felt good to be needed. If they could just hold each other long enough, maybe the storm would pass.

"The heart of him that hath understanding seeketh knowledge."
—Proverbs 15:14

chapter thirty-nine

G rief settled like a blanket of fog over Stoney Creek and residents mourned the loss of their golden quarterback. A double whammy came when Stoney Creek lost the quarter finals and all hopes of winning the state championship went down the drain. For Sydney and Kendall, it was their own personal losses that welded them together, the merging of two souls that experienced tremendous loss.

For Sydney, the hurt was all too familiar. How many times had she promised herself she would never laugh again, never celebrate another holiday, never open herself up again to hurt? Perhaps she would have had a chance if only time had stood still. But it grinded on and on and she was forced to run along behind it, always trying to catch up.

Before she realized it, Thanksgiving had come.

* * * * *

The aroma of turkey and dressing, mingled with freshly baked apple pie, filled the air as Sydney stepped into Mrs. Fletcher's kitchen.

"Hey Sydney." Emma sniffled, looking up. She used the back of her sleeve to wipe away the stream of tears pouring down her face.

"Emma, it's okay. You don't have to cry about it," Sydney teased. She pointed to the onions Emma was chopping.

"Gee thanks," Emma said and then started sneezing repeatedly.

"Are those onions causing you to do that?"

Emma shook her head. "No, it's my allergies."

Sydney remembered the case of allergy medicine she'd seen at Kendall's cabin. "It must run in the family. Kendall has bad allergies too."

Emma cocked her head. "Kendall? Allergies? Humph! Kendall has never had an allergy problem a day in his life."

Sydney wrinkled her nose. "What?"

"No, he's the lucky one. I'm the one with all the problems." Emma motioned to the pan Sydney was holding. "What's that?"

"Ta da!" Sydney proudly unveiled the cake that Stella had painstakingly instructed her how to bake over the phone. "It's Mississippi Mud Cake. Kendall said he likes chocolate cake."

"Wow, that looks good," Emma said, mixing the chopped onions into a container of broccoli casserole.

"What are you making?" Sydney took a handful of walnuts and stuffed them in her mouth.

"Broccoli casserole, sweet potato casserole, and seven-layer salad." Emma dumped a cup of shredded cheddar cheese into the broccoli mix.

Sydney looked at the freshly baked pies, the gigantic bowl of fruit salad, and the mashed potatoes that were heaped a mile high. "What can I do to help? It looks like you've already fixed enough food for an army."

"Well, first you can get me a couple of casserole dishes from the top of the cabinet." Emma pointed. "On the right."

"Okay."

She handed a dish to Emma. "Where's Kendall?"

Before Emma could answer, Mrs. Fletcher came into the kitchen carrying a basket of freshly cut mums.

"Sydney, I didn't know you were here." She smiled and set the flowers on the counter. She came over and gave Sydney a hug. "How are you doing?"

"Great. I was looking at the leaves on my way over. They're absolutely breathtaking. I can't remember the last time I saw an autumn this beautiful. In Texas there are only two seasons. Summer and winter."

Mrs. Fletcher chuckled. "We're so glad you could spend the day with us and that Emma and I get you all to ourselves this morning."

"Where is Kendall, by the way?" asked Sydney.

"Oh, he didn't tell you?"

"Tell me what?"

"He and Walter go quail hunting every Thanksgiving morning. It's a tradition. The men go out and hunt while the women slave over a hot stove." Mrs. Fletcher laughed. "It doesn't seem fair, but I can't imagine having to eat a Thanksgiving meal prepared by Kendall."

Emma hooted. "That's for sure."

"Kendall didn't mention anything about going hunting," Sydney said. "He just said to come on over." She had the uncanny sense of déjà vu. Avery and Walter used to go hunting on Thanksgiving morning while her mom and a sober Maurene cooked lunch. Somehow, the fact that Kendall was taking Avery's place made her feel slighted. She didn't know why she should be surprised. Hadn't she been drawn to Kendall because he had those same attributes that Avery possessed? Why shouldn't Walter feel the same way?

"I guess Walter and Kendall are pretty close, huh?"

"Yes, they've been close ever since Kendall lost his dad." Mrs. Fletcher spoke the words without looking up as she arranged the yellow mums in a vase filled with water.

"Are they coming for dinner?"

"No, I've invited them several times, but Maurene always has plans of her own."

Sydney tried not to let her relief show. "The flowers are beautiful, Mrs. Fletcher."

Mrs. Fletcher stood back and admired her handiwork. "Thanks. Let's go out back and cut some for the dining room table. Emma, we'll be right back."

"Don't take too long. I'll need some help shortly," Emma said.

Sydney bent and examined each flower before selecting the ones to cut.

Mrs. Fletcher cleared her throat. "I've wanted to talk to you for a while about Kendall."

Sydney stood and looked at Mrs. Fletcher in the sunlight. She was very attractive in spite of her age. The lines around her eyes and mouth did not mar the inner beauty that shined through. Sydney wasn't sure what to expect next. "Oh?"

"Let's sit over here where we'll be protected from the wind." Mrs. Fletcher pointed to a bench nestled close to the house. "In high school Kendall was a fun-loving boy. I'm sure he's probably told you that he was the quarterback on his high school team." She trimmed the dried leaves from the stems. "Well, after his dad died, he changed. Walter was the only one he would even talk to."

"I had no idea that Walter was such an important part of your family."

Mrs. Fletcher nodded. "Oh yes. You see, Walter and J. W. were close friends. They had been ever since J. W. went to work at the mill. When J. W. died, the life insurance company didn't want to honor the claim because J. W.'s death was suicide." Mrs. Fletcher looked off in the distance, and Sydney could tell that remembering was painful. "If Walter hadn't stepped in, we would've lost everything. He convinced the insurance company to pay us."

Mrs. Fletcher gave Sydney a sad smile. "I'm sorry. I don't know why I shared that with you."

Sydney was touched. "I'm glad you did. It helps me to understand Kendall better."

"After J. W. died, Kendall was so sullen and withdrawn that I worried about him all the time. He was mad at J. W. and at the world. But lately, he seems more like his old self. I think a lot of that has to do with you, and I just wanted you to know that."

A lump formed in Sydney's throat, and her eyes grew moist. She could only imagine the anguish this poor woman had suffered, first over the death of her husband and then worrying about her son. She wished they had had this conversation several months ago. For the first time, she felt she was getting a true picture of Kendall and his family.

She thought about Jarilyn and what she must be going through this holiday season. Sydney was glad that she'd gone to Knoxville to be with her sister. At least Jarilyn would be surrounded by family. She felt a twinge of guilt that she was here with this wonderful family and would be with Stella tonight while Jarilyn was mourning the loss of Reggie.

"I'm glad we had this conversation, Mrs. Fletcher." She gave Kendall's mom a hug.

"We'd better get back to the kitchen before Emma comes looking for us." Mrs. Fletcher stood and brushed away a tear.

* * * * *

Hazel's curtains opened and closed when Sydney drove into the driveway. In a few seconds she was hollering out her door and waving one arm at Sydney while bending down and picking up Dixie with the other.

"Sydney!"

Sydney got out of the jeep and walked over to greet Hazel. "Hi, Hazel. Did you have a good Thanksgiving?" Sydney thought back to the first time she saw Hazel peeking out. It had been so annoying back then. It was amazing the difference a few months had made. Now she looked forward to coming home and being greeted by Hazel.

"Oh yes, I did, Sydney. Did you?" Hazel said, ushering Sydney into the house.

Sydney smiled and reached to stroke Dixie. "It was wonderful. I spent the day with Kendall and his family and afterwards, I—" Sydney stopped, realizing that she'd almost told Hazel she'd spent Thanksgiving evening with her grandmother.

Hazel looked past Sydney to the street. She whispered. "Not out here. Let's go inside."

Sydney looked back, trying to see what had caught Hazel's attention.

"The eyes are watching. Let's get away from the eyes."

A shiver ran up Sydney's spine. Was someone really watching them or was she letting Hazel's paranoia draw her in?

Once inside, Hazel was back to her normal self. "I brought some cake from Wally's house for you."

"Wally?"

"Yes, Louellen and I always go to Wally's for Thanksgiving, and he was so nice to us this year, but Maurene was really, really ugly." Hazel moved a stack of magazines out of the chair so Sydney could sit down.

"Maurene? Hazel, do you mean Walter and Maurene?"

"Yeah, you should have seen her. Every time I asked for seconds on the rolls and cheesecake, Maurene would roll her eyes at Wally and blow out her cheeks like a blow fish, but he just pretended he didn't see. Wally knows I love rolls and cheesecake. That's why he always has them for me on Thanksgiving. Louellen even got mad at Maurene this time."

"Hazel, how are you and Louellen related to Walter and Maurene?"

She moved some pillows and sank down on the sofa. "He's our brother, but we never call him Walter. We call him Wally."

Sydney let the information sink in. The fact that she didn't know that Walter was Hazel's older brother was very unsettling. Why hadn't she made that connection? There was really no reason why Walter or

Louellen should have told her, but it just made her wonder what other connections had she missed. What other surprises did Stoney Creek have in store for her? Hazel interrupted her thoughts. "Sydney, do you want some cheesecake? Wally gave me all of the cake that was left!" Hazel put her hands on each side of her mouth and giggled. "Ooh, this made Maurene really mad."

"Yes, that would be great. I'll take a small piece."

"Good," Hazel got up and went into the kitchen.

* * * * *

Doubts raced through Sydney's mind. She ran her fingers through her long hair. Maybe she should have called Walter instead of just showing up on his doorstep. Her leg ached, and she willed the pain away as she held her breath and rang the doorbell. Please let it be Walter, not Maurene who answers the door.

"Sydney, what a nice surprise," Walter said and motioned her in.

Her face flushed. "I hope I'm not catching you at a bad time."

He waved her comment away. "Oh no. Maurene has gone to Glendale to shop."

She followed him to the den where he settled into the sofa and crossed his legs. As usual, he looked impeccable in khaki pants and a plaid button-up shirt. He reached for the remote and clicked off the television. Sydney smiled, not surprised that he was watching a football game.

"What can I do for you, young lady?"

She could feel her palms going sweaty. "I wanted to talk to you about a couple of things."

She began by telling him about Helping Hands and how she wanted to help people in the community. When she finished, he looked at her in admiration and shook his head.

"You're so much like Avery. This is a wonderful

thing that you're doing. I would love to help. Do you have a building yet?"

"Well, no. I'm still working on that part."

"I'll hook you up with a friend of mine, Tess Lambert. She'll find you a good deal."

"Yes, I know Tess. She helped me find the house I'm renting."

"Great. I would like to be one of your sponsors."

"Wonderful. By the way, I just found out that I live next door to one of your sisters."

"Hazel?"

Sydney nodded. "I didn't know that she and Louellen were your sisters. I just love Hazel."

Walter laughed. "That Hazel's a character."

All the while she and Walter were making small talk, Sydney's heart was pounding. She cleared her throat. "There's something else I need to talk to you about." For the hundredth time, Sydney prayed she could convince Walter to believe her. He'd already done so much to help her, but she needed him now more than ever. She was up against a brick wall with nowhere else to turn. There was no dancing around the issue.

"I've been investigating Avery's death." She watched Walter's eyes to see his reaction before continuing. His expression was unreadable.

"And?"

"I'm more convinced than ever that Avery was murdered."

She saw it then, the guardedness in his eyes. She willed herself to remain rational—to take her time and lay out the facts.

"Shortly before his death, Avery wrote a letter to my aunt, asking her if I could stay with her. He told her that he was very worried about some things."

"Did he say what?"

Sydney shook her head. She knew how flimsy this must sound. "No, he was vague. I think he was planning to tell her everything when he saw her. Unfortunately, he never got the chance." She switched gears. "And then there's Buford Phillips."

Walter's eyebrow arched. "What about Buford Phillips?"

"I found the accident report at the mill that Avery filled out. It said that Buford was killed by a chunk that split off from a log."

"That sounds about right from what I can remember."

"Someone else added that Buford had been drinking. Mrs. Phillips swears he was sober. She told me that Buford became religious prior to his death and that he'd given up alcohol. Mrs. Phillips believes that Buford was involved in some sort of illegal activities going on at the sawmill. She thinks that he wanted to come clean. According to her, he tried and was killed for it."

"What sort of activities?"

Sydney shrugged. "I'm not sure."

Walter scratched his head. "It's only natural for Mrs. Phillips to want to defend Buford. I don't blame her for wanting to protect his memory. I must tell you, though, this sounds a little far-fetched to me."

"I know how it must sound."

Walter ran a hand through his silver hair. "Honey, I can't even begin to imagine what it has been like for you to lose both of your parents. But putting yourself through this won't bring Avery back. His death was an accident. Sometimes things just happen."

"No!" The word exploded from her mouth. "No," she repeated softly. "I don't think so."

He was about to interrupt again, but she stopped him. "Just hear me out...please?"

He nodded, then waited for her to continue.

"I spoke to Lewis Jackson." She saw Walter's eyebrow twitch and knew this was a possible sore spot because Lewis was Walter's ex brother-in-law. "I confronted him about the accident in the log yard and how Avery thought the chain had been cut. I told him that Avery suspected him of short-changing the loggers. When I asked him about it, he practically threw me out of his store."

Walter was sitting with his arms folded. "Yes, Avery told me about the accident in the log yard, but how did you know about it? Did he tell you about it before he died?"

"No." She looked him in the eye. "That's the clincher. I read it in his journal."

"What! Avery kept a journal?" He stood and walked to the fireplace and reached for the poker and began stoking the fire.

Sydney scooted to the edge of her seat. She'd finally caught Walter's attention. She gave him a moment to let the information soak in. He turned toward her but kept one hand on the mantle. "Where did this journal come from?"

"It was in a box of things that Stella, my grandmother, gave to me when I first returned to Stoney Creek."

"She had it this whole time?"

Sydney nodded.

Walter shook his head. "I had no idea."

"Avery wrote that he had an appointment with Judge Crawford from Glendale. The appointment was scheduled for the day that Avery was killed. And get this. Judge Crawford was killed that very same day. My Aunt Judith had a newspaper clipping of Avery's death that she kept with the article about Judge Crawford. Don't you see? Both the Judge and Avery were killed the same day. And they both died in explosions."

Walter stroked his chin. "Sydney, that could be a coincidence."

"Two men in towns right next to each other? No one ever found out who killed Judge Crawford." Before Walter could interrupt, Sydney rushed on. "I've spoken to Judge Crawford's widow. She said her husband told her that he was headed to an appointment. He also said that he'd gotten a major break in a case he was working on."

She shook her head. "I'm sure there are other clues in the journal."

"Did you bring it with you? I knew Avery better than anyone. Maybe I could take a look at it."

"That would've been good, but it's impossible now."

"Why?"

"It was stolen."

Walter rocked back. "What? When?"

"Someone broke into my house and took it."

"Well, that's convenient."

His comment sliced her to the core, and Sydney jumped to her feet. "You wanna talk about convenience? I'll tell you about convenience. Do you think it was convenient when someone ran me off the road or threatened me with a switch-blade?" She paced back and forth in front of the sofa.

"Why didn't you tell me all this was going on?"

Sydney threw up her hands. "Oh, I don't know. I'm just so sick of it all." She stopped pacing and looked at him. "I was trying to gather enough evidence so that you would believe me."

He moved toward her and put a hand on her shoulder. "Let's sit back down, and I want you to tell me about the knife and how you were run off the road."

He listened without comment while she related all that had taken place. Finally, he shook his head. "I had no idea you've been going through so much."

"It has been rough." Her mind went back to that day on the boat. "Avery asked me to check the bilge for fumes." She bit her lip to stay the emotion. She'd not planned on telling Walter all of this, but somehow it just felt right. "I've replayed that day over and over in my mind so many times, trying to remember if I smelled gasoline. I keep thinking that if only I'd checked more carefully then maybe..."

Walter touched her arm. "Oh, Honey, it wasn't your fault."

She blinked back the tears. She wasn't looking for sympathy from Walter. She just wanted him to understand. "I know how all of this must sound. Believe me, I've even had my doubts. There was a time—before the journal and the threats—when I feared that I was looking beyond the mark, trying to find something that wasn't there so I could ease my own conscience. But now there are too many unanswered questions. Too many things that just don't add up."

She sat up. "Look, here's what I think happened. I think Avery found out that something was going on at the sawmill. He went to Mrs. Phillips' house shortly after Buford's death because he suspected that it might not have been an accident. I think he told Judge Crawford, and that's why they were both killed."

"Why would Avery go talk to Judge Crawford? If he suspected foul play, he would've told me. Avery was like a brother."

Sydney shook her head. "I know. You're right. There are so many holes, but I have this feeling that I'm on the right track. I'm sure that's why I've been threatened. There's something missing, but I don't know what. Walter, you were the general manager of the sawmill then. Can't you try to remember?"

"You can bet your bottom dollar that if something had been goin' on at my sawmill, I would've known about it."

"I believe that something's going on at the sawmill right now."

Walter's eyes widened. "What?"

Sydney told him about the fight between the two men and how she found the drug apparatus nearby. "If the guys at the sawmill are taking drugs, then that could explain all the random accidents. Look what happened to Reggie Kelly. He was out of his mind when he climbed on top of the bridge. And then there are the trucks."

"What trucks?"

She told him about seeing the trucks leaving the sawmill late at night.

"Have you told anyone your suspicions?"

"Yes, I've talked to the Sean O'Conner, the manager, about the drugs. He told me that he would check into it."

"Well, I guess we'll have to trust that he will."

Sydney smirked. "I'm not holding my breath on that one. I don't believe that Sean O'Conner has a clue about how to run a sawmill. He makes too many obvious mistakes."

Walter chuckled. "Spoken like a true safety consultant."

Their words got lost in silence and they sat staring at the fire. Walter spoke first. "I'm glad you told me about Avery's journal. You've raised some good questions. And you don't have any idea who stole it?"

"No."

"I want you to know that I'm going to do everything I can to get to the bottom of this, but you have to promise me one thing."

"What's that?"

"If I come up empty-handed, you have to let it go."

Sydney stared into the fire and watched the flames devour the logs. She thought of Avery, then looked up to meet Walter's eyes.

"No, I won't let it go. I can't. I have to find the answers...even if I die trying."

"...a time to keep silence, and a time to speak."
—Ecclesiastes 3:7

chapter forty

Whenever the stress in Sydney's life became unbearable, she could count on a good hard run to ease the tension and clear her mind. Today even that had not done the trick. Hot water from the shower pounded on Sydney's back as she replayed her conversation with Walter over and over in her mind. Then her thoughts shifted to Kendall. He'd called and awakened her at 8 o'clock this morning, saying that Walter wanted to take them out on his boat. It was so frustrating to try and explain why she didn't want to go without revealing all the facts. There was no way she could make Kendall understand. Why would Walter even suggest such a thing? Surely he knew how she felt about boats. Maybe Walter was trying to help her face the fear, but he was certainly going about it the wrong way.

Sydney stepped out of the shower and wound a towel around her hair. The phone was ringing. She threw on her robe and rushed to answer it. "Hello?"

Silence.

"Hello?"

The words were garbled and husky, like they were all wrapped up in barbed wire. "They know! They know who you are! Get out now while you can!"

Hot prickles pelted Sydney. She gripped the receiver. "Who is this?"

The line went dead.

Sydney's hand was shaking when she put down the phone. She tried to place the voice. Something about it was hauntingly familiar.

The sound of the door bell jolted her and she moved to open it.

"Kendall, you're early."

He stepped into the living room and glanced at her attire. He looked at his watch. "I told Walter we'd meet him at two."

She swung around, causing the towel to fall off her head. The nerve of him. The phone call, her conversation with Walter—it all melted to the razor-sharp tip of an arrow. And that arrow was pointed at Kendall. "If you're in such a big hurry to get there then maybe you should just go on without me!"

An arched eyebrow was his only reaction. "No, I'll wait." He sat down on the sofa.

How could he be so oblivious? Couldn't he tell that something was wrong?

Sydney stomped to her bedroom and slammed the door. She threw on a pair of jeans and a sweatshirt and retrieved her tennis shoes from the closet. Any other time she would have put more effort into her appearance, but she'd be darned if she'd put Kendall out any further by making him wait an extra minute! She reached for a hairbrush and raked it through her hair in jerky movements. She was going to take her jeep instead of riding with Kendall. That way she could talk to Walter for a minute and then leave. If Kendall didn't like it, that was tough. At least one good thing would come out of the whole ordeal. She could tell Walter about the phone call.

When she returned, Kendall was pacing back and forth in front of the door. "All right," she said, "let's go. I'd hate to keep your dear friend Walter waiting." She reached for her jacket and purse and stormed out the door with Kendall following close behind. She noticed Hazel's curtains part as she approached the driver's side of the jeep.

"What are you doing?"

Sydney's chin raised a notch. "I'm going to follow you to the dock. I told you earlier that I don't want to go out on the boat."

He shook his head and rolled his eyes. "Why would you not want to go? It doesn't make any sense. It's a beautiful day, and we'll have a wonderful time. It means a lot to Walter. I want the two of you to get to know each other better."

She had to stop herself from laughing out loud.

"Come on, it means a lot to me."

Normally, she would give in. Kendall didn't know, couldn't possibly understand, what he was asking of her. She raised an eyebrow, letting him know that she still wasn't convinced.

"Look, I'll make a deal with you," he said. He came around, opened her door, and practically placed her in his truck.

Well, that was a first. He'd never opened her door before.

"You ride with me, and if you still feel the same way when you get there, then I'll bring you back."

She searched his face, trying to decide if she could trust him to really bring her back. "All right," she said. She got in and he closed the door.

* * * * *

Not two minutes after Sydney walked out the front door, her phone rang and Ginger's voice came across the answering machine. "Sydney, it's me...hello? If you're there, pick up. This is really important." There was a pause, followed by a deep breath. "I really wish I could tell you this in person. Anyway, Mark finally got a hold of Dustin Akin, his friend from The Woodlands. Get this: He's never heard of Sean O'Conner. He gave Mark the name of some other guy who was the starting quarterback. He even asked some of his former teammates to make sure that he wasn't missing something. None of them had ever heard of Sean O'Conner either. Something's fishy here, Syd. Mark's really worried about it and so am I. I have a bad feeling about this. You need to stay as far away from Sean O'Conner as possible. Call me as soon as you get this message. I'll try your cell phone."

*   *   *   *   *

A stony silence settled over Sydney and Kendall on their way to the dock. Sydney kept running the strange phone call over and over in her mind. She tried to place the husky voice. What was it about it that was so familiar?

It was when her cell phone rang, causing her to jump, that she realized that her nerves were raw. She reached in her purse to retrieve it and saw that it was Ginger. She looked at it for a moment, trying to decide if she was going to answer it. There were no short conversations with Ginger. And Ginger had an uncanny way of sensing when something was wrong. She would be asking questions that Sydney couldn't answer—not with Kendall sitting next to her.

"Aren't you going to answer that?"

She shook her head. "No, it's a friend of mine from Texas. I'll call her back later."

*   *   *   *   *

Tuesday rinsed off the last plate and watched the sudsy water slide down the drain. The voices of her two teenage grandsons drifted into the kitchen.

"Momaw, the game's about to start!"

"I'm almost finished." She reached for her oven mitt and took the pan of hot cookies out of the oven. She breathed in the familiar aroma and listened to her grandsons laughing in the next room.

"Come on, Momaw!"

Tuesday hurried into the room, carrying a plate heaped with chocolate chip cookies just as the pre-game ceremony began. She stopped in her tracks. All thoughts of the game fled. There it was right in front of her—the very thing she'd been racking her brain to remember.

"What's wrong?"

Tuesday looked down and realized she was gripping the plate.

"Boys, y'all go on without me. I'll be right back. I've got to make a phone call."

* * * * *

By the time she reached the dock, Sydney's pulse bumped up a notch. In her mind she formulated her excuse for not going on the boat. Her one consolation was knowing that Walter would back her up. He of all people would understand her reasons for not wanting to go. In fact, it seemed strange that he would even suggest such a thing. This time Kendall didn't open her door. He exited the truck so quickly that he was halfway down the pier by the time she got out. She shook her head. What was it with him, anyway?

A blast of cold air slapped Sydney in the face when she got out of the truck. She pulled her coat tighter around her. She glanced up at the sun that was shining in the thin sky. It was one of those deceptive days where you see the sun and think it'll be warm until the wind hits.

She gazed over the sparkling water and breathed in the faint fishy smell. It was all so familiar—too familiar. Her thigh began to ache and a wave of nausea engulfed her. Her time with Judith had been a buffer to the pain, but standing here, almost in the same spot she'd stood all those years ago, her world seemed to contract, as if she were living it all over again. She had to get a grip. She was safe here with Walter and Kendall, and she wasn't getting on the boat. She was going to have a conversation with Walter, and then Kendall would take her home.

It was a short walk on the pier to the boat, but it seemed like the longest of her life. If Walter had owned a sailboat, the similarity might have been too much to bear. Thankfully, what Kendall had referred to as *Walter's boat* was in actuality a petite yacht. Walter was moving around on the deck and performing what she knew were last-minute checks before leaving the dock. The radio was turned up full blast, and she recognized the garbled sounds of a football game. Any other time, she would have smiled. Of course: Alabama was playing today. Walter would never miss that. The band was playing their fight song, "Yea Alabama." Walter whistled along. Her childhood floated to the surface of her mind and she remembered going to Walter's house with Avery on countless occasions to watch the game. Walter was always whistling that tune.

Walter's back was facing her as she approached. Kendall was already on the boat beside him. Would it have hurt Kendall to wait a minute for her? She moved to the edge of the pier and Kendall extended his hand. At least he had the decency to do that.

Rather than taking hold of it, she stepped back. Kendall gave her a questioning look, which she ignored. The trick was how to talk to Walter about the phone call with Kendall right beside him. She cleared her throat. "Walter, I'm afraid I'm not going to be able to go on the boat today. I just came to apologize."

A look passed between Walter and Kendall. Before she could continue, her cell phone rang again. She reached in her purse and retrieved it. The caller ID read Tuesday Phillips. "Excuse me for a minute," she said. Walter nodded.

"Hello?"

"Sydney, I'm so glad I caught you. Do you remember when you asked me about Buford's death?"

"Yes."

"Well, remember how I told you that Buford was mixed up with somethin' illegal with the guys at the mill?"

"I remember."

"That tune that kept coming to me. I just realized what song it was: Yea Alabama. You're probably not familiar with that, but it's the theme song for the University of Alabama. I just heard it on the television."

For a moment Sydney felt like she was having an out-of-body experience. White lights exploded in her head. Hot prickles covered her as it all came together. The husky voice on the phone that had sounded so familiar was Maurene's. Images of Maurene clicked through her mind. Maurene standing on the landing. Maurene's eyes boring into her at the football game. Was the call some twisted way to try to warn her? Was she trying to ease her own guilt but lacked the courage? She fought hard to stave off the look of horror that was sure to form on her face. How could she have been so blind? She thought of her most recent conversation with Walter. His words rose like a mocking banner. "If something had been going on at my sawmill, you can bet your bottom dollar I would've known about it." Of course he would have known about it. Walter did know about it. Like a dot-to-dot picture, her mind ran through all the evidence and connected it. An image of Hazel on the back porch flashed in her mind. The mean brother who drowned the kitten. All of the color drained from her face. She looked at Walter and Kendall and realized they were studying her intently. Her head started spinning.

"Sydney? Sydney, are you there?" Tuesday asked.

"Yes," she croaked, "I'm here."

"Are you all right?"

"Yes, thank you." She couldn't let the terror overtake her, not with Walter standing there, listening to every word she spoke. She couldn't let him know that she knew it was him. "Just keep things under control as best you can. I'll be there in a few minutes."

"What are you talking about?" Tuesday asked.

"Thanks. I'll see you in a few."

"What's going on?" Sydney heard Tuesday ask as she disconnected the call.

Sydney looked at Walter and Kendall. "That was Sean O'Conner. There's been an accident at the mill. I have to go there right away."

Walter's eyes narrowed. "An accident? What kind of accident?"

"Uh, I don't know. He didn't say."

"I see." Walter paused. "Sean O'Conner, huh? Who was it really?"

A calm stillness much like death came over her when she looked into the face of her father's killer. Then came the rage. Oh, how she would love to rush at him to tear him apart—make him hurt like he hurt her. Her voice became steel. "I told you. There's been an accident at the mill." Even as she spoke, her mind went over the alternatives. She was all alone in a remote area with Walter and Kendall. Could she race to Kendall's truck and beat him there? No, when Kendall got out of his truck earlier, he took his keys with him. She could try to run, but they would catch her. Was Kendall involved or just an innocent bystander? Her only chance was to make Walter believe that she didn't know about him. "Kendall, I need you to take me home so I can get my jeep," she said with a voice of authority. Sydney's heart dropped when Kendall looked to Walter for permission.

Walter nodded.

"I'm sorry I have to leave," Sydney said. Kendall hopped off the boat and onto the pier.

There was a pang of sadness in Walter's eyes. "Yes, me too."

* * * * *

Sean beat on the door for the third time then turned and looked at Sydney's jeep parked in the driveway. Where could she be? He caught a movement out of the corner of his eye and turned to see Sydney's neighbor peering at him through her window. When she realized he'd caught her staring at him, she slinked back and let the lace curtain cover her. Sean put one hand on his hip and ran the other through his hair. The old woman was always watching Sydney's house. Maybe she'd seen Sydney leave.

He rushed next door. The front door was open but the glass storm door closed. He grasped the metal handle, only to find it locked. He cupped his hands around his eyes and strained to see inside. The woman saw him the same instant he saw her. She was standing in the middle of the living room. He knocked on the glass door, but she made no move to open it, remaining fixed to the floor.

"Hello?" he said through the glass. "I'm looking for Sydney."

She shook her head and looked like she might bolt to a back room. "Have you seen Sydney today?" he asked. She didn't answer. He felt something brush across his leg and looked down to see a cat. He bent down and picked it up.

"I have your cat," he said loudly.

In a flurry of motion, Hazel rushed to the door. She unlocked the storm door, opened it, and reached for Dixie. She attempted to close the door, keeping Sean at a safe distance, but Sean stuck his foot in the door.

"I've got to find Sydney. She may be in danger. You've got to help Sydney."

Hazel's eyes grew wide, and her head began shaking from side to side. "Can't hurt Sydney. Shouldn't make Sydney go on that boat. Sydney didn't wanna go. He shouldn't have made her."

"Boat? Who made Sydney go on a boat?"

"Shouldn't have gone. No, she shouldn't have gone. Bad. Bad. Don't hurt Sydney."

Sean caught hold of Hazel's arm. "I need to know who she went with. You've got to tell me!"

Hazel raised her eyes to his and studied his face. Panic contorted her features and she squeezed Dixie so tightly that the cat screeched and leapt from her arms.

"Don't hurt Hazel. Please don't hurt Hazel," she whined as she backed away from him.

"What! What're you talking about?"

She pointed her finger at him. "I know you. You broke into Sydney's house. You're the eyes! You're the eyes that have been watching me and Sydney!"

"A time to weep..."
—Ecclesiastes 3:4

chapter forty-one

Kendall and Sydney sped down the highway toward town. She had the feeling that none of this was real, like she'd been thrown into the climax of a horror movie. A part of her was still clinging to the hope that Kendall was an innocent bystander in this whole ordeal. She couldn't question him, though, because if he were involved, he would know that she was onto Walter. She had to make small talk. This wasn't really her, and it couldn't be Kendall, tearing like a madman down the highway. She glanced at his face. It was set in stone.

"I hope no one was seriously injured."

Silence.

"Sean said a chain broke on one of the saws."

"Better get your story straight. A few minutes ago you didn't know what kind of accident it was, and now it's a broken chain." He shook his head. "Give it a rest, Sydney. You know as well as I do that there was no accident at the mill. Who called you?"

"I told you. It was Sean. There was an accident and—"

Sydney's voice stopped mid-sentence when Kendall raced past the road that led into town. Panic filled her throat. So much for Kendall's innocence. "What are you doing? Where are you taking me? Why are you doing this?"

Kendall remained silent. "Answer me!" she shouted.

"Just sit back and shut up. You don't have a clue do you?"

She could feel her body shaking like a sewing machine, and she fought to get control. "No, I don't understand. Not completely." Kendall had been a teenager when Walter killed Avery. How could he be linked to that? "Kendall, you don't have to do this. You don't have to do what Walter tells you to. I know you. You're a good man."

Sydney could almost see the wall that Kendall was building between them. He gripped the steering wheel harder, causing his knuckles to grow white. His jaw was so tight that the veins on his neck protruded like roots of a tree. Who was this person? How could she make him listen to reason?

"You don't owe Walter anything," she pleaded.

Kendall looked wild-eyed at her. His face was flushed. "You'd better shut your mouth because you don't know what you're talking about. Walter's been like a father to me. When Dad died, the insurance company refused to pay Mom the money they owed her." He spat out the words. "They said they didn't pay for suicides. Dad was weak. He would've left us penniless if Walter hadn't stepped in. I don't know what would have become of us if it hadn't been for him."

Sydney's heart was hammering in her chest, and her breath was keeping time. He was not rational. How could she have missed all the clues about Kendall and Walter? It was right there in front of her the whole time. Why could she not see it? Sydney looked out the window. Her heart lurched when she realized that Kendall was headed to the river. It was the same route he'd taken on his bike. She had to get away from him, but how? She gripped the door handle.

Kendall clucked his tongue. "I wouldn't do that if I were you. We're going too fast. You'll never survive the fall."

She let go of the handle. She had to get through to him. Keep him talking. Make him change his mind. "How long have you known about me?"

"Known who you were?"

She nodded.

"Since that first night we went to Walter's together. I wanted to introduce my new girl to Walter, and surprise, surprise: he already knew you."

Kendall's voice was returning to normal, and he'd loosened his grip on the wheel. She tried to keep her voice conversational. "I remember that night. You were showing Walter some plays for the game. I fell asleep in the study. When I woke up, I heard you and Walter arguing over football."

"Not hardly. It was over you. I was stunned when Walter told me who you were." He glanced at her. "I mean you're so much prettier than you used to be. I convinced Walter to let me have you." There was no apology in his voice, only a plain statement of fact, as if it were completely normal that he was referring to her as an object. "Walter gave you to me under the condition that I keep you under control. Plus, you kept me up to date on the events at the mill. It was like having another set of eyes."

"What does any of this have to do with the mill?"

There was a hint of amusement in his voice. "Don't you know?"

She strung it all together, trying to make a connection. The random accidents, the men taking drugs, the trucks leaving at odd hours. Then, as swift as a bolt of lightning, it all became clear. "You don't have allergies, do you?"

"What?"

"I said you don't have allergies."

"No, I don't. What does that have to do with anything?" Kendall turned onto a dirt road. Sydney's heart skipped a beat. She recognized this road. It led to the abandoned coal warehouse by the river.

She needed to keep him talking. That was her only

chance. "That time you took me to your cabin and I went in the laundry room. I thought you were angry because I saw Jessica's picture. That wasn't it at all, was it? It was because I saw the allergy medicine and bottles of iodine you were using to make meth. You've been using the sawmill to transport the drugs. The drugs that killed Reggie! Oh, Kendall. How could you?"

"Just shut up!" Kendall raised his hand to strike her. He balled his hand into a fist and lowered it to his leg before it reached her face. "You don't know what you're talking about. I never sold any drugs to Reggie or any of my other football players. He got it from someone else."

"That doesn't matter. You're dealing the drugs. You might as well have given them to Reggie yourself!"

Kendall didn't respond.

"What about your mom and Emma? Don't you care about them? Think what it'll do to them if they ever find out what you're doing. You said you didn't know what would've become of you and your family if Walter hadn't stepped in. Well, maybe you wouldn't have become a drug dealer! Maybe you wouldn't have that cabin in the woods and the four-wheelers and all those other toys! You just might've been the kind, decent person I thought you were!"

Kendall brought the truck to a squealing halt in front of the warehouse. "There's been enough talk! Get out!"

*   *   *   *   *

Sydney threw open the door and bolted from the truck. She made it a mere hundred yards before Kendall tackled her to the ground.

"Dumb move, Sydney. Real dumb." He jerked her to her feet and held her by the arm. They both looked toward Kendall's truck. Walter pulled up behind it and got out.

"I'm sure sorry it had to come to this," Walter said, walking toward them. "And you can wipe that hateful expression off your face, young lady, because this is all

400

your fault. I gave you a job because I felt sorry for you."
He shook his head. "I should've known better. You're
just like Avery. He was like an old dog, always sniffin'
for that bone. No matter how hard I tried, I couldn't
convince him to let it go."

"And you killed him for it."

"Yes, it was one of the hardest decisions I ever had
to make. Avery was like a brother to me."

Sydney scoffed. "Some brother."

"A couple of days before he died, Avery told me that
he'd gone down to the log yard in the middle of the night
and saw some of the men stealing from the mill. I told
him to let me take care of it, but he wouldn't listen. Now
whether or not he suspected that I was behind it all, I
don't know. He told me that he'd already spoken to Judge
Crawford from Glendale and that he had an appointment
to meet with him. That's when I knew that I had to do
something. His death was a senseless waste." His eyes
met hers. "Just as yours will be."

She turned to Kendall. He was her only chance. "Are
you hearing what he's saying? He's a murderer. You're
not like him, Kendall. Listen to me!" She saw something,
perhaps it was a flicker of compassion. Maybe she was
getting through to him.

She glanced at Walter. He was eying Kendall with
concern. Perhaps he had seen it too—that momentary
hesitation in Kendall's expression. Walter's eyes met
Sydney's. "You and Kendall have more in common than
you realize. Who do you think rigged up the boat that
killed Avery?"

The very air seemed to hold its breath and Sydney
waited for Walter to continue.

"It was J. W., Kendall's father."

Sydney's mind reeled. She wondered if this was the
first time Kendall had heard this. Images of J. W. ran
through her mind. J. W. and his boisterous laugh. J. W.
making a fire in the pasture so she and Emma could
roast marshmallows. J. W.'s kind eyes and broad smile.

"No, I don't believe it. Don't listen to him, Kendall.
He's lying."

Walter's voice went smooth like velvet. "Why would I lie about that? J. W. worked for me at the mill before he went to work for the highway department. He knew explosives like the back of his hand. He took care of both problems: Avery and Judge Crawford."

"Is that why J. W. committed suicide?"

Walter ignored her comment and looked at Kendall. "Son, I should've told you about that a long time ago. You were so torn up over J. W.'s death." Walter's voice broke. "I just couldn't stand the thought of seeing you hurt any more than you already were."

"W-what?" Sydney directed her words to Kendall. "What kind of rubbish is Walter feeding you? Surely you don't believe any of it. J. W. probably committed suicide because he couldn't live with fact that he'd killed two innocent people. If that's the case, then Walter's responsible for his death too."

Kendall gripped Sydney's arm harder. "You'd do best not to talk about things that you don't understand. My dad killed himself because he was weak."

Walter reached in his jacket and retrieved a pistol. "Well, now you know the full story. There's only one point of interest left." He pointed the pistol at Sydney's chest. "Now where is the journal?"

She swallowed hard. Her eyes remained fixed on the pistol. "I told you. The journal was stolen."

"Not good enough," Walter said. Kendall took his cue and jerked Sydney's arm, pinning it behind her back.

She bent over in pain. "Kendall, you're hurting me."

"Tell us where the journal is."

"I'm telling you the truth. I don't know."

"It's a pity you won't tell us," Walter said. "But I'm sure Stella will...one way or the other. Now I'll have to take care of Stella, and she can thank you for that."

Walter's words were like a red flag in front of a bull. Sydney went wild. She stood up straight and ground her heel into Kendall's foot. Kendall loosened his grip on her arm just long enough for her to lunge at Walter, knocking the gun out of his hand. Walter scrambled to pick it up and she took off in a mad sprint.

"Get her," Walter yelled.

She could hear Kendall's heavy footsteps behind her and felt his breath on her back. Then came the vicious yank on her hair that jerked her backwards.

"I'm getting tired of chasing you down," he said, dragging her back to Walter.

"If we weren't trying to make this look like an accident, I'd shoot you right now," Walter said. "You're a foolish girl, just like your father."

Sydney's chin jutted out. "You're right. I am just like my father, and I'll die fighting the same evil he did."

"Well, you got the dying part right anyway." He looked at Kendall. "I've got some rope in my truck. Tie her up and then put her in the warehouse. There's going to be an accident—a fire. No one'll ever question it. For years people have been saying this old warehouse is a tinderbox." Kendall let go of Sydney and Walter leveled the gun at her. "If you so much as move a muscle, I'll shoot."

The sound of an approaching vehicle stopped Kendall in mid stride. Walter turned to look. "Who is that?"

Sydney's heart leapt when she recognized the driver. It was Sean. He was coming to rescue her!

"It's Sean O'Conner," Kendall said.

Walter's eyes narrowed. "What's he doing here?"

Kendall shook his head. "I don't know."

By the time Sean got out of his truck and walked to the unfolding scene, Kendall had returned with the rope. Sean's expression never changed as he looked from the gun Walter was holding to Sydney's panic-stricken face.

"What're you doing here?" Kendall asked.

Sean's eyes cut to Kendall's truck. "I saw you tearing up the pavement back there and thought I'd better see what was going on. Walter, I didn't know you were part of this."

"Well, what did you think? That an operation of this caliber runs itself? You've been given everything on a need-to-know basis."

Sean nodded. "Gotcha."

Walter's eyes met Sean's. "I guess the question is can I trust you with this?"

Sean straightened to his full height. "I believe I've proven my worthiness on many occasions." He looked at Kendall. "Isn't that right?"

Kendall shrugged. "He does have a point."

"All right," Walter said. "We're wasting time." He motioned. "As you can see, we're having a little unexpected trouble with our lady friend here and could use your help. Kendall, hand him the rope so he can tie her up."

Sydney's eyes flew open wide. "You! I should've known!"

Walter looked at Sean with a raised eyebrow. "She really hates you."

Sean chuckled. "I seem to have that effect on women." He stepped behind Sydney and tied her hands. "You've got enough rope here to tie up ten people."

Walter lowered the pistol and looked at Kendall. "Let's go get the stuff."

* * * * *

Sydney struggled against Sean with all her might. "Would you be still?"

"I wouldn't give you the pleasure, you low-down double crosser." For some strange reason, Sean's betrayal hurt more than Kendall's, even though she'd halfway suspected Sean of something the entire time.

"I said hold still! I'm trying not to hurt you!"

Tears sprang in her eyes. "I hate you!" That's when his words registered. She stopped moving and tried to make sense of what he had just said.

"Listen, Syd. I've been playing along with these thugs to gain their confidence, but I'm on your side. If you'll shut up and trust me, we might just both get through this alive," he whispered in her ear.

Kendall came back. Sydney cried out when she saw that Kendall was carrying a container of kerosene.

"Come on," he said to Sean. "Let's get this over with." The abandoned warehouse loomed over Sydney like the gate to hell as Sean dragged her to it. Her mind clicked through the scene like the frames of a camera. She saw the ripple of water as it lapped against the shore, felt the icy air whip her cheeks, saw a cluster of black birds flying overhead. Was this where it was destined to end? Here in this isolated place?

When they reached the building, Kendall tugged on the wooden door. It was so swollen with moisture that it took him a couple of tries to get it to budge. The damp scent of decay hit Sydney full force. Sean shoved her inside.

"Sit down." His voice was so brutally forceful that she feared she'd only imagined the words he'd spoken a few minutes earlier.

He made her sit on the cement floor with her back against the wall as he tied up her feet and then wound the rope around her legs, holding her in a sitting position.

"I'm going to spread this kerosene around the outside," Kendall said.

The horror of it all was swiftly overtaking Sydney. Even though Kendall hadn't ignited the kerosene yet, she could already feel the searing heat and smell the burning flesh. Her breath was coming faster now, and she knew it would only be a few seconds before she started hyperventilating. The door was open, allowing enough light into the dark building so that she could see the outline of Sean's face.

He touched her hair. "Breathe in through your nose and out through your mouth," he whispered.

"Don't leave me."

He leaned in so close that she could feel his warm breath on her face. "I'll be back. I promise."

And with that, he was gone.

*　*　*　*　*

405

Sean left the building and Kendall came around the corner. He held up the empty container of kerosene. "I didn't have enough to put around the entire thing, but I think there was enough to do the trick. Did you get her taken care of?"

Sean nodded.

"Good. Now all we have to do is close the door and barricade it." He placed the container on the ground and turned his back to Sean.

"Where's Walter?"

"At the truck getting the matches."

It was now or never. He only hoped he had enough time to take them one by one. Sean pushed Kendall hard, smashing his face into the side of the warehouse. Kendall stumbled to the ground, but it only took a minute for him to get his bearings. He swore under his breath and jumped to his feet and faced Sean, his eyes blazing.

Kendall lunged at Sean, knocking them both to the ground. The two traded blows, rolling in the dirt. Kendall was the first to get to his feet. Sean got up on his hands and knees and Kendall gave him a vicious kick in the ribs that was so powerful Sean felt like his body was being ripped in two. He braced himself as Kendall kicked him again and again. Sean did a side sweep with his foot and tripped Kendall, dropping him like a brick. Sean pinned him to the ground and pounded his face. Kendall reached to grab Sean in a choke hold but couldn't get a strong enough grip to do any damage.

Just when Sean knew he had Kendall under control, a sharp pain tore through the back of his head and everything went black.

*   *   *   *   *

Sean went slack, and Kendall looked up to see Walter standing above him. It took Kendall a moment to realize that Walter hit Sean in the head with the handle of the pistol.

406

Walter's eyes took in Kendall's bloody face. "Looks like I got around here just in time. A few more minutes and he would've taken you."

"He turned on me."

"Yeah, I never was too sure about him anyway. It just goes to show that you never can trust an outsider. He was always a little too good to be true."

Kendall used the sleeve of his jacket to wipe away the blood that was still trickling from his nose.

Walter nudged Sean with the tip of his shoe. "He's out cold. Put him in the warehouse." He paused. "Make sure you get his keys and cell phone. The last thing we need is for him to come to and try and make a phone call." He motioned to Sean's truck. "Take his truck and drive it into the river. It will have sunk to the bottom by the time anyone sees the fire."

But Kendall just stood there, looking at Walter. The world stopped spinning as their eyes met. Kendall's face crumbled. "I can't do it."

"What?"

He ran his hand through his hair. "I just can't do this to Sydney."

Walter took a deep breath. "Let's think this thing through. You know I'd never ask you to do anything that wasn't necessary."

Kendall looked at the ground.

"Kendall!"

His eyes met Walter's.

"You know that, right?"

Kendall nodded.

"Now that she knows, she won't stop until she brings it all down around her."

"But I can convince her, make her understand."

Walter paused one awful moment, long enough for a twinge of hope to flicker in Kendall. "No son, I don't think you can," he finally said. "You've got to think of your mama and Emma."

Doubt flashed in Kendall's eyes. "What do you mean?"

"Look, I don't care all that much what'll happen to you or me if this gets out, but think what it'll do to them. Think would what happen to your sweet mama if she realized what J. W. did. You've got to be a man and disassociate yourself from this thing. Sometimes you have to see past the unpleasantness to hold victory in your hands. Kendall! Look at me!"

Kendall's eyes met Walter's as the latter spoke. "You know what you need to do."

*   *   *   *   *

Sydney struggled to free her hands from the ropes, but Sean had tied them too tight. Her eyes were growing accustomed to the darkness, and she tried to get a feel for her surroundings. The first thing she saw was the faint light coming in from a window up above. The window was so corroded with dust that it was barely visible in the darkness. Next she saw light spilling in around the edges of the door. She managed to half roll, half scoot, and work her way toward it. She'd almost made it when the door burst open. Kendall stepped in and threw an unconscious Sean on the floor. He paused when he realized that Sydney was right there.

Tears were streaming down her face when she looked up at him. "Please help me!"

He bent down and cupped her cheek, and she noticed that his hand was trembling.

"Kendall, don't do this!"

He looked at her for one long moment. His eyes grew soft, and she thought he was going to help her. He backed away. "Goodbye, Sydney."

The door slammed shut, sounding like the closing of a tomb. Darkness enveloped her.

*   *   *   *   *

The igniting kerosene sounded like rushing water encircling the building. A giant fist was choking Sydney. She lay on the floor, gasping for air. It was like she was watching herself in slow motion. Please, she prayed in her mind. Lord, please help me! Her mind cleared for a second, and she managed to propel herself to a sitting position. She hit her body against Sean's. "Wake up! The building's on fire! Sean! Sean!" It took what seemed like an eternity for him to respond.

He rolled over and opened his eyes.

"Get up! The building is burning!"

He sat up and winced, holding his rib cage. He rubbed the back of his head and squinted his eyes.

Smoke was pouring into the building, and Sydney knew it would only be a matter of time before the fire sucked out all the oxygen. She was no longer in a building with Sean but on the burning boat with Avery. A high-pitch scream started in her throat and then echoed through the building.

She felt hands on her arms, shaking her. "Listen to me! Get ahold of yourself! We've only got a few minutes before the building collapses! Sydney, listen to me!"

All she could see was Avery. "Dad! Dad! Don't hurt him!" She felt a sudden slap on her face and came back to the present. Sean had not left her. She tried desperately to stave off the panic.

Sean reached for his phone, but came up empty-handed. He then pulled a pocket knife from his boot. "I'm going to cut you loose, and then we're gonna find a way out of here."

Sean repeatedly threw his body against the door, but it wouldn't budge. He swore. Smoke was pouring in around them, burning their eyes and causing them to double over in spasms of coughing. He took Sydney's hand.

"Stay down low!"

She was sobbing again. "It's no use! They're going to kill Stella! Everyone I ever loved has died! And now she will too...all because of me."

"Sydney, I love you. I believe I've always loved you," Sean said, then a fit of coughing overtook him. "I called for backup. They should be here in a few minutes."

"Backup? What're you talking about?"

"Try to stay calm. We'll get through this together. I just hope they get here in time."

The next words that flowed into her mind seemed to generate from outside of herself, almost as if she could hear someone else speaking them. It was the verse from the Bible that Stella had quoted. "Peace I leave with you, my peace I give unto you: not as the world giveth, give I unto you. Let not your heart be troubled, neither let it be afraid." Peace. Blessed peace. Was this the Lord's way of telling her that she going to die and that it was okay? Sean loved her. Stella loved her. She had to help Stella. This wasn't just about her anymore. It was bigger than that. It was then that an idea flowed into her mind as clean and pure as the freshest water. She looked up at the window.

"Sean, I know how we can get out of here."

"How?"

"We're going to climb out that window and get on top of the roof. Find something heavy to tie around the end of the rope. We can sling it over that metal rafter and propel up."

"What?" He shook his head. "It's no good. Even if we could climb up, which I doubt because the wall's too slick, we'll die of smoke inhalation before we get to the top."

There was no time to explain the miraculous peace she'd experienced or the knowledge that had flowed into her mind. "That wall is made of cinderblocks. It won't burn like the rest of the walls. We have to at least try. Sean, I can climb anything. You have to trust me."

"All right," he said, reaching for the rope. He felt around and found a short two-by-four piece of lumber. "You hold this end of the rope. Don't let go." He tied the wood to his end and then tossed it up. It took him three tries before he managed to get the wood over the rafter. It came back down, sending the rope with it. She handed him her end, and he tied it to his.

He yanked on the rope to make sure it was secure. "I'll go first and then pull you up."

"Oh no, I'm the climber. I'll go first." She grabbed the rope out of his hands. "There's no time to argue."

Her eyes were burning as she looked up through the smoke. She turned her face to her shirt and attempted to breathe into it. Climbing the cinderblocks would be like walking on hot coals. An intense pain shot through her thigh when she thought about the flames from the burning walls that were closing in around her. *This is not about you. Think about Stella.* It was a short climb, no more than fifteen feet, but it would be the most difficult of her life. The rope cut into her hands as she used it to propel herself up. She willed herself to go higher and higher into the thick smoke. The heat from the walls burned her feet through her tennis shoes. She paused and breathed into her shirt.

"Are you all right?" Sean yelled.

"I'm fine...almost there." Her head was spinning wildly, and she kept repeating the same prayer over and over. *Please, help me.* With a superhuman effort, she climbed until she was even with the window. She held onto the rope for dear life and kicked the window. "Sean," she yelled down. "I made it to the window." Her foot broke through the glass. She kicked it again and again until she felt the cool air rush in. A shard of glass dug into her heel. She winced and put her foot on the window frame and used it to pull herself toward the window. A moment later, she stood on the window sill and climbed through the broken glass and onto the roof.

She let the rope fall back through the window. She laid on top of the roof for balance so she could help Sean up. Smoke used the window as a means of escape and started billowing out.

"Sean!" She coughed through the smoke then waited. "Sean! Are you okay? Answer me!" she shouted into the smoldering inferno.

Her only answer was the roaring fire.

The seconds seemed to last hours. "Sean!"

She heard the coughing first and then her name. "Sydney!"

"I'm here," she called. She looked through the window and saw the top of Sean's head. "Just a little farther!"

He looked up at her.

"Give me your hand!"

He caught hold of her hand and she helped pull him up on the roof. He rolled over and a string of coughs racked his body.

A loud bang caused them both to flinch. They looked in horror as the far side of the roof disappeared.

Sydney stood. "The roof's collapsing! Get up! We have to get off!"

"But how?"

Sydney looked out at the water. Her eyes locked with Sean's. He grabbed her hand and they ran to the edge.

"Are you ready?"

"Jump!"

*   *   *   *   *

The sound of the sirens was so faint at first that Sydney felt she'd only imagined it. She was alive! Swim! She needed to swim!

*   *   *   *   *

Several men were waiting for Sydney and Sean when they reached the bank of the river. They helped pull them from the water where they both collapsed on the ground. Sydney's body was shaking like jello. She tried to sit up. A policeman in his mid twenties knelt beside her and draped a blanket around her shoulders. Under different circumstances, Sydney would have recognized him as the man who questioned her after the journal was stolen. "Your hands are bleeding and you're in shock. We need to get you to the hospital."

Sydney looked down. The rope had cut into her hands, leaving bloody streaks, and she hadn't even noticed. "Stella! I have to help Stella!" She struggled to her feet and stumbled. The police officer moved to steady her.

"Whoa. Take it easy ma'am. You're not going anywhere. We need to get you to the hospital." He looked down. "Your foot is bleeding."

412

She slapped his hand away. "They're after Stella! I have to warn her!" She took a step forward.

The officer held out his hand to stop her. "Hold it."

Sean was at her side in an instant. He rose to his full height and glared at the young officer. "I know you mean well, but it would be in your best interest to let the lady be."

"And just who do you think you are?" He eyed Sean's disheveled appearance. Drops of water were trickling down his face. His torn shirt was clinging to his chest, and a swollen purple bruise was forming around his left eye. A cut followed the line of his cheekbone.

"I'm Special Agent Sean Corbin, FBI.

"You're *who?*"

"I don't have my badge on me, but I'll be happy to supply the number so you can verify it. Also, I'll give you the number of my office."

The officer went to jot down the information but fumbled with his pen and dropped it. Sean had to lean down and retrieve it for him. The police chief stepped into the conversation.

Sean extended his hand. "Sean Corbin, FBI."

After shaking Sean's hand, the chief shook his head. "Well, I'll be."

He patted the young officer on the shoulder. "Son, I'll take it from here. Why don't you go and take some statements from the onlookers? I reckon you'll find one of them who saw most of it." He looked at Sean. "Let's you and me walk over yonder to my car, and you can tell me how it is that you happen to be here in these parts."

Now that her adrenaline was wearing off, Sydney realized that she was freezing. She turned to Sean. "I have to get to Stella," she said through chattering teeth.

"Officer, the men who attempted to murder the both of us threatened to harm her grandmother. If it's all the same to you, maybe we could continue our conversation on the way to Stella McClain's house."

The officer's eyes widened as he looked at Sydney, who at the moment looked like a drowned rat that was trying to shake itself dry. "I've known Stella McClain for years. I was good friends with her son...um, I mean her late son. She's your grandmother?"

Sydney clenched her fists. "Yes, she's my grandmother! Could we please go? Every minute we stand here talking puts her at a greater risk!"

"Certainly ma'am."

"And please, blast the heat. We're freezing to death!" Sean said, hugging his arms.

"...a time to heal..."
—Ecclesiastes 3:3

chapter forty-two

Stella had just popped a frozen pizza in the oven and was fixing a glass of ice water when she heard the knock at the front door. She placed the glass on the counter and went to the door. Her eyes widened when she saw not only Sydney but Chief Butch Miller and another man standing beside her. It only took her half a second to figure out it was Sean. She'd heard Sydney talk about him often enough.

Sydney cried out and rushed into Stella's arms. "Stella! You're okay! I was so worried!"

Stella's eyes darted back and forth between Chief Miller and Sean. She held Sydney at arm's length and looked her over. "You're soaked. What happened to you?"

"Has anyone been here this evening?" Chief Miller asked.

"No, I've been all alone. Why?"

Sean pointed to the phone resting on the coffee table. "Is your phone working?"

Stella's eyes grew round. "I believe so."

Sean walked over and checked it. "It's fine."

The officer looked at Sean. "I can call my deputy up here to watch the house."

Sean shook his head. "No, that won't be necessary. I'll stay here with the two of them. I just need you to take care of the other matters we discussed."

Stella's forehead wrinkled and her brows knitted together. "What's going on here?" Her eyes went to

Sydney's and then Sean's. "What happened to y'all? How did you cut your foot?"

Sydney was still shaking. "Everything's going to be okay," she said and hiccupped.

Chief Miller looked at Sean. "Well then, I'll get out of your hair. If anything—and I mean anything—comes up, *you will call me,* right?"

"You have my word."

Stella put her arm around her granddaughter. "Let's get you into some dry clothes and take care of that foot." She looked at Sean. "I don't have anything that will fit you, but take off that wet shirt and I'll bring you a blanket to wrap up in."

Sean nodded.

Stella's eyebrow arched and she peered at Sean. "And after that, young man, you're going to tell me what in the world is going on here."

Sean chuckled. "It's a deal."

* * * * *

Kendall felt like a part of him had died right along with Sydney. He drove up his long driveway and glanced at her purse that was lying on the passenger seat. He would have to burn it. An image of Sydney and her pleading eyes flashed in his mind, and he tried to block it out. His only hope was that she died quickly and without too much pain. He did what he had to. It was as simple as that. He walked through the living room and tripped over a footstool that either his mom or Emma had left in the middle of the floor. He kicked it with all his might, sending it crashing into the wall. He then sat down on the couch and buried his face in his hands.

The noise sent his mother running into the living room. She stopped when she saw Kendall. "What's wrong?" She gasped at his appearance. "What happened? Where have you been?"

He shook his head. "I got in a little brawl. Nothing serious."

"Well, from the dried blood all over you and the look on your face, it certainly seems serious."

"I don't want to talk about it!"

She left and came back with a wet paper towel. She stopped short before she reached him, and he could hear the quick intake of her breath.

"Kendall, why are police cars coming up the driveway? And why do they have their lights on?"

Kendall looked up at her and saw her wince when she met his eyes. He knew he had seen that expression on her face before: when she looked at his dad. Then it hit him. He had hated his dad's weakness, couldn't understand what could have possibly motivated him to kill himself. Now he knew. There was only one thing, and it was the same guilt that was now eating him alive piece by piece. History was repeating itself. He was all of those horrible things he hated. It was his worst nightmare—the thing he feared the most. He had become his father.

Gail's eyes filled with tears. "Son, what's going on? What have you done?"

* * * * *

Walter poured the shot glass full of whiskey. He replayed the events of the day. He was getting much too old for this crap. At least this had been easier than it was with Avery. There were still a few loose ends to tie up though. Avery's journal would have to be found and Stella taken care of. He closed his eyes, threw back his head, and let the hot liquid burn down his throat. All in good time, he told himself. All in good time.

The situation with Kendall had been touch and go, but it turned out fine in the end. He'd seen the turmoil churning in Kendall, and he understood it well. Today was the first time that Kendall had been forced to get his hands dirty.

"Please tell me you didn't hurt that girl."

Walter didn't turn around but kept facing the wall. "Go to bed, Maurene." His voice sounded as tired as he felt.

"Did you hurt her?" she asked again, her trembling voice raising a notch.

Walter took another swig of whiskey. "I'm not sure how you found out about any of this, hon."

"I hear things, Walter! I overheard you and Kendall. I'm a drunk. I'm not stupid! You didn't hurt her, did you?"

"It's all taken care of, if that's what you mean. Now go to bed. We'll talk about it in the morning."

The click of metal made his eyes pop open. He put down his glass and turned slowly to face a wild-eyed Maurene holding a revolver. Her eyes were red and swollen from crying, and streaks of black mascara ran down her pale cheeks.

"Put down the gun, Maurene. You're drunk."

Her hands began to shake as she took a step backward. "I've never been more sober in my life. You got rid of her, didn't you? First it was Avery and now her! You just couldn't leave it alone! I called her!"

"You what?" Walter's eyes narrowed as he studied Maurene. In the past he'd always been able to control her, but she'd never held a gun in her hands before. He lowered his voice as if he were talking to a child. "Honey, I did what I had to do for us. You know that. I loved Avery and Sydney, but they just wouldn't listen to reason. It takes money to buy all those fancy clothes you like...and the booze you can't live without."

"Don't you dare drag me into this filthy mess! We're like cannibals, you and I, living off the flesh of others. Well, it's gonna stop. Do you hear me? It ends here!"

"Yes, dear."

She lowered the gun.

Walter took advantage of the opportunity and stepped forward just as she jerked the gun back up. This time it was aimed directly at his chest. "You killed Avery and Sydney. How many more people have to die because of you? You're destroying innocent lives. Those kids you're selling drugs to have done nothing to you!"

"Maurene, honey, you're not making any sense." His eyes pleaded with hers. "Nowadays all kids take drugs. If I weren't furnishing drugs for them, someone else would be."

She shook her head. "No, that's not true." Her voice was barely audible.

Walter started walking toward her. "Now give me that gun." The sound of the shot vibrated through the house. He stared at Maurene, then fell to the floor. There was a moment of silence. Maurene stood looking down at him. "I'm sorry Walter...for both of us," she said softly. She turned the gun to her head and pulled the trigger.

* * * * *

The three of them made a cozy picture, with Sean and Sydney wrapped in blankets and all of them sipping hot chocolate. Sydney was sitting next to Sean, who had his arm draped comfortably around her shoulders.

Stella's eyes widened as she listened to them relate the events of the day and how they'd barely escaped with their lives.

Stella clucked her tongue. "Walter and Kendall. Who would've thought it? Both of them sure had me fooled." She sighed. "What will happen to them?"

"The authorities are on their way to pick them up right now," Sean said.

Sydney turned to Sean. "Was Louellen involved?"

"No, but Lewis Jackson and Buck Gibson are a different matter."

Sydney nodded. "Thank goodness for Louellen's innocence. Otherwise, I couldn't begin to imagine what would happen to Hazel. It will be bad enough for Mrs. Fletcher and Emma."

Stella took a sip of her drink. "Yes, it is going to be hard on them." She paused. "But time is a great healer, and they have each other." Stella placed her cup on the table. "It's funny how people think they're an island unto themselves and what they do only affects them. It's like ripples in a pond. Everything we do touches the lives of those around us." Sydney's eyes caught Stella's and a look of understanding passed between them. She knew Stella was thinking about Avery.

A comfortable silence filled the room. Sydney stared off into the distance. Something extraordinary had happened to her today, something even more powerful than the fire. She'd been in the depths of despair and had received help straight from heaven, right when she needed it most. The Lord was mindful of her. He'd given her peace. It was a feeling that she wanted to bottle up and clutch next to her heart forever. Her thoughts went to Kendall and his trembling hand when he touched her face for the last time. Her feelings for him were so complex and mixed up that she wasn't sure what to make of them. "Kendall was a good man in so many ways."

Sean scowled. "Yeah, except in the ways that really mattered. The most frustrating part of this whole case has been watching Kendall pull the wool over your eyes and the whole town. You know, Syd, Kendall was a big boy. No one held a gun to his head and made him do the things he did. He made his own choices. I'll tell you another thing too. He didn't become a murderer overnight. What you saw today was the end result that he built layer upon layer over a long period of time."

Sydney sighed. "He just reminded me so much of my dad."

Sean was quick to counter. "No, you're wrong, Syd. They were very different. Avery had conviction and died for what he believed in."

This won him a look of admiration from Stella. "You're a man wise beyond your years. A drop of water, harmless enough in itself, yet over time, those tiny droplets, one upon the other in a continuous flow can hollow the face of stone."

Sydney let this sink in. For her it would never be that black and white. Kendall would always be linked to her tragic past, a mixture of good and bad. One whose inner demons got to him in the end. "You're right, Sean. I guess I just assumed that because Kendall was such a good person when he was young that he was the same now. I never really understood him." She could follow that train of thought further and add that because Sean was so handsome and suave that she'd automatically assumed the worst of him, but she wasn't ready to say that out loud...at least not yet.

Sydney's mind raced to another part of the puzzle. She looked at Sean. "How did you know that I was in trouble today? And how did you know where to find me?"

Sean withdrew his arm from around Sydney's shoulders and shifted on the couch. "To answer your first question, I know this may sound strange, but all I can say is that I had a terrible feeling that something was wrong. I've learned to trust that inner feeling."

"Me too," Sydney said.

"Now the second part was more concrete."

Sydney's eyebrow arched; she waited for him to continue.

"Hazel told me."

"Hazel?"

"I went to your house to check on you and saw Hazel watching me. I went next door to talk to her. I told her you were in danger and that I needed to know where you were. She told me how Kendall had insisted you go on the boat with him. I was headed to the dock when I saw Kendall speeding down the road."

Sydney chuckled. "Well thank goodness Hazel was eavesdropping again. And to think how aggravated I used to get because she was always poking her nose into my business." She smiled at Sean and used her elbow to give him a slight jab in the ribs.

He winced in pain. "Careful. I'm a little sore there."

"Sorry." A sheepish smile crept over her face. "I knew you were a lousy sawmill manager, but it never dawned on me that you worked for the FBI."

He made a face. "Was I really that bad?"

She nodded.

"Ouch!"

This brought laughs from Stella and Sydney.

Sydney's eyebrows knitted together. "I'm just having a hard time seeing you as an FBI agent. I mean, does the FBI really put people in positions like that?"

Sean chuckled. "Absolutely."

"But how did they put you in a management position? Who else knows about you? Does Jake Roberts know? Is he involved?"

Sean laughed and held up his hand as a shield. "Whoa, one question at a time."

She waited for him to continue.

"Well, for starters, we have informants all over the place." He raised an eyebrow at Sydney. "And no, I can't tell you who they are."

She laughed. "And Jake?"

Sean shrugged and made a motion like he was zipping his lips. "I'll never tell."

"Well, why not?"

"Oh, he wasn't trafficking drugs if that's what you're asking. Other than that, that's all I can say."

Sydney huffed. "You're impossible!"

"Anyway, back to the story. Our informant told us that drugs were being run from the sawmill, so the bureau approached the owners of Chamberland Mills about putting me in that position." He paused. "It took me a while to figure out who the players were and to gain their trust."

Sydney mulled this over. "Well, I'm really impressed with how you solved this case."

"I never could have done it without you."

"What do you mean?"

"There's been a growing concern for a few years about the large-scale meth operation in this area, but no one could find out who was really running it. Drugs are being run all over the Southeast from here. That's what prompted the bureau to get involved. My contact was Buck Gibson, who then led me to Kendall. But Kendall was very careful to hide Walter's identity, and even though he let me be a part of operations, I was still considered an outsider. Without you, we would've indicted Kendall eventually, but Walter would've gotten away. Then when I started reading Avery's journal, I found out about Avery and his connection to Walter."

422

Sydney's face paled. "Wait a minute. What do you mean when you started reading Avery's journal? How did you get hold of it?"

Sean searched Sydney's face for a moment. "I stole it."

Sydney's mouth dropped. "You're the one who broke into my house?"

He nodded.

She slammed her cup on the table and jumped to her feet. "How could you do that? Do you have any idea what that journal meant to me? You invaded my privacy!" Her voice grew soft. "You took the only tangible thing I had left of my dad."

"I'm so sorry I hurt you," Sean said.

Stella cocked her head. "No one knew about the journal. How did you know to go searching for it?"

"That's a good question. I didn't know about the journal...at first. I broke into Sydney's house to learn more about her." He looked up at Sydney. "When you first came to work at the mill, I knew there was more to the picture than met the eye. I mean, why would a girl like you leave Ft. Worth to come and work as a safety consultant in a sawmill in Alabama?"

"And just what is so bad about Alabama?" Stella asked.

He held up his hand in defense. "Nothing. I mean no disrespect. It's just that something about the whole picture didn't seem right. So I had Sydney checked out."

"You what?" She glared at him.

Sean's eyes met hers in a direct challenge. "Yes, I did." He kept his voice level. "There was too much at stake to take any chances. When I found out who you really were, I had to learn the real reason why you came back to Stoney Creek. I broke into your house, not really knowing what I would find. That's when I came across the secretary with the locked drawer." He held up his hands. "It just goes to reason that anytime someone locks a drawer, I figure—"

"There must be something of value in it," Stella finished for him.

His eyes met Sydney's in a plea for understanding. "Exactly."

She studied his face for a moment as the full picture began taking shape. "You were the one who made the bogus call that sent me on that wild goose chase to the outlying woodlands."

He nodded.

She ran her fingers through her hair. "You made me feel like such a fool for going out there, and all the while you're the one…" She shook her head. "You were the one who was always watching me. The eyes, as Hazel says. It was no accident when you showed up just in time to rescue me that day in the park, was it? You were also at the cockfight. I saw you."

"Yeah, Syd. I was there all of those times, but if I hadn't been, you might not be alive right now."

She thought about the man who had threatened her with the switchblade. "You were my guard dog."

"Yes."

She felt so betrayed. So used. "I have to think about all this."

"Honey, Sean's right." Stella stood and put her arm around Sydney's shoulder. "He did what he had to do to take care of you." Stella turned and looked pointedly at Sean. "You are giving the journal back to her? Right?"

"I want my articles back too," Sydney said.

Before Sean could respond, the phone rang. Stella moved to answer it. A small furrow appeared between her brows and she handed the phone to Sean. "It's for you."

"I see…yes, I understand. No, everything here is okay." He hung up the phone.

Sydney's hands went to her hips. "Who was that? What happened?"

"That was Chief Miller. Kendall, Buck, and Lewis have been arrested, but when they went to pick up Walter, they found him and Maurene dead."

Sydney and Stella looked at each other in horror as Sean continued. "Apparently, Maurene shot Walter and then turned the gun on herself."

chapter forty-three

Sydney spent the night at Stella's, and Sean went back to his apartment. Sydney slept late the next morning and felt like a new person when she awoke. She and Stella piddled around the house and had breakfast together. Then Stella accompanied Sydney to the police station where she filled out a seemingly never-ending barrage of paperwork. Next the two drove into Glendale and had a late lunch at the Mexican restaurant. There was only one thing left for them to do before they could close this chapter of their lives. They needed to visit the cemetery.

They drove up the hill and were greeted by the giant magnolia trees holding their bare branches high in the sky. In an unspoken agreement, they walked the distance from the jeep to the graves in silence. The only sound they heard was the crunching of their feet through the brown leaves on the ground. When they reached the tombstones, they heard the hum of a vehicle and looked back at the road. Sydney and Stella watched Sean open his door and stride toward them.

Sydney was surprised, but Stella seemed to be expecting him. "Sorry I'm late," he said.

Sydney looked to Stella. "He called this morning while you were still asleep. I told him that we were planning on going to the cemetery, and he asked if he could join us. I thought it would be okay. He's as much a part of this as we are."

Sydney considered this for a minute and then relaxed. "Okay."

She turned and looked at the tombstones. Everything else around her seemed to disappear as she read the tender inscriptions. She felt again the incredible peace that she'd felt the day before. She remembered her last visit to the cemetery and the hatred she'd felt. She didn't know how or even when it had happened, but the hate was gone. She didn't hate Walter or Kendall for what they'd done. It was the closest that she could come to forgiveness, and somehow it was enough. The Lord, in his infinite wisdom, had accepted her feeble gift, and in a way that she didn't understand, He'd made up the difference.

The song started as a sigh in her heart, barely discernable to her consciousness, and then it began to swell until it filled her being. "God Be With You Till We Meet Again." Though she spoke no words aloud, she knew that her song had reached heaven on the wings of her spirit. She looked at the still, silent graves of her parents and knew they weren't there. They lived—just as she did, and she also knew that she would be with them again someday. It was that knowledge that gave her the strength to let them go. "God be with you till we meet again," she whispered.

Sean put his arm around her, and Stella took her hand. "You never have to be alone again," Stella said.

"I know," Sydney said. "I know."

They stood for a few minutes in silence until Sean looked up at the sky that was brushed pink and purple in the setting sun. "Would you look at that sunset?"

Sydney looked at Stella and smiled. "It looks like a cotton candy sky to me."

Stella smiled back. "Yes, it certainly does."

Sean looked at Sydney. "Would you mind walking back to the truck with me? I want to show you something."

Sydney shrugged. "Sure." She turned and waited for Stella to go with them.

Stella shooed them on. "Y'all go on. I want to stay here by myself for a few more minutes."

Sydney and Sean walked to his truck. He took her hand and linked her fingers through his. She still hadn't gotten over the fact that he'd broken into her house and stolen the journal. She thought about jerking her hand away, but let it ride.

When they reached the truck, he let go of her hand and retrieved Avery's journal from the seat. "I believe this belongs to you, ma'am. The articles are tucked inside."

She clutched the journal with both hands and held it to her chest. "Thank you."

He leaned against his truck and took one of her hands and pulled her to him. "So where do we go from here."

She shook her head. "I don't know. You tell me."

He traced the curve of her cheek with his finger. Her face grew warm under his touch. No matter how hard she fought it, she never could overcome her strong attraction to him. His hand moved to her hair, and he took a section and wound it around his finger and then let it go.

"I don't even know who you are," she said, her breath coming a little faster when his arms encircled her waist. "Are you really this Sean Corbin, or whatever you said your name was?"

He laughed. "Yes, I am."

"Are you even from Texas?"

He nodded, a glimmer of amusement sparkling in his dark eyes. "Yes, I'm from Texas, but Austin, not Houston." He grew serious. "Sydney, I meant what I said to you yesterday. I love you."

She searched his eyes. "Do you really?"

"How could you even question it?"

She withdrew herself from his arms and shook her head. "I don't know. I don't even know who you are."

"Oh, I understand, Sydney...or is it Cindy?"

Her eyes grew large. "Wait a minute! That's not

fair. I had a very good reason for concealing my true identity."

He nodded. "Bingo!"

"Okay, maybe you've got a point. But what will you do now? You've solved the case. Won't you go on to someplace else?"

"Yeah, that's the plan." His eyes met hers. "Unless I decide to change it."

Those words kindled a hope that surprised her. "What do you mean?"

"I've spent the last five years hopping from life to life, always undercover. This never bothered me until I met you. I always knew the right girl would come along someday." He paused. "Look Syd, I don't have all the answers. I just know that I want you to be a part of my life."

Oh, how she loved hearing those words.

He put his arms around her waist again. This time he linked his fingers so she couldn't get away. "Are you telling me that you don't have any feelings for me?"

A tingle ran up her spine.

"Well?"

She was warm all over. "Okay, I do feel something for you. It's just all so confusing right now."

He looked hurt for a second. "I guess I can live with that."

She tried to explain her feelings. "I've always been attracted to you, and I've spent the last few months trying to rid myself of those feelings."

He chuckled.

Her eyebrow arched. "Oh, so you think it's funny, do you? It's like this: A part of me wants us to be together, but the other part of me thinks that maybe I'd be better off if I got rid of you."

He smiled. "Is that right?"

"Yeah."

"Oh, Syd, you'll never be rid of me."

"Well, aren't I the lucky one?" she said as her lips met his, and for the first time, she meant it.